PHANTOM
PAINS

M.A. Dash

ACKNOWLEDGMENTS

Funny, I rarely used to take the time to view this when reading a book. Yet, I hope for you to do so now. Call it irony I guess. But a promise is a promise.

First off, shout out to Josie Steffey for being an amazing editor and the first person to set eyes on this story. The discussion we had at Panera gave me the boost I needed to make this dream a reality. Also, wanted to give credit to Hannah B, for allowing me to bounce ideas off of you.

Next, thanks to the friends and family that gave me encouragement, advice, or support along the way.

Finally, thank you to you the reader, for giving this story a chance and joining me on this journey. Let's have some fun and hope you enjoy!

Chapter One

*L*eave the kid out of this!" The voice desperately cried out into the darkness. "You've already won."

"My dearest hero, what you fail to understand is that I'm not here simply to beat you, I'm here to end you," The other voice replied, oozing with southern charm as the desperate cries of a boy began to descend further away from them.

"No!" The first voice yelled as it followed closely after the boy.

What comes next is the scream of a child followed by the horrid sound of barbed wire, ripping away at the skin of its unfortunate victim. Blood trickled down a lifeless hand and silence followed.

My screams reverberated throughout my bedroom as I woke up from my nightmare, lying in a pool of sweat and blood.

"Same dream?" A small figure stepped out from the corner of my room as the shadows seemingly peeled away, revealing a boy with a torn rose red firetruck t-shirt. "Don't you think it may be a bit problematic at this point?"

"You know I'm not in control of it when I have nights like yesterday," I responded groggily as I rose from my reclined position to focus on the kid that couldn't have been any older than twelve. "Besides, I think 'good morning' is the proper term you're looking for."

"I only do as I am allowed, my liege," He replied in his best medieval knight impression, bowing to emphasize the sass.

At that moment, a Himalayan cat bounded into my bed, securely taking residence in my lap and rubbed his head reassuringly against me. Once again, Mew was helping me during one of my morning episodes.

Gently stroking Mew's head, I took a deep breath and began counting by three. By twelve, I felt my heart beating at its normal pace. Though I had calmed myself, I couldn't deny the dream along with my nighttime activities were starting to take their toll on me. The nightmare's relentless recurrence felt like a wary warning of an event yet to come, but there was no reason to panic. My reality is only what my brain makes of it, just like everybody else.

At least that's what I keep telling myself.

"I thought our relationship was in a better place, Sammy?" I pondered aloud, glancing back towards him.

"We're leaps and bounds ahead of where we were since you decided not to test gravity's mercy, but one day you'll have to play that dream out all the way through," Sammy replied simply. I winced at the mention of my lowest moment, but Mew elicited a placid purr that managed to repacify me.

"You're right, little buddy. That was a long time ago," I said to him, reminiscing about how that formerly drenched, mewling kitten and those helpless royal blue eyes managed to get me down from that ledge.

Looking back at Sammy, I realized that I was accompanied by the two closest entities in my life. *Strange bedfellows indeed.*

"Besides," Sammy interrupted, placing a proud hand over his heart. "If it weren't for me, you'd be late to work every morning since you never set your alarm."

"Fair point," I responded in a hurry as I lightly tapped my pet to get off, so that I could get dressed. "I need to feed Mew before I leave though."

Fortunately, the blood wasn't mine, so it washed off easily enough although it had dried and crusted overnight. Afterwards, I quickly changed and checked myself in the mirror before heading to my office. Investigating my face, I spotted no major blemishes on my mocha latte-colored skin except for a faint scar running vertically along my left emerald colored eye. I was content until I touched the wound gingerly, a sobering reminder of a past trial and the ones yet to come.

I brushed my short curly hair, while attempting to put on my khakis at the same time, an unfortunate consequence of running late. Finally, I finished buttoning up my favorite sky blue dress shirt, equipping a navy blue tie to match. I remembered to grab my rectangular-rimmed glasses off my nightstand and went to deliver Mew his breakfast before I left.

 Mew purred as I walked over to his perch to which he had returned, planted on top of my mahogany dresser, which held his feather-lined sleeping basket. Before you ask, no I didn't buy it like that. Mew loved to bring back pieces of his prey as if they were hunting trophies.

"Don't worry, Your Highness," I bowed as I grabbed his food, "Your sustenance is being provided according to schedule."

After I finished pouring the *Nibletts* into his food dish and replenished his drinking bowl, Mew hopped down and let out a trill while rubbing against my legs.

"I love you too, buddy," I said as I bent down to scratch his ear.

I wished him farewell one last time and checked the time. There were only two minutes left before I needed to be in to work and it was a five-mile drive.

Although, with my ability, distance is almost irrelevant. With my left hand outstretched, I opened an indigo shaded portal to my office and entered.

Okay, admittedly I may have buried the lede. You see I'm an Irregular, and no, that doesn't mean my bowels are out of control. An Irregular is the term that replaced the old phrases of the ever popular superpowered, hipster Metahuman, or the now somehow less offensive mutant.

How'd we get stuck with the name? Let's just say that people possessing special abilities were treated no differently than your average Jane Doe up to a point in America, but one unfortunate cataclysmic event changed that for all of my kind.

The exact details are admittedly still murky, but essentially in the year 2025, an Irregular with nuclear capability detonated and took Wyoming with him, all of it, making the former state a no-man's land, which kick-started a period of civil strife that even three decades later left many of us to pick up the pieces of what once was.

As I stepped out the other side of my portal, I buzzed my assistant, Sofía, to notify her that I was in the office. Sofia is also an Irregular and a trusted friend, so I could teleport in and out of my office without making any elementary excuses. Working with a Normie, a person without enhanced abilities, could have its complications.

"Mr. Jenkins called and said he will be here shortly," an Argentine accent lightly tinted her svelte voice as she replied through the intercom. "Also Devin, if you show up early enough, you can say 'good morning' like a proper gentleman."

"You know I don't like to be disturbed in the morning, Sofia," I replied in a matter-of-fact tone.

"But what if I was incapacitated and you coming through the front door was the difference between life and death?" Sofia mused aloud in a child-like manner.

"Consider it an occupational hazard," I said in jest. "Send in Mr. Jenkins when he arrives."

As our customary morning banter concluded, I glanced around the office, which was bigger than my apartment. Various paintings adorned the walls in an attempt to give the room a refined ambiance. I wasn't much of an art enthusiast, but my former therapist and mentor, Dr. Green, previously owned them, and in my admiration, I decided to follow in his footsteps. Bookshelves filled with epic poems such as Homer's *Iliad* and *Odyssey* lined the walls. I turned towards my desk and looked up at the plaques hanging overhead.

If you couldn't tell by now, I'm a therapist. Why? Like me, there are other people hurting in this world. I want to be there for them in their darkest hour, just like Dr. Green had done for me. My plaques loom over the office as a daily reminder to not only carry the weight of my hardships, but also help shoulder the burden of others.

An insistent buzzing sound went off in my office, alerting me that Mr. Jenkins had arrived. I rose from my chair and went to the door to greet him.

Mr. Jenkins is both my most beloved and least favorite patient. Some patients can be hesitant to get open, so they'll give shallow answers that prevent further questioning, but as someone trained in guiding conversations, seeing a 'Do Not Enter' sign on a topic alerts me that this is the exact door to probe.

The trouble with Mr. Jenkins is that he makes a mule look compliant by comparison. At times, it's forced me to put aside my feelings and weather the storm until I made it out on the other end. I believe somewhere behind his surly visage stood a kind-hearted man, which is why I'm typically willing to overlook certain remarks.

"Hello, Mr. Jenkins. Pleasure to see you again," I said in my most professional voice while extending my hand in greeting.

"Prince," he replied gruffly, not bothering to add the honorific, "I still wait for the day that the actual doctor shows up to help."

Mr. Jenkins crossed the soft blue carpet before giving me a limp fish handshake. His worn calloused palm scratched against my own as he headed for the velvet chaise lounge to lie down, dusting off his customary faded denim overalls as he tried to get comfortable.

I looked down at my hand, bit back a sharp reply, took a deep breath, and returned to my smooth linen armchair with a strained smile on my face.

As I looked Mr. Jenkins over, not much had changed since I had last seen him. Jenkins was an elderly man. Based on his liver spots, he was probably somewhere in his sixties if I had to venture a guess.

"No straw hat today?" I asked to ease his initial tension.

"No. If I'm going to have one of you quacks work my brain, might as well rest my body," He responded while fidgeting with his khaki trucker hat that covered his thinning gray hair.

"Well, the world will always need farmers, Mr. Jenkins."

"You got that right, doc," he let out a long sigh as the briefest hint of a smile touched the corner of his lips. "You know, I'm still surprised you're a therapist. I mean you're -"

"So *young*," I quickly interjected, "I actually get that quite a lot. Nice of you to notice."

With being one of the few African-American therapists in the city, my credentials were constantly in question. From our very first meeting, Mr. Jenkins would always slip one sly comment about my qualifications. I had grown accustomed to it, but one's patience can only run so thin. Better to stomp the embers out before they can become a forest fire.

"How have you been since our last meeting?" I inquired, officially beginning our session.

"I came back, so I guess you didn't fix me," he barked back, but this time with a little less bite.

"As we discussed before, therapy isn't a sprint to run away from your problem. It's a marathon, in which we intend to identify, address, and confront the problem."

"Well, can't you just give me one of those happy pills instead of all this talking? I identify I'm upset, we address it with the right prescription, and then the pills confront my stomach."

I subtly covered my lips with my clipboard to conceal my burgeoning smirk.

"Pills are a temporary solution to a persistent problem, Mr. Jenkins. Plus, if you overdosed, I wouldn't be able to overcharge you for our sessions," I jokingly retorted.

"The quack finally reveals the truth. Fine, let's get this over with," the smile on his lips revealed to me that the mutual humor had overcome his grumpy, old man demeanor.

"Have you been exercising as one of the methods I suggested?"

"I'm a farmer. What do you think?"

I adjusted my glasses nervously at his retort. The question was a lapse in attention to detail on my part. "Fair point, but what is your go-to, as we discussed?"

He let out a deep breath and began rubbing his chin while he mulled over his answer.

"I do enjoy taking the scythe to the wheat. Keeps me calm."

"Good," I scribbled down his response on my notepad. "What do you think about when you're swinging the scythe?"

"Is this where I'm supposed to say, 'I feel like I'm cutting all my problems away'?"

"Just share what's on your mind." *You usually don't have a problem with that.*

"I don't know. Just cutting wheat, nothin' special."

"Come on Lee," I urged him gently. "I know there's more to it."

"Alright, you got me," he conceded, his southern accent more apparent as he became increasingly animated. "I think of the bastards in this world, that think they can jus' take and take from us. This world was different when I was younger. We didn't have this madness, but people jus' sit there. Pretend it ain't there. Sticking our heads in the sand, hoping that we're not next. So, I cut and cut and cut, till I feel better."

Looking over at him, the wrinkles on his skin appeared more pronounced, a haunted look reflected from his eyes that now had even deeper bags beneath them. He seemed to have further aged in the little time we had spent together. It was like Mr. Jenkins's rebelliousness was his only chance at staying young in spirit, a way to prevent his years from weighing on him. At that moment, I started noticing the cracks in a man that kept his middle fingers up to the world to keep from breaking.

"Is it because of Beth and the boys?" I asked, careful not to offend or force an answer from him. Broaching this topic is usually how our sessions go off the rails.

His body stiffened, but his face showed no reaction to my question. I wondered if he was deciding on whether to answer or ignore me. He opened his mouth momentarily then just as quickly closed his jaws. The ball was in his court now, so I put down my notepad and waited.

"I'm lonely," was the answer he offered that broke our silence. "The Conflict. The Purification. They took my family."

He grimaced as every word left his mouth, as if each of them delivered a sharp blow that only he could feel. The Conflict he was referencing, was the label given to the deadly civil strife I mentioned. Although there was never an official decree of war, there was hell to pay, and the currency was blood.

Given our capabilities, Irregulars held the advantage. That is, until the Purification.

The Purification marked when current Secretary of Defense, Ryder Watson implemented a brilliant strategy that ultimately led to the birth of the Irregular Police Force (IPF). Watson called for the "unmitigated eradication of Irregulars and those that would aid them against the pure" unless they were willing to join him or submit, which turned the tide until the Irregular threat was quelled.

Unfortunately, the entire period took its pound of flesh from a lot of citizens, Irregulars and Normies alike.

You see, Mr. Jenkins had a wife, Beth, and two boys, Eli and Zacheriah. Being on a farm meant they were away from people, avoided the majority of the fighting, but still couldn't avoid the eye of the IPF. Their two boys were both Irregulars and the IPF have always had questionable methods for identifying and locating our type dating back in those days.

He hadn't given me the full story, but from what I managed to piece together, Jenkins's entire family had been murdered by IPF agents as well as the normies.

So tell me, how does a man under those circumstances benefit from the Purification in the end? That's a question that a lot of people had to ask themselves post-Conflict.

"That damn Watson," Jenkins continued, "He knew he would profit the most from it all. Beth, Eli, Zachy, all of them died, and for what? The country is basically under military control. The IPF ain't giving up power and Watson is gonna take over. Mark my words."

He paused for a moment. Tears began welling up in the corner of his visible eye.

"I'm a coward," he spit those words as if it were a bitter taste he were trying to rid himself of, "How could I let them die and do nothing? Mary Beth wouldn't let them get to our sons. 'Not our boys' she told me before they came, and I let them all die. I did nothing."

At this confession, he gently pulled down his hat over his face as if trying to hide from his shame rather than the tears. I would've offered him tissues, but this was a proud man and the least I could do was allow him his dignity.

Once he stopped, I simply said, "Lee, It's not your fault."

The elderly man wiped his tears away then forced a smile, a sign that the cinders of his rebellion had not fully been stamped out yet.

"Look at me, crying like a newborn babe," he said, while putting his tough guy face back on. "Just cause you got them fancy degrees behind you, you think you're a movie doctor now?" He questioned in jest.

I returned his smile.

"I'm required to give a quote during each session, so I've reached my quota for this one," then leaning in as I switched to a more serious tone, "The Conflict took an immeasurable toll on this entire country, Lee. You can't blame yourself. Retaliation only makes the wound worse."

At this, he rose up to a seated position and looked at me soberly. "So you're just asking me to move on, forgive and forget?"

"No," I said sharply, "but what I am asking you is to not to do something stupid and get yourself killed."

I pinched my nose beneath my glasses, letting out a low sigh before continuing, "But more importantly, what I'm asking, is for you not to swim in guilt and drown in sorrow. I never met your family, but Beth and your boys wouldn't want you to suffer. I want you to go home and list why that's the case and bring it back so we can discuss it next time."

Mr. Jenkins nodded in confirmation then stood up. I rose with him.

"I'm a bit too old for homework assignments, but I think I can do that," he fixed his hat as he prepared to leave, giving me a toothy grin in the process. "You quack."

"I look forward to seeing you again Mr. Jenkins," replying with a smirk of my own, offering out my hand in farewell.

This time, he shook it firmly.

I told you. Sometimes you have to weather the storm and hope you come out better on the other side. Thinking over our session, I realized we all have our own tempests to navigate. I just hope he makes it out for the better once he does.

As Jenkins reached the door to exit my office, he hesitated and peered back towards me.

"Hey Doc, that thing you said about retaliation, with all the kidnappings, have you ever wanted to go out there and do something about it?"

"Every day," I answered calmly as I took my glasses off to look at him. "But that's not for me to handle."

I'm not sure how he felt about my answer, but he acknowledged it with a neutral nod and proceeded to walk out.

"You know you shouldn't lie to people," A voice spoke from behind me.

I flinched and turned around to find Sammy at his desk going through his coloring book.

"I thought we agreed you wouldn't sneak up on me anymore."

He glanced up for a brief moment, tapping a black crayon against his chin before settling for a shrug. "Take it up with your brain," He replied, going straight back to his coloring.

I sighed, turning from my door towards the window. The late afternoon was beginning to kick in as the sun descended from its apex. Its rays hit the surrounding skyscrapers, the shadows stretching out as they tried to envelope the light and those that walked in it.

Sammy's comments and morose tone suddenly put a damper on my already tenuous mood. I furrowed my brow and exhaled as I prepared to respond to him.

"I'm not sure what you mean," I lied.

"About retaliation and how it makes things worse. Doesn't that make you a hypocrite?"

"What I do is different, and you know that," turning to face him, "Plus, you know that *he* won't leave me alone if I let certain things sit."

At this, Sammy stopped coloring and looked up at me. "How do you think I feel? When I go away, I'm left with him. Creepy dude if you ask me."

"That's why I didn't ask you," I replied dryly, "If no one steps into the dark to help, how can those suffering in it know of light?"

Sammy tapped his crayon on his chin and stared at the ceiling, in what I could only assume was to ponder his answer. After a minute, his eyes came down, resting on mine.

"Two questions. One, if someone willingly steps into the dark themselves, who's there to get them out when they've stayed too long? Two, if you lost someone you loved, could you resist the urge for revenge?"

I was slightly thrown off by his questions. It was surprisingly well thought out, considering someone his age shouldn't have been able to discuss moral equivalency so eloquently.

I settled for a snort of disgust at his simplistic line of questioning before turning back to the window. "I'm tired of being questioned by my own hallucination. Can you leave me for a while?"

"You got it, but just so you know *he's* here."

I glanced over my left shoulder towards the non-descript navy blue door in my office.

"Well, I guess you are here," I commented in that direction.

The *he* that Sammy and I were referring to, is the second most prevalent member of the motley crew taking up residence in my mind. Hovering in front of the door, was a figure sporting an unbuttoned long black coat with the design of silver flames encircling the bottom that reached about a quarter of the way up the coat, around the shoulders, steel colored flames coiled along the arm like a snake.

The figure inside was vaguely humanoid in appearance, with his "body" resembling that of a shadow. His features seemed to subtly change based on lighting or position in which you observed at him. *He* didn't possess any legs, thus the hovering. There was a torso, with arms that poked out of the coat sleeves into his pockets, but I hesitate to assume that means *he* had hands. There wasn't much of a face. I mean it possessed all the normal features that most humans have, the only notable difference being that the eyes were golden orbs. *He* is called the Spectre.

"The time is soon upon us," The Spectre stated, his voice oscillating somewhere between a whisper and a moan.

I patiently rubbed at my temples. Interactions with Sammy are one thing, but the Spectre is an entirely different beast. Sammy was right about this guy being creepy. Courtesy to my mind, I assume.

Lowering my hand, I looked to the Spectre. "What is soon upon us exactly?"

"The time."

I glared back towards him. I forget sometimes that you must be specific in dealing with the Spectre.

"The time to do what exactly?"

"To go out into the dark. We've been idle for too long recently."

"You've been listening to Sammy and me again, haven't you?"

"The boy and I don't discuss trivial matters."

I hesitated for a moment before responding. "You know this takes its toll on me."

The obsidian colored fedora on his head managed to stay in place as the Spectre drifted over towards me and stopped behind my back to whisper in my ear.

"The toll is heavier for those that can't lift the weight of their burdens."

I nodded as he used my own words against me yet again, then headed towards the door he previously guarded. My hand rested on the handle for a moment. Letting out a heavy exhale, I summoned my resolve and twisted the knob.

You could describe what lay behind the door as a walk-in closet. There were more bookcases and suits inside, but they were mostly just window dressing. Sifting through the suits, I stopped on a coat similar to that of the Spectre's and gazed upon it for a moment.

"It's the right thing to do," The Spectre encouraged me, freeing me from my momentary trance.

"At least you're not as moralistic as Sammy," I stated. After covering the coat with the remaining clothes on the rack, I began groping underneath the bookshelves till I found the items I was looking for. I pulled out my pair of tonfas and examined them.

Now for those not familiar with weaponry, tonfas are weapons that are similar to batons, but with the grip handle perpendicular to the longer base which covers the forearms. Usually they're made of wood, but thanks to a generous patron I've been able to upgrade the material. The exterior was made of palladium due to its malleability, with a high-grade Kevlar core for shock absorption purposes. I appreciatively ran my fingers over the built-in trigger that releases the hidden obsidian blade, for when the situation calls for something a little more lethal.

Like I said, I have a very generous patron.

Finally, underneath a shelf adjacent to the previous, I withdrew my .44 Magnum Desert Eagle. Carrying the pistol to the small table within the room, I gently set it down, beginning the process of polishing the gun and inspecting the rounds.

"The lost thank you," The Spectre whispered as he levitated above the table, the lamp overhead now making his cloak and form appear luminous in the dim room.

I grunted in acknowledgement as I finished preparations and placed the Desert Eagle back in its hidden compartment.

"Not tonight," I looked at him pleadingly, "Just information."

"The Safe Haven?"

Nodding in confirmation, "Yes."

"Acceptable," as he answered, he floated towards the door and began to fade, "Tomorrow then."

I left my "lair" and returned to my desk to review my notes from my earlier session with Mr. Jenkins and prepared to go through my upcoming appointments for the week.

After a while, I heard a timid knock on my door.

"Come in," I called to the door without looking up from the papers spread out in front of me.

The door slowly opened, and the subject of Sammy's question poked her head in.

"Hey boss!"

Sofia came in wearing her usual white button up collar shirt to go along with a business casual black skirt, which greatly accentuated her curvy build. She adjusted her butterfly glasses as she gave me a cute, hesitant grin. *Long live the shy nerd look.*

It was evening now. The sun was currently filling the room and when the light hit her bronze skin, I could've sworn I was in the presence of a goddess. Terms like hot and sexy do a disservice to someone like Sofia because she was breathtakingly beautiful and deserved the treatment of a queen.

I briefly glanced up at her to wave her in. My gaze hurriedly shot back to my work as I realized how thankful I was that my complexion doesn't allow for obvious blushing.

"Hey Sofia, did you need anything?"

"It's getting late, and I was wondering if you had any plans for tonight?" she asked, slightly turning her head away from me, "Since we don't usually get early morning patients on Fridays, I thought you might be free later?"

"You know this might be construed as an HR violation," I joked to set her at ease.

"It's only the two of us. So would you be reporting to yourself or to me since I basically do everything else around here?" A smile widened on her face as she matched my energy and countered with a quip of her own.

I reclined in my chair, letting out a huff of mock laughter, "Wow, now is that anyway to talk to your boss? You were in line for a raise, but this current display of insubordination is unacceptable. I'll just have to hold off for now and maybe dock your pay if this conduct continues."

"Now, I'll have to contact my union rep for a potential breach of contract," twirling her long, cerulean accented hair as she came to stand before my desk, "I'll own this place in no time."

"Great, I'd love for you to be able to take our *clients,*" I emphasized to correct her earlier choice of words, "off my hands."

"What else do you love?" The playful smile remained on her face, but the sudden drop in her voice hinted that the question was searching for a more serious answer.

Nervously averting my gaze, I distractingly gave my chair a full spin and placed my palms on my desk.

"I'm going to Mr. Romani's place tonight," I stated, avoiding her question.

"Oh," she replied. Her face remained neutral, but her tone couldn't mask her disappointment. "Well, I'm glad you're not cooped inside as usual. I'll go home for the night then."

Sofia hung her head slightly before turning on her heel to head out.

"It's possible for people to run into each other by chance," I called out to her before she reached the door.

Hey, I'm not a completely insensitive jerk.

Sofia stopped in front of the exit, twirling around which revealed that room brightening smile on her face. She paced back towards me, stopping at my desk, bent forward, arms behind her back.

"By chance, huh?" She parroted thoughtfully. "Can I get a quick lift to my place then?"

"Of course," I rose from my desk and opened a gateway from my office to her apartment and bowed my head at her, "Your chariot awaits, *mi reina*."

"Maybe I don't need to speak to HR after all," stepping through the bridge to her apartment, she turned around and gave me a wink, "Thanks Dev."

I closed the portal and created one of my own, headed for my apartment. I crossed over into my dwelling place and began to prepare for the night's upcoming festivities.

Chapter Two

One of the very few positives of the Conflict was that it led to the eventual birth of megacities. Some states even underwent supermergers, leading to the conception of Dakota, Virginia, and Carolina, no cardinal directions needed.

My home of Peach City, encompassing both Atlanta and Athens, is the hub of the entire northern part of the Peachtree region. The city at night is a vibrant change of pace from the worker bee mentality the day brings. A far cry from the still nights brought about from the terrors of the Conflict and Purification.

Curfews and general fear kept citizens inside, but over time the rules became more lax causing Peach City's nightlife to thrive, which is one of the benefits that the birth of megacities eventually intended to accomplish in the long term.

Think of it similar to a bedtime or curfew when you were a child. The younger you were, the earlier you had to be in your house and in bed. As you got older, hopefully you showed your guardian you were able to handle being up later until you generally outgrow the restrictions.

Well, the city had plenty of time to outgrow its bedtime and is one of the more successful metropolitan areas in the United States now. Unfortunately, I can't say that for many other godforsaken places in this country.

As I continued my walk, I looked up at the Peach transit overhead. Flying cars still aren't a thing yet, but advancements in magnetism and machinery allow for high-speed travel that covers cities from end to end, which significantly cuts down on commute times.

Below on the streets, I observed the cars zipping by. Every car now drives itself, working on a hive mindset, which eliminated human error and if we're being honest, was probably the biggest cause for accidents in the past.

You could hardly tell that it was night, with all of the lights that brightened the roads and walkways. The lampposts, placed about every third block, were like beacons with all of the folks congregating around them. The problem is that some of these blocks offer their own personal bite from the Fruit of Eden. We all possess our vices, and each corner would gladly help you scratch those personal itches.

You might think that doing this in the open would invite the authorities, but with such a wide area to cover it taxes resources, especially for what are considered trivial matters in the big picture. Consider it a silent admission to a truth most of us wouldn't admit to others. If people didn't use and abuse drugs there wouldn't be a need for drug dealers and if people weren't obsessed with sex, the world's oldest form of employment wouldn't exist. Heck, you might even see some of the authorities there if you look close enough.

There did exist two overarching rules to this menagerie of chaos though. No blood, no killing, at least not in broad daylight. Other than that, it's mostly self-policing. I mind my business like most people these days. They're all trying to eat out here, just like the rest of us.

A sudden gust of cool wind breezed past me, causing the tail end of my silver blazer to lift up similar to that of a cape. I put both of my hands in my pockets, kept my head down, and trudged along.

I finally arrived at my destination and glanced up at the neon sign, hanging above the entranceway. It read *Rifugio*. Italian for a safe haven. I looked down to find the bouncer stationed at his usual spot.

"Hey Leo," I greeted him with a friendly smile. "Busy night?"

"No busier than usual," he replied disinterestedly.

Leonardo Russo was a stout man, appearing as if he did bench presses with garbage trucks for fun. Surprisingly, his suit fit him just fine. All black, which added to the 'I'll crack your skull' vibe he was giving off.

Nonchalantly pulling a comb out of his suit pocket, he began straightening out his silver hair and whistling to himself. Clearly, he believed I posed no threat to him.

Truth be told, I didn't.

I presented my left hand before him, showing him my ring finger. On it was the sigil of my patron, a scorpion sitting upon the back of a frog. Because in the end, we are all slaves to our nature.

He nodded, opened the door, and held it open with one of his gigantic hands for me. "You know you don't have to show it."

"I know, but I'd be making your job more difficult if others saw me just walk in without acknowledging you. They might try to waltz right in also."

He started to dig in his ear with his free hand. The hint of a smirk appeared on his face almost as if he enjoyed the thought. "That would make my job more interesting."

I barely managed to suppress a shiver in response to the yearning expressed in his reply.

Walking into the door, I pulled out an action figure from a bygone era and held it out to Leo. "I think this will complete your collection. Nice taste, I heard the Red Ranger is the best. Hope your son likes it."

He took the figure from my hand and grunted what I believe was a thank you.

After my typical exchange with Leo, I entered the building and headed for the bar.

Rifugio could be thought of as a mixture of bar and club, but it didn't exactly cater to the scum of the earth. Nor was it a high-end place that's a first choice for the snooty among us, which I guess is covered by the scum of the earth criteria. If you have the means of entering, you'll be able to enter, but it's up to you how you exit.

I walked over to the bar, hands in my pocket trying not to draw too much attention, observing my surroundings while I was finding my way.

The place was big enough to have a good time and some semblance of privacy, but also small enough for a family feel while also having the ability to keep an eye on everyone. The bar and club area of the establishment were dimly lit, most of the clientele seemed to be enjoying the confidentiality. The club portion comprised of circular booths with ruby colored seats encapsulating the tables. Turning to the restaurant section, I saw what I presumed to be a couple, laughing while sharing one booth bench together. Another table had an old-timer that kind of reminded me of a much more affable Mr. Jenkins.

Arriving at the bar, I took a seat in one of the turquoise bar stool chairs. One of the bartenders recognized me and came over.

"Hey Clara," I greeted her.

Clara was Italian, just like her uncle, the owner of this establishment. She was a relatively tall blonde and definitely would be looking over me in heels.

"Hey Dr. Prince," Clara returned the greeting as she began twirling her right pigtail in an enthusiastic manner. "How are you?"

"Please," throwing my hands up in mock protest, "I prefer not to be addressed as Doctor when I'm in public. When people find out I'm a therapist, they try to get free sessions out of me on the spot."

"I think that's awesome, I'd have people call me Doctor everywhere I went. I'll go get *Zio* for you."

"No need, he's a busy man. I can wait till he's free."

"Nonsense, I always have time for my favorite customer," a voice boomed, as a portly Italian man in an emerald *Armani* suit came bursting through the door to the back room where the real business happens.

This was Toni Romani. Mr. Romani was one of the most famous Capos in Peach City. At the end of the Purification, people recognized that having an agency as powerful as the IPF being the sole policing force in the country could mark the end of democracy and lead to the birth of a dictatorship as history has shown. This led to the rebirth and creations of factions, old and new. The Romani family was stationed here and is one of the many different overall factions that occupied Peach City. The difference now is these factions were more about self-preservation than gain.

The IPF was always lurking.

Mr. Romani was the one you called if you needed protection or if someone needed to be taken care of. I heard that he was even underboss for a time, but when he met his wife, he transitioned into a more conciliatory role and took a step back from the day-to-day business for the Romani family. The birth of his kid led to him opening his bar and going as straight as one can go in his line of work.

It's hard to differentiate what are facts or rumors about him because word is that the truth is more terrifying than the stories. Don't let the jolly fat man routine fool you, Romani had a switch that seldom few ever get to see. I've seen the other side of his switch before just as I've been on the other side of his gun. So I knew he was a man to be respected, but also wary of.

He smoothed out his mustache as he marched his way over to me, grabbing a bottle of Sprite before pouring a glass for me.

My favorite. That's why he's my patron.

"Mr. Romani," I rose to meet him. "A pleasure as usual."

"*Smetilla,*" he scolded me. "You're family."

He greeted me with a kiss on both cheeks. I've grown accustomed to this form of welcome, doesn't mean I like it though.

"That doesn't mean I'm calling you Papi."

"And remind me of my age, *Dio no,*" he made the sign of the cross on his heart. "Many more years to go. I see you came for business today," his eyes rested on the ring he gifted me.

I took a swig of my Sprite and nodded.

"I didn't want to rush right into it," then in my best *Godfather* voice, "You've done nothing to make me treat you so disrespectfully. I come to you out of friendship."

Romani bellowed in laughter at this and hung one arm around my shoulders and started shaking me.

"You know most people wouldn't have it in them to do that to my face, but not you kid. That's what I love so much about you."

Romani wasn't exactly one for personal space. I was in the middle of having an up-close meeting with his herbal cologne when Clara rescued me.

Addressing her uncle, "You know auntie doesn't tolerate you treating the customers in such a manner."

"It'll be fine," he pawed his hand at her, dismissing her concerns, "She won't get mad since it's Devin."

"Thanks Toni," I responded flatly as he finally released me. "How's Mia Bella doing?"

His eyes started to mist as I mentioned his daughter.

"Oh, she's doing wonderful! She's always asking when she can see her Uncle Prince again! I can never thank you enough," he put both of his hands on my shoulder and bowed his head.

Either no one else in the building saw the display of emotion from this proud man or they had the sense enough not to acknowledge it.

"She's a fighter," he continued, "I gifted her your old weapons. It helps to calm her down after what happened."

He lowered his voice at this, a somber expression painted his face.

About a year and a half ago, his only child Mia Bella Romani was kidnapped. Even though Toni nor his wife are Irregulars, Mia Bella just happened to be born as such. Post-Purification there's been a spike in Irregular related kidnappings and my belief is that they're being sold as pets to shady individuals, or maybe worse.

That night was the first time I remember putting on the Spectre's coat. Luckily, I was able to rescue her and ever since then Toni's been my patron. He told me it was a matter of principle and honor. Plus, it's not the type of offer you can refuse if you know what's good for you.

I calmly placed my hand on his shoulder and offered him a gentle smile.

He collected himself, then continued in a near whisper, "She's getting pretty good at it, maybe one day you'll be in the market for a sidekick, and she can -"

"She will do no such thing!" The voice of a woman commanding absolute authority interrupted him. Accompanying that voice was Toni's wife Susan, who was carrying a silver round tray with one hand and a notepad in the other.

Susan Romani, unlike most of the Family, isn't Italian. She's a no nonsense fiery redhead, Georgia blue-blood through and through. She lost both of her parents during the Conflict, and as the eldest remaining member in her household, had to rally and take care of her remaining siblings. Kind of fitting since she seemed like she's used to carrying one child in her arms when she's at home while herding the others.

It seemed pigtails were the theme today. Her ginger hair, flamelike in appearance, flickered as the lights danced and played with her hair upon approach.

"Nothing gets past you dear," Toni said in submission, "We were discussing Mia's training to be a therapist just like Devin here," he pleadingly looked at me for assistance.

I suddenly found my Sprite to be the most interesting thing in the room at the moment. I respected Toni, but I feared Susan.

Glaring at Toni, hands on hips, "You expect me to believe that load of cow dung. Even Mia could spin a tale better than that. I could hear you blubbering halfway across the room. Have some dignity. And why are you bothering dear Devin?"

I looked back up from my glass, "Pleasure to see you again Ma'am. I'm always blessed for you to grace me with your lovely presence. Forgive me, unfortunately it seems tonight I needed to bother Toni."

She smiled with the corner of her eyes. "Ah, we have a gentleman among us," then shooting a withering scowl at Toni, "See, why don't you flatter me instead of groveling like a pig?"

Susan Romani does not pull punches.

"Clara, will you be a doll and handle the tables for me? There is business to discuss."

Susan knew fully well the type of business that Toni was into, but she loved him unconditionally. Very few people have clean hands these days. That's why I work with Toni, to protect the ones that do.

"Yes, Auntie I'll get right on it," Clara answered before bounding out to converse with the customers.

Susan whispered to Toni, motioning to the room he had exited from earlier. He nodded his head grimly, gathered himself, looked back at me and headed to the back room.

Glancing back towards me, Susan asked, "How is my favorite adopted son doing? Are you eating well?"

"I'm doing well Ma'am. My practice is doing good and as you can see," lifting up my arms to present my body, "I'm not skin and bones just yet."

"Good to hear sweetie," she started handling the other customers at the bar while continuing our conversation every time she stopped by. "Forgive Antoni, he blames himself for Mia being...*taken*." she paused before saying the last word, "Someone hitting him so close to home, makes him feel helpless. Weak, like he failed as a father and a husband, but you, you've given him inspiration to try to prevent other parents from feeling the same."

"Nothing to forgive. I'd probably be in the same boat if I had a family of my own."

She rested her hand gently upon mine, "You are family, dear."

It was warm, like your favorite blanket wrapping you up in the middle of a chilly winter. I wondered if my mother ever comforted me like that in the past. My memory really didn't allow me to recall either of my parents, but it was little moments like this that brought about that sense of longing.

With her other hand, she slid me an orange juice filled shot glass. "Speaking of which, I think there's a little missy over there that's dreaming of a family of her own," she gestured with her head with this statement.

I looked in the direction of her gesture. Sitting at the opposite end of the bar was Sofia. Her left eye was completely covered, hiding behind her now fittingly royal blue dyed hair as she wore her lovely mane down for the night. When she knew she had my attention, Sofia brushed her hair aside and wiggled her fingers at me in 'hello'.

I met her gaze with a smile and whispered to Susan. Correspondingly, Susan poured a shot of Fernet and Coke then placed it in front of Sofia. Susan started to talk to Sofia, but she had her back to me, so I couldn't make out what they were saying, but when she turned around the two of them started giggling.

We both raised our glasses, saluted, and knocked our shots back.

"Go and talk to Toni," Susan suggested as she came back over. "You shouldn't keep a girl like that waiting, you know."

"We shouldn't be long," I replied. "Maybe a few minutes."

Susan leaned towards me and in a hushed voice, "You know that's not what I mean," she eyed me knowingly.

"I know what you mean," I grinned halfheartedly, "I'll go talk to Toni."

I stood up from the stool and headed to meet Toni. I had to pass the opposite end of the bar to reach the back room and as I arrived at the door a hand suddenly grabbed my wrist.

Sofia looked at me with concern in her eyes. "Are you sure about this?"

She was the only person that's seen the true cost that the task before me had on my well-being.

I offered her a reassuring smile, though I'm not sure how convincing it was. Patting her hand, "Yeah, I'm sure."

Then, I walked into the lion's den.

"Is your timeout over Toni?" I asked, taking a seat across from him at the square table where he was settled. The single light bulb in the room, hanging above, alternated back and forth like a grandfather clock, manipulating the shadows in the small space.

"Ha, I trust my Susan's judgment more than I do my own most days," he clasped his hands together and began speaking in a more deliberate tone, "So, let's discuss what you came here for."

"The Underground," I responded, matching his timbre.

He leaned back in his seat, running a hand over his face.

Withdrawing a piece of paper from his suit pocket, "I got information for you."

After sliding it across the table, Toni sat back, arms folded, waiting for me to finish reading the message.

I glared up from the note, "I have to talk to *him*?"

"He's never been wrong before," he took time to ponder his next words carefully, "He's a little eccentric, but you see worse on a daily basis."

"If he was my client, I would quit being a therapist."

"Don't kill the messenger," Toni put his hands up in surrender, "plus I heard you'll blend right in with the dress attire."

I decided my attire wasn't the hill I wanted to die on. Waving my hand dismissively, I responded, "Regardless, how have your, um, interviews been going? Any information on where this leads?"

Smirking at my PG description of his interrogations, "The interviews? Right. The culprits in question sing like my *mamma* while cleaning during the Italian spring. I thank you for selecting the candidates."

He bowed towards me to emphasize his gratitude.

"Well, it is a part of our deal that I leave a few crooks alive, so you can question them," I glanced at the light swinging above, "Probably better for them if I just killed em."

In agreement, "You're probably right about that."

"How far are we getting with The Underground anyway?"

"Well, first we need to find their actual name. The Underground has power because no one's dragged them to the surface and exposed them yet."

"And MyKey can lead us to them?" I peered back questioningly.

"If he wants his stream of income to keep flowing, he better?"

Sighing, "Well, I guess I'll pay him a visit tomorrow. Do you have any guesses how The Underground works?"

He began rubbing his mustache in contemplation, "My guess, how most organizations work, somebody at the top is calling the shots, but you won't ever see him."

I tilted my head askingly.

Acknowledging my confusion, "Meaning he can't afford to get his hands dirty with something as deep as this, so you'll never see or hear from him. But with an operation this big, assuming all these kidnappings are connected to a single boss, which is unlikely but still. There will come an overseer. Especially with the disruption you've been over the past year. You find this overseer, then you can possibly find the big boss."

He paused for a bit. I didn't interrupt.

"The problem though is that he's probably selling the goods," he spat, "*Perdonami* for the choice of words, which means that this is much bigger than Peach City, but I can deal with that when the time comes. I just need to know where to aim before I fire."

"And you have the Family's blessing to use these resources?" I inquired.

"The Underground is an affront to the Family and all that we stand for!" Romani suddenly pounded his fist on the table. I was certain the thunderous reverberations could be heard in the bar area.

"Plus, they made this personal. I have the Family's full support and there will be hell to pay," he snarled.

"Understandable," I placated him before my eyes sunk to the floor.

"Why do you seem so down, *mio amico*?" His demeanor and voice softened.

"Seeing all these people get taken," shaking my head in disbelief, "I go out, punch a couple of minions, rinse and repeat. We're just playing a meaningless game of Whack-a-Mole unless we find a more permanent solution."

In resignation, I placed my head in my hands.

Toni came around the table and placed one of his giant paws on my shoulder. With his other, he tossed a few pictures on the table.

"Look," he ordered firmly.

I let my hands slip from my face and scanned the photos he had displayed before me. The pics contained images of children and young adults, men, and women alike. Smiles painted their faces. Some photos had children appearing to be reunited with family, others had young adults apparently in work uniforms.

Toni had a penchant for hiring those that I saved. A lot of Irregulars that get snatched, are children, minorities, or come from poor socioeconomic backgrounds. Toni believed by putting them and their families in positions where they can better their standing in society, then it would be less likely for them to be targeted.

People won't ask questions when a homeless vagabond goes missing, but when John Doe doesn't show up at the office to consult a client or attend a meeting with the board then they'll care.

Toni also believed by being connected this way, it would put a network of support in place. It also didn't hurt to have an informal gang of pissed off Irregulars at your beck and call, ready to strike back at their captors.

"This is just a fraction of the people that you've saved," he said reassuring me, "You go out there in that bar and you'll see those you've helped. Natasha gets a chance to be the first one in her family to go to college, Joey is going to be a lawyer soon," referencing the couple I had seen earlier.

He continued, "You saved my Mia Bella," before nudging me with his elbow, "and now you also got the world's best and most underappreciated assistant."

I chuckled at this. "Everyone takes her side, but you're right. Thanks for this. All of it."

I picked up a picture of a small little red-headed girl with deep green eyes, missing one of her front teeth, and holding a soccer ball, while smiling at the camera. Admittedly, that made me tear up a little.

"Mia's grown up a lot since then," I reached out to hand the picture over to him.

He held up a hand to stop me. "Keep it, so you'll remember *whom* you're really fighting for."

"*Grazie!*" I thanked him, slipping the photo into my coat pocket.

"*Prego!*"

I stood up, our meeting over. We shook hands, with his huge hairy hand swallowing mine. Toni placed his arm around me as we headed towards the exit.

"Have fun," He patted my back as we returned to a livelier atmosphere than when we had previously left. Business was truly picking up now.

"My wife, dance with me," Toni playfully begged Susan before leading her to the dance floor.

"Sure, I'll let you make it up to me," Susan responded and began taking her apron off. "Clara, handle the bar!"

I leaned into Sofia's ear, "Do you want to get a booth?"

Offering me her hand, "Yes, I do."

***

Later in the night, we said our goodbyes to the Romani's and left *Rifugio* together.

Walking arm in arm in the vibrant night, I noticed that Sofia was clutching my arm tightly and her eyes were darting around nervously.

"It's okay, no one's coming for you," I stated, trying to assuage her fears.

She looked towards me and smiled in gratitude. Thinking back to the photo of Mia Bella, I was convinced now more than ever that I had to protect those smiles.

"I could've just opened a way for you to go home," I offered.

Shaking her head in protest, "And turn this down? No way! I'm not going to let them control my life. I'll be fine, I just need a couple of moments."

Tough woman.

"Alright," I gave her a grin. "We'll keep walking then."

She began snuggling her head in gratitude onto my shoulder and we continued on.

"You're quieter than usual," I noted a while later. "Normally, you would've made a joke about my out of work attire by now."

"The night is still young," she replied before slowly peeked my way. "I was wondering why we haven't progressed yet?"

"You know why," I said, trying to keep my voice even.

Rolling her eyes, "It was one time. I didn't know then."

"That one time almost got you killed," I exhaled looking at my free hand. We've still yet to completely bridge the gap from that day.

"I've forgiven you," she replied, her voice barely above a whisper.

"And I, you."

"Yet, there's still that rift," her head lowered to the street as she said this.

We stayed that way for a few minutes as we walked down the street. I really needed a way to lighten the mood. Every time one of us would look in the other's direction, they would quickly avoid eye contact.

"Well, at least I don't have to report to HR that I have a relationship with one of my employees. That would be a public relations nightmare."

Sofia playfully punched my arm at this. "Jerk."

"Ouch," I rubbed my arm, feigning pain, "I need someone to rescue me from this abusive relationship."

"Too bad," she said, the grin returning to her face. "you're stuck with me."

We eventually arrived at her apartment complex. A nice, multistory, brown brick building. Her particular apartment located on the seventh floor had a great view, overlooking the nightlife below.

"Thanks again Dev," she gave me a peck on the cheek before bouncing up the stairs.

At the top, she turned around, "Oh yeah, that blazer looks ridiculous on you. I figure you as more of a sweater guy."

"You never miss an opportunity, do you?" I asked dryly.

"Can't help myself," she shrugged, sticking her tongue out before going inside.

I watched her walk in while shaking my head, a smirk on my face.

"You made the right decision," The Spectre suddenly whispered into my ear.

I jolted back in shock at his abrupt appearance.

"Really?" I asked in disbelief.

"Yes."

"I meant appearing out of nowhere," I retorted. "Don't you have any sense of personal space?"

"I appear from your mind," he replied simply.

"I would've preferred Sammy in a moment like this, but at this point whatever."

Still fuming, I turned and began walking down the street, looking for an alley I could step into to head home. I'm not officially registered to use my powers, so I couldn't afford to be so blatant about using them out in the open.

Once I found the appropriate spot, I checked my surroundings then opened a portal. I stepped into my apartment and began preparing for the following day.

Tonight I rest, but tomorrow, I hunt.

Chapter Three

How come we just don't just make our own way in there?" Sammy looked at me quizzically as we both gazed at the steel door before us. It was the following night and thanks to Toni's tip I was exactly where I needed to be to get more information.

"This is a place that doesn't like unwanted guests," I answered with a grimace. "Plus, I don't feel like chasing this guy."

"Then we knock?" He frowned at me. "That kind of messes up the whole hero bit."

"Don't say that word!" I snapped at him. "They don't exist anymore."

"Sorry," a glum look came on Sammy's face as he started kicking the ground in front of him.

"Always the bad guy," I muttered to myself. "Hey, do you want to knock on the door together?" I leaned down to ask him in order to cheer him up a bit. The last thing I needed was a disgruntled illusion going rogue in a place like this.

"Really?" His face brightened.

I nodded in the affirmative and we knocked together.

"I like your outfit by the way!" He observed as we waited to be let in.

I glanced down, looking at myself. I was in my ensemble for my second job, the one that's off the books. My black, long coat was only buttoned towards the top, causing the bottom to flutter in the wind. The white flame design looked like a raging fire in the night. My fedora was slightly tipped in the front to hide as much of my features as possible and I had silver Steampunk goggles covering my eyes. I was also wearing my light gauntlets, which simply covered my hands from the cold. Honestly, they're just gloves, but gauntlets sound cooler.

"Thanks, I guess," I quickly took a glimpse of him as another gust of wind blew inside the holes in his unintentionally ripped jeans. "I would compliment your attire, but you always wear the same thing. It would be pretty redundant."

"Fair enough," he said before attempting to whistle, "What's taking so long?"

"One sec," we began pounding on the door this time, clearly knocking lightly wasn't working.

"MyKey, you know it's me!" I shouted at the steel impediment, "Open up or I'll just let myself in."

I heard the sudden unlocking of the latch coming from behind the door. Soon the entrance opened, revealing a socially conservative person's worst nightmare. Strobe lights were flickering back and forth, loud undecipherable dubstep music blaring, and a crowded enclosed space.

"Close your eyes," I advised Sammy as we headed into not a cloud of mystery, but a mist of marijuana.

I completely walked past the goon holding the door, flashing my Desert Eagle as a warning that I preferred not to be messed with. You have to keep up certain appearances in any line of work. I lightly pushed a couple of party goers out of my initial path and eventually people started getting the idea.

Now where to find him? I thought.

Sammy and I turned down a corridor until I found the room I was looking for. A cage was placed in the center and the audience was going rabid over the competitors scrapping in the center. I had to give it to MyKey, he knew how to appeal to the masses.

"Ahh, the Peach City Phantom! To what do I owe this pleasure?" A voice crooned from within the midst of the crowd.

A second later, just the man I needed appeared. Along with the unnecessary phonetically correct spelling of his name, his sense of fashion was also in poor taste.

He came through the crowd towards me with slicked back magenta hair, pink leather trench coat, and so many tattoos that I thought someone was using his body as the blueprint for an escape plan.

"Why does he look like a knockoff Joker?" Sammy inquired. I suppressed a smirk and waved for him to be silent.

"Yes, announce to the world that it's me," no inflection in my voice as I addressed MyKey.

"Relax, look around," he spun to show off his domain. "No one can hear us. Plus, your attire matches the theme of my establishment."

He was right. MyKey's setup was an off the grid entertainment center. A hodgepodge of a fighting rink, dance club, drug haven, high stakes card games, and another service that we'll just say is best left unsaid. Was any of it legal?

Absolutely not.

Too much money changed hands here for the higher ups not to take notice. Problem is that this is the type of place that the higher ups love. Remember what I said about we all have our vices? MyKey was just the first to consolidate them all together under a single roof.

In light of this, it goes without saying that discretion is of the highest order. Everyone in attendance had some form of attire that hid their true identity. Fortunately for me, the general theme was Steampunk, add a touch of a Victorian Masquerade vibe with a sprinkle of pop culture characters of today thrown in and you're all set. In other words, every cosplayers dream.

Even though most rival parties don't particularly like MyKey, trying to take him down would be a waste of time. At this point, he was nearly too big to fail. The attempt to fill the vacuum of vice he would leave behind would lead to near anarchy.

What I will say about him, is that he treats his employees fairly. None of the blackmail or unpaid debt stuff that you typically see for those that work in these conditions. He's just merely a conduit for their secret cravings. Another plus is that he despises the ongoing kidnappings just as much as me and he's willing to do something about it, which is all I truly cared about.

"Mr. Romani sent me your way," I looked at the fighters in the cage disapprovingly. The female fighter was close to clawing the male fighter's eyes out. "You couldn't have just given him all the information?"

His eyes followed my gaze, a sleazy smirk creeping onto his face. "Oh that. Don't worry, the ref will ring the bell soon, maybe. It's a shame you missed our champ though. They always put on a show," he started shadow boxing next to me, sound effects and all.

"The information MyKey!" I whispered harshly, trying to refocus him.

"Right, right. Can I get you a drink by the way? You look parched."

A growl started to form in the back of my throat.

"Sorry," he glanced around skittishly. In a lowered voice, "I couldn't get this information to Mr. Romani directly because I don't trust anyone to carry it. And a guy like me can't just walk into a fine place of business such as *Rifugio*. The missus would shoot me on the spot."

I couldn't disagree with him on those points. If you own a restaurant, you don't want a rat walking through the front door on the way to the kitchen, and Susan would most definitely shoot him before the door could even close behind him.

"The Underground, they operate in the dark," MyKey stated.

"Now is not the time to be metaphorical," I warned him as my patience began running dangerously thin.

"You got me. But not just figuratively, literally as well," he guided me to a more secluded spot as our discussion continued. "The docks, old MARTA tunnel ways, secret passages in destroyed stadiums and theme parks, what do they all have in common?"

"Ever since the end of the Purification, most of those places got abandoned or turned into spots that people could gather in secret," I answered, going along with his train of logic.

"Exactly, but ever since their destruction post-Purification, no one could comprehend how complex it is, it's almost like those weird hamster tube mazes."

"A habitrail?" I threw out.

"*Gesundheit*. They thought they were clever, but no one's outsmarting MyKey," tapping his belly, "I got the keys right here."

My eyes widened at this realization. That slickster, he was walking around with the treasure map in plain sight.

Noticing my amazement, he nodded in self-gratification, "Exactly, and tonight they'll be here," pointing to a particle spot within his belly button.

I certainly hope he isn't messing with me. I thought as I started making a mental map of where I needed to be later when suddenly, a hooded figure bumped past me.

"Out of the way Edgelord!" They called back angrily, continuing on.

"Forgive the champ, they're usually moody after a fight," MyKey advocated, his eyes following the cloaked figure. A half smile slowly donned his face. "But I do get the feeling things may have just gotten interesting."

"It's nothing," I said, brushing off the lack of hospitality. "Thanks, MyKey. This really helps." Those words stung like vinegar coming out of my mouth.

"Takes a cockroach to find a cockroach," stepping closer to whisper in my ear, "Exterminate them all, every last one."

I nodded grimly in confirmation then departed Sodom and Gomorrah as quick as possible.

Chapter Four

I think that went well," Sammy opined to me once we were outside.

"As long as you didn't see that much, we're good," I replied.

"Do I get to run point this time?" He asked hopefully.

"No, get Spectre. I gotta feeling this time might be a little different."

"Aye-aye, Captain," he saluted. "Just try not to get distracted by the other."

I winced at his mention of my most dreaded hallucination. "I'll try."

Opening a portal, I then headed for the tunnels. Since I've had to travel these passageways a lot over the past year, I had a general idea of where I needed to be. I stepped out of my opening, welcomed to a pitch black stillness. I heard what I hoped were rats scurrying and squeaking in the distance around me. Reaching up, I enabled night vision mode on my goggles, another perk gifted to me by the Romani family.

"You there Spectre?" I called out in a low voice. With my ability, I'm not a powerhouse nor am I particularly skilled fighter, so stealth is vital to my success.

"I'm with you," The Spectre affirmed. I didn't need to see him, I just needed him to confirm my reality.

"What about Barb?" Fear started creeping into my voice.

"It is loose," a hint of concern tinted his tone.

"Oh well," I shook my anxiety off, "We have to press on."

"Agreed."

MyKey was right about the tunnels becoming mazes. The deeper I went, I started to find more passages that clearly weren't being used for commuting or maintenance. I kept my guard up for any welcoming parties. At this point, I was definitely an uninvited guest.

Soon, I started to see dim lighting in the distance. Silhouettes produced by the light danced on the walls before me. From what I could count, there were about six figures present. Voices were coming from these shadows and from what I could tell, one of them wasn't happy.

"Sloppy," the voice derided, "The higher-ups aren't happy with the recent handling of the shipments, so they dispatched me to find and fix the problem."

"But boss," another voice spoke up weakly, "It's the P.C.P, he ambushes us too quickly. Nobody can get a good look at him and there's never any survivors."

A sharp smack rang throughout the tunnels, causing me to pause my approach, and hide behind a rundown railcar.

"Excuses. Cowards like you are the reason we're behind schedule. This agitator aims to usurp everything we've built. Headquarters will not have it anymore. If his continued presence persists, I will deal with it personally. He won't be able to hide from me."

I started to notice that the assumed alpha of this group had a familiar southern twang, but I couldn't quite place where or how I heard it before.

"Toni," I radioed him in a hushed voice, "I think I found the overseer you were talking about. I'm sending you my location now. Send your squad. Doc out."

I touched the beacon on my goggles, signaling my coordinates for Toni to find me. I didn't want to reveal myself too quickly, not knowing the extent of this new threat's ability, but I needed to get a look at him and capture his appearance.

As I sidled the railcar, I also tried to keep a lookout for the kidnapped victims. I couldn't risk them getting caught in a firefight. Pebbles started to fall from somewhere up above, but even with my night vision there was nothing to be seen after a brief scan.

"Please don't be it, please don't be it," I chanted quietly in order to calm myself down.

"It is not," The Spectre appeared, reassurance in his voice. "Another may be among us."

"Also," Alpha voice continued, "If you want to play with the merchandise that's fine, but don't damage it!" His voice rose to a shout.

"You're not the only angry one, you bastard," I whispered. These guys were about to get a masterclass in pain tolerance.

As I peeked around the corner, I could see him. This dude had me by at least six inches. He stood at least six foot six and strapped to his back was one of the largest swords I've ever seen, a claymore I believe. He had gloves that you would see in colonial times where men would challenge each other to duels. A dark brown trench coat adorned his body. The *crème de la crème* of it all is that this man was wearing, of all things, an orange ascot.

Unbelievable, who does he think he is?

I decided that maiming him would be the best course of action. Take out the minions, then leave him to Toni for questioning, seems like the most efficient way to handle this. I withdrew my Desert Eagle from its holster and paused.

First priority, the taken.

They had to be close. No way you took all six guards away from the hostages for what amounted to an employee pep talk. The sound of chains clanking could be heard from another railcar, not even twenty meters away from me.

"Are you going to let them die too?" A scratchy voice murmured in my ear.

I spun on it, my Desert Eagle pointed at the ready.

Nothing was there, but I knew to whom the voice belonged. My breaths were ragged, sweat began seeping from beneath my hood unto my brow. I needed to calm down before I blew this.

"You're not going to get me Barb. Just let me save them first," I wasn't sure if I was trying to convince myself or Barb more.

Now that the taken were located, I gathered myself and took aim at the alpha's hamstring. He posed little threat if he couldn't move.

My finger began pulling back on the trigger when suddenly a column of white flame came crashing down on the unsuspecting assailants.

"Play with this, like the way Cardinal John played with you, choir boys," A cry came from above the fire.

I had to barrel roll in order to avoid the roaring flames. Trying to locate the source proved unsuccessful, the flame was too blinding.

I turned my night vision off and equipped my tonfas.

Reminding myself, "No blades yet."

"Don't let them die too," Barb had finally revealed itself.

Barb, the third member of the triumvirate renting space in my brain. Barb was feline like in its nature, moving around on all fours, with its body completely comprised of barbed wire. It prowled about as if it owned the place and constantly leered at me as if I were prey. Its bulky frame seeping with blood and scarlet cat eyes glowed from where slits existed within the head. A reminder that not all nightmares exist when we sleep.

"Get out of my way," I scowled, but there was a lack of conviction in my voice.

"I'm sorry my dear prince," Its sharklike teeth dripping with red plasma as the cruel smile taunted me, "How could I miss this fun?"

"Leave him be. Your presence is unwanted," The Spectre quickly came to my aid, challenging the abomination standing before me.

"I'll be around Devin," the sinisterness in Barb's voice made clear before it faded away.

"Thanks, Spectre." Nodding to him in gratitude, while trying to collect my breath.

"I am here to serve," looking towards the other railcar, "and so are you." He then flew out of my line of sight, leaving me alone.

"Right, time to move," I opened a portal and leapt into action.

I popped up behind thug number one and cracked him in the base of his neck with one of my palladium tonfas, rendering him unconscious.

"Good one, your highness," Barb sadistically commented.

"Shut up!" I yelled.

Thug number two wasn't as lucky. With my escalating agitation, my aggressiveness also increased. The now external expression of my internal conflict gave him time to point his Uzi towards me.

Yet, that's all he had the chance to do.

I created a portal in front of me with the opposite end appearing behind him. I reached into the entryway and yanked him from behind on the other side. When he came through before me, I admittedly may have struck him in the face more than was necessary. I tossed his limp body aside and examined the surrounding chaos.

The flames were starting to die down, but more of the goon squad started to appear. Four more came from around the bend in the tunnel, which leads me to believe that must have been another entrance or there were more captives. That would explain how the mystery person got in. The alpha, it seems, must have chased after them.

In the flames were four other captors. Their para-military garb, smoldering post-attack. I didn't have time to fully check their equipment, but these were the most professional bunch I've seen yet, and with this overseer coming through they must've had serious backing.

"What happened here?" One of the female guards asked.

"I don't know but check the merchandise," another guard ordered.

With one leaving the group, I put into place my favorite trap. This time I made a triangular gateway below their feet and the three standing within fell through. They then dropped from another gateway above and into the previous one below.

Okay, so admittedly unless your power requires an invocation, naming your moves is pretty childish, but I call this one the Infinite Loop.

While the three stooges were experiencing one of the trials that many computer scientists face on a daily basis, I snuck up on the guard heading to the railcar of the victims.

"Stop!" I called out.

They turned on me quickly. I was expecting a frightened man, but what I got was a slightly morphed individual now with claws and razor teeth. They came at me with animalistic intent, knowing I had them backed into a corner.

"Great, a theriomorph," I muttered.

I raised my weapons to take the brunt of the initial attack, though my forearms still managed to feel the vibrations from the blow. I needed to end this quickly. Focus is the key to creating and maintaining my wormholes and fighting the theriomorph before me was going to be a challenge.

"Come on Air Bud," I mocked him with my arms behind my back, "I got a treat for you."

Insults, a consistent classic that never fails on low level idiots. He became enraged and charged again. This time though, I did have a surprise. I pressed the triggers on my tonfas which unsheathed both of the blades.

This time when I rose to block his attack, his hands were pierced by my blades.

A yowl of pain rang throughout the tunnels. At this, my Infinite Loop finally found its end and the other three of his cohorts dropped. They were barely moving, but it wouldn't be enough to keep them down.

Gotta move quick.

I let go of the stick in my left hand and withdrew my gun to deliver a gutshot.

Once my attacker slumped to the ground, I put two bullets in his brain. In this business, always double tap.

"I wonder if he had a family?" Barb inquired as I stood over the now lifeless corpse.

I immediately shot in its direction. A stifled cry followed my weapon's discharge. Only then did I realize that I had shot the railcar holding the captives.

"No," I started to run over, but realized the three I had been holding were now stirring. "Focus, Prince. Focus!"

I holstered my gun and picked up my other stick. I resheathed the blades and quickly dispatched two of the guards with blows to the temples. The female guard had managed to recover her senses quicker than the other two. When I spun towards her, she began blasting at me with a six-shooter revolver.

In a movie, I would've blocked the bullets with my tonfas, and defeated her soon thereafter while she was still in awe of my awesomeness. In reality, I took three bullets to the chest.

Fortunately, I was wearing a Kevlar vest underneath. Unfortunately, it still felt like a professional slugger hit me with a baseball bat three times.

I fell ungracefully behind an isolated cinder block, to avoid another barrage. She didn't fire another round. Must've thought she killed me, or she was saving ammo. I thoughtfully created a portal underneath me and fell on top of her.

Pinning her down, "It's over. Surrender."

"Please don't kill me!" Her hands opened in submission.

"Don't play scared broad now."

Who says broad anymore? I thought disapprovingly to myself.

"Please, I just wanted to make some quick cash. Support my family. No one gets hurt. You know how it is, right?"

To say the blissful ignorance of that statement enraged me would be like saying the Sun is a little warm. It took every ounce of self-control for me not to unload the rest of my clip into her right there and then.

I picked her up by the vest, slamming the crook against the storage railcar. Frightened whimpers came from within.

"Look at them," I demanded, pressing her face to the cold metal. "Do you call this no one getting hurt? Do you think there are no consequences for your actions?"

"Who are you to judge us?" She spat back, "You pop up, kill some guards, and then leave the rest to be tortured by the mob, and get to call yourself a hero?"

I jammed one of my sticks onto her neck, stifling her breathing while I contemplated whether to end her pathetic existence.

"Heroes are dead," my voice dropped deadly low as I kept her pinned. "Only a demon like me is left to protect the innocent from monsters like you."

"Yes, kill her!" Barb lustingly cheered me on. "What's one more?"

"To protect, we must do what we must," The Spectre concurred.

"To be, or not to be: that is the question!" The voice from earlier interjected, "To kill, or not to kill: that is the question before you."

"Damn it," Barb cursed, spinning towards the voice. It gave me a cursory glance before disappearing. "I'll see you later tonight my prince."

"Do their actions justify your own?" The voice inquired again. As it drew closer, I noticed that it sounded feminine.

Peering over my shoulder, I noticed that it was the hooded figure that bumped into me earlier at MyKey's spot. As the figure lifted the hood, it revealed a customized smiling silver Greek theater mask.

"Can I help you?" I questioned them evenly, while still pressing the guard to the car.

"Just knock her unconscious. Don't ruin the name of the Peach City Phantom over trash."

"I hate this trope so much," I muttered, mostly to myself.

"She's not leaving alive anyway, is she?" Looking inside the windows, "Plus, there are children. Be a light to them, the same as you were to the others before."

The figure made two good points. Toni, as far as I know didn't exactly let people walk out and leave once he was done with them. I never had the nerve to ask anyway.

I peered inside the windows also. There was a combination of scared and confused faces staring at me, waiting for my next move. My gaze rested on one face that was different from the rest. It was a little boy, even younger than Sammy, gripping a teddy bear. He slowly shook his head at me, almost as if begging me not to kill his captor. Mercy, to someone that's keeping him locked and soon to be sold off as a slave.

My shoulders slumped, the will to kill now gone.

"Coward," the guard spat at me.

The figure stepped up and punched the captured assailant square in the nose, rendering her unconscious. I let her limp body fall to the ground.

"We met earlier, right? I thought you would want to rip her head off?"

"You could say there's another part of me that wants to remove her spine, but it's sleeping right now."

"Thanks, by the way. That was a tough chick."

"We prefer not to be called chicks," she said pointedly.

"Uh, I'm sorry I guess," apologetically rubbing the back of my head with a mix of confusion.

"Bahahaha, you should see your face right now," she burst into laughter and began imitating a robot, "'we prefer not to be called chicks' and you bought it."

I found the Infinite Loop to be very tempting right now.

"Anyway," moving along, "Let's get them out of here."

"Of course."

By the time we finally finished removing all of the chains and tying up all the unconscious guards, the first signs of the arrival of Toni's cleanup crew began to show, with Leo leading the charge.

"I must leave soon. It was great getting to work with you," she said turning to me.

"Same to you as well. I'm not really in the field with others a lot. What happened to the claymore guy by the way?" I asked.

"Oh, I created a flame double and it led him down one of these tunnels. I think he thought I was you. There weren't any other hostages, so I turned around. By the time I got back, you were about to perform acupuncture on her jugular, so he might still be around. At least I get to say I worked with the Peach City Phantom," she browsed around the area as she said this.

I performed a brief scan also before returning my focus to her. "People call me by that ridiculous name, but I didn't catch yours."

"I'm Angelus," she bounced cheerily, the motion resembling a child getting ready to go to the candy store.

When she stopped bouncing, she became very still for a moment.

"Is everything okay?" I asked, confused by her sudden shift in demeanor.

I couldn't see her expression, but I had the sense she was examining me very closely. Angelus stepped forward quietly and lifted a hand to my left eye. I wanted to flinch away from her, but I didn't detect any malice in her approach. She ran the hand smoothly over the scar as if she were trying to recall a memory.

"My muse," I heard a faint whisper escape from behind the mask but couldn't quite understand what she said.

"What?"

After a moment, the masked figure stepped back and enveloped herself in those white flames, rising off the ground.

"Don't worry about it, Edgelord," she called back as she took off, "I'm pretty sure we'll be seeing more of each other. Bye-bye."

"That's a weird one," I spoke to no one in particular.

"An interesting one indeed," The Spectre replied as he appeared beside me.

"Was she real?" I asked.

"As far as I can tell, yes," he answered, "So far, Sammy is the only pure human that appears to you."

"She did have a mask," I pointed out.

"Indeed, she did."

I shrugged, "Oh well, let's go home."

"Are you prepared?"

I sighed, "I knew what I signed up for."

***

As soon as I arrived in my apartment, I fell on my bed writhing in pain. Not only from the bullets from before, but I also felt a shearing agony emanating from my back which spread all over my skin as if it were being removed from the muscles below it.

"Your reward, my prince. A hero indeed," Barb teased me as I lay gasping for air. "Oh, you didn't call sweet Sofia to soothe you. I do hate when she interrupts, doctor. Maybe I should've just had you finish the job the first time. Only I can truly protect you."

I reached over to my nightstand and grabbed two bottles of pills. At this point, blinking caused me intense pain. I took one to stop the hallucinations and the other to sleep.

"Have a sweet dream Devin, I'm sure it'll hold you over till the next time we meet," Barb whispered in my ear as my consciousness began to fade.

Chapter Five

*L*eave *the kid out of this!" The voice desperately cried out into the rain, "You've already won."*

Standing across from him was a man in a trench coat. His face and features barely visible in the torrential downpour.

"My dearest hero, what you fail to understand is that I'm not here to simply beat you. I'm here to end you," The figure in the trench coat replied, his voice oozing with southern charm as he dropped the boy.

"No!" The first voice yelled as it followed closely after the boy.

The owner of the first voice ran past the offender to the ledge. He caught a quick glance of his weapon, revealing it to be a longsword of sorts. Then he leapt down to save the boy. The boy was falling head first, but a quick flash of his rose red shirt was visible. A portal opened before the boy and a hand reached out to grasp him.

What comes next is the scream of a child, followed by the horrid sound of barbed wire ripping away at the skin of its unfortunate victim. Blood trickles down a lifeless hand and silence follows.

I gasped as I woke up. Once again, my sheets were drenched in perspiration.

What was that? That dream isn't usually that vivid. I thought to myself as I tried to mentally recover from the night terror.

I pondered over these thoughts until I felt a licking sensation on my cheek. I turned over to find Mew. I guess I disturbed him from his sleep.

"Thanks pal," I scratched behind his ear, "It's only you and me for the next two days."

The pills will halt my hallucinations for a couple of days, which was currently a bummer. I really needed to talk to Sammy about what I just saw. The color scheme of clothing was similar, but I couldn't see the boy's face or if there was a firetruck. Also, what was with the sword and the portal? Post-mission was when my nightmares were the worst, but the one last night seemed abnormal compared to usual.

Mew purred as I petted him before he went back up to his perch, his mission accomplished.

I rolled out of bed, clutching at my ribs in pain. With all the mental anguish, I had forgotten that I was physically exhausted as well. I went to the restroom and from the cabinet pulled out a syringe. I jammed the needle into my stomach, releasing the nanites into my system, so they could start the repairs. Bless the benefits of modern day technology.

"I guess I'm not jumping through any hoops today," I pointed out to myself, but I still needed to get answers. Luckily, it was a Saturday so I may be able to talk to just the guy I needed to.

***

"Hello Dr. Green," I greeted my former therapist and mentor. "Thank you, nurse. We'll be fine from here," I thanked Nurse Gooding, a heavyset, middle-aged black woman, with a kind smile and an even kinder heart, who had walked me to Dr. Green's room.

"Is that you Devin?" Dr. Green, who was sitting in his reclining chair, turned to me.

"Yes sir. I brought a pack of cards and the chocolate bar that you're not supposed to have," I put my index finger over my mouth, playfully indicating that this was our little secret.

"Thank you, my boy. They never let me have either these days. Say it enables my bad habits."

"Well, how many times have you gotten in trouble for gambling?" I questioned him. "I have to beg them not to kick you out every time. You're lucky that I work with some of the residents here for free."

"Ah residents, not patients?" He lifted an eyebrow.

"People first, just like you taught me."

"Seems even today I taught you well," he nodded to himself in approval.

I pulled the table in his room up beside him and sat down in a wooden chair.

I examined him a little bit to see if he had any physical changes since last week. He was wearing his favorite green sweater that I had gifted him once I earned my certification. His feet were dancing around in his slippers while he sat. Clearly, he wasn't going out today. His gray hair was thinning a bit at the top and his widow's peak was becoming more pronounced, but he still seemed to be in great physical shape. I could see his old man muscles outlined underneath his sweater. Like he said, "Take care of the body and may the mind follow."

"I have a question for you regarding something doc."

"Well, open up the pack and let's get a game going," he pointed to the deck of cards. "I'll see what help I can be to you while we play."

I opened the pack and we started playing a game of Crazy Eights.

"Do you remember much about me when I first came to you?" I asked him while dealing.

He put on his reading glasses and picked up his cards, "I know you were scared," he reflected for a bit, "and I suppose scarred. You kept mentioning a boy and something about a ghost."

"I already had my ability when I came to you right?"

"Yes," he grimaced when he saw the cards in his hand and then gave me a quick suspicious glance. "You rarely wanted to use it, like every portal you made brought you pain. Look at you now though, saving the innocents that are stolen off the streets."

"Was there someone before me?" I leaned in, looking at him pleadingly. "Dr. Green?"

He was off staring into space, unblinking, unmoving.

"Dr. Green?" I waved, trying to get his attention.

Dr. Green slowly turned to me and then a smile spread across his face.

"Is that you Devin?" He asked.

I put on a fake smile and then answered him. "Yes, Dr. Green. It's me."

"It's good to see you, my boy," he repeated.

"Yes, I brought you a pack of cards and chocolate," I said, my mood deflating.

Dr. Green was in this nursing home because he was suffering from dementia now. It was probably Alzheimer's, but we wouldn't know until…after.

Advancement in technology can only go so far sometimes.

"That's great, let's get a game going," he stated, oblivious to the fact that we were in the middle of a game currently.

"Yes," I agreed with him, "How about Crazy Eights?"

"Perfect."

I waited a couple of minutes for him to reset and then repeated my line of questioning until I got back to where we left off before he drifted.

"Was there always someone fighting like me? With my abilities, I mean."

"I suppose so," he furrowed his brow as he was thinking, "But maybe it was always you. I mean you look young my boy, but I never did know how old you were when you first came to me. You barely look any different from when we first met and with how the education system is today, you can fast track to your preferred field. That eliminates adding years from college."

Shaking his head, "Sorry kid. I know where but not sure when I am most days. I don't know if that helps you or not?"

I rubbed my chin, trying to start putting the mental puzzle pieces together. His information, though limited, was still helpful, but I was still missing key information.

Dr. Green's head shot up suddenly as something had just come to him. "There was a time where that outfit you wear now was prevalent in the news a lot. A vigilante, post-Purification. Then suddenly no one heard from him again after a while. Shortly after, you came to me. Maybe that's why you can't remember. IPF probably got to you. Either wiped your memory or beat it out of you."

That insight proved to be interesting. He was right about my age being a wild card. Many Irregulars age slower than most Normies, or at least the effects are less noticeable. Plus, with the Conflict a lot of records were destroyed in the fighting. If I'd been in the field before, that could explain why I feel compelled to fight now. It would also explain why I chose my specific outfit. I remember how each piece of the attire came into my possession, but I'm fuzzy on why exactly each piece held such significance to me.

"Thanks Dr. Green," I dealt another hand, once our game finished, "Any bit of information helps at this point."

"No sweat off my back, kid. Happy to help a former mentee."

"What a lovely image to think of."

He began laughing at my sarcasm before it turned into a bout of coughing. It sounded hoarse, the kind you would expect from someone that was under the weather for a prolonged period of time or at death's doorstep.

"Are you okay Dr. Green? I'll get you some water," I stood and went to pour a glass.

As I returned from the sink with his cup, he was looking at me with that faraway look from earlier.

"Is that you Devin?" He questioned.

"Yes doc, it's me," the false smile from before returned to my face, but with a little less enthusiasm this time.

"It's good to see you, my boy. What brings you here?" He asked as if I had just walked through the door.

"I came to give you something to drink before you take your nap," I offered him his cup of water and he accepted it gingerly.

"Nap? Right," he nodded to himself. "I wish we had more time to talk. Maybe you can bring cards like usual next time."

"Of course," I concurred while ushering him to bed.

As he was laying down, I drew the cover over him. He added, "Oh and that chocolate that I like too."

"Chocolate, got it," I answered him. "I hope you get some good rest doc."

"Thanks, Devin. I can always count on you," he grinned up at me in gratitude before closing his eyes to rest.

Quickly thereafter, he was sleeping. He seemed uncomfortable, so I picked up one of the pillows to adjust it for him. I looked at the pillow, then towards the sleeping elder before me.

I thought about how much I hated seeing him like this. His condition was getting steadily worse, even week to week there was serious decline. Dr. Green shouldn't have to suffer like this after all of those he's helped. Maybe it would be more merciful if his pain could end as quickly as possible before he was no longer himself in the end.

I suddenly snapped out of my trance and found myself with the pillow just inches from his face.

"What am I doing?" I asked myself in mild shock. I shook whatever thoughts I was having out of my head and placed the pillow back under his head.

"Bye Doc," I left the room to tell Nurse Gooding I was departing.

As I was wiping my eyes leaving the building, I noticed two text messages from Toni.

The first one read:

Hey Devin! Good work yesterday. There will be more updates this week as information is extracted. Also, we wanted to invite you over for dinner tomorrow a little after we come back from mass. Mia Bella would love to see her uncle. Addio.

That sounded reasonable enough, but I wasn't sure if I was in the mental state to be around people. My world was growing a lot more complex, and I didn't want the distraction of company at the moment. I went to text him back that I wouldn't be able to make it, but then read his second message.

Susan invited you personally.

I quickly responded back: *I'll be there.*

Chapter Six

Sunday at 4 pm on the dot, I was standing outside of the Romani estate, although castle would probably be a more accurate description. The electric gate in front, ensured that no one would be climbing over or trying to pick any locks. The main building in the background was made of marble, with a granite roof. The sheer scale was enormous and even though I've been inside before, I still didn't know how many rooms were within. To the left of where I was standing was the guest house, a scaled down version of the main residence but with more windows on the side.

Near the front right of the house they have a miniature forest, complete with Redwood trees and a pond that hosts a plethora of fish. The real kicker though is that one of the Romani's employees is an Irregular with the ability to communicate with animals, so Toni decided why not have a bear for security. She hides somewhere within the forest.

Good luck trying to break in. The only thing missing was a moat filled with gators.

I pressed the button for the intercom to alert them of my presence.

"Um, hello. I'm here," I nervously reported into the microphone.

A buzzing noise from the intercom signified that my entry was approved. After parking, I walked up to the front door and knocked.

"Devin!" Toni greeted me at the door, "Joy to see you. Glad you came!"

"How could I turn down your hospitality?" I looked around before lowering my voice to a whisper, "Susan would temporarily ban me from the bar if I didn't show up."

He chuckled at this then gestured for me to come in. "You're right about that, *mio amico*."

"Uncle Prince!" A young voice from within the house cried out to me.

I spun towards the voice which belonged to a sweet little ten year old girl currently running towards me.

"You're finally here!" Mia Bella exclaimed, leaping into my arms.

I caught and twirled her around. "Good to see you, Mia Bella. How's my favorite niece doing? I haven't seen you since our last session."

"I'm your only niece," she pouted, folding her arms to make clear her displeasure once I placed her back on the ground. "You should come over more."

"Now, now, you know Uncle Prince is busy these days," Toni came over, mildly reprimanding her. "But he decided to pay us a visit for a while today."

Her smile returned as she beamed up at me. "Do you wanna play? Daddy got me new toys."

"We will eat before any playing occurs," Susan interrupted as she strolled into the room, wearing a sunflower yellow apron, and wiping her hands with a towel as she joined us. "I don't recall approving of these 'toys' that your father bought you," she glared at Toni.

"Susan, good to see you. I brought some sugar. I know your famous sweet tea usually requires a considerable amount," I said, saving Toni from certain peril.

"Thanks Devin, you can have a seat. The food will be out soon," she took the bag of sugar from my hand thankfully before glaring back over to Toni, probably indicating that their conversation wasn't over.

"Can I sit next to Uncle, Mama?" Mia Bella pleaded to her mother.

"Yes sweetie, but help mama set the table first."

Bubbling with joy, Mia Bella skipped over to help her mother.

"Hey Devin, good to see you," Clara welcomed me as she strolled down the mahogany staircase, wearing a plum blouse and jeans. A perfect combination for either chilling at home or going out with friends. From her relaxed demeanor, she seemed to have been enacting the former. "Are you joining us for Sunday dinner?"

"Yeah, I guess I am," I rubbed the back of my neck as I watched her come down the stairs. "Always hard to turn down free food."

"Right about that," she giggled before giving Toni a peck on the check. "I'm going to help Auntie, *zio*. You both can probably come in after a minute."

"Thanks Clara," Toni took off his coat and set in on the coat rack before putting a beefy arm around me leading me to the dining room. "Come Devin, let us not keep the ladies waiting."

When we reached the dining table, Toni took his seat at the head of the table. Susan sat to his right; they held each other's hand tenderly as the rest of us took our places. I sat opposite Toni at the table. Mia Bella was firmly planted between me and Susan, with Clara sitting to Toni's left. The smell of pasta sauce tinted with a hint of southern home-cooking permeated through the room as the food sat in front of us.

"So Devin, how was your event last night?" Toni asked me once we started eating.

I peered from him to Susan then gestured cautiously with my eyes towards Mia Bella who was happily eating pasta while humming to herself.

"It's fine," Susan waved her hand in approval, "She knows enough. Just leave out details."

"Okay, well I met someone new," I replied.

Mia Bella's eyes suddenly widened, and she gawked at me. "You mean like a girlfriend?"

Even Clara glimpsed at me in surprise before politely covering a smile with a hand.

"Mia Bella!" Susan snapped, "Don't be rude at the table."

"Sorry Mama," Mia Bella apologized sheepishly.

"Um, no not like a girlfriend," I answered Mia Bella, "It was a woman though. She inadvertently assisted me with the problem. There was another interesting development. I guess you could say I met two new people. I don't know if you received the image I sent you?"

"I got it," Toni answered grimly, "Looks problematic."

"We know you can beat this, Devin," Susan added, her grip of Toni's hand tightened as she spoke, "You're one of the few real symbols of hope left in this city."

I opened my mouth to object, but she lifted her hand to stop me.

Pointing to her daughter, "That little one right there is proof enough."

I looked down to see her beaming up at me, pasta sauce staining the left corner of her mouth.

"Can we play now?" She asked.

***

"So, how have you been sleeping?" I asked Mia Bella.

She was currently leading me by the hand around her room. It was about the size of my office and was covered in posters that I assume were of her favorite characters and pop star idols of the day. I didn't recognize any of them, not really one to be in the know of what's cool in the world of ten year old girls. And that was probably for the better.

"I still get nightmares," she replied glumly as her head drooped.

She was still suffering from the scars that the night of her kidnapping had left her. Mia Bella was my client also, as I wanted to help with her healing process. I offered to help for free, but Toni and Susan were hearing none of that, part of the reason why I'm under their patronage.

"I'm sorry, but don't worry we're going to keep working at it," I encouraged her, putting one hand on her shoulder comfortingly. "In time, hopefully they'll go away soon."

She stopped and turned back to me, "I kinda don't want them to stop."

Shocked, I asked, "Why? Don't they scare you?"

She shrugged and gripped my arm a little tighter, "You always save me at the end."

There are rare moments that occur in life where you feel like your existence is validated. This was one of those moments for me. First, a scared boy teaches me about mercy for his own captors and now Mia Bella was teaching me about strength. Leave it up to kids to teach the most basic of lessons.

I patted her head and she proceeded to show me all the wonders in her room.

She pulled out a box from her closet and sat on the ground. She tapped the ground beside her, inviting me to sit. I joined my niece, waiting to see the surprise she obviously wanted to show me.

"These are the toys Daddy got me. Don't tell Mama," she put a finger over her mouth.

"Your secret's safe with me," I answered before zipping my lips.

She lifted the top of the box and scooted it over for me to see.

Inside were my old bamboo tonfas that I used before Toni made me upgrade. I picked one up to examine it. The tonfa seemed smaller than before. I'm guessing he was fitting it to a particular ten year old's dimensions. Also, in the box were my original steampunk aviator goggles. Admittedly, I looked more ridiculous then than I do now. I guess that's why I don't like being seen when I work. At least my bowler hat was no longer part of my active fit.

"That's cool Mia. Do you ever use them?"

Putting on the goggles, she started running around the room imitating a plane until she landed right back beside me. "All the time! They help keep the bad guys away. Daddy said I can be a hero like you one day."

"I don't know if I would call myself a hero Mia, but you would make a great one someday."

"I've been working on controlling my powers. Look!" She stood up, both hands outstretched towards her lavender covered bed. The bed slowly started vibrating, which turned into violent rattling and then eventually rose slightly off the ground. "See."

When Mia Bella switched her focus to me, the bed suddenly dropped and made a loud thud as it crashed to the floor.

"Mia Bella Romani! What did I tell you about using powers in this house!?" Susan could be heard screaming from below.

"Sorry Mama!" Mia Bella apologized with a sly smirk on her face.

Voicing my concern to her. "That was impressive, but it's dangerous out there."

She lifted the goggles from her eyes, letting them rest on her forehead. Considering me seriously now, she asked, "Do you ever get scared?"

A brief smile touched the corners of my lips, "All the time, but I think about all the other little Bellas I need to save and that makes me brave."

"I want to be brave just like you," she responded, laying her head upon my lap. I began gently stroking her hair as she began to doze off.

"You're already braver than I'll ever be, kid," I whispered in her ear as her chest rose and fell rhythmically, her soft breathing was the only noise that could be heard in the room as she slumbered. Carefully carrying the little one to her bed, I placed her under the sheets before running my hand across a loose strand of hair. "I'll do my best to make you don't to grow up too fast Bella."

Chapter Seven

How come you don't drive more often?" Sammy asked as we rode in my vintage red Dodge Stratus on the way to work the next day.

Responding to my recently returned aberration, "Did you miss the part where I teleport?"

"I guess you have a point," leaning back in the passenger seat, "Did we miss anything while we were gone?"

"Nothing definitive, but the dream is becoming more," I paused, searching for the correct word.

"Clearer?" He offered in his youthful voice.

I shook my head. "Let's say pronounced, still got more questions than answers."

Sammy simply nodded in acknowledgement then proceeded to stare out the window.

I sighed, "The time where I need you to be talkative is when you shut down on me."

Still fixated on the world outside the window, "The truth has many different perspectives. Depending on the one you see, it may destroy you."

"Well, Barb is already doing a great job at the destruction part," I responded caustically, "Not exactly like you're helping me with the truth part of it," I sniped back.

When I glanced towards the passenger's seat, Sammy had already vanished.

"Typical," I rode in silence the rest of the way as I waited for my Stratus to get me to the office. Since I had no clients scheduled for today, hopefully work would be less eventful than my personal life.

***

"Boss, we have a bit of a situation," Sofia informed me over the intercom.

Lifting my head groggily off of my desk, I checked the clock overhanging my desk. It was currently thirteen minutes pass three. I only had a little over an hour and a half before I could go home.

"Here I was, thinking that I'd get the entire day to myself," I groaned, still groggy from my brief respite from reality. I patted the side of my head, trying to get the cobwebs out, then pressed my intercom to reply to Sofia's perceived hiccup.

"What is it?"

"There is a client that wants to speak with you, but they didn't make an appointment."

Switching to my telephone, I called Sofia so that this potential client wouldn't be privy to our conversation. Wouldn't want them spreading nasty rumors of our lack of hospitality, that would be bad for business.

"Walk-ins don't start till four. She can wait or come back at that time."

"I shared this information," Sofia paused. I'm guessing she was looking at whoever walked in and was doing her best to be courteous while still coding her language. Professionalism at its best.

"They insist that they meet you now. They say, 'the situation is of the utmost importance.' Waiting isn't exactly an option for them?" Sofia stated, questioning the proper course of action that she should take.

"What's their name?"

"One sec," Sofia put me on hold, presumably to get our guest's name. "She said it is Em Mortalle." I asked her to spell the name out for me, so that I could record it.

"You have gotta be kidding me," I sighed when I looked down at the notepad. I really wasn't in the mood for one of these types this close to getting off. "Leaving isn't an option?"

"Unfortunately not, on both accounts," she replied. I could hear her straining to maintain the politeness in her voice.

"Gimme a sec and I'll be out there," rubbing my forehead, I forced myself to rise from the comfort of my chair and went to go see who this client was.

I placed my glasses on before striding over to open the door.

"Excuse the delay. I was a bit, um, occupied." Not necessarily a lie.

"Every second is of infinite value," the reply came from a young brunette with a pixie cut standing in front of Sofia's desk.

She was wearing a green and yellow horizontal striped shirt that had sleeves longer than her arms as they dangled down where her hands should have been.

I considered her for a moment. She seemed old enough to be here without a legal guardian, but young enough to still get a guy in trouble. There seemed to be a youthful exuberance to her demeanor, yet there was something about the steadiness within her hazel eyes that told me she was much more mature than her appearance would suggest.

"Right. Thanks for your patience. You can come inside," I welcomed her politely.

Before I even finished my sentence, she trotted by me and into my office. I felt a sharp jolt of static as her shirt sleeve grazed me. I glanced towards Sofia pleadingly. She looked past me in disgust to the girl inside, shook her head, and went back to her laptop.

My shoulders slumped in disappointment, but I turned around to meet my inevitable fate.

When I re-entered my office, she was already laying down on the lounge chair. *Interesting, most first-timers usually prefer to sit upright.*

"I'm glad you're comfortable," I said as I sat down across from her.

"I'm just kind of surprised," she remarked, idly picking at the holes in her ripped jeans.

"Surprised about what exactly?" I asked.

She pursed her lips, "You're not what I was expecting. I may have been mistaken in coming."

I bit my tongue, before letting out a retort. You don't exactly demand entry into one's house unannounced and then insult them before they can even offer you something to drink.

Remember, professionalism. I reminded myself before putting on my best doctor's smile.

"What would you be surprised about? You came to me."

She considered me for the first time since I entered the room. "You look like a dork."

Professionalism.

"I'm afraid most of my colleagues in this profession lean more to the proper and prim side of the clothing spectrum. Keeping up appearances as they say."

She shook her head, I guess she didn't agree with my stance. "Not exactly what I meant, but since I'm here, I guess I could use a therapist's opinion."

"Well, that's what I'm here for. What do you need?" I offered.

"I'm an Irregular," she confessed.

I did my best not to let out a cough of surprise, taken aback by the simplicity of her admission. Even though I have to abide by physician-patient privilege, admitting to being an Irregular was not something that you would just tell a stranger.

She shifted her eyes back to me, noting my response, "You can pick your jaw up off the ground doc. You have to honor my privacy. I heard you're one of the few therapists that'll help people like me anyway."

There was truth to this statement. Depending on the stability of your socio-economic status, your standing in society could drop based on your interactions with a non-IPF registered Irregular, let alone an unregistered. Many therapists would feel compelled to rat out their clients in order to protect their status, so most of my colleagues denied them service to protect themselves from the potential backlash. This isn't much different than any time period where mass discrimination was *en vogue*.

"Sorry, I'm a bit surprised most of my clients don't usually admit to that so freely," I responded after getting myself together.

"It's okay. Why would they?" Her mood soured for a sec, then just as fast gained a sense of cheerfulness again.

"So...um ....Ms. Mortalle?" I started.

She waved her hand dismissively, "Just call me Emma."

I nodded affirmatively, "So, Emma how can I help you?"

She adjusted her body on the couch, making herself more comfortable, "I have these abilities and I hadn't used them for a while until about a year and a half ago. It seems I forgot the extent of them, but recently I feel reinvigorated," a purposeful smile crossed her face as she spoke.

"If I may, what happened a year and a half ago?" I questioned.

"I've found my muse," Emma's eyes brightened.

Not understanding, "Your...muse?"

"Yes, my muse. The source of my inspiration. The rumor that floats around this city, the one who comes in the night, rescuer of the lost, the one who brings judgment upon the wicked, and I think I may have just met him," she was nearly bouncing uncontrollably as she spoke.

I was still uncertain as to what she was talking about, but I felt like I'd heard those words from somewhere before. Adjusting my glasses, I refocused my attention on her. "I'm not seeing the problem yet?"

Quickly, her head snapped towards me, and she looked me directly in my eyes, "Isn't that what your damn job is!?"

I visibly flinched at her dramatic shift in demeanor. The voice that came out of the young woman before me was not that of the Emma who was laying there a minute ago.

"So," I put on my best attempt at a disarming smile, "You're dealing with dissociative identity disorder."

Her eyes widened in confusion. I guess Emma had taken back the reins from whomever else previously had them. She smirked apologetically, "Sorry, I'm back. You can say that I consider it as more of a split timeshare."

"No, forgive me. I may have provoked you. If you don't mind me asking, what exactly are your triggers?"

"Well," she folded her arms and pouted in contemplation, "We both have our purposes, but I'd say agitation, head trauma, death, or if I call upon her."

"Excuse me, but you said death?" I interjected.

"Yes, I've been alive over one hundred thirty years," she replied casually to my query.

I nodded at her answer, then began jotting in my notepad. *Also delusional.*

"You can continue."

"As I was saying I met my muse and now I know how I can help him."

"How?"

"Well, we were at the abandoned MARTA station in the tunnels, and we worked together to save this group of civilians. It was awesome. Even my other is invested. It's the first time we've seen eye to eye in decades. When the villains were captured, I doubled back to hear what they were saying when they got questioned. They mentioned something about there being an underground structure before the old Georgia Dome was destroyed. I'm going there tonight to investigate."

At this point I was leaning in, hanging onto every word that escaped her lips. If what she was saying was true, then I was looking at the flame bringer from the other night. This was the outcome that I feared the most, that my actions would bring about a copycat or fanatic follower.

"Are you entirely sure you want to do this? Maybe your muse isn't exactly looking for a partner?" I asked trying to direct her on a different path.

"And how the hell would you know what they want?" That same biting voice from before came back, sniping my hopes at redirection.

I adjusted my glasses nervously, "I don't, but maybe you should exercise caution. Emma did say that you just recently had a rebirth with your powers."

"We've had more rebirths than I wish to remember," the new persona responded.

"If I may ask, what is your name?"

"Don't worry about it," she huffed, shooting down my inquiry. "We won't be seeing each other after this anyway."

Their pupils dilated again, which I presumed meant that Emma had returned.

"Don't worry about her, she's a bit of a grumpy pants."

"Grumpy pants?"

"Grumpy pants," she affirmed with a nod, "Anyway I think I can help. I'm stronger than him anyway."

I don't think I could really disagree with this point, but I couldn't help but feel a bit insulted anyway.

"So, you're asking me if you should get involved?"

She took a bit of time before answering. For the first time Emma sat up, glaring directly at me. I felt a part of my spine disintegrate as she held me with that withering gaze.

"I'm asking if I made a mistake in coming here?"

"I think only you can answer that. I hope I helped somehow though."

"The miserable have no other medicine, but only hope," Emma jumped up from her spot, trekking over to the door in her green and yellow polka-dot Vans. She looked back over her shoulder, "The Peach City Phantom provided that to me and others. Have a good life doc."

Sofia immediately came in after she left.

Exasperatedly she asked, "What was that about?"

"Nothing good," I replied, glancing at the clock and it was currently ten past five. I can't believe we spoke for that long.

"Anything you can talk about?" Sofia asked.

I sighed, "I think she wants to copy a certain someone's nighttime activities."

Sofia came over and placed her hand on my arm reassuringly, "Well, I'm pretty sure a certain someone won't let them get hurt."

"That's not my responsibility," I protested.

Sofia leaned into my ear and whispered, "Neither was saving me," with that she rose from my desk and glided smoothly to the exit, "Later Dev."

Thirty minutes later, I put down my notepad and was preparing to go home for the day, until I lifted my head and was met by an unwanted visitor.

"Why are you here?" I asked contemptuously.

The Spectre floated before me, his coat fluttering as if there was a current of air blowing around him.

He tilted his head, "Are you going to abandon her?"

"Abandon her? At no point did she say she needed help," I scoffed at his question.

"Doesn't your client's mere presence admit that they need help?"

I rolled my eyes until I felt that they touched the back of their sockets, "That's a very prideful way to think of it."

"We only do what we're allowed to do," a different voice interjected somewhere from behind me. Twisting around to the corner of the room, I found Sammy sitting there working on his coloring book.

"Great, is this an intervention?" I threw up my hands in annoyance as the two hallucinations came together. Very rarely, does more than one of my hallucinations show up at the same time. I'm very grateful that's the case because one by themselves is enough to give me a migraine.

"Consider it a meeting of the minds," The Spectre suggested, hovering beside Sammy.

"Earlier, I wanted answers, now you expect something of me? I think not," I grabbed my jacket off the back of my chair and ungracefully threw it onto myself before storming towards the exit. "I'll be seeing the two of you later."

As my hand touched the door knob, Sammy said, "This may be the path that leads you to the answers you seek."

I let my head drop down and hang for a few moments. "No kid speaks like that."

"I've been learning," he said, proud of himself.

The Spectre flew over to my secret closet and waited.

"Observation only," I groaned in defeat. "I only step in if it's serious."

Sammy and Spectre look at each other, then back at me. In unison, "Deal."

Chapter Eight

W hat have I gotten myself into?"

I was atop the Mercedes-Benz Stadium, overlooking where the former Georgia Dome used to be. The state had attempted to do many things with the spot over the years, but post-Conflict they pretty much gave up. Now it was just a patch of empty concrete, not even suitable enough to serve as a true parking lot. Yet, given its downtown location, there were still plenty of citizens in the area and with any number of events possibly taking place, the number of potential onlookers could increase substantially.

I thought it odd that The Underground would pick a spot with so much foot traffic, but that's the best location I suppose, in plain sight.

"She didn't even give a time," I complained, swatting at a fly that kept buzzing around my head.

"You sure are complaining a lot today," Sammy pointed out as he sat on top of the roof next to me.

"How observant of you. My head hallucination has been cryptic the entire day, a copycat is running around imitating me, and Barb is probably going to show up later. What more could I ask for?"

"You know sarcasm is just a defense mechanism of those lacking wit."

Tired of his flippant attitude, I walked over to Sammy and kicked him off the edge of the roof. "See you later Sammy!" I called down after him.

As I peered over the edge to admire my handiwork, I suddenly felt a sharp, piercing pain in my head. I had flashes from my nightmare. All that could be heard was screaming and the tearing of flesh. I fell to my knees from the agony, clutching at my head.

"You didn't even need me to convince you. I would have done the same. Good job, my prince," Barb said sinisterly as it appeared next to me, in what it must have interpreted as its form of comforting me.

"Stop," I cried to myself, "Stop, please stop."

I was currently in the fetal position and shivering now. The pain was too intense for me to move. Barb prowled towards my head and considered my pitiful state for a moment.

"Oh, don't worry. It's far too soon for one of our sessions. I want to savor it more. So don't die on me, my prince," with that Barb was gone.

"Three, six, nine," I chanted to myself in order to regain my composure. By the time I got to seventy-eight, I was up and ready to go. I slowly made my way back to my feet and tried to refocus simply on breathing. When I had myself together, I turned back to the abandoned lot.

Overlooking my intended destination, I reached out my hand, creating a portal before me, then leapt off the roof of the stadium.

***

Stepping out of any of my portals can be a tad bit disorienting at first, but over time I've grown accustomed to it. Still, transitioning from descending rapidly out of the sky to landing into the pitch black of being underground required me to take a second to get my bearings.

I stuck both hands out to my side and took a deep breath.

"Okay, hopefully this isn't a waste of time," I said before reaching up to my goggles. "Night vision, activate."

I could once again see clearly as I traversed the subterranean space. I heard that the Georgia Dome used to be a very popular place back in the day, but it got torn down for the new stadium. I feel like the money could've been better spent elsewhere, but people were more frivolous spenders in those days.

I ended up at the conclusion of my current path. Before me, there was a brown rusted door. Opening the door would probably be too risky, so a little tact was needed. I placed my hand on the door and made a gateway just big enough for my head to fit in. I took a gander inside and was greeted with a stillness that started to give me goosebumps. I increased the size of the opening for my entire body to enter and stepped through, quiet as a church mouse if I may add.

A steady *clinking* noise came from somewhere below my feet. I peered over the handrail in front of me. The building I was in seemed like some sort of factory.

"Weird. Why would this be here?"

As I got closer, I realized why I was having apprehension about this place. This was an Irregular Police Force staging area, where they implanted chips into their Irregular agents before sending them out into the field or a different branch of the IPF. These facilities were guarded almost entirely by their wolves, agents that had the agency to operate on their own without supervision. Meaning chances were high that everyone in this facility was either a dangerous Irregular or highly trained in killing one.

At that moment, it was as if time froze along with my body. I couldn't afford to be caught here. For now, my *other* persona was mostly still a rumor. Admitting that citizens were being kidnapped and sold on the black market under their nose, would be a stain on the organization's reputation. They couldn't afford to be seen as weak, especially if that meant there were third parties potentially creating their own personal army of Irregulars. I was merely a necessary evil as long as my activities didn't become too public or interfere with their affairs.

The workers below were going about their business, my presence unbeknownst to them. There had to be easily over a dozen guards on standby, this wasn't even counting the recruits. Some of the new recruits, or dogs as they were called, were currently being either tagged or collared to ensure they would follow instructions and prevent any rogue behavior. The rest of the recruits received tattoos similar to barcodes. This way they had freer reign, but their whereabouts could still be monitored.

Emma had to have gotten bad intel. Unless the Underground was working with the IPF, it wouldn't make sense for them to have that information, especially an underling. Romani might've had a point about it all being connected then, which lent credence to the fact that they wouldn't be able to acknowledge me. The days of dragging suspected citizens out of their houses ended along with the Purification.

I spun on my heels to exit through the door that I came through, when suddenly I heard the crunching of glass.

"Please don't be her," I begged whoever was currently authoring my fate. I peeked back hopefully, but it only ended up validating my fears. "Oh expletive."

Below, near one of the collar stations I saw Emma once again wearing her comedy mask and cloak. She had broken one of the collaring displays and was not only surrounded by shattered glass, but also IPF agents, whose cuts would go so much deeper.

I inched nearer, peering through the rails to see how the scene would unfold.

"Hands up," one of the operatives commanded her. He must have been the leader of the bunch because the others moved out of his way as he marched towards the now exposed intruder.

"What exactly do you think you're doing here?" He called out in a deep, baritone voice.

She shrugged her shoulders before responding meekly. "Um, I heard that there was a party and was disappointed I didn't get an invitation. So, I decided to invite myself."

I shook my head in disapproval. Not only did she drag both of us into this mess, but that was a terrible joke. The delivery could've been much better.

"You have two options; Join or die," the operative spoke again. My view was slightly obscured so I couldn't see his face directly, but I did detect a faint trace of a British accent in his voice.

"What kind of benefits are we looking at? Medical insurance for people like us is skyrocketing these days," she retorted.

Better. I nodded slightly in approval.

"You get the benefit of not dying. Put a collar on this one, a dog like her needs to be under control," he spun on his heels and proceeded to let his lackeys do the heavy lifting.

It was either my imagination or a trick of the light, but suddenly Emma's mask spun around and morphed from a smile to a frown and her cloak became much darker, as if someone had turned the contrast down.

Then the other voice that I heard earlier, Not-Emma, spoke, "You wanna make me one of your dogs, huh? Well good luck getting this bitch under control! "

Now, that's how you banter. I thought to myself.

Just as soon as the transformation occurred, Not-Emma pulled out what appeared to be a knife attached to brass knuckles on both hands and leapt at her would be attackers.

The first two got dropped before they even had time to react. She slashed their throats and moved onto the next wave before her victims' gushing blood had time to stain the floor. With the element of surprise gone, these new opponents had a bit more luck. They both whipped out shock batons and eased forward, the others assumed a defensive perimeter around them and started to encircle Not-Emma like a frenzy of sharks ready to feed.

Her next two opponents appeared to have a lifetime membership to shop at Big, Tall, and Bald. Tattoos covered most of their heads.

I guess you have to have something up there at a certain point.

Baldy number one swept low at her feet, but she gracefully leapt over his attack and placed an incision on his shoulder as she flew over. Baldy number two went for a bear hug as she landed, but what happened next was an informative commentary on why brains will usually triumph over brawn. Once he had her within his grasp, he accidentally shocked himself with his baton as his arms touched.

Admittedly, this made me chuckle.

With his partner dropping unconscious, Baldy number one's eyes dilated, and he howled towards his target. His surrounding pack of companions spread out, giving him room to operate. I've seen this once before from a kid that I rescued. The guard was about to go into berserker mode. The IPF agent started beating the ground, growing even more muscle, and then charged towards Not-Emma.

She attempted to slash his hamstrings, but with his increasing muscle mass, her blade couldn't puncture skin. He turned around and continued his charge. The others easily could've blindsided Not-Emma with an attack, but that would've put them in the crosshairs of their rampaging ally. This time she tried to halt his charge directly. I'm guessing she was even stronger than Emma because her resistance slightly impeded his rush, but he was still able to drive her into a containment pod. She yelped as her back collided with the metal structure.

Baldy number one paced backwards, never turning from his prey. He was preparing for another charge. He lowered himself into position and began preparing to perform another blitz.

"I guess I should get involved now," I mumbled to myself.

The one benefit of my current predicament is that I know how to stop a berserker. I also know how to disrupt a pack. Cause absolute and utter chaos.

A second before he flattened Not-Emma even further into the pod, he ran into one of my portals. The big bruiser came out from behind his compatriots, bowling over at least six of them.

"Perfect," proud of my work, I pulled my tonfas from their holsters and hopped over the rail to Not-Emma's aid.

As the guards were gathering themselves and trying to make sense of what happened, the rhino of a man was now attacking indiscriminately. Gunfire could be heard in his direction. With that distraction, I ran over to the pod to check the status of my one-time client.

"Angelus!" Calling her by the name she gave me at our first meeting, "Can you stand?"

The mask switched to comedy again, so I was currently with Emma.

"Is that you?" She asked, puzzled.

"Yes, you've gotten us into a big mess," I informed her as I stuck out my hand. "This had to be a trap."

Rising to her feet with my aid, "The web of our life is of a mingled yarn, good and ill together."

"Excuse me?" I asked her, perplexed.

"We're in this together," turning her smiling mask towards me, "For better or worse."

Angelus put her knives back and pulled out a pair of butterfly swords.

"How many weapons do you have?"

"Enough for two. Try to keep up," she replied before she rushed back into battle.

While the guards were distracted, she sliced one who had their back turned to her and then shot white flames in the direction of another.

My shoulders sagged in resignation as I watched her fight with renewed fervor, "I was saving you so that we could leave. Guess I don't have a choice now."

I re-equipped my weapons and was confronted by another two agents with shock batons.

"Did all of you call each other about matching weapons before you came here? That's so cute," I mocked the two of them in my perfect high school mean girl voice.

They must not have appreciated my joke because the first one came at me yelling, rod raised. I sidestepped the charge before chopping them in the neck with my sheathed-tonfa. Watching him crumple to the ground, I then gave his partner a challenging look. *Works every time.*

My opponent returned my challenge with a minacious grin, their mouth showing from the hole left in their ski mask. They touched the end of their baton, the electricity flowing from the weapon to throughout their body, forming a layer of electrical armor.

"Great, electricity manipulation," I benefited since the core of sticks were Kevlar, which isn't conductive, but the trouble was Palladium is. Prolonged contact with my opponent would provide me an up close and personal lesson in the dangers of high voltage. I steadied my will and raised my guard, bracing for the incoming onslaught as they rushed at me.

They were more skilled than I anticipated. The tonfa, my weapon of choice, isn't a commonly used tool for combat these days. The principles of the martial arts used behind it are often practiced, but most of the time when you see the actual sticks it's mostly for show. Meeting someone not only this skilled with a baton, but also able to maintain control over an ability such as theirs was impressive.

It was dawning on me that Angelus and I were sorely out of our weight class here with this many adversaries.

My opponent and I traded a sequence of blows, neither of us gaining an advantage over the other. If I could've seen their face, I might've gotten a read on their exhaustion levels, but all I could study was their breathing. The problem was that his rhythm was steady, while I was starting to huff for air. In time, I would wear down fighting them this way.

This was my mistake. Never fight the fight that your opponent wants. I'm not used to prolonged melee combat, so there was no point in trying to best them. My ego got the best of me, one of the reasons I despise people calling me a hero. Heroes eventually succumb to their own arrogance.

Realizing my error, I hopped back into a portal below my feet and disappeared from their view. In their confusion, I dropped down from above with my arms together ready to slam my weapons down upon them just as a gorilla pounds the ground when trying to assert dominance.

They raised the baton to block, but the aided force from my fall caused them to drop to a knee. Slowly, he looked up at me and there was a "gotcha look" being expressed from their smirk. The electricity transferred from them to me, and I writhed from the convulsions. Then my opponent landed another blow to my previously injured ribs, temporarily knocking the wind out of me.

"I win," he said in a voice so low that I could barely hear his words as he stood over me.

"Not yet," I responded defiantly after I had a moment to collect myself. Abruptly, he dropped through a portal I designed especially for them and collapsed from above next to me.

He landed with an audible thud, the breath temporarily leaving his body. I unsheathed my blades and rolled over onto him victoriously. With myself mounted unto him, I put each tonfa on his chest, to show that I would puncture both of his lungs if he so much as breathed aggressively. That was when I realized I might not have been fighting a him.

I curiously poked with my weapons at the chest again and I got a lot more feedback than I was expecting. Tenderly, I peeled back the ski mask from my opponent's face in the dimly lit room enough to reveal the traces of a blonde female looking back at me. And she was *pissed*.

A few moments passed with us staying there, unmoving. Eventually, her cheeks became flushed, turning a bright pink color. I couldn't see the color of her eyes clearly, but they read murder and I was the intended target.

"What do you think you're doing? Release me you pervert," she started squirming to get out from underneath me, but unfortunately for the both of us my weight was planted firmly upon her.

"I'm totally sorry, but with the ski mask," I gestured to the article of clothing, "I thought you were a guy. I really didn't mean for this to happen."

This probably wasn't the best time for my apology, definitely a poor choice of words, but it's still the thought that counts.

Still wriggling beneath me, "I am Lt. Vitoria Tudor of the Wolf division of the IPF, and I will not tolerate this affront! Kill me now or I will hunt you down! I'll take a serrated knife and remove your testi-"

I knocked her unconscious with the handle of my tonfa. It was probably better for the both of us if she forgot this incident happened. This is why you never assume gender.

"Hopefully Emma is doing better than I am," I muttered to myself. Looking up, this turned out to be the case. Codename Angelus was spreading fire all around, kindling the flames of the chaos that I had started.

At this point, the other IPF operatives were focused mostly on the berserker. He had taken out a good majority of his coworkers for us, so we were mostly on cleanup duty.

"You will cease this behavior at once!" The voice from earlier commanded.

Stepping forth was a ginger male, around his mid-thirties with the stripes of captain on his SWAT inspired IPF uniform.

His subordinate turned to him and then growled.

"I beg you to make my day, Davis," the commander replied coolly.

Davis charged again and as he reached out to snatch his commanding officer, an invisible force slammed down upon his head, rendering him motionless. Whatever hit him so suddenly, looked like it was giving a tutorial on the relationship between a hammer and nail. The floor beneath Davis was indented and cracked from where his skull impacted the floor. The captain walked over to him unhurriedly and bent over to examine him.

"You'll be fine later. Latrine duty for you in the morning though," he spun on his heels, now facing Angelus.

Angelus stopped her fighting and flew down to oppose him.

The captain, hands behind his back, calmly peered over his shoulder to acknowledge me, "I knew you weren't a rumor. Your time will come," then he returned his steady gaze to Angelus.

"Your associate didn't kill anyone, so he is free to depart, but you on the other hand," he looked distastefully at the bodies around him, "Are not leaving this facility."

"May I inquire as to what your name is?" Angelus requested, butterfly swords in hand while she waited for him to make a move.

The officer inspected his fingernails before bringing his attention back to Angelus, "Captain Jack Woods."

"Pleasure to meet you," not sure if she was serious about that comment or not, but she had completely dropped the playful tone. She was now considering Captain Woods, (no, I am not calling him Captain Jack) more meaningfully.

Suddenly, one of the pods was lifted out of its entrenchment and launched at Angelus. She dodged the incoming projectile and ran circles around Captain Woods. I'm not speaking figuratively here, she was literally running around him in a circle, probing at the periphery of his defense. Her speed had increased significantly. She wasn't going Flash level quick, but I would venture to say that she could give a cheetah a run for its money.

In her movements, I started to notice that earlier she was mostly stationary and when she did avoid attacks, she appeared to be maximizing her distance from her would be attackers. Now, she was avoiding blows by the slimmest of margins, not because she was slower but because she was now more agile in her approach. This gave her greater opportunity to counter-punch whenever Captain Woods got too close.

For some reason, I got the feeling that these two combatants were enjoying themselves. I couldn't see Angelus's face because of the mask and Captain Woods hadn't even so much as taken a step during their confrontation, but there was a focus that one had reserved for the other that I had yet to experience in battle.

Angelus then stopped on a dime and unleashed more of her white flame, this time it spiraled towards Woods. He lifted his palm and the blaze crashed into a translucent obstruction, roaring in all directions as it failed to torch its prey.

For the first time, Woods moved and jumped towards Angelus, attempting a Superman punch. Not one to let a moment pass her by, Angelus moved away her cloak and then launched three daggers into his chest so quickly that I was barely able to detect it.

Seriously, how does she have all these blades?

The piercing daggers weren't killshots as they were probably intended, but they did dull his attack. I'm guessing he was going for a full-scale frontal strike with his ability, but it only turned out to be a glancing blow. Yet, it was still strong enough to send Angelus crashing into carts about five feet behind her, rendering her motionless.

As Woods landed, he extracted the daggers from his now revealed armor and dropped them on the ground, the clattering of steel reverberated in the hollow space.

"Good effort," he commented as he strolled over to the downed Angelus unhurried, "but your precision is still off. Unlike your partner, you have real experience as a warrior."

He didn't even glance back to acknowledge me. I have to say, I was starting to get highly offended by the flippant comments on my fighting skills.

I noticed as the captain was starting to prepare for the final blow, the IPF agents around us were beginning to stir. I needed to leave, but at this point leaving without Angelus, Emma, Not-Emma, or whatever else she calls herself would be a sunk cost. I was already here, so I guess I needed to help somehow.

I noticed one of the hanging lights above beginning to swing. There was no draft this far below ground and there was no reason for it to be swinging unless...

Hurriedly, I created a portal in the direction that the light was initially swayed some distance away from it. Next, I made the exit portal underneath Woods. When he tapped into his powers to attack her again, he was thrown upwards into the ceiling. The accompanying smacking sounds of his ascent and descent were quite sickening. I didn't have time to check his status, so I dashed over to Angelus and made a doorway for us out of there and to the world outside.

Barely escaping with all of our faculties intact, I returned to the top of the dome in which I originally was observing from before our grueling encounter.

"What were you thinking?" I asked incredulously. I stood up to look at the horizon. Night had set in and was now being lit by the buzzing city below, the activity below moving randomly through the streets like electrons.

"I thought it was fun," Angelus chuckled in response, tilting her head back as she looked at the starlit sky above.

"We have varying definitions of fun," I sighed. Looking towards her now, "Do you have any idea what the IPF is going to do to us now?"

Teasingly, "I think a certain someone may have you on their hit list more than me."

Embarrassed, I turned away. How she saw that during the fight is beyond me. Now the incident couldn't be swept underneath the rug.

"A situation that could've been averted had you avoided the most basic cliché of stealth," I recovered enough to lecture her.

"In my defense, have you seen my powers? I'm not exactly a cape that goes tiptoeing around, no offense."

I sighed. What's done is done. No point in arguing with her about events that couldn't be changed.

"So, does that mean we're partners now?"

Not even my goggles could hide the puzzled look on my face as I glanced back at her.

"What would give you that idea?"

"Oh come on, we've teamed up twice already."

"Twice is a bit of a stretch," I grumbled.

Angelus, stomped her feet in exasperation, "What? First, the MARTA tunnels and now tonight. We definitely teamed up twice."

"Sneak attacking an unsuspecting group, of which I was a part of, if I may add, then running off till the fighting is over, does not qualify as a team-up. And tonight, tonight was more of a 'we each fight our own opponents' situation."

"Setting the berserker loose on his fellow men in tights and saving me is a form of collaboration. Plus, I've dragged the big bads away from you each time."

Her line of reasoning caused me to furrow my brow. With her taking on all the boss battles, I had been relegated to minion duty recently.

"What?" She continued, "You think that you're the conquering hero and I'm the damsel in distress."

"I don't remember you actually beating the 'big bad' either time," I pointed out in retort.

Angelus balled her fists together and stormed to the edge of the roof. "This isn't over. You'll be seeing me sooner than you expect."

Slowly, she turned back to me and in a hushed voice said, "Thanks by the way."

After that, she swan dived off of the roof, plunging towards the concrete below. I rushed over to gaze over the edge. Someone would have to stop her from attempting a re-enactment of a fly splattering against a windshield. As I peered below, I was met by a blinding light before seeing Angelus flying away, white flames forming wings upon her back.

"Angelus, huh?" Impressed with what I was witnessing, "Yeah, that makes sense."

Chapter Nine

H ey Mew," bending down to scratch behind his ear, "How are you buddy?"

Mew purred as he rolled onto his belly and yawned. Absolutely adorable.

"Really, good to hear. You're the only normal thing in my life these days."

I had just finished returning my outfit to the office and was currently trying to decompress in my apartment. Mew was one of the few beings that was consistent in my life. He's been saving my life since the night we first met, my own personal form of therapy.

Rubbing his belly, "You never change on me. Never hurt me."

"Is that why you fail to love me?" A slithering voice intruded on my conversation.

I froze mid-stroke while petting Mew. That voice. I should've expected it, but something was different this time. Nobody ran point on the mission earlier, but there was no need. So why now?

"Barb?" I whimpered into the previously empty room.

Mew quickly scurried away towards my bedroom.

"Who else?" Barb paced before me, red eyes staring daggers into mine. Its gaze violated the very essence of my soul.

I gulped, "What do you want?"

"What I've always wanted, to help you," its mouth twisted into something that could be mistaken for a grin but was more similar to a wolf baring its teeth before it chomps into its prey.

"How?"

"By delivering what the others refuse to give you, truth," this was perhaps the most extensive conversation we've had since Barb first appeared. I couldn't help but notice how grating its voice truly is. The sound of nails running across a chalkboard came to mind, and the prolonged exposure felt like a hammer driving a spike into my brain, seducing me closer to madness.

Sometimes in life you know that you should take the blue pill, the choice that helps you sleep at night, living in blissful ignorance. But there's something about the red pill that's so darn enticing.

"The whole truth?" I glared at it intensely, watching as Barb stalked patiently, luring me deeper into its rabbit hole.

"The truth is relative. I'll give you all the pieces of the puzzle," Barb's razor grin widened. "The usual way, but I'll allow you to put them together. That's infinitely more than the boy or the ghost has ever offered you. They fear what the truth will do to you. They say you aren't ready, but have you run around in ignorance. I shall free you of it."

I narrowed my eyes at its statement. Nothing Barb said was outlandish, but for some reason I couldn't help but feel like a prize carp caught on a hook.

"What exactly do you want?" I investigated.

Barb stopped its pacing. It was currently on all fours, partially hidden in the shadows of my apartment. Its spiked face and crimson eyes were the only aspects of its being that were visible.

"What I want?" Barb tilted its head in consideration. "When all the cards have been shown, I wish to run point once. Are those terms satisfactory, my prince?"

My blood instantly went cold. Every time I go out in the field, Barb pays me a visit just like tonight. Every. Single. Time.

The Spectre and Sammy usually run point to decipher what's real and what's not. They keep my mental state in check. It's like a Spidey-Sense aimed at internal dangers.

For Barb to want to guide me on a mission was disconcerting. It's an unwelcome distraction and in its presence is when my condition becomes most intolerable. I thought back to my first night trying to save those taken and Barb's interference. I did my best to suppress a shudder, but you can only hide so much from yourself. There were only two reasons I could think of for Barb to make this request of me. Either for me to kill or be killed.

How deep was the truth, and why would Sammy be so secretive about it?

I let out a deep sigh with my eyes closed. "Deal."

I knew that I couldn't put the toothpaste back in the tube now. We were going to have to ride this one until the wheels fell off.

"Perfect," the way Barb stretched out that word with sadistic pleasure let me know that I was probably making the wrong choice. "I'll leave you be until the time arises."

With that, my most feared figment faded away, leaving me alone to stand in the silence of my living room. I shrugged my shoulders and walked towards the kitchen. No point brewing in my own stupidity.

As I entered the kitchen, the lights switched on, activated by the new motion in the room.

I searched my cupboards and fridge to see what there was to prepare. There were some pork chops that I had let thaw out earlier. Peering down, I also found a head of cabbage sitting there.

"Score."

This was the first time since the Spectre appeared a couple of days ago that I had a chance to settle down and try to piece together what had happened.

Clearly, my constant interference had forced the Underground into action. They sent an emissary of sorts to make sure that the situation would be handled. The man with the southern accent and Claymore sword. Something told me that I should be wary of trading blows with him. Speaking of exchanging blows, my encounter with the lieutenant was definitely going to put me in the crosshairs of the IPF. The reason for me being there was because of a false tip received from an Underground goon and this was information received from Emma, who's an enigma herself.

In summary, at some point I needed to confront the Underground's representative, while staying under the IPF's radar which was going to be a near impossible task. On top of this, Barb's presence was about to get a whole lot more pronounced, and my sanity was probably going to decrease with it. Also, the one potentially capable ally I could recruit was probably more unstable than me.

Typical first world problems.

If I was going to survive, I needed to find out more information about Angelus and her whereabouts. Then it hit me that we met at MyKey's joint. She must have overheard the conversation and started snooping around the tunnels until she happened upon me. The quest for information, just like a lot of other questionable substances in Peach City flowed through MyKey, meaning he required a visit. I didn't want to delay this, so tonight would have to suffice and I knew where he would be.

The timer from the stove alerted me of my meal's completion, snapping me back to my current surroundings.

"No point in wasting a good meal," I commented to myself. Grabbing a lime green plate from one of the cupboards, I sat to eat before I began playing detective for the night.

***

One of the things that makes MyKey so loathsome is that he lacks subtlety.

I was currently standing in front of one of MyKey's many hiding holes. This establishment was located in the section of the city formerly known as Bankhead and time nor the city had done much to turn things around in the area. There was litter plaguing the streets, glass from broken windows of rundown homes crunched beneath your feet if you weren't careful, and people generally looked past each other with hardened expressions in their eyes. No one wanted to get caught with their guard down in this part of the city, Irregular or not. I was currently wearing a gray hoodie and black sweats with non-brand running shoes, so that I wouldn't stand out too much. But I was wearing aviator goggles and a navy blue bandana over my mouth, bandit style, so that I could still protect my identity.

I tilted my head up to get a better look at the neon red sign above me which read, In Da Cut. Now for those of you not familiar with this type of verbiage, the term 'in the cut' refers to a secluded place that's either hard to find or off the map. It's not necessarily a bad thing, most speakeasies during Prohibition would be considered in the cut. You could also use the term if you went off road in the middle of nowhere, which is definitely a bad thing for a person in my position.

MyKey's spot was in a back alley and the actual inside of which I've unfortunately been inside of before had literally cut a piece out of the original buildings of which it formerly belonged. Again, this was a man that was too on the nose for me to ever truly get along with.

I checked my surroundings to make sure that no one would try to sneak up on me from behind and took my right hand out of my hoodie and rapped quickly on the door. A small rectangular slit within the door slid open and a pair of beady yellow eyes stared at me.

"Whatchu want?" From the tone of the questioning voice, it was clearly perturbed by my presence. The unblinking predatory eyes continued staring at me in an eerie way.

"Um, I wanna talk to MyKey," I answered.

The slit closed soon after I finished my reply. A few seconds later it reopened.

"Who asking?" The floating eyes asked.

I hesitated for a second. I really hate going by this name, but I knew it would be the quickest ticket to getting me inside.

"P.C.P," I settled on the initials. I really hated the name this city has given me.

The eyes squinted for a bit and the slit closed yet again. I could hear muffled noises somewhere inside the room. Then the door creaked open and there was MyKey dressed as a steampunk version of the Mad Hatter. He even had an orange cane to match the wig he was clearly wearing.

Extended his hands out in greeting, "What have I done to be graced by your presence yet again in such a short period of time?"

"The displeasure is all mine," I replied, rolling my eyes. It's kind of hard for the gesture to carry the same weight when your eyes are distorted by eyewear and a hoodie. "Are you going to invite me in?"

"Of course, where are my manners?" He turned his body sideways, welcoming me in.

Behind the door, I was able to see the owner of the floating eyes. There was a menacing mongoose perched on a stool that allowed it to peer through the slit.

"Can I help you?" It inquired of me in a sardonic tone.

Yes, I was speaking with a mongoose. Before you roll your eyes, ask yourself, in a world where people are genetically imbalanced to the point where they have the power to essentially travel through wormholes like me, do you really think that Mother Nature would skip over animals and itself?

"No, I'm good," I responded quickly, moving past the mongoose.

I entered deeper into the space and found that it had the same tint as the neon-red sign that I had seen outside. The room had wooden pews with soft crimson cushioning grouped into threes throughout. They formed triangles all throughout the room. There were even black triangles painted on the red walls throughout the room. A steady low humming played within the room giving the setting a spooky type of ambiance. On the back wall of the room there was just a desk, similar to the one I had in my office. It gave off the impression that he simply monitored what was occurring around him, like some kind of sick overseer.

To be honest, I couldn't even comprehend what I was seeing. There was a group of middle-aged patrons holding hands in their triangle praying, but I couldn't make sense of the language. To my near left, there were three men around college age laying outstretched on each pew like a surfer before he stands on his board. Each of them lay on their individual pew unmoving, their hands nearly touching the foot of the one before him. In the far back left corner, um, let's just say that I'm thankful that this was the one spot in the room that was dimly lit.

My mouth was gaped. I don't think any explanation would've proved beneficial to me.

MyKey must've got a kick out of my face because he started chortling. He must've been so used to his underworld dealings that my reaction would've been a foreign concept to him since most of his customers probably knew what they were getting into. I made a mental note to myself: when in a room full of crazies, don't assume you're the normal one.

"Sorry, I didn't clean up beforehand," he said putting his arm around my shoulder to shield me from the horrors in the room.

He guided me to the center of the space and pulled out a remote. MyKey pressed a button and continued leading me. We started to descend down a wooden staircase that deposited us into a room below. The lighting was still red, but in this room, there were two couches facing across from each other.

He plopped down on one of them and gestured with his hand, inviting me to sit on the couch opposite him.

Beaming towards me, he asked, "What can I do for you?"

"I need to know about your champion," I responded.

Seemingly confused, he tilted his head. "Who?"

I had to give him the benefit of the doubt. No telling what was in his system. I kind of got the feeling that MyKey lost the ability to get high off of normal drugs. His blood was probably tainted with a litany of substances needed for him to get off, so I decided to be more specific.

"Your fighting champion," I bobbed my head towards him as a teacher leads a student to an answer. "The one that bumped into me when I was at your club."

"Oh, Angelus. What a lovely girl. I make so much money off of her. Usually you try to bet on the underdog, but I mean come on. Why throw away free money?"

Inquisitively, I tilted my head sideways. "She's that strong?"

MyKey nodded his head enthusiastically. "Stronger. In fact, I don't know why she wastes her time in the pits. She came to me just over a year ago, said she was preparing to meet someone or something like that."

I raised an eyebrow. "She say anything else? Any other interesting facts like big changes in personality?"

He stroked his chin for a bit, pondering over my question. "Her personality is typically a combination of bitter and mean with a sprinkle of abrasiveness. Other than that, I would say a thank you is considered out of the normal for her."

"Interesting," his answer gave credence to the outbursts that came from Emma when she visited me, but it's possible that it could've been an act and the aggressive side of her was the base personality with the more personable one being a front. She did outline how the other personality worked which would make sense how the change occurred after Captain Woods slammed her into one of the pods, but I'm not sure if I could say there was a consistent trigger otherwise. So, I could've been dealing with an Irregular who is also a con artist or whose powers are triggered by her personality. The hard part would be determining which.

"I heard you had a run-in with the IPF earlier," MyKey interjected, releasing me from my current trance.

"How'd you know about that?" I asked, perplexed. "It only happened a few hours ago. Plus, it was in a secluded area."

"Please," he waved his hand dismissively, "you're one of the few people that don't come to me for a release. I provide a lot of services, but information is the one that people don't take advantage of."

"How does that explain that only so many people had access to said information and none of them have any incentive to speak a word of it?" I pressed, genuinely curious about the inner workings of his intelligence network.

He rested his head on one of his shoulders and pursed his lips. I'm guessing he usually never took the time to consider how his process worked and was having a hard time figuring out how to explain it. It would be similar to an Irregular explaining the exact science of how their powers worked. They could tell you what it does and how they use them, but how it happens is second nature.

Finally, MyKey's eyes flicked back to me. "Papers are signed in the boardroom, deals are made in the dining room, and the real juicy details come out in the privacy of the bedroom," he made air quotes as he finished the last part of his statement.

I took a moment to think about his answer then shrugged my shoulders. It was probably the best answer I was going to get on the subject, so I accepted it.

"I guess that makes sense," I conceded. "But yeah, we pissed them off. Like that's not the last thing I needed."

"They'll probably get over it. The details came from a huge guy that said his captain was putting him on toilet duty, but he doesn't remember much other than fighting Angelus."

"Baldy number one," I muttered to myself.

MyKey perked up, raising both of his eyebrows. "What was that?"

"Nothing. I have something you might be interested in though."

"Ooh," he leaned in, both hands on his cheeks like a kid seeing the latest toy on television. "You should've told me you came bearing gifts."

"The Underground and the Irregular Police Force may be directly connected."

He let out a long whistle. "Juicy indeed. I thought they would be opposing forces. Romani has a theory that the Underground is kidnapping and selling Irregulars on the black market, but that's merely for resources and to curry favors and not the actual goal. The real tea though is that they're stockpiling enough Irregulars to create a militia big enough to take down the IPF."

"He's said about as much as that to me before. Could it be a mole? I mean one of the kidnappers we took gave us that location, so clearly it was a trap."

"I wouldn't put it past the IPF. You can't gain this level of power without a lot of influence and having your hands in a lot of cookie jars," he crossed his legs as he leaned back, arms resting on the top of the couch. "There's another problem for you though."

I frowned. "What would that be?"

He inclined his head back to look at the ceiling and spoke. "The IPF isn't just located in Peach City. They're all over the country. If the Underground is building an army, how far are you willing to take this?"

I let the question linger for a bit. Honestly, I hadn't really given the subject much thought. This all started because I wanted to save a little girl. If these two entities went to war, there would be a litany of Irregulars and Normies alike that would be able to put me down. Even if I could handle a one-on-one battle, that would be one gauntlet I wouldn't be able to run. You can only come up all sevens so many times.

I ran a hand over my head, unsure of how I should respond. Regardless of what the Underground and IPF did, innocents in Peach City were having to suffer. I wasn't simply going to stop protecting them. I knew what I signed up for. This is a line of work where you typically get carried out on your shield.

My eyes shot back to MyKey, face hardened. "Peach City is off limits to the Underground."

He finally looked back at me and nodded soberly, "And the IPF?"

I shrugged my shoulders. "I have no love for them, but they do serve a purpose."

"You're one of the few people to admit that," he leaned forward, resting his forearms on his knees. His usual nonchalant demeanor had faded. His eyes seemed more serious like he was looking at something that only he could see. "Their methods aren't popular, but what can you do when the country is scared, and everyone is looking at their neighbor sideways? At least they're less 'violation of the Third and Fourth Amendment and more of the Patriot Act' these days."

"I guess," I half-heartedly agreed so that we could move on to a different subject. I got as much useful information as I could from MyKey and after what I saw upstairs earlier, I certainly wasn't trying to stay in this place any longer.

"Thanks for your help," I rose to leave and MyKey stood with me.

"Getting a visit from Peach City's Phantom is always my pleasure. You increase my notoriety. I look forward to our continued partnership," he extended his hand.

I reciprocated the gesture, and we shook firmly. As I turned to leave, I quickly replayed my conversation with MyKey, and one question stood out to me.

I stopped and looked over my shoulder, "What are you exactly?"

He didn't respond at first. Then that carefree grin of his returned. "Some secrets are better left untold until a later time," he answered with a chuckle.

I rolled my eyes and turned back to leave. "You're probably right about that."

Chapter Ten

How nice of you to show up," I remarked to Sammy as I was fixing my silver tie in the mirror while he sat on my bed, observing me. I could feel his petulant gaze staring daggers into me from behind.

"You pushed me off a dome!" He replied, his voice rising to that of a whine.

"You're not even real. Get over it," I stated, rolling my eyes. I wasn't really in the mood to deal with his childish behavior today.

"Then why are you talking to me?" He retorted, sticking out his tongue.

I glared at his reflection in the mirror. "Do I need to call Barb?"

Sammy stiffened at my threat, hurriedly looking towards the window. The morning dawn was breaking through the curtains, signaling that the workday was soon to begin.

Still glaring at the window, "When did you and Barb get so chummy?"

I closed my eyes. "It's not like that. We weren't exactly on the best of terms at first either," I sighed, referencing our complicated relationship.

"Then what is it like?" He swung his feet and hopped off the bed, "Why would you just let it in so easily?"

"I gave you a chance," I reminded him, my voice lowering.

"But Barb causes you so much pain!" He pleaded with me. I could see the desperation in his eyes as he stepped beside me.

Somberly, I responded, "I almost jumped because of you."

"That's not fair," he choked back a sob, lowering his head.

A long awkward silence fell over us. The tension was unusual because of all the tenants renting space in my head, my relationship with Sammy was by far the best despite our rocky start. Recently though, I couldn't help but notice that he was hiding something crucial from me. My irritation over the matter was simmering and I was doing my best to conceal it, but kids have a way of detecting these kinds of things and it was having a strain on our relationship.

"Be the adult," I muttered to myself. "Look Sammy, I'm sorry. I have a session with Mr. Jenkins today and with everything else going on I'm just stressed. You can sit in today if you want?"

His head snapped back up and his eyes brightened. "Really?"

"Yep," I answered, "I might even use one of your pieces of advice if it's relevant."

At this point, Sammy was too busy bouncing with joy to give me a proper reply. I don't know why, but he loved getting to be present for the entirety of my appointments.

"Yeah, yeah, yeah. What are we waiting for? Let's go," he said, grabbing my arm to reinforce his urgency.

"Alright. We can head out," I lifted my hand to prepare for the two of us to leave. I dipped my head to say a little prayer before going to the office, "Hopefully nothing eventful happens today."

***

When we arrived through a portal, I could immediately tell that something was off. I was looking at my desk and the chair wasn't pushed in as usual. That was my tradition at the end of the day to signify that my work was complete. The drawers in my desk were pulled out as if someone were looking for something. Sofia wouldn't have so blatantly done this, so that eliminated the only reasonable person that would have access to my office.

I suddenly felt a breeze which lifted my tie. I had to press it down with a hand to prevent it from blowing in the wind. I glanced at my window and saw that it was open. The latch was broken, hinting that it had been tampered with. I closed it the best

I could and immediately got the sensation you get when you feel that someone is in the room with you despite not being able to see or hear them. It's similar to a deer that stops what it's doing and perks up, trying to detect if any predators are around. It doesn't run because it doesn't know the direction of the danger, but it's aware it's out there. Maybe it has something to do with the unnatural stillness in the air, or a sound that seems out of place, but you know you're not alone. That's how I felt now.

"My muse!" A voice happily exclaimed from behind me.

Surprised by the shout, I swung around defensively preparing for a battle only to find Emma behind me near the door to the walk-in closet. She was wearing a retro Atlanta Braves baseball hat which caused her to put her hair into a ponytail. She also rocked a black and white striped jacket, along with denim jeans. Once I recognized her, I noticed that her hazel eyes were wide with elation.

"I knew it had to be you!" She blissfully bounced towards me. "You do a great job at hiding it though. After seeing you the first time, I couldn't believe a stiff like you could be the Peach City Phantom."

I looked down at Emma in bewilderment. The young woman was looking up at me with a mix of excitement and expectancy like she had just found out Santa's real identity and wanted him to give her a tour of the entire North Pole operation. I didn't really know how to respond. Only six people knew both of my identities and four of them came from the same family. Granted, we were in the same boat now because we both knew who the other was behind the mask, but I didn't know if she could be trusted yet.

"What are you doing here?" I demanded. I closed the windows and checked all the doors just in case anybody else planned on intervening in our conversation.

"I had to confirm my suspicions and you just did that for me," she replied coolly.

"Technically, you haven't confirmed anything yet. You're just an intruder that happened to get caught by a renowned therapist that happens to be an Irregular."

Emma sucked her teeth and made a face. Clearly, she wasn't buying my poor effort to conceal my exposed identity.

"Oh please, the second you came to help me with the IPF I figured it had to be you, or at least someone close to you."

"What brought you to me in the first place?" I conceded.

"Oh right. My *other* told me she heard you talking to MyKey about kidnappings. Along with your outfit, she figured it might've been the Peach City Phantom, so she placed a tracker on your coat, and we followed you to the MARTA station and here to your office. You do a really good job with the whole Clark Kent routine. I definitely fell for it."

I'm an idiot.

It's one thing to put your costume in a secret lair hundreds of feet below your place of business. It's another to simply place it in the closet of your office. Every time I placed my coat up, I was giving Emma a beacon to my stronghold. On top of that, by following the tip that she directly delivered to me, it was the equivalent of me volunteering to tell her about my secret.

"So at the end of your first visit, you were just testing me?" I inquired.

"Yep," she confirmed.

I growled internally. My carelessness may've dragged me deeper into a mess of my own making.

"What now?" I asked. The ball was clearly in her court and with her constant snooping I suspected she had no plans of just walking away quietly. My identity was totally at her mercy.

"Well, obviously we have to talk about this," she exasperatedly pouted like this was supposedly an everyday occurrence for me. "You know, share our tragic backstories which led us down our respective paths, we come to some deeper understanding of each other then we kick butt."

"Sounds pleasant," I replied sarcastically.

"Right," she responded, missing my insincere tone. "But I skipped over the most crucial part."

"And what would that be?"

"I'll ask you to team up, but you'll be all 'I work alone'," she mockingly made a deep voice while imitating me, "I'll walk away, down but not out. I'll probably follow you to the next battle or jump headfirst into another and you'll have to save me then our partnership will be official."

I folded my arms and leaned back against the wall. "Considering the fact both of those events already happened can we skip the clichés?"

She took a moment to consider this, hand on her chin. "We did kind of go out of order. So, partners then?"

"Sorry, but I work alone," I answered her in the same voice she mocked me with earlier.

She threw her head back and laughed. "I already get the feeling we're going to make a great team."

Dropping down to her knees and clutching her sides, this young woman that had intruded upon my office continued to bellow in laughter.

I didn't think my joke was that funny, but her reaction did cause me to chuckle a little bit. I had to admit her easy-going personality made her enjoyable to be around. I'd deny it if she ever asked though.

"Are you okay in there, boss?" I could hear Sofia call over the intercom.

I recalled that Mr. Jenkins was coming in soon and I needed to dot my I's and cross my T's. The shock of my identity being found out was going to throw me off my game. After all the progress I've made with him I couldn't afford that.

"Everything's fine Sofia!" I shouted back, hoping that she wouldn't come in. Sofia was a smart cookie. I hadn't walked through the front door this morning which meant she would have known I teleported in and if she saw Emma here, she would know that I had been found out which could put both of us at risk.

"How come you didn't tell me you were in?" She questioned. "I could've been here with my boyfriend doing Lord knows what."

"One, you would need a boyfriend for that to be the case. Two, you most definitely would be fired. What kind of business would people think that I'm running here?" I joked in response.

Teasingly, "Jealous much?"

I then remembered that Emma was here, and my eyes slowly traveled back to her, the way a child looks at an adult when they realize they've been caught scrounging through the cookie jar.

Emma was still on the floor but was staring at me in pure amusement. She held one hand over her mouth, fighting back the giggles.

"Umm, what time is Mr. Jenkins scheduled to arrive?" I replied back to Sofia, changing the subject.

"Oh," disappointment clouded her voice now that I had ended our routine morning exchange so abruptly, "The schedule says he should be here at eleven."

"Right, thank you."

"Someone has the hots for their secretary," Emma cooed as she rose from her spot on the floor to her feet.

"Drop it," I grunted.

"Well judging from her voice, she definitely wants to fu…"

"I said drop it!" My voice rose harshly.

Emma threw her hands up in surrender. "Any moment might be our last. Everything is more beautiful because we're doomed. You will never be lovelier than you are now. We will never be here again."

"No Shakespeare this time?"

She lifted her eyebrows in shock. "You can tell the difference?"

I shrugged one shoulder, "I read *The Iliad* in college, freshman English."

Emma walked over to my desk and tore a sheet off of my notepad. Then she took a pen and started writing something down. She returned to me and slipped the note into my shirt pocket.

"This'll probably work after all, but we still need to have that chat. Meet me here at seven," she headed for the door but stopped and spun her heels back towards me. "On second thought, she might flip out if I walk through that door. Can you make a way out for me?" She asked me sheepishly.

My shoulders sagged in annoyance. I know my ability is rather useful, but I'm not a taxi driver. Now that I think about it, I'd probably make a fortune if this were my side hustle, but never mind that now.

Not bothering to hide my mood from her, "Where to?"

"Just outside."

"Fine."

"See you later, my muse," Emma said before she left, then jumped through my portal to whatever location I had randomly decided upon.

"Mr. Jenkins is here for his appointment boss," Sofia notified me.

"Great," I muttered to myself, running a hand across my face as I went to my desk to prepare my notes. "Send him in."

***

"Hello Mr. Jenkins. How have you been since we last met?" I adjusted my glasses as I asked the question.

"Younger," Mr. Jenkins replied gruffly. He was lying on the chaise lounge chair, but his upper body was sitting up and he had his arms folded, his eyes not looking at me. He was wearing his usual faded denim overalls. This time with an orange plaid shirt underneath. No hat this time, so I could see the thinning gray hair atop his head which was losing its battle with baldness.

"It's barely been a week since we've met."

He grimaced as he adjusted himself on the chair. "Not long enough. You had me doing that stupid homework assignment like I'm back in junior high."

I tilted my head slightly confused. "Middle school?"

"Whatever you wanna call it. You're supposed to be the smart one," he grumbled.

Mr. Jenkins was a bit surlier than usual today. I let his comment sit in the air, so that I could analyze him for a moment.

He had kept his arms folded since the moment he had sat down. It was weird because Mr. Jenkins was almost always on the offensive, but this posture was a defensive form, a way to close himself off to others. His left index finger was consistently tapping on his elbow, similar to how a student anxiously taps their pencil on their desk during an exam. His face would range from a frown to a wince as if there were a series of thoughts that were mentally striking him with the same effect as an open-palmed slap to the jaw. I was going to have to be gentle with my approach or risk a setback.

"Maybe you should give him a balloon," Sammy interjected. He was sitting at his desk with his own yellow legal notepad and a black coloring pencil. There were also a set of spectacles resting on the bridge of his nose.

"Keep it down," I sniped back.

"Excuse me?" Mr. Jenkins looked at me puzzled. Apparently, he had heard me.

"Forgive me," I apologized then shot a dirty look back at Sammy.

He ducked his head down and started scribbling notes on his notepad. What notes he possibly could have had at this stage is beyond me.

Turning my attention back to my client, "So Mr. Jenkins, about the list, what were you able to put down?"

"The non-suffering list?" Mr. Jenkins replied. He seemed so much older, tired,…defeated. "I don't know how much I want to talk about this, doc. I want the pain to stop, but my head. These thoughts, they're so vivid. Memories, fresh."

He fell silent and just sat there. I had to start throwing my best stuff because I was currently flailing.

"Name one thing on the list. Then we can talk about it. How does that sound?" I urged, hoping to get some type of response out of him.

He let out a resigned sigh. "I guess if I'm payin' ya for it anyway, might as well not waste my money. The first thing I wrote is that the animals would suffer too?"

I raised an eyebrow. "The animals?"

He nodded, suddenly proud of himself. "If my work suffers then the crops suffer. The crops suffer, animals don't get proper nutrition which makes my work harder. It kind of works together, like a loop."

"Circle of Life?" I tried to add.

He looked at me with a baffled expression. "What?"

"Never mind."

"He's never seen the Lion King?" Sammy yelled exasperatedly. "No wonder he's depressed."

My lip twitched but I forced myself not to smile. Mr. Jenkins would probably think that I was making fun of him, and I couldn't afford that.

"What's next on your list?" I transitioned to his next point.

For the first time since he sat down, he unfolded his arms. A smile managed to break through his grim demeanor. He adjusted himself yet again to lie down completely, making himself comfortable.

"My home," the deeper meaning within that statement had the effect of briefly lifting his spirits.

"Continue," I replied simply, lifting my notepad to prepare to take notes.

"My home," he repeated. "Beth and I met in college, back in 03'. I was a brash kid from Athens, and she was a sweet daughter of farmers. I didn't really know what I wanted to do, but I wanted to make as much money as possible, so I majored in Business. She wanted to help the Earth as much as possible, so she majored in Natural

Resources and Conservation. She handed me a flyer for one of the marches they were going to have on campus. I stopped because I thought she was pretty, and I ended up going to the rally. To be honest, I had no interest in 'going green' and all that jazz, but when I heard the passion with which she spoke, I knew I wanted her to be my girl."

He paused briefly to take in his memories. It was good for him to relive these positive memories. Most of our sessions involved dredging up the traumatic ones and figuring out how to accept and move on, not from, but *with* them.

Mr. Jenkins lifted his head and continued. "I remember she told me that she just wanted to live on a farm. Live a simple life with family, so I switched my major to Architecture. I didn't know a thing 'bout buildings, but I managed to find a plot of land and secretly started building her dream home. When I proposed, I surprised her by bringing her there for the first time. She said yes before I could even pull out the ring."

He looked at me the way a friend looks at another after venting over a few drinks. He smiled weakly with his mouth, but there was a light in his eyes that shone through strongly. I managed to return the smile. Usually, I kept the tissues close by for clients, but this time I almost needed one for myself. Almost.

"That was so happy and sad at the same time!" I glanced over my shoulder to see Sammy sobbing at his desk with his head buried in his folded arms.

I looked back to Mr. Jenkins who was now twiddling his thumbs. I assume he was waiting for me to transition the conversation to the next phase, which worried me because I knew I needed to crack the shell of what was bothering him when he initially walked into my office.

"May I ask what was troubling you earlier?" I inquired of him as tactfully as I could.

His expression immediately stonewalled, and I could feel him expeditiously closing off to me. I needed to worm my way through before I lost him.

"Lee," I said, trying to be as comforting as possible, "Please talk to me."

I witnessed his eyes widen and mouth open as if he wanted to share what was on his mind before clamming up again. "I got nothing to share that you wanna hear," is what he settled on.

"Try me."

His eyes twitched to the silver watch on his left wrist. Then he sighed, "Maybe next time, doc," he started to roll off the chair in order to get up.

I rose before he could stand. "Lee, whatever it is, you can tell me. You don't have to stew on this alone. It's not what Beth would want."

That proved to be the wrong route to take. Thick veins pulsed throughout his face, and he scowled at me to which the likes I've never experienced with him before, showing that I had struck a nerve.

"And how the hell would *you* know what Beth would want, what the boys would want?" He agitatedly started brushing himself off and smoothing the wrinkles in his overalls. "Did you ever meet them? Do you commune with the dead?"

He jammed his finger into my face. "Jus' cause you got those papers hanging up on that wall behind you, don't mean you got the right to act like you know *me*! *I* married Beth. *I* raised dem boys. *Me*. Everyday. And you think you can assume you know dem better than *me*. Who the hell do you think you are?"

He began storming towards the door. I jumped from my seat and ran to beat him there. I placed a hand on the door, positioning my body between it and Mr. Jenkins. Impeding his exit probably wasn't the best way to reach him, but I needed to do something. I didn't want a repeat of what happened to a previous client of mine to happen to Mr. Jenkins.

"Please, forgive me," I pleaded with him. "I would never assume to know them better than you. Please, just sit back down. We can talk about something else, anything you want."

His eyebrows furrowed so much that I was afraid the skin on the top of his forehead would start peeling from his skull. His voice dropped to a harsh whisper, "Son, get out of my way."

Defeated, I stepped aside, removing myself as the last line of defense for his departure. He brushed past me to the doorway. I pulled out the business card that had my personal number from my wallet and slipped it into his shirt pocket.

"If you need to talk. Please call, anytime, I'll pick up," it was the last lifeline I could think to offer him.

He glared back at me then looked down at his pocket begrudgingly. "Maybe."

Before he walked out of my office, I managed to catch a glimpse of him patting where I had placed the card before slamming the door behind him. I wanted to smile, but I couldn't bring myself to do it. The truth of the matter is that today was an abject failure, and it was my collective shortcomings as his therapist that caused Mr. Jenkins to leave so abruptly.

I sulked back towards where he was sitting previously and plopped down onto it. I placed the back of my hand over my forehead and just lay there.

"That went really bad," Sammy said from his desk.

"Go away," I wasn't in the mental space to start talking about what happened yet and didn't feel like going through the headache of talking to Sammy right now.

"Do you want to talk about what just happened?"

"Now you're mocking me? I said go away!" I snapped.

"Sorry boss. I didn't mean to disturb you," I leaned up to see Sofia poking her head through the doorway. By the time I opened my mouth to apologize, she had already closed the door.

"Great. How many more people can I alienate today?" I dropped my head back down and mercifully napped until it was time for me to leave.

Chapter Eleven

T hat bad, huh?" Toni asked as he poured me another glass of orange juice.

"Even worse," I took the glass, raised it towards him, and knocked it back.

Toni peered down at me while cleaning one of the mugs. "Are you sure you don't want anything stronger?"

"I think the last thing I need is alcohol," I replied, aimlessly circling my finger around the rim of the glass, thinking over what my next move should be.

I had arrived at *Rifugio* a couple of seconds after I left my office. I was still beating myself up over the failed session with Mr. Jenkins and having my identity discovered by Emma. Normally, Sofia would be my go-to in a situation like this, but we hadn't spoken since I mistook her for Sammy. So currently, I settled for the next best thing, *Rifugio* and the Romanis.

"My advice is that you give the old man time to come around. I've dealt with my share of temperamental old farts in my time."

"No potty talk at the bar!" Susan shouted towards us from the opposite end of the counter.

"*Mi dispiace*, my love," he looked back at me and like a student not trying to get caught whispering in class, leaned in, "As for the other issue, I've had my fair share of tiffs with Susan over the years. I suggest you apologize in grand fashion then grovel for forgiveness."

My eyes briefly darted towards Susan, who was thankfully paying us no mind. I looked back at Toni, grinned slyly, and nodded.

"Thanks again for your sage advice, Toni."

He spread his arms in acceptance of my gratitude. "Of course. What kind of council would I be if I couldn't lend my expertise to an ear in need?"

"Always one for humility, aren't you?"

"One of my many fine qualities," he started patting my chest in jest. "When did you start carrying your business cards in your shirt pocket? Usually, you pull it out of your wallet."

"What?" I questioned. He was right. I do keep all of my cards in my wallet. I started feeling around the pocket and pulled out a piece of paper. Then it hit me that this was the paper Emma slipped me earlier. With all that had happened, I hadn't taken the time to check the contents of what she had written.

I started to read the note she had left. It contained an address and a time.

Russ's Joint

2340 Peach Street

7:00 Tonight

"The plot thickens," I muttered to myself. To Toni, "You ever heard of a Russ's Joint?"

Toni pursed his lips and stared at the ceiling. "Susan took me there once. I'm not really sure how Americans describe it. I believe diner is the appropriate term."

I glanced down to look over myself. If I was going to a diner, my therapist attire definitely wasn't going to help me blend in. I checked the clock on the wall behind Toni. I was going to need to go home to change and according to that clock, I only had about forty-five minutes to prepare if I wanted to be there on time.

I started to shuffle my way off of the stool and started gathering my belongings from the counter top. "I'll probably be seeing a lot more of you. Send Mia Bella my regards. *Grazie.*"

He inclined his head towards me with his billion-dollar grin. "I'll do that. Good luck."

***

I pulled up in my Stratus to Russ's Joint with three minutes to spare. I had made a gateway from the bar to my place and hurried to get myself ready for the evening. Due to the amount of energy I exerted the past couple of days by using my power so extensively, I decided 'driving' would probably be in my best interest.

I stepped out of the crimson car and examined the diner. From the outside, it looked like your classical throwback diner. The bright neon blue exterior is the first thing I noticed even though the sun was setting in the late Georgia evening. The name was emboldened in the center of the diner on silver metallic letters.

I walked through the entrance and the first thing that hit me was the scent of burgers on the grill. The familiar smell of charcoal diffused through the air, causing my stomach to rumble.

Aesthetically speaking, the inside matched the feel of the exterior. There was a sky blue counter accompanied by twelve silver diner stools with baby blue cushions. By the front entrance, were three booths of similar color to the stools on each side of the door with views outside of the window. The left wall contained the bathrooms, while the right wall had two booths more spaced out with one of them near the back wall, the furthest seat from the only entrance.

Next to the last booth, was a rustic brown jukebox, currently blaring "Can't Take My Eyes Off of You" by The 4 Seasons. I took notice of the person sitting in the back booth. They were the only customer in the restaurant and were singing their heart out to the song. As I drew closer, I noticed it was Emma. She was still wearing the exact same attire from earlier. The Braves cap was still sitting atop her head and her zebra-striped jacket swayed back and forth with her as she belted out the tune. I waited for her to finish before I accompanied her.

"Nice pipes," I said, awkwardly trying to slide my way into the booth without bumping the table.

"Thanks," she replied with a quick grin. "Glad you were able to make it. I'm surprised someone of your stature had time to dine with us Plebs after hours."

"You do know most of my clients would be considered 'Plebs' by some?" I pointed out to my rambunctious dining companion.

"I guess your attire brings you down to our level," she was referencing the *Bleach* anime t-shirt that I was currently wearing.

I twisted my mouth to one side, slightly amused. "Must every encounter begin with you insulting me?"

"Sorry, I'm a bit of a joker, but I am truly glad you came," Emma paused, and a silence fell over us until the waiter came over.

He appeared to be in his late teens, probably working your typical kind of side job while still attending school. An old school high top fade was his hairstyle of choice, and he was wearing a retainer in his mouth. The uniform for this establishment was apparently khakis with a baby blue shirt that had the name of the diner located in the top right corner. On the opposite side of his shirt was his name, Russell.

"Um, excuse me, but are you two ready to order?" Due to the retainer, Russell's speech slurred when he had to pronounce the letter s. He held up his notepad and a pen to take down our requests. I noticed his hand shaking while he waited for us.

I offered him my most professional therapist smile that I use to put nervous patients at ease. He returned it and the shaking subsided.

"Yes, I'm ready. I'll have the Russ Burger and a side of onion rings," I told him while holding up the menu to select my meal.

"What type of drink?"

"A Sprite."

"Russ Burger, onion rings, and a Sprite?" He checked with me.

"That's right," I affirmed.

During this exchange, Emma watched me with curious intensity, but without saying a word or giving much attention to Russell, like when your boss sits in on you to examine your actions at work. It was quite unsettling.

"And you ma'am?" Russell turned to ask Emma.

This snapped her out of her trance. She shook her head to clear the cobwebs, looked at the menu briefly and then ordered.

"The usual," she answered, handing the menu over to Russell.

"Right. Your drinks will be right out," Russell responded before leaving to give our orders to the kitchen.

He quickly returned with two Sprites, set them down, then departed back to the kitchen.

We both sipped our drinks awkwardly, and generally avoided making extended eye contact with the other. The sense of mutual discomfort dragged along as time passed.

This wasn't how I imagined this meeting going. Emma was practically bouncing off the walls earlier and now she seemed conflicted with uncertainty. I wasn't sure how to lead the conversation, considering the fact that I was kind of at her mercy since she had found me out and was the one to initiate the time and place of this get-together.

I had a feeling that this was more important to her than it was for me. Eavesdropping on my conversation with MyKey, crashing and initiating fights with the two most powerful organizations in not just Peach City but also possibly the country, and God knows how many times she had been snooping in my office. I needed to give her something, but I wasn't sure what she wanted or needed. It would be best if I put myself in a position to open up to her first.

"So, is there anything you wanted to talk about in particular?" I offered her, trying to cut the burgeoning tension between us.

Emma beamed at me, before her eyes nervously shifted back down towards the wooden table between us.

"Can you give me a sec?" She requested.

"Sure."

"Can you take over now?" She lowered her head and whispered. I had enough experience with talking to beings that no one else can see to notice that she wasn't talking to me.

Emma closed her eyes and inhaled deeply. When the young woman reopened her eyes, I knew the person sitting across from me was no longer Emma. Her normal hazel eyes had changed to gray, the first time I noticed the switch since meeting her, but the look within them was much colder. Her face post-change took on an air of annoyance as if she wanted nothing to do with this encounter.

"Forgive her," Not-Emma sighed. "She's being a baby all of a sudden."

"You might not believe me, but I know exactly what you mean," Sammy has had his fair share of temper tantrums. "First, they do something impulsive then ask you to bail them out when they can't handle it."

"And have the nerve to pout when you let them know how displeased you are," she added. Briefly smirking, she withdrew the straw from her cup, tossed it on the table, and drank the soda straight from the cup.

"What is your name by the way?" I asked.

She eyed me while finishing her drink before placing the cup down. "She can give you the whole life story melodrama. I'm not much of a conversationalist. Get out here, Emma. He's alright."

Their transformation occurred again, and Emma returned from wherever the non-dominant personality resided. The warm, playful look in her hazel eyes returning with her.

"Not nice," she ridiculed her alter. "You were supposed to handle this, but I guess I did push for this more than you," she noticed me watching her internal dialogue play out and suddenly clammed up.

So, that's what it looks like. It's really weird being on the other side of it for a change.

She arched her back and rose within her seat. "Right, I had questions for you. First, why do you keep your suit in your office closet?"

I've been punched by Irregular henchmen that have had less impact than Emma's words. She always seemed to know the exact button to push to agitate me.

"Er, it was the simplest place I could put it without it being at my home. I never really considered anyone putting a tracker on me. I guess it's something to think about now."

She bobbed her head back and forth considering my response. "Next question, what's with your costume?"

My eyes narrowed at her lack of seriousness. I wasn't sure if she took pleasure in mocking me or genuinely wanted to know, but I'm not a huge fan of having my time wasted. "Next question," I said, trying to keep my voice even.

"Sorry, it's the jitters," she rubbed the back of her neck and looked towards the kitchen. "I'm not really good at interacting with others, especially someone like you."

I swear a vein almost burst in my head when she finished that statement. Gritting my teeth, I considered leaving on the spot, but I wanted to give her the benefit of the doubt.

Emma must have caught my reaction because she instantly had an apologetic look on her face. Putting both hands up in defense, "No, not like that. I'm doing a terrible job at this."

She took a deep sigh then continued, "You're a therapist, right? By now you must've noticed that I'm not the only one in here," she tapped the side of her skull with her finger. "So, you probably know that some conditions are a product of trauma. My trauma derived from guys slightly older than me, brother-like figures."

A look of sorrow was cast all over her face as her eyes dishearteningly drooped down away from me. This was the second time today I had put a woman on the verge of tears. I'm not always the most chivalrous person at times but this was pretty ridiculous. I wanted to crawl in my bed at that moment, hide under the covers, and try this day over again, but I couldn't leave this situation as is.

"Sorry, I get it," I apologized, reaching my hand out slowly to rest on hers. The warm sensation of her smaller fingers tightening around my own, gave me assurance that my apology had been well received. "To be honest, I think my costume is pretty cool. It's much better than the original design."

Emma perked up at my acknowledgment of her previous question. "You're right about that," she laughed. "The first one was pretty silly. I think you were trying way too hard."

"How'd you know about my first outfit?" I asked her, perplexed.

She placed her right elbow on the table and slid towards me. In a deliberate tone, she whispered, "That's what I'm here to talk to you about, my muse. The roots of the Underground predate your genesis."

"You were there that night?" Referencing the first time that I wore the outfit in my attempt to save Mia Bella Romani. My eyes widened in bewilderment as I leaned back against the booth.

"Indeed," she affirmed. Her voice was now starting to reveal the maturity that I detected when she first visited my office. "You returned me to the path that I'm currently on now, but I'll leave it up to you to remember the details."

"Two Russ Burgers. One with a side of onion rings, the other with potato wedges." Russell interrupted as he placed our food down before us.

"Thanks Junior," Emma said as she took her plate.

"Junior?" I raised an eyebrow.

"Yeah. His dad owns the place. Some of the best food in the region. Hey, Russ!" She waved to the cook who had just walked out of the kitchen.

Russ, who I presumed was the owner of the place, was an older African American man. From the looks of him, I'd say maybe in his mid-fifties. He wore a blue apron over the same type of shirt his son wore and a chef's hat on his head, blocking the view of his hair. His face seemed to be a bit weathered, but his eyes remained unhardened by time. There was a playfulness in them that had seemed to skip over his son's 'I'd rather be anywhere than here' look. But teenagers, am I right?

Russ returned her wave. "Hey there, Miss Emma. How's my favorite customer?"

She lightheartedly rolled her eyes at him, "Please Russ, you say that about every customer that comes in here more than once."

"Ouch, you got me there," he put his hands over his heart, imitating that her words had pierced him. Then he turned to me, "Be careful with that one. Her bark is as bad as her bite."

"I'm finding that out the hard way, but I'll try." I promised him as he and Junior returned to the back.

"You know the dog references are starting to pick up over the past few days. I don't like it," Emma interjected to me.

"Now you know how I feel when people make fun of my sense of fashion," I replied.

She pursed her lips. "Fair enough, now back to the Underground. Another reason that I was so desperate to find you is because I have information that I think would be of great interest to you."

"I'm listening," I responded as I started applying ketchup to my onion rings.

"Remember the dude you saw in the MARTA tunnels, wearing the ascot?" She gestured towards where the ascot was placed.

I nodded in confirmation before digging into my food.

"Well, his last name is Bennett, but he also goes by the name of the Southern Gent when working. He acts as a kind of proxy for the Underground in the south, thus the name. I've managed to do some reconnaissance on him and it's not good," she pulled out vintage Polaroid pictures with notes written in sharpie on the bottom and slid them over to me.

"You know we're halfway into the twenty-first century now?" I said as I collected the photos which contained better images of the presumed alpha I had seen in the tunnels a few days prior. "You could probably use some better technology than this."

"Excuse me for being old-fashioned," she retorted. "Anyway, before the rude commentary, I was going to say I know exactly where he's going to be at the next few days."

"And where would that be?" I asked.

"Augusta," she said proudly. "Pack your things, we're going to the National!"

"Wait a minute," I nearly choked on my food. "I missed the part where I agreed to go anywhere with you."

"Come on," she griped, "Don't you want to figure out what the Underground is up to? If we catch him in the act, imagine how much information we can obtain."

I definitely had my reservations about this, but I didn't exactly have a reason not to go. Mr. Jenkins was my only scheduled client this week and I'm pretty sure he didn't want anything to do with me currently. I just needed to tell Sofia that I would be out of the office for a few days, but that would mean I wouldn't speak to her for nearly a week, leaving the situation from earlier unaddressed.

As I was mulling over what to do, I felt the wind in the room change. Something was hovering behind Emma's shoulder. The Spectre's expressionless face loomed in the background of our conversation.

"Bennett is the key," he implored me in his moaning, ghostlike voice.

"Not now," I grimaced at him, looking past Emma.

""Excuse me?" She tilted her head in confusion, "I can't just go up to him and ask him to reschedule."

I looked back to her and shook my head. "Sorry, you're not the only one dealing with *others*."

She looked at me understandingly and reached out, asking for the ketchup. "Did they tell you anything helpful?"

"You could say that," I passed her the ketchup bottle. "I'm in."

"Great!"

She couldn't contain her excitement as she started to glow. And I mean she literally started glowing, the white aura that I've seen surround her during battle was now sitting above her skin, simmering in response to her emotions.

"Take it easy," I motioned with my hands towards Emma to caution her about using her abilities in public. I was pretty sure that she wasn't registered, and it was going to put Russ in a tough position since business owners are highly recommended to report unchecked Irregular activity, if they wanted their business to continue flourishing that is.

"Relax, they know who I am," she dismissed my concern and started drenching her potato wedges with ketchup. "Plus, after the beating we handed the IPF, no way they would want to take us on again."

I thought back to my interaction with the lieutenant and shuddered. Unfortunately, I got the feeling that they probably wanted to take us on much more than Emma was giving them credit for. Not only did we overcome their skill, but worse we wounded their pride. It would probably be in both our best interests to be keener of our surroundings in the future.

"Are you sure you should be using that much ketchup?" I observed as I could hardly see her potato wedges anymore.

She gave me a look and kept adding ketchup, even more deliberately now.

I rolled my eyes, annoyed. "Okay, one thing before we go. I gotta make sure if we have to fight your *other* doesn't come out and decide to burn me to a crisp. Am I going to be okay around her?"

She fidgeted with her ball cap before answering me. "She doesn't hate you and I have the conn right now, so as long as those remain unchanged you should be fine."

Not exactly the most comforting answer, but since the Spectre was still there it meant that I was on the trail to not only the Underground, but to potentially finding out more about my past. "What's her name? Something tells me speaking to her in second person or calling her Not Emma might grate on her nerves."

"Not Emma, that's great. I have to call her that now," Emma tossed her head back and laughed at this. She brushed a tear away from her eye, "You're right though. That would piss her off. She goes by Angel."

"Angel?"

She considered my reaction for a second. "Ahh, I get it. When you met us in our costume form, we told you to call us Angelus," she grabbed the salt and pepper shakers to help illustrate her description. "Well, you see the thing is her full name is *Angelus Mortis,* which is Latin for 'Angel of Death', but after decades of getting to know each other, I decided to nickname her Angel and as a compromise our caper name would be Angelus. The costume changes slightly, depending on who's in control, giving us a darkness and light kind of vibe."

"How come you don't just go by Yin and Yang?"

She looked at me in shock. "Are you kidding me? That's cultural appropriation!"

"I guess you kind of have a point there."

"So, we good?" She asked me.

I looked to Spectre then back to Emma. "Are you going to ask me about my others?"

She shook her head. "No. It's not a terms of service agreement for me. You'll tell me if you want to."

"I guess we're good then. When do we need to leave?"

She pulled out a wad of cash and threw a couple of bills on the table. "Thursday. We'll be gone for the entire weekend. Meet me here at three in the evening. Pack your finest attire."

"Should I drive?"

She thanked Russ and Junior on her way to the exit. "No, we're going to need something more conspicuous if we want to blend in."

"That proved to be quite useful," The Spectre fluttered next to me. "This could be mutually beneficial."

I said my farewells to the staff and made my way to the Stratus. "You're probably right, but I don't know why she's going after the Underground so hard."

"Maybe the past is coming into play?" He offered.

"I don't remember her though. You know I don't think or talk about my first night in the field that much."

"It wouldn't kill you to do it. All threads flow from two points in your life, but you fear to trace them back to the origins."

"The dream?" I asked.

"Indeed, but now is not the time. Predators disguised as prey lurk in this hunt you're about to begin."

"Fitting," I stopped in front of my car. Thinking back to what Emma said about blending in, I observed my Stratus. "Other than the red, I think this blends in pretty well."

Chapter Twelve

How is this conspicuous?" I exclaimed at Emma. It was late Thursday afternoon, and I was standing in front of Russ's Joint in awe that she had pulled up in an orange Lamborghini. The roar of the engine reverberated through my insides as she settled into a parking spot.

"We have to be as pompous as possible. We're not exactly a part of the good ole boys network," she commented as she stuck her head out of the driver's side window.

I made a face at her, grabbed my bags, and started heading to the trunk.

"Wrong way!" Emma called out. "Bags go in the front." she popped the hood for me to place them.

Technology was constantly evolving to the point where today's advancements can seem light-years ahead of yesterday's inventions, but it's still the simple things that can blow you away sometimes. I put what I brought inside and found that Emma had no luggage of her own. I closed the hood of the luxurious sherbet colored car and walked back to the driver's window to check on Emma.

With the late summer breeze blowing her short pixie brunette hair along with her designer sunglasses, Emma looked like she was the heiress of a Fortune 500 company. The simple violet skirt dress which she wore was a departure from her preferred striped shirt and jeans combination. This was the first time where I truly looked at her without all of the distractions that usually thwarted us.

Admittedly, she looked very cute but to me more in a squeeze your cheeks kind of way rather than want to date type of way. It was one of the few times where I've seen her fully enjoying her youth even though in terms of appearance, I was probably only slightly older than her, but according to her she more than quadrupled my age. Emma's past was still kind of fuzzy to me. She dropped enough hints over the course of our few interactions, but I hadn't really gotten the full picture yet. Hopefully, I would be able to find out more during this reconnaissance mission, but I would also probably need to give her a piece of myself also. That's the thing about trust, it's a two-way street.

"What exactly is the event we're attending?" I asked from the passenger's seat.

"Unimportant," she said nonchalantly, "I've been to plenty of these before. They always have some immaculate title that's named after somebody or some foundation. We'll call it the Unnecessary Pompous Get-Together of the Wealthy."

I gave her an uncertain look. "Rather dismissive, don't you think? Shouldn't we at least be able to give a quick one sentence blurb about the event?"

"Don't worry," she said assuredly, pressing the engine to initiate auto-drive mode. "Everybody comes for different reasons. They just need an official title to put on the tax write-offs, business trip proposals, and to get away from spouses. Money changes hands behind the scenes, deals are agreed to at dinner tables and over glasses of wine, and –"

"The juicy details come out in the privacy of the bedroom," I finished for her.

She raised an eyebrow approvingly. "Someone's been hanging out with MyKey."

I tsked. "I'd prefer not to, but he provides valuable information."

"What brings you to dislike him so much, but you're more than happy to associate with the mafia?" She glanced down accusingly at my ring finger where I was wearing the ring that Toni had given me with his family insignia on it. The gold reflected from the sunlight as I twisted my hand to examine it.

"It's more complicated than that," I said, trying to keep my voice neutral.

"It always is with criminal organizations," her voice strained as if there was something more she wished to say but was holding back.

"And what MyKey runs isn't a criminal organization?" I shot back.

"I get it," she raised her hands in defense. "I'm just saying some people are led into dark places and there's no one there to show them the light. Others run into it willingly without hesitation," she leaned back in her chair and turned her head to look out the window. I let out a huff of air and reclined back in my own seat.

We sat there, not speaking. The silent tension sat there with the two of us. She had really hit a topic that was a bit of a silent neglect of mine. Few groups had insignias as notable as the Romani Mafia in Peach City.

It's not like I randomly team up with the Romani family from time to time. A lot of my current gear had either been improved upon or gifted to me by them. I don't really associate with the entirety of the mafia, but Toni and his family had welcomed me in like one of their own. I may consider it a necessary evil at times, but I'm not going to say that I don't enjoy being around them or the benefits that come from being associated with them.

The real problem is that I knew at least a little of what they did beyond assisting me. They make their money in a lot of different ventures, not all of them on the straight and narrow. I have my own unvoiced suspicions about added ulterior motives Toni may have with aiding and assisting as much as he does with the kidnapping victims. Hell, I deliver the captors to him so they can be "interviewed" for helpful intel. After Wyoming, the moral compass of the country had shifted, and everyone was still deciding which way it was pointing. Directly associating with the Romanis would be viewed as honorable to some and make enemies of others, but the thing is, I was more interested in saving people's lives rather than their souls.

"So, why'd you become a therapist?" Emma, still looking out the window, asked me, breaking the silence between us.

I didn't answer immediately, taking time to mull it over. I had a specific reason why I chose my path but hadn't verbalized it to anyone else other than that person, so I wanted to phrase it in a way that made sense.

"When I was broken, someone gave me a chance to put the pieces back together. I want to give others the chance to do the same," I responded thoughtfully.

She looked back at me for the first time since our earlier tiff. "Do they?"

"Sometimes," I answered in a sullen voice. "Not all though."

"Maybe if we stop the Underground, more can get that chance?"

"Maybe," wanting to change the subject I asked, "What's our story for being there once we arrive?"

"Simple. Have you heard of the Celestial Theatres?" She countered with a question of her own.

"You mean the only theatre to come close to rivalling Broadway?"

"That's the one," she confirmed. "Let's just say that the story is that my *great grandmother* started it years ago and I inherited it."

"Were you an actress back in the day?"

"Back in the day," she covered her mouth, mocking being insulted. "You could say I'm still one of sorts today. But I did act in plays in the past. That's how my family got by. We travelled a lot but once my mother left my dad, it was just me, him, and my three brothers. I had to play the lead female role in every play. Eventually, I learned to love it."

"Amazing," genuine interest in my voice, "So, what brings me along?"

"Right, that was a slight oversight on my part. You're my personal therapist that I keep on retainer, and I requested you accompany me to reward you for your excellent dedication."

"I guess that's reasonable," I nodded. "At least we're not pretending to be a couple."

"I would say I'm offended, but you're right. The types of people that we're going to be around will have their condemning eyes glued to us. This way we can operate separately," Then eyeing me disapprovingly, "Plus, you're too frail to be my type. I'm more of a bodybuilder kind of girl myself."

"Really?"

She shrugged her shoulders. "What can I say? I love the apex of male masculinity."

"More like toxic," I muttered to myself, sneaking a glance at my own biceps. I wasn't exactly The Rock but calling me frail was going a step too far.

"The itinerary for today, is they'll give a fancy speech and dinner, but it'll let out early so everyone has time to meet their buddies and make plans. Friday, you'll hit the links in the morning, and I'll work the ball at night. Then-"

"Wait, how come I'm not working the ball?" I interrupted.

"Can you dance?"

I shut my mouth and motioned for her to continue.

"Thank you. As I was saying, on Saturday is when we'll make our move and look for whatever it is we're looking for."

"Whatever it is we're looking for?" I repeated.

"All will be revealed. This Southern Gent is there to either set up a future deal or make sure that a current transaction goes through smoothly. This is the true purpose of banquets like these, either over or under the table deals."

Questioning the desired scenario of the Southern Gent's involvement, "Which one better suits us?"

"If it's the former, we won't be able to go in guns blazing. Can't get away with punishing someone for something they haven't done yet," Emma paused briefly before adding, "unless you're the IPF. If it's the latter, we can catch him off guard and bust him on the spot. The Phantom rarely visits these parts of the Peachtree region."

"Good plan," I concurred before a question popped into my mind. "Can I ask what made you think I was coming along?"

"Other than you telling me you were?"

I narrowed my eyes and made a face.

She raised her hands in mock surrender. "Okay, you got me. Let's just say that broken people always have a way of finding each other. Talk to you when we get there."

Emma turned in her chair towards the window and proceeded to take a nap.

"Yeah," I said to her back. "Talk when we get there."

I closed my eyes and reclined yet again in my seat, listening to the sounds of the radio and nature blend together as they coaxed me to sleep.

***

"We're here," I felt a tap on my shoulder, pulling me from my evening *siesta*.

I snapped to, checking my new surroundings, and let me tell you I've been around rich people before, some might even say that I'm pushing the boundaries of that status, but this was next level. The oft whispered about one percent were here in full force, and it was incredible. There were cars of each color of the rainbow here. There was even a rainbow car. Men were getting out of cars with multiple women. One woman was sitting on a throne being carried by four men, one for each leg post. Many of the outfits were well-fitted, sharp, and probably made by a designer whose name I had little chance at pronouncing. I think I even saw one person in a peacock outfit.

And *the course*, the course was beautiful. I stepped out of the Lamborghini to get a better view. The sun was soon about to set, so I couldn't see too far off in the distance but the way the ponds reflected its light was mesmerizing. The greenery in the area was a nice change from the city where you'll be lucky to find three trees in a row. It was a close look at what nature once was and intended to be.

I turned back to look at the club house. It was a white two-story building with a granite colored roof. Patches of people stood on the second floor balcony chatting away over a few drinks barely giving any care to their surroundings and new arrivals.

"Close your mouth. Try not to look so out of place," Emma told me as she opened her own door and extended her hand out patiently.

I took it and helped her out of the car. She didn't require the assistance, but she was right. For this weekend to produce the desired outcome, we were going to need to blend in as much as possible. She reached back into the vehicle to retrieve a matching velvet shawl. Dramatically draping it over her shoulders, she proceeded to greet a young auburn-haired woman that seemed to be going for a Marilyn Monroe impersonation sans the hair.

"Don't look out of place, got it. Let the Unnecessary Pompous Get-Together of the Wealthy begin," I said mostly to myself and walked into the clubhouse.

When the security at the door moved towards me, I simply flashed my rings towards them and kept walking. They hesitated, looked at each other and then stepped back. You don't cross the Romanis, and this was the type of function where everyone here would know what that ring meant.

"I guess I'll fit right in," I said smugly as I looked for a seat for when the banquet officially started.

I selected a table in the far left corner of the room. We were far enough to get a good look at who was coming and leaving from the mahogany coated banquet hall, but close enough to others that we didn't look suspicious. Her friend, Jessica, the auburn-haired woman from earlier sat with us along with her companion Jerry. A bald man in his early thirties, his dark pinstriped suit was tight enough to accentuate his muscular build, and the suave manner in which he conducted himself made him very likeable though he was a man of few words.

Emma was right about the occasion being more about hobnobbing and elbow-bumping than the reason for the actual event itself. The patrons were attempting to respectfully not listen to the speaker like when you're in class or work and you're going through the motions when you're being given instruction. You nod when you're supposed to, laugh on cue, even make a couple of faces to give the impression that you're really mulling it over, but your mind is elsewhere. I could tell this was the case because I was sitting in a room full of people that are used to giving the speeches and they were doing a terrible job at imitating the behavior that their subordinates had perfected.

I listen for a living so whenever the speaker, a thin, nerdy looking young man with curly hair and glasses, would make eye contact with me and see my reassuring therapist smile, his charisma increased, and he would continue their speech to the others more emboldened than before.

See, I can fit into high society.

The club seemed to be honoring one of their highest giving donors who had passed away years prior, parasailing in the Alps. I was just as confused as you are when I heard. How he thought that was a good idea is above my reasoning. It was the eighth official time the event had been held. You'd think they would have honored him enough by now, but what do I know?

"Yes, I was telling Jerry here of all the wonderful vacation spots I've been to in the past five years, Monte Carlo, Barcelona, my own personal island in the Caribbean," Jessica, who had been incessantly talking since we sat down, turned to me. "You're a therapist, right? You must've seen some amazing places recently?"

"I went to the Savannah district of Seaport City about four months ago," I said seriously.

"Oh," Jessica responded disappointedly. "I heard it's nice there."

Suddenly, a sharp pain shot up my foot. I turned to examine the source only to see Emma with an annoyed look on her face. She was methodically rubbing her thumb against the edge of her butter knife. My answer was clearly not up to par, and she was notifying me of this. Keeping up appearances is something that I'm used to in my profession, but I wasn't in the office right now. This was a different playing field, and I was going to have to start learning the rules of the game quickly if I wished to survive.

I grimaced a smile at her, letting her know that her message was received loud and clear.

"Jessica," I turned to the starlet of our table. "How did you meet this lovely woman?"

"Ahh, my dear Emma," she affectionately put a hand over her heart as she said Emma's name. "I am the star of the Celestial Theatres. She rarely visits these days, but she always puts me in the leading role."

"Yes, Jessica is certainly one of the best we have," Emma smiled. I had done this long enough with my clients to tell that Emma was forcing the smile. It was sincere in nature, but fake in appearance, only there to put the one on the receiving end at ease. Simply, like a parent telling a child that there's no monsters under the bed or in the closet but neglecting to tell them about the monsters with human faces outside the door.

Jessica continued on about her many appearances and future roles she wished for with Jerry mostly on the receiving end of her monologue. The look on his face gave off the impression that he was used to this but was still genuinely interested in hearing what she had to say. *Good man, Jerry.*

"... and now we'd like to welcome our next speaker. Captain Jack Woods of the Irregular Police Force," the current speaker announced on stage in his nasally voice.

Emma nearly spit her drink out all over me while I almost choked on my hors d'oeuvres.

"Are you two okay? Was there something wrong with the food and drink?" Jessica asked, concerned. "I'll notify a waiter right away," she got up to leave the table and find the hired help, Jerry followed close behind.

"You didn't tell me the IPF would be here," I whispered harshly to Emma.

She shrugged, shocked as I was. "Didn't know he would be here. Call it situational irony."

Sure enough, it was the ginger haired captain that we had fought almost a week ago. He was dressed in ceremonial IPF uniform, wearing pure white dress pants that went well with his polished black pointed toed dress shoes. Cpt. Woods's midnight black dress coat and gloves gave him a deadly aura. He carried his onyx colored hat in his right arm and coolly strolled to the stage. Underneath one of the lights, I noticed him grimace slightly as he moved, possibly a residual effect of our previous encounter.

When he reached the podium, he calmly put his hat down, his medals shined from the fluorescent light above. Woods looked over the crowd and waited. He seemed like the type of man that required absolute obedience and he was not going to speak over anybody. The gathered attendees received the message and the pockets of conversation in the room died out instantly.

"Good evening esteemed guests," he started in his commanding voice, "It is my pleasure to represent the IPF here in this weekend's festivities. I hope to meet you and make new allies in the quest to stop unchecked Irregular behavior in this country," as he continued to speak, I noticed his slight accent yet again. From my guess, somewhere in the UK.

"I know some of you may be concerned about the recent upstart behavior from a particular individual in Peach City," his gaze swept in my general direction, and I swear my heart nearly burst from my chest and started running for the safety of home. I had to stop myself from letting out an audible sigh of relief when his gaze swept over me and back to the center of the room. "But rest assured, it is merely someone playing dress up and is of no concern to anyone here."

Emma tilted over to whisper in my ear, "Why would that be a concern to people here? You're only a rumor and the rumors consist of you stopping human trafficking."

"One cockroach may be excusable, but two means you have an infestation. We fully intend to exterminate these pests before it reaches that point," he continued grimly.

"He's totally talking about us," Emma whispered again. I nodded silently. I swear, Cpt Woods tone indicated that if he knew we were here he would kill us on the spot.

"We ask for your support and resources. Thank you," he finished speaking and was met with a standing ovation. Taken aback by the reaction, I stood up a couple of seconds later than the rest of the crowd. I didn't think the audience would be this anti-Irregular. There had to be a few like Emma and I in the crowd, but most likely they were registered and had no intention of using their abilities in public. Something told me though that this same crowd was more than happy to use us to line their pockets and advance their agendas. I clapped, but secretly seethed within.

I felt a hand grab my arm. I followed the arm to the owner and found it belonging to Emma. Her eyes met mine. She offered me a sad half-smile and shook her head, warning me not to do anything rash. I returned her smile with a twitch of my lips. It was all I could manage. I had the feeling that this was going to be a long and challenging weekend.

"Thank you for that speech Captain Woods," the emcee for the night said, "Our final speaker for the night will be Hamilton Bennett."

"What?" I exclaimed, but not loud enough to overcome the dying down of the applause. I knew we were here for him, but I wasn't expecting him to be a speaker. He was going to be trouble enough when he was just an attendee operating from the shadows, but a public face along with Cpt. Woods being here. If Emma and I weren't careful, the only way we were getting back to Peach City would be in body bags.

As Cpt. Woods was leaving the stage, his path crossed with Bennett in the walkway. The older Bennett seemed to dwarf over the younger man, but Woods never blinked and held his gaze unnerved. Bennett extended his hand to his counterpart. Woods took it in his hand and the two shared a brief, tense handshake. Bennett leaned in and whispered in his ear. For the most part Woods didn't respond, but there was a slight twitch of his lips, indicating whatever was being said wasn't a mere joke between friends. Bennett patted his back firmly with a smile, causing Cpt. Woods to wince in pain, before proceeding to the podium himself. My pulse quickened as I realized that Bennett must've noticed his discomfort also.

Bennett wore a black tailcoat, one button done, over a white dress shirt that somehow fit his massive shoulders and gray khakis for trousers. Of course, he had his customary orange ascot. Unlike Woods, Bennett wore his hat upon the stage. It was a tall top hat similar to that of a ringmaster which seemed apropos considering the circus I had been dragged into.

"Good evening gentlemen, ladies," he made a face that I'm guessing was meant to pass off as charming to some of the women in the audience. They cooed in response causing bile to rise in my throat.

"Can we give another round of applause for Captain Woods?" He implored the crowd on and began clapping himself. The crowd followed suit. I don't know why, but something about his tone and mannerisms almost seemed mocking. I looked to where Woods was sitting. No reaction.

"I too have had my fair share of issues with rogue Irregulars," he drawled in his thick gentlemanly southern accent. "As a former IPF member I saw the ugliness that some of their ilk produced. Countless innocents have been lost to their senseless rampages."

"You normies were doing a great job at senseless killings way before we became mainstream," I grumbled low to myself. My anger was starting to leak out and I could start to feel the rage that Barb begs me to tap into.

Emma tightened her grip on my arm to calm me. I folded my arms and leaned back in my chair, not saying another word for the duration of Bennett's speech.

"But have no worry, y'all are in good hands, my new friends are working to also aid the IPF in their eradication of this infestation. This weekend though, is for fun, nourishment, new friends, and new memories. To Wyoming," he toasted to end his speech.

"To Wyoming!" The crowd saluted back.

"What did you bring me to?" I whispered, trying to hide the growing franticness in my voice.

My mind was racing about all the potential ways that this could go sideways. From what Bennett said, was it true that the Underground and IPF were in cahoots? If that was the case, Peach City was as good as lost unless I wanted to be the catalyst for another Conflict and most Irregulars didn't have the spirit to go through another Purification. Had Emma set me up?

No, she would have had plenty of opportunity. Unless her aim was bigger than me, which would explain her comments about the Romani family.

"Breathe," The Spectre commanded as he glided from the ceiling towards me.

I heeded his advice and took three short breaths, then three long breaths, alternating until my mind had settled.

"Can't talk now," I muttered, trying not to draw attention to myself, "later though."

"Agreed," And with that the Spectre faded from sight.

"Are you okay?" Emma asked me, concern painted her face.

"A lot to take in," I responded, not meeting her eyes.

"Maybe you should head in. I can take it from here tonight," she drew closer so only I could hear. "Hit the golf course tomorrow. Try to be around Bennett, watch who he talks to, that's probably what we're really after. I'll meet you before the banquet."

I looked at her and nodded. Pushing out my seat, I rose to my feet. I bowed respectfully to our recently returned table mates before leaving. "Jessica. Jerry. Nice to meet both of you, but I must retire to my room, clients really exhausted me this week."

"Of course, dear," Jessica said understandingly, empathy in her eyes. "Please, get as much rest as you can."

Jerry simply nodded back at me.

I said farewell to Emma and started making my way to my hotel room nearby. It was nightfall outside now and the Georgia breeze blew its cool air on me. The sounds of nature played its nightly tunes. The crickets customary hum, owls hooting in the distance, and the faint splashes of creatures going into the ponds could all be heard. I stood and reveled in it for a moment. It was the most at peace I'd been since arriving here and I wanted it to last for as long as possible.

"Are you okay sir?" One of the guards from earlier asked me as I stood idly by.

I ignored him at first, not wanting to interrupt the moment. Then, I faced him and gave him a reassuring grin with a thumbs up. "All good."

Chapter Thirteen

T his is not good," The Spectre silently observed as I outlined my fears to him. His gaze followed me as I paced back and forth in my room. "I don't know who this Bennett is, but I think he's the one from my nightmares. If that's the case, I think I already lost to him before or I'm going to lose to him in the future."

"Your fears are probably justified," The Spectre offered.

I stopped my pacing. Turning towards him, I asked, "And?"

"And they are justified."

"Aargh," I moaned. "You can be borderline useless sometimes."

"Maybe you'll find Sammy more suitable for tomorrow?" Spectre suggested.

"Hmm," I pondered the thought over. "It may put me slightly at ease, but we haven't been on the same page lately."

"I suggest you start. Lives are at stake."

"Lives are always at stake," I retorted. "If I'm not at peak mental focus, which I can rarely ever trust that I am, then mistakes happen, and people still die."

Spectre moved in the room behind me and stared into the mirror. There was no reflection of him, but I saw myself. My eyes were bloodshot and frantic. My dress shirt was hanging off of me, tie loose but not completely undone. I looked shook.

That's because I was. My work the past year consisted of fighting in dark alleys, tunnels, abandoned buildings, and the sketchiest of areas. The past week or two and especially tonight, had shown me the negative consequences that resulted from my actions. Don't get me wrong, I'd save those innocents every time, but I was finally starting to see the real face of my enemies and it terrified me. I was realizing that I much preferred a guard with a gun than a businessman with a grin.

I took my tie off and jumped onto the bed. "Maybe you're right. Sammy tomorrow, then see you Saturday."

"Agreed," The Spectre said, unmoving from his spot.

I leaned my head back and waited for daybreak to wake me in the morning. I had my eyes closed, but I kept hearing a swirling sound in the room. It was like the noise you hear at the beginning of a tornado, but on a much smaller scale, almost negligible.

"Why are you still here?" I asked the Spectre, my eyelids still shut.

"Barb is quieter than usual," he said, concern in his voice.

"Isn't that a good thing?"

"Don't make deals with that devil," he warned.

I groaned and rose to look at him. "If the two of you won't give me answers, I'll get them from Barb. This is the game you've forced me to play."

"A dangerous one at that. You know extended exposure to us affects your mental state," he reminded me cautiously. "That's why the boy usually speaks for us."

"I'll deal with the consequences when they come," I plopped back down on the bed and closed my eyes yet again. "See you Saturday."

The miniature whirling slowly began to fade away, letting me know that the apparition had disappeared, and I was left alone with my own thoughts and dreams.

***

I awoke to the sun's rays beaming down on me. I reveled in the warmth that they provided, few better ways to start the day in my opinion.

I rolled out of bed and walked to the bathroom. Compared to the near manic mood I was in last night, it was a nice change of pace to go through a basic morning routine. I could now appreciate the beauty of the room. Maroon carpet on the floors, systematic paintings of various colors decorated the walls, with two queen size beds in the room. I noticed that the other bed was left undisturbed, meaning that Emma had probably stayed somewhere else last night, presumably with Jessica.

After throwing some cold water on my face, I checked my suitcase for my golfing attire. I'm not much of a golf player, but my putt-putt game is solid. Emma told me to bring cash or a checkbook because these outings usually end in gambling. Since this was going to be a gentlemen's activity, Emma wasn't going to be available as my out if anything occurred. It was just going to be the other golfers, Sammy, and me.

"Sammy, please don't mess this up for us," I pleaded to myself. After getting dressed, I examined myself before leaving. I was wearing an emerald-green polo which matched my eyes, khaki pants, and some black Nike tennis shoes for comfort.

"Are you ready?" I called out to Sammy, putting my green golfing gloves and visor on to finish the ensemble.

"Ready as ever!" Sammy happily responded. I blinked when I saw him. He happened to be wearing the same attire as me. This was the first time I had seen him in a different outfit outside of his ripped firetruck shirt and jeans.

I raised an eyebrow questioningly. "When did you get an upgrade?"

"I dunno," he extended his palms upwards and shrugged. "I guess I have you to thank."

I sat on the bed to come to eye level with him. "Do you understand the plan for today?" I spoke to him the same way a parent would speak to their child before going to a public event. Hopefully, I could protect him while at the same time ensuring that he wouldn't embarrass me.

"Yes," Sammy bobbed his head excitedly. I guess he was really ready to go. "Keep an eye out for suspicious behavior, try not to talk to you when others are in earshot, and provide useful quips when they're being jerks."

"The last two kind of contradict," I pointed out to him, "but you more or less got the idea."

"Let's go then," he ran to the door and waited for me to open it.

"To be young again," I muttered, walking over to him.

Emma was present at the first hole. She had the in with most of the individuals there and after listing off some of my "accomplishments" as her personal therapist she was able to get me in a group with just who we came for, the Southern Gent.

As I approached, I could see that he was wearing pure white golf shorts and a white polo of his own. He seemed more like he was getting ready for a tennis match rather than to go golfing. The rest of the party of middle-aged men were milling about and talking amongst themselves.

"Devin, it's good to see you!" Emma greeted me with a warm smile and a hug. "I was telling Hamilton here about you."

"All good, I'm hoping," I happily replied.

She slowly pulled back and gave me a slight approving nod before turning back to Bennett, "Of course. There's nothing but good things to report."

Bennett took off his gloves and extended his hand to me. "Pleasure to meet you Mr. Prince. To be honest, seeing you now, I was quite surprised that Emma here had such glowing things to say about you."

I took his hand in my own, forgetting to take off my gloves and gave it a light squeeze. His responding squeeze was much less light.

"Dr. Prince," I corrected him. I rarely make that distinction, but this wasn't the place to be lax about titles. "You'd probably be surprised Hamilton, but I get that a lot. My age always seems to throw people off."

Slight disappointment that his jab hadn't landed as he intended flashed across his face, but just as quickly, that insincere smile of his returned. "You're *age*, right. That's always a contributing factor. You can call me Bennett, only friends call me Hamilton."

I returned his comment with a fake smile of my own. "Well, hopefully by the end of this we'll be the best of friends, Bennett."

The handshake lasted a little too long, so Emma moved to Bennett. "Hamilton, sweetie. Do be nice to my doctor. You have no idea how hard it is to find one that takes your money while actually producing results."

"I wouldn't imagine anything less. What kind of gentleman would I be if I did?" He responded, putting his hand over his heart. "Scouts honor."

"Thank you, much appreciated," Emma walked towards me and stood on her tippy toes bringing her mouth close to my cheek. With her back to Bennett, it appeared as if she were giving me a friendly farewell kiss, but she quickly whispered, "Be careful."

I gave her indication that I received her message loud and clear then bid her farewell.

"Are you always so friendly with your patients, doctor?" Bennett questioned me.

Remembering the bio she had given me when we were on the road here, I replied, "Emma is hardly considered one of my patients now. She keeps me on retainer mostly for her actors when they get stage fright or need encouragement for their acting. Come, let's go with the rest of the group," I gave him a not so friendly pat on the back and walked forward.

"Hamilton, I didn't know you had your own personal caddie?" One of the members of the early bird special club called out to us as we approached closer.

"What is he talking about? I don't see a caddy," Sammy remarked, looking around in surprise. He wasn't exactly familiar with the history that this particular club had, and I had no desire in walking him through it. You have to try to preserve a child's innocence as long as you can. It's one of the last pure things in this world.

My eye twitched at the comment, but then I forced another grin. "I didn't know that the End of Days Nursing Home had let the octogenarians out today. You should've brought your nurse. That way we'd all have something better to look at than your ugly mug all day."

The commenter bowed his head embarrassed and started idly messing with his clubs as his friends failed to stifle chuckles behind him. Sometimes you have to match ruthlessness with ruthlessness, step to the baddest man in the yard and punch him in the face. That way you'll shut down the nonsense quick, fast, and in a hurry.

I felt a huge hand press down on my shoulder. "Impressive," Bennett whispered in my ear, "but he nor his friends will forget that slight."

"Nor will I," I responded.

He gave me a toothy grin then invited me to ride with him in his golf cart for a chat.

"Tell me Dr. Prince, do you ever take in Irregulars as patients?" Bennett asked me as we drove to the next hole.

"There are times when I do," I answered him curtly. Speaking about Irregulars in general, was a near taboo subject unless you were cursing their existence. I didn't want to give him too much insight on my personal feelings on the topic nor did I want someone associated with the Underground to start targeting my clients.

Bennett looked at me then away and wore a pout on his face. "They are dangerous, you know."

"So are the nor-" I caught myself before I used the term Normie, a dead giveaway of being an Irregular, "normal people that gunned down their fellow man way before the Irregulars started popping up or the same people that still put others in cages," my last statement had venom in it, but I made sure not to direct it in his direction.

"You have a point," he conceded. "Many of us forget what it was like before Wyoming. We got too concerned about our abnormal differences with one another that we forgot what it was like beforehand. Humans, bound to repeat the same mistakes until we eventually go extinct."

"Well, that was morbid," I rested a hand on my cheek before turning slowly to him. "Is there something you would like to get off your chest?"

Bennett gave out a hearty laugh. "Nice try doctor, but then you'd have to charge me."

"I can lend an ear for a continued cart ride."

"Persistent. I like it," he turned to me. "I wish to rid us of that pain, but I fear we must first go through more suffering. Something that you're probably familiar with."

"I am," I affirmed. "You were IPF right?"

He sighed deeply. "I was. A long time ago. The Conflict and Purification forced me to see that neither side is particularly innocent in this world, but I do concede that with such powers Irregulars need to be kept in check. I bet you're wondering why I left though. I was one of the highest ranking officers in the force, which allowed me to get to talk with administrators. I met General Watson and let me tell you, that is a madman lacking any honor. The plans he had at the time were concerning. I can only imagine how those plans are progressing now."

"Is this where your friends come in?" I pressed.

This time it was him that gave the curt response. "Yes, but a man of your principles wouldn't want to meet them, nor they you."

I grunted in acknowledgement, and we rode on in blissful silence.

***

"Why is golf so boring?" Sammy complained.

We were hanging out by the golf cart. He was sitting in the driver's seat, imitating that he was operating the machine. I was leaning against the back of the vehicle. We were finally on the back nine, thirteenth hole, and there were three men in front of me before I had to go up to the tee.

"It's not boring, just," I mulled over the proper word, "slow."

"I'm bored and why do they keep calling you Tiger?" He asked.

"Famous black golfer," I answered him, doing my best to disguise my talking. The last thing I needed was them seeing me talking to a golf cart.

"Couldn't they call you something else? I'm scared of tigers. They remind me of Barb."

I glanced over my shoulder to see Sammy hunch under the wheel, gripping it tightly as if he were hiding from something that was on the road as he pretended to drive.

"I need you to hold on for just a couple more holes," I implored him. "Then we can have fun at the banquet if Emma lets us go."

His eyes lit up as he turned to me. "Oooh, a banquet."

"Yep," I answered him happily. "You're doing a good job. We're at least getting something out of Bennett. I don't know how helpful it is in the short term, but it's better than nothing."

"You're right," Sammy turned away from the steering wheel, his legs dangling above the ground from the side of the cart. Gingerly, he jumped down from the driver's seat and trotted beside me, imitating my stance, arms folded, one foot on a wheel, and reclined back on the cart. "Plus, Chrome Dome seems to be one of his friends."

Chrome Dome was the one from earlier that had "accidently" mistaken me for a caddie. I hadn't bothered to remember his name, so Sammy affectionately started calling him this when the elderly man took his visor off and the sun hit flush on his head, reflecting off his dome towards us. I try my best not to burst into laughter when Sammy mentions it.

"Good point. Nice work," I discreetly patted his head and looked back to the tee.

"You're up now, Tiger," Chrome Dome called out viciously to me.

"Guess it's my turn," I withdrew my driver and carried it with one hand over my shoulder.

I lined myself up and drew back to swing.

"Wait!" Chrome Dome exclaimed. He trotted confidently down from where his gaggle of guys were towards me. An ugly sneer painted his face. "You've been fairly decent. How about we make this more interesting?"

I placed the driver down and leaned forward on it towards him. Disinterest painted my face, and I didn't bother trying to hide it.

"How so?" I asked lazily.

"Let's say whoever gets the better score out of the two of us, gets some kind of compensation. I win, you leave tonight, with or without your lady friend and I get five thousand dollars. That should be pocket change for a doctor of your status, right?"

Comparing bank accounts, the equivalent of comparing a certain body part of the male anatomy and a favorite pastime of people like him. They only see the world in terms of dollars, lacking any sense.

"And how do I benefit from this? You already have me by four strokes with five holes to go," I pointed out to him. I needed to inflate his ego as much as possible in order for retribution to hit home as hard as I wished it too.

"Oh, I guess you're right, wasn't really paying attention," he lied in an insincere tone. "You can pick. I'll do anything you wish if you somehow manage to win."

"Anything?" My voice rose a little as I simulated suddenly becoming more interested. He must have thought he had me now, which if I didn't golf the best holes of my life, he probably did.

"Anything," he rubbed his grubby fingers together, confirming his willingness.

"I'm starting to get the feeling that you may not want me here," I complained mockingly.

"Just a wager among men. You know how it is," he replied.

"Believe me, I do," I stepped up to him, getting in his face.

I'm not the tallest or most intimidating guy in the world, but the thing about stereotypes is that they can work in your favor if you know the right time to tap into them. I'm pretty sure the only people like me that Chrome Dome talked to, either worked for him or was in his social class, so there was a lot of wiggle room I had in terms of how he viewed me.

I slightly hovered over him. Shocked by my sudden intrusion into his personal space, he took a step back. I took a step with him to close the distance. He couldn't retreat too much or risk looking weak in front of his friends. The arrogance he had earlier left his face, replaced by uncertainty.

I looked down at him and put more bass in my voice, slightly altering the cadence, I told him my terms. "I'll take your stupid deal, but when you lose. Five million dollars, to a charity or organization of my choosing. Also, you'll attend tonight's banquet in a speedo. If you don't have one, I'll have one of your errand boys deliver it to you and when people ask, you'll tell them exactly why you're wearing it," my voice dropped to a deadly tone. "Because I'm superior to you, mentally and physically. Got it."

He nodded his head nervously and I gripped his hand firmly to seal the deal. He waddled to return to his group. For a second, I thought I saw a stain on the back of his trousers, but what do I know, I hallucinate.

I managed to par that hole which didn't really help me with four holes left, but thankfully he went after me and bogeyed his turn. Must've been the nerves.

"Very bold of you," Bennett said as we rode in the cart headed to the fifteenth hole.

"Yeah, we showed him," Sammy agreed along with Bennett.

I rode with my arms crossed. There was no way I could keep relying on him to bogey if I wanted to win the bet and stay on the premises. That would throw a wrench in Emma and I's plan. She would beat me to kingdom come if I got kicked out now.

"I'm a therapist. I know how to read people. His type is probably the easiest," I answered.

"And what about me?" Bennett asked.

I tilted my head to him, curious, "What about you?"

"Can you read me?" The question was innocent enough, but at the same time it felt like a subtle challenge. Bennett was telling me that he wasn't easy prey like Chrome Dome, and I would be mistaken to treat him as such.

I shook my head. "You're not his type."

He smirked at this and looked back to the course as he drove. We passed another lively pond and a garden filled with color, ranging from various pinks to vibrant oranges. The sun was descending from its apex, so it would be in our face now as we shot, slightly blinding us. This gave me an idea, a devilish smirk creeped onto my face.

"Oooh, I like that," Sammy commented in understanding, one of the benefits of sharing a brain.

"May I ask," Bennett interrupted my scheming, "Why do you find his type so repulsive?"

"Do you mean him specifically or wealthy people in general?"

"In general?" He clarified.

I pursed my lips to think over how I wanted to phrase my reply. "The unspoken answer to why most people hate the wealthy, envy. Because they know that no matter how hard they work, invest, and apply themselves, that's a level in which they'll never attain. The simple answer here, homeboy literally wanted to get rid of me the instant he saw me. He probably donates to places that'll give him a banquet in his honor or building with his name on it, so he thinks he can just insult me. Granted his friends would probably be doing the same, but he happily volunteered as spokesman first."

"Is that a fair judgment on your part?" He asked me while banking around a corner.

"I don't exactly see you stepping up to stop him and is it fair of you to question my credentials as a doctor?" I asked him pointedly.

He mostly hid any visible reaction to my poignant comment, but I did see a slight twitch of a nerve in his forehead.

"Touché," he conceded. "Tell me, what would make *his* type better?"

"Don't get me wrong, ninety-nine percent of people screaming about sacrifice would be doing the exact same thing. It's not my right to tell someone what to do with their money, earned or inherited," I paused. "Except in this case."

Bennett peered at me. We were approaching the fifteenth hole and he began slowing down even though we would have had plenty of room to stop at our previous speed. I figure there was something else he was searching for in this conversation that he hadn't quite found yet.

"So, you assert that it's the degree of sacrifice that determines one's moral standing?"

"That's an oversimplification in my opinion," I idly adjusted my gloves and continued. "But I do think greater sacrifice is required for decisions that oftentimes conform to our principles. Where that falls on the general moral spectrum is above me though."

"I see."

"Can I ask you something?"

"It's only fair. Go ahead."

"Have you lost someone?"

Bennett's grip on the wheel tightened, his jaws clenched together, and he focused on the road. The deep resignation in his eyes gave away the answer before his mouth did. "We've all lost someone. I wasn't willing to make the necessary sacrifice because of my morals," he turned to me, and those resigned eyes now burned with anger. "I haven't made that same mistake since."

I turned away and gulped. Emma was right. I needed to be a bit more careful around him. Trading theological stances with a friend is one thing, but he made it clear in no uncertain terms that we were not friends.

We finally pulled up to the hole. I grabbed my clubs and left without saying another word.

"I don't like that man," Sammy was huddled against me while I walked to the tee.

"Me neither," I whispered under my breath. I took my handkerchief out in order to wipe sweat from my brow. The heat was starting to get to me and the others as well.

Chrome Dome was up and preparing to swing. His face was a bit more determined than before. The initial shock of me standing up to him must've worn off with the realization that all he needed to do was be consistent and I wouldn't be able to bridge the gap. The rest of the crew of men were holding their hands up to block the sun from their eyes, which is exactly what I was hoping for.

As he hit the ball, it flew into the direct path of the sun, out of the line of sight of anyone trying not to bake their eyeballs. Suspiciously though, his ball ended up landing amongst the trees. I don't know how it happened, but it's almost as if the path of the ball mysteriously changed.

I came up and clapped him jovially on the back. "Don't worry, happens to the best of us."

He ended up double bogeying and I broke even. I was only one shot back with the two holes to go. It was doable.

We both parred the seventeenth hole, so as usual it came down to the final hole, the eighteenth.

A big cloud rested in front of the sun, providing us all with a piece of cover from the heat as we all prepared for the final round. Unfortunately, that meant I wouldn't be able to use the same trick, I mean technique, again on this hole.

Chrome Dome did what he had to do and yet again broke even, putting all of the pressure on me. I could feel the vultures' gazes behind me as they waited for me to fail. That's when the jeers would really come out and they'd probably pack my bags for me on the way out, or at least get their servants to do it.

"Don't worry Prince, I'll be sure to at least give you cab fare when you leave," he jeered, his confidence now returned. I hadn't birdied the entire time I was here and that would be what was required for a tie at minimum, let alone give myself a chance to win our wager.

I was starting to get nervous. Maybe this was the one time where I should've conceded, kept my mouth shut, and played a cordial game of golf, but like Dr. Schultz in *Django,* "I couldn't resist," I fidgeted with the driver unsure of how I was going to do this.

"Hit it in the sand," Sammy advised.

"What?" I looked up at him. He was standing opposite me. A green apple colored putt-putt club in his hand. He was in a stance of his own, club hovering next to his own tee and ball.

"Hit it in the sand," he repeated. "Trust me."

He smacked the ball and landed in the sand trap just how he suggested. The ball bounced and was hidden from view. I didn't really see how this would benefit me, but when Sammy is confident, I can usually trust what he says. He's a part of me after all.

"What's taking so long? Is the heat starting to make you delirious?" One member of the Peanut Gallery called out to me as the rest chuckled.

"I hope you're right little buddy," I muttered to myself and hit the ball, mustering all of my strength to send it as far as I could. The ball took a curved path to my intended destination. In appearance, it appeared as if I hooked it badly. The ball landed near the same spot that Sammy's landed and sat there, out of sight.

I peered over my shoulder, and they were having a grand time now. Pats on the backs, high fives, I'm surprised they didn't do a group hug and start jumping around in a circle. Now that would be a site to behold. The only one not celebrating was Bennett. He was sitting on the back of the golf cart and leered at me. Maybe he made a side bet with the others and put his money on me, or he was still upset over our previous conversation. Either way, he didn't hide his displeasure.

I approached the bunker, while the rest waited a few yards behind me. "Why on Earth did you tell me to hit it here?" I complained to myself. "It's going to take one hit to get it out and another to go in the hole just to tie."

"Or maybe just one for both," Sammy was sitting on the top of the bunker with his legs crossed, peering down at me. The smug grin on his face showed that he was very proud of himself.

I looked back down then glanced over my shoulders. The memory of the ball landing and almost immediately being obscured from view by the sand played in my head.

They could see me but couldn't see the ball. I figured out Sammy's plot.

Sammy bent his head in acknowledgement at my realization.

"Alright let's finish this," the devilish smirk returned to my face.

I grabbed my putter and prepared to wrap things up here. As I swung, I made a portal underneath my golf ball, so that it could fall through. The purpose of my swing was merely to hit up as much sand as possible as a diversion. The resulting cloud of sand sent some particles into my eyes, causing them to sting. The others behind me covered their faces or coughed from the dust. Luckily, I remembered enough about this particular hole that the ball came out of another portal just above, but outside the bunker I had been in. Rolling down the side of the incline, it was on just a perfect enough trajectory that it rolled directly to the cup, circled around and then dropped into the hole for an eagle, securing my victory by one stroke.

I gave a fist pump and looked at my opponent, the thrill of victory in my gaze. Chrome Dome matched my stare with a look of misery. His eyes clouded and his head drooped down. He took his newsboy golf cap off to hide his face, showing his barren scalp. I walked by him and rested my hand on his shoulder.

"Don't fret," I reassured him. "I'm pretty sure you look good in a speedo. I'll have it delivered to you by the evening."

His head drooped so low that I thought he was trying to bury it in his chest.

"Oh," I stopped as I was walking away from him. "And don't even think about backing out now. You wouldn't want everyone to believe that you're not a man of your word."

I continued my triumphant stroll to the clubhouse. As I walked past Bennett, he simply nodded at me when I passed by. Looking towards his defeated companion, he sighed, a look of disgust on his face.

"Maybe golf isn't so boring after all," Sammy cheerily commented as he reappeared to stride next to me.

Chapter Fourteen

ahaha. Wait, wait. What was his face again?" Emma couldn't contain her laughter while I recounted the events of earlier to her. "I'm totally taking pictures tonight. Blackmail still goes far these days."

"I'm just glad I didn't screw this up," I said. "Did you find anything last night or today?"

"Hmm, let me think for a minute," she began vigorously brushing her teeth while wearing a fuchsia pink robe with matching slippers and her hair wrapped. The night's ball was in about three hours, and she was already prepping for it.

"Jessica doesn't stop running her mouth, so I found out a lot of juicy details about some of what people around here get into," she went to the sink to spit and walked back into the room to continue her debrief, "Bennett's dealings are mostly legit. He seems to have a lot of friends here."

"Apparently, so do you. When do you find the time to moonlight as an heiress to one of the most famous theaters in the world?" I asked.

"The world is more connected than ever before," she turned to me. "Plus, just because I fight at MyKey's ring doesn't mean I'm homeless."

I thought it over for a bit. I didn't know much about her personal life, so it would've been wrong of me to assume anything based on her initial appearance, same as what Chrome Dome and company did earlier to me. "Good point."

I took my shoes off as I finished with her. I was looking forward to calling it an early night and start preparing for tomorrow since my part of our deal had been completed.

Sorry Sammy, I thought to myself. No ball for me.

I twisted onto my side and let my head hit the pillow.

"What do you think you're doing?" I heard Emma's voice, breaking me from my respite.

"I don't think I need to explain the concept of sleep to you," I groggily retorted.

Next thing I knew, I felt a pillow hit the base of my spine. It didn't hurt but was annoying, nonetheless, causing me to flip over to look at her.

Her hazel eyes glared at me, brow furrowed, and her cute nose was scrunched up. The deep frown on her face and hands on her hips added to the overall look of indignation.

"You can't go to sleep now," she informed me.

Incredulously, "Why not?"

"You're accompanying me to the ball," she ordered.

"You told me you're going to the ball alone," I reminded her. "That it would be best for our cover."

"That was before the wager you made with George."

"Who?"

"Chrome Dome," she corrected herself.

"Ahh," I said. "I still don't see why I need to go."

Emma tilted her head and gave me a look like I was the densest person in the world. She opened her mouth then closed it again. I guess it takes time explaining things to idiots.

Finally, she settled on saying, "Everyone is going to want to see and talk to the man that bested George Adkinson, owner of Adkinson's Poultry."

"Wait," I interrupted. "The chicken man?"

She nodded impatiently, unhappy that I had interrupted her explanation.

I had a fit of laughter. "That's great. I know exactly the type of speedo I'm getting him now."

Emma tapped her foot as she waited for me to finish. "Like I was saying, everyone will be asking about you and if you're not there that means they'll hound me, which ruins my investigation. Telling them you went in for an early night isn't a suitable excuse. Get up and get ready."

I groaned loudly and turned back on my side away from her. "Five more minutes mom."

Another pillow hit me in the base of my spine, this time sending me to the floor. I soon began grooming for the night's ball. Never let it be said that I'm not a quick learner.

***

"You shouldn't stuff your face," I advised Sammy as we stood near the bar of the banquet.

"Mind your business," I could barely hear him over the amount of food he was gorging into his mouth, even though I knew he wasn't really eating anything. The brain is a strange muscle.

For the night, I had assumed wallflower duties. My sage colored tuxedo helped me blend into the surroundings, yet I still got bombarded with unwanted conversation from time to time. Emma was right. People wanted to talk to the man that showed up George Adkinson on the golf course, forcing me to listen to the story of my triumph every time I heard someone recount it back to me. I would mostly just smile and nod, no point in bursting my own bubble. I had gifted him a turkey themed speedo, feathers and all. How was that possible on such short notice? Don't question the resources of the wealthy.

Adkinson walked by me and paused. This was first time we had seen each other tonight. He turned to me and the look on his face told me that if murder were legal, he would commit it on the spot. I made a mental note that I would possibly need to watch my back moving forward.

I calmly met his gaze and tipped my glass to him. "You fill that out much better than I expected. You should be happy, you're the belle of the ball."

"This is far from over, you ni-" he started.

I quickly shifted from my position on the wall to get directly in his face. I glowered into his eyes and bared my teeth at him, Barb style, "I dare you to finish that sentence."

He backed his head away from me but stood his ground. "This is far from over. I don't care who you have backing you. I'll ruin you."

I rolled my eyes. "And you would've gotten away with it, if it weren't for this meddling kid and his stupid dog."

He blinked, puzzled by my quote.

"Scooby-Doo," I sighed. People don't appreciate the classics anymore.

His sneer returned to his face as he stormed off to chat with the rest of his smurfs.

"You shouldn't be so quick to create enemies here," a voice warned.

I turned to find Captain Jack Woods standing next to me. He was in full IPF attire, same as yesterday. I stiffened at his appearance. Of all the people that I expected to come up to me, he was probably the last.

"Captain Woods, what an honor to meet you," I reached out my hand towards him. He returned the gesture, grasping my hand in his and gave me two perfunctory pumps.

"I've gotten that all day, Dr. Prince," he replied. "You must be wondering why I came up to you."

"Not rea-" I started.

"I wanted to meet the one that upstaged Mr. Adkinson," he continued. I guess I was supposed to know his previous comment was rhetorical.

"More importantly," his voice tightened, "To see what kind of man you are."

Being this close to him, I could feel the intensity radiating off of him. I could also see some of his features up close. Some would probably consider him handsome, in a G.I. Joe kind of way with his jagged vertical scar crossing over his right eye. He must have received it years ago, for it had lightened considerably. His ginger hair was crew cut, adding to his whole militaristic vibe. His jaw was very defined and since he always seemed to be clenching his teeth, I could see his cheekbones. This was a man that had seen some things, and nothing was going to get in the way of him fulfilling his duty. I had to be cautious of not giving him any indication that Emma and I were Irregulars. I got the feeling that he was used to sniffing these types of things out.

"Hopefully, you find me to be a man of honor," I matched his tone. "But I have no intention of kissing up to you."

The corner of his mouth twitched upwards. "I wouldn't want it any other way. What brings you here?"

"Duty," I replied simply. "I planned on staying in Peach City, but Emma insisted that I accompany her. She said that she could possibly need my services when around such a crowd."

"Understandable. I had a similar experience in getting me here," Woods clasped his hands behind his back and looked back towards the crowd disapprovingly. "These aren't exactly my kind of people."

I thought of a leprechaun joke, but now wasn't the time. Instead, I took a sip of water from my glass and replied. "I know the feeling."

"You seem rather apprehensive," he noted. "Is it because I'm IPF?"

The strobe lights in the room left my face at that exact moment, hiding my initial shocked expression. He was good at reading people and wasn't going to hide it like I usually do. His own version of a lie detector test.

"Not every day you see a captain," I told him a version of the truth. "I'm guessing you're one of the wolves."

He clenched his jaw. "Yes, I find the moniker distasteful, but it is the name that we were officially given."

Unbeknownst to him, I understood that sentiment completely. "I take it then that means you're an Irregular?"

"Yes," his response was noticeably terse.

"Then how come you spoke the way you did about them at last night's event?" I continued my line of questioning. Even though he was IPF, most of the Irregular agents they have don't hate others It's more like they feel like the privileged to be one of the good ones.

Woods folded his arms and looked toward the crowd again. "Look at these people. What would they think if some Irregular went on a rampage or walked around freely without contingencies in place? How would they react? *Unchecked* Irregular activity will force them to turn to a man like Bennett?"

"Did you serve with Bennett?" I asked.

"Bennett," his voice strained at saying the name, like it was a curse. "Is one of the best agents to serve in the IPF and it was unfortunate that he left."

I raised my head, curiously. Something about his answer felt rehearsed, like it was a company mandated response. He also never answered my question. "I see."

"It was nice meeting you Dr. Prince, but I'm not much of a conversationalist. I may be seeing you in the future," he nodded in farewell before marching away.

"Looks like you scared him off," Sammy noted as he put another shrimp into his mouth. "You're really good at doing that."

I let a puff of air out of my nose and went back to my position on the wall. I observed the crowd to see what Emma was up to. I scanned around the room until I found a table with four partygoers sitting there. She was with Jessica and Jerry, who happened to dress as if they were in the Great Gatsby, the other guest with them was the man we came for, Bennett.

They seemed to be in the midst of an enjoyable conversation. Laughs all around, oblivious to their surroundings, seeming to have no other cares in the world. The way Emma was so chummy with Bennett made me think that they had known each other their entire lives. They were laughing over their perfectly weaved trap, and I was the fly that got caught within the web. I shuddered at the thought.

I shook my head to get that idea out of my head. "I got to trust her."

Deciding that I needed a seat, I worked my way the short distance to the bar, avoiding the fanboys and girls as I found my stool. The only available seat was next to a short haired strawberry blonde who seemed as disinterested in being here as I was. I would've preferred to sit elsewhere, but all of the other seats were blocked by people standing by the bar.

"What can I get you?" The buff, bearded bartender asked me as I sat down.

"Orange juice, please," I answered.

"With what?" He asked.

"Plain."

He raised an eyebrow, questioning my order.

"Designated driver. You know how they can get sometimes," I jabbed a thumb towards a middle-aged man who was passed out on the bar counter.

The bartender nodded understandingly and then went to the unconscious man. "Mr. Wilson, wake up. You know that you can't sleep here."

I gingerly sipped my juice, hoping to save it for as long as I could. Sammy was rattling off all of the sights that he saw in the crowd. I began questioning if I made the right decision in allowing him to come. The later it got, the more drunk partygoers became, and with that the raunchier the evening became. There are just some things kids shouldn't be allowed to see.

"Are you going to hang here all night?" The bartender came up and asked me. From his tone, it let me know that he wasn't intending to be rude. He wanted to know if he should start a tab or not.

"Sorry, I'll probably be a while," I replied. "Not my kind of crowd."

Out of the corner of my eye, I thought I caught a glimpse of the blonde sneaking a glance at me. I quickly turned away and focused back on the bartender, but he just simply nodded and started attending to the other customers.

"What is your kind of crowd then?" A diffident feminine voice asked me.

I turned to the direction of the question and found it belonging to that of my bar neighbor. This was the first time I saw her face full on. She was actually quite striking. Her rich jade green eyes seemed to drag you deep into them while also giving the impression that she was able to see into you. She had an athletic build which went well with her sapphire dress, yellow streaks of lightning were impressively embroidered into the dress which ran from the bottom of the dress all the way up to her hips. Her blonde hair was short and stylized in a way that gave her a tomboyish look. Pearl earrings were the only jewelry she wore to go along with the light blue eyeshadow and lip gloss which passed as her only form of makeup.

The problem was that her face seemed rather tight though as if she were used to frowning a lot. She still seemed rather disinterested and that she was only talking to me because she couldn't sit in her own silence anymore.

"Well, with my job, I'm used to people trying to hide the truth from themselves, yet still they search for a solution, but the people here seem perfectly content with being..." I stopped, not entirely sure of the word I was looking for.

"Fake," she finished for me.

"Yeah, maybe that's what I was going for. It's kind of like that movie that came out a year ago, *Artificially Synthetic,* I believe was the name."

At my mention of the movie, her eyes immediately lit up. She put both elbows on the table and leaned towards me, gifting me with a whiff of her pleasant peach aroma.

"You know that movie?" She asked eagerly. "No one ever mentions it. I fell in love with the acting and the story?"

"It was a well thought out plot," I agreed. "The ending was a bit of a brain bender though."

"Yes, so many people miss the hidden meaning," she giddily replied. We both met eyes for a second before nervously looking away.

The blonde caught herself and started smoothing out her dress. It was a habit many of my patients would do when they were emotionally amplified. This was usually a calming mechanism to regain their composure.

"I'm Vee, by the way," she slowly extended her hand toward me before quickly withdrawing it.

"V, huh?" Most of the night had gone terribly, so I wanted to push my luck. "Are you going to give me the speech about your personal *vendetta*?"

She flossed her pearly whites at me. "No. It's Vee. V-e-e, my name is longer, but my friends call me that. And I could totally repeat that entire speech back to you."

"So we're friends now?" I asked.

"One of few. Consider yourself lucky. What do you do for work anyway?" She had fully dropped the air of professionalism and was actually being surprisingly friendly to me. She was the only person other than Emma to act this way towards me without expecting something in return or sucking up to me tonight.

"Therapist."

Her eyes widened and she looked from Adkinson back to me. "Ah, you're the one that put that pig in the turkey speedo?"

"I am," I sheepishly sipped from my glass. I had discussed this subject enough for the night and I didn't feel like going too much in depth with it.

"Well, let me thank you for every woman in here," she put her hand on her heart in gratitude. "Some of these men think they can just touch whoever they want and not face the consequences."

The look of disgust on her face and venom in her voice seemed familiar, but that familiarity quickly passed as the lovely smile returned to her face.

"So, what do you do?" I asked.

She bit her lip nervously and looked away from me. "Private sector."

"I see. Can't talk about the job. I kind of know how that is, doctor-patient confidentiality."

She looked back at me. Her eyes wrinkled into a smile, though her lips did not, which is harder to pull off than you think.

"Yeah, I don't really talk about work, but I'm glad you understand," she beamed. "So, are you here with anybody?"

It was me that looked away this time. I highly doubted that this was going where I thought it was going, but I also needed to stay on task, so I couldn't afford a major distraction or risk drumming up suspicion. "You could say that."

Vee's face became blank. "You could say that?" Her voice turned flat, suiting her expression.

I rubbed the back of my neck nervously. "My boss dragged me along. I didn't really want to go, but duty calls."

"I know how that is," she rolled her eyes in concordance as she perked back up a bit. "Want to share another drink? Alcohol-free of course?"

"Of course," answering both of her inquiries.

"To Wyoming," she saluted.

"To Wyoming," I toasted back. We clinked glasses and talked for another hour.

The ball started wrapping up and the last call for drinks was given out.

"We're down to the final two songs. Fellas grab your ladies because it's couples only," The DJ belted out over the speakers to the crowd. The lighting in the room changed to a more comforting ambiance. The kind of comfort that makes you want to snuggle up for warmth under the covers during the winter.

"I guess it's almost time to leave," Vee was looking towards the DJ.

"I guess so," I answered simply.

"They seem to be having fun," she remarked, looking at the dancers now.

"I guess they are," I responded in the same tone.

"Did you want to get up?" Her eyes flickered with annoyance for a second before she gestured her head to the dance floor.

Silly me, I wasn't really paying attention to her subliminal messages. "Oh, yes. Would you want to, um, dance?" I'd probably never see Vee again so it wouldn't hurt. I was only doing this to keep my cover. Yeah, that's exactly the reason I asked her to dance.

"I'd love to," she extended her hand out to me again, the way royalty would, this time without hesitating.

Just as I rose from my seat and reached out my hand to take hers, we were interrupted by a clearly perturbed voice. "Dr. Prince! It's time to go!"

Emma was standing before me, arms folded. She was still sticking with the violet theme. Aside from her brunette beehive hair, her entire wardrobe was that color. A different dress, but violet nonetheless combined with her violet stilettos was her attire. I was tempted to call her a crayon, but the frown she wore on her face dissuaded me from that course of action.

"Miss Emma, I was just about to provide the lady here with a final dance."

"I'm in the midst of an urgent situation that requires your immediate assistance," she flicked her eyes from me to the table she previously occupied.

I tried to read her face. She clearly was in a bad mood, but her abrupt timing made me question if it was as pressing as she was making it out to be.

I turned back to Vee apologetically, "I'm terribly sorry."

A buzzing sound started occurring from somewhere on the bar top. Vee pulled her cell phone out of her purse and looked to check the message. She gave a face that's reserved for finding out that you're either being called in to go to work unexpectedly or a text from a clingy ex.

Annoyed, she placed the phone back in her purse and slid off from her seat. "No worries, people like us always have to put duty first. Hopefully, our paths will cross again."

She put her hand on my shoulder in farewell, slowly letting it linger as she walked away.

"You totally should have asked her for her number?" Emma said to me when Vee was finally out of earshot.

I looked down at her and made a face. "Oh yeah, and say what? Excuse me, I know my boss ordered me to leave and I immediately jumped up to go, but if you don't mind, can I have your number?"

"Yes, exactly!" The fiery brunette exasperatedly told me in response.

"You could've waited five minutes," I replied, my shoulders slumped in annoyance.

She shrugged. "With your usual demeanor I thought you were just trying to gather information, not whatever it was you two were doing."

"One, that would've been even more reason to give me a few minutes. Two, my usual demeanor? We just got on a first name basis less than a week ago."

"Yet, it feels like we've known each other our whole lives. Come my muse, we have much to discuss," she started walking towards the exit as the music wrapped up and the lights in the room began to come back on. "Plus, she looked like she could totally kick your butt. I was protecting you, call it motherly instinct."

I snorted before hurrying to catch up with her. "More like an annoying little sister."

Emma looked up at me, a bright smile on her face. She didn't show any teeth which somehow gave her young face a sad aura that adults give to children when all the chips are down, yet they find the strength to tell them that everything is going to be okay. I still found it reassuring, so I returned it with a half smirk of my own.

***

"Alright, this is what we've got so far," I was writing down notes on a Dry-Erase board that I had quickly jumped to my office to retrieve. "Bennett is here in some capacity for the Underground."

I drew a circle with his name in it at the top of the board and proceeded to do so with the following names that I would list, drawing a line to connect them. "The majority of Bennett's time was spent talking with Chrome Dome and his pals. For some reason, he talked to Jessica and Jerry a lot."

Emma raised her hand while sitting on the other queen bed in the room. Her other hand was preoccupied with the cheese pizza she was eating, a staple food of proper detective work.

"You don't really need to raise your hand, but yes?"

"He mentioned that he hoped to make new friends in his speech," she recalled. "From your outing earlier with them, would you say that they had just met or had an established relationship?"

A very good question. Even when Chrome Dome had been making his jokes with his buddies, Bennett was more of an indifferent observer rather than an avid supporter. Most of his insults had been made directly to me away from the others.

"Hmm, if I had to describe it," I started, still thinking, "Bennett came off as more of a person entertaining a potential client rather than a friend, but I never saw them introduce themselves as if they never knew each other."

"Did he seem like he was in control?" She questioned.

Considering the fact he never jumped in to intervene, which I never expected, and he seemed upset over the fact that he felt the need to be the one to calm the client down, I would say he clearly was there to ensure Adkinson signed on the dotted line.

"Bennett always seems like he's in control of the situation, but I'd say he maintained that persona here without that being the case, so no."

Emma jumped from the bed, pizza still in hand. She erased the names with her free hand and then patiently held out her hand for the marker. I placed it in her hand, wanting to see where her head was at with this. She reorganized the names and stepped back for me to see.

The new board this time had Bennett in the second tier. Above him was C.D., the initials for Adkinson's generous nickname. Next to his initials was an empty circle, but a line drawn horizontally from that blank directly to Adkinson and also had a separate vertical line connecting to Bennett below.

"What exactly are you showing me?" I asked.

"This," she pointed to the blank circle. "Is the boss. One option is that he's here in disguise watching everything as an innocuous figure and Bennett is trying to facilitate secret meetings with new clients."

"What's the other options?"

"Well, only one really. Since Captain Woods is here representing the IPF instead of, say, an area director or the local commissioner, this event isn't big enough for the head honchos, so most likely the boss is still, for lack of a better term, underground. Either way, Bennett has contacted him already."

I stepped back beside her to look at the board. One hand held my elbow, while the other rested underneath my chin. The web was starting to become less tangled, but we still needed to trace the right thread to its source.

"Do you think I messed the deal up?" I asked Emma without taking my eyes off the board.

"If the Underground is what you suggest it is and Bennett is as calculating as I've heard..." she paused for a brief moment to shiver. It wasn't cold where we were, so I knew her reaction wasn't because of the temperature, but I didn't comment. Instead, I waited till she was ready to continue. "If he's as calculating as I've heard then he's going to use today's situation to his benefit, and your detriment."

"I'm guessing this leads to one man then?"

We looked from the board to each other, nodded and in unison. "Chrome Dome."

Chapter Fifteen

I thought we weren't going out until tomorrow," I remarked while examining our current all black matching attire. My traveling companion had brought ski masks, hoodies, cargo pants, and stealthy tennis shoes that we could use for reconnaissance before Saturday's mission.

"We were, but we still don't know where to go. The last thing we need is us showing up announced somewhere and having Bennett or Woods on our case. That's why we're spying on Adkinson tonight while he's still enraged. He's going to be sloppy and slip up, trust us."

"I do," I conceded. "But you could have at least gotten clothes that were less tight. These are choking me." The wool interior of the clothing was making me itchy. The ski mask had a thin slit running horizontally from ear to ear, but with nothing to hold it open, our sight was going to be significantly hampered.

"Had to make do with the time we had," she said, "Now stop moving before I drop you."

I was suspended above Adkinson's room with Angel grasping me. Emma didn't have the strength to hold me up for such an extended period of time, so they switched out before starting our espionage. We had gotten Adkinson's location from Jessica, one of the benefits of having loudmouth associates, and I was currently maintaining a miniature portal through which Angel's hand was holding me through while the rest of her was in our hotel room. When I gave her the signal to pull me back, I would expand the portal large enough for my body to fit through and she would yank me in.

Adkinson was staying at one of the more upper end hotels as well. It was about a ten minute drive away from the clubhouse and was in a rather secluded location. The theme of the room seemed to be the Renaissance era. Some of the paintings on the walls were familiar in style to the paintings I had in my office. The bed was fashioned with a canopy. White satin linen not only served as sheets, but also as the curtains that surrounded the bed. On the wooden floor, lay a zebra pelt, which isn't even indigenous to this country mind you.

"How pretentious can you get?" I grumbled as I dangled in the air.

When Adkinson appeared, it didn't take me being a therapist to see that he was livid. He burst into the room, still wearing the turkey speedo I had provided him. I had to do everything in my power not to retch in my ski mask. Even as repulsing as the sight was, I still whipped out my camera and took pictures. Like Emma said, blackmail goes a long way.

The grumpy bald man was on the phone and whoever was on the other side of that call was probably going to have long-term ear damage once it was done.

"That so-called doctor thinks he can come here and embarrass me! ME!" He screamed into the phone. "That's it. I want the deal and speed it up!"

He grabbed a hotel provided vanilla robe and slippers then began pacing frantically.

"What do you mean you can't move up the shipping date?" He yelled belligerently. "Bennett said the products would come as I requested them. I want those Irregulars now!"

Interesting, just as Angel said, in his rage, Adkinson slipped up and revealed just enough information for me to lock on to the Underground's dealings.

"Thanks Chrome Dome," I whispered to myself.

Below, he was still frothing at the mouth. If I hadn't known better, I would've feared that he might've been bitten by a rabid squirrel on the course.

"Two deliveries?" He stopped pacing. "I suppose that'll work. One, next week. Second, the week after. View and memorize the code from the stronghold this weekend, and don't take it with me. Got it, thank you."

He hung up the phone and placed it on the mirror. Slowly, he looked up into the mirror and displayed one of the evilest sneers I had ever witnessed. It was Barb level scary. At that moment, Adkinson revealed to me perhaps one of the ugliest souls that I'd ever come across in my life. A lot has to go wrong in one's life for a person to get to that point, wealthy or not.

I gave the signal for Angel to pull me up and just like that I was back in our hotel room.

"Thanks."

"Whatever. Tell Emma, I'm not her personal errand girl," just like that, the cold callous gray eyes faded away, replaced by the energetic hazel ones that signaled Emma was with me now.

"What's the situation?" Emma asked, waiting expectantly for the details of what I had seen and heard.

I reported the details to her and gave her a second to chew everything over.

"What do you think the stronghold is?" I asked her.

"Well, that tells me he's not keeping the codes on him, neither is Bennett. It's definitely not at the clubhouse. It's probably far enough away that you wouldn't stumble into it, but close enough that you can drop off and deliver them without being gone too long."

She urgently started digging through her bags as a thought apparently hit her and pulled out an honest to God map. She scanned the map before pointing to a spot. "Here."

I came around to observe the location she marked. "Fort Gordon? I thought it got destroyed in the Conflict then was used as torture chambers during the Purification. It's defunct now."

"Which makes it a perfect location. Think about all the places you've fought so far; the Underground isn't exactly out in the open about this," she pointed out.

"You have a point. So, Fort Gordon tomorrow. Get the codes and we're in business."

"Then we have two weeks, two opportunities to expose the Underground," she tapped her chin thoughtfully before turning to me, a rare serious expression on her face. "You think we can do this?"

I nodded grimly in affirmation. "It's not a matter of can, we have to."

She put her hand on my shoulder and clenched it encouragingly. "Then lets."

As cool as it felt to finally be on the same page with someone out in the field as committed to stopping the Underground as I was, one thing was still bothering me though ever since we left the ball. "Hey, how come you were so adamant about leaving earlier?"

"I already told you, instincts," she said evasively.

I narrowed my eyes. "Be serious," I've sat across plenty enough people to know when they're hiding something from me. Clearly, whatever was bothering her then was still troubling her now.

"Ugh, you got me," she crossed her arms as if she were physically trying to shield herself from what she was about to share. "It's Bennett. Jessica asked him about his time in the IPF and when he initially left. He told stories about the Irregulars that he killed. It was the way he told it though. No care, no remorse, it's like he didn't feel anything or think twice about. Killing was just as simple as going grocery shopping to him. He killed..." Emma choked back a sob, tears were forming in her eyes. "a child," she finished weakly.

The beautiful, carefree young woman that had come into my office was gone at that moment, supplanted by an overwhelming pain that couldn't be healed by any physical means. I already disliked Bennett, but this made me hate him. We were going to stop him, stop the Underground, and anybody else associated with them.

I slowly walked over to Emma and did something that I rarely do. I gave her a hug, burying her head in my chest, shushing her whimpers to calm her. "It's going to be okay. Like you said, two weeks, two opportunities, we'll get it done."

After a few minutes, her sobbing stopped. "I don't want to do anything until tomorrow night. Can we just stay away from them?"

"Sure," I said. I let my voice be as soothing as possible, trying to maintain her now more stable mood. "One thing though."

"What?" She asked, trepidation in her voice. I could feel her body tense up as I finished my sentence. She was holding her breath now.

"We get to wear our own suits tomorrow night. Deal?"

She looked up at me. Her eyes were red from the tears, but she smiled. It reminded me of when Mia Bella told me about her dreams, another validation of my existence. "Deal."

Chapter Sixteen

S ee this is much better," I pointed out to Emma.

"No need to throw it in my face," she responded hastily.

We were wearing our usual evening costumed attire. I had my silver flamed, black coat, studded gloves, and steampunk goggles with the lenses up. Emma was in her Angelus persona, the comedy theater mask letting me know that she was currently in control. Her silver cloak fluttered along with mine in the cool Georgia breeze.

We were standing before what was left of Fort Gordon. The building was barely visible in the moonlight, but you could see patches of ground where the grass differed. Some of the worst fighting during the Conflict had occurred here. Irregular forces tried gaining access into the fort in order to get weapons and provide a stronghold in which they could defend themselves. Unfortunately, this assault came too late in the campaign when the tides of war were swinging back in favor of the Normies. Once the Irregulars ultimately failed, Fort Gordon was used as an interrogation and experimentation site during the Purification. It had thankfully been decommissioned and presumed to be abandoned, but I doubted that the Underground would leave this site unattended if they were using it to store information.

The one thing Emma and I had going for me though is that since Fort Gordon was a government sanctioned No Man's Land, security here would have to be light which would be more than manageable for the two of us.

"Come on, we don't have much time to waste before sunrise," I flipped the lenses on my goggles down, initiating night vision mode. I started walking to one of the holes in the gate to reserve my energy and ability for when I would really need it.

"As you wish, my liege," Emma answered mockingly while trudging along behind me.

We stepped over the chunks of debris littering the ground and entered the walls of the fort. As we came closer to the building itself, I heard a whooshing noise overhead.

Suddenly, the Spectre descended down in front of the two of us. "I suspect others," he spoke to me, Emma none the wiser.

"Can you walk around and see if there is a door?" I asked Emma in order to send her away. Even though we had grown closer the past couple of days, I still wasn't comfortable with anyone seeing me consort with my hallucinations.

"How come you can't just make a portal on the wall for us to go through?" She questioned before adopting an annoyed tone. "And I'm not your sidekick, so don't give me orders."

"I believe I asked you nicely," I replied facetiously.

She folded her arms and turned her masked face away from me. "I believe you're missing something."

Leaning towards her with a huge grin on my face, "Would you be able to walk around and see if there is a door, please?"

"Hmph," she pouted before heading off.

I waited till she was out of view and then turned to the Spectre. "I figured someone would be guarding the place, but how can you tell?"

Spectre moved to a spot on the ground that led to a trail of two sets of footprints, both of which were very odd. The first set began with two large footprints, but then got progressively smaller and alongside the smaller prints was a hole in the ground as if they were using a walking stick of some kind. The next set had four prints in all that looked as if someone were crawling along the ground.

"Interesting," I noted to myself, taking the clues in.

"Interesting," he echoed me. "Two organisms."

"Or just people," I corrected him for my sake. "Possibly three, look at how these prints change."

I pointed to the heavy set of footprints that led into the smaller pair of prints and presumed walking stick.

"How what changes?" Emma asked. She was coming from the opposite side of the wall in which she disappeared, indicating that she must have looped around the entirety of Fort Gordon.

Without hesitation, I pointed towards the footprints below. "There, others are here or were not long ago."

She came over and tilted her head to get a good look. She didn't give any advanced notice, but suddenly her hand started glowing white from her flames. Squatting down to glance at the set of footprints, she ran her non-illuminated hand over the disturbed dirt.

She rose up, turning to me. "Safe to assume they're still here. I found a door on the east wall. It's cracked, but most likely it's going to creak when we open it."

"Thanks, I think we can take whoever's in there, though."

"Look who's Mr. Optimistic all of a sudden," she mused at me.

I shrugged. "I'm as surprised as you are, but they wouldn't be able to keep their strongest or a bountiful of fighters here. It would cause too much of a commotion and bring attention. If the Underground got exposed here, it would ruin them."

"All right," she said confidently. "Let's get to it."

"Agreed," I affirmed and looked back to the Spectre, his gaze unchanging.

"Be careful," he whispered while fading from view.

"Will do," I whispered back and proceeded to follow behind Emma as she led us to the eastern wall.

"I don't remember all of these walls being here," Emma pointed as we stepped into one of the facilities. It appeared to have been used as some type of garage for larger vehicles in the past.

"With the Conflict and Purification, better defenses were added to places like forts, battleships, and other military bases of operations," I explained. "The government couldn't afford for it to fall into the hands of Irregular forces."

She nodded at my response as we pressed on. The inside of the abandoned garage was huge. It would have been possible to put two basketball arenas inside. This made examining the room difficult, especially with the lack of lighting. With my night vision, I could make out some of the details in the room, but not enough to rule out any impending danger.

The floor was scuffed with tracks that I could only assume was because of the constant coming and going of the vehicles that had previously been here. There were a couple of equipment parts on the floor also. Broken glass, two hubcaps, a hood of a car, and engine were all visible on ground level. Along the walls were your typical workbenches, shelves, and tools. Nothing was too out of place here. I didn't know whether that should've given me comfort or if the hairs on the back of my neck should've been standing.

"I have a question for you," Emma broke me from my investigation. Her hand was still illuminated in her white flames, serving as a light source to guide her in the darkened room.

"Go for it."

"Were you around during the Conflict?" She asked me sincerely. There was no judgment in her voice, and I couldn't sense any ulterior motives that she might have in asking me that.

That time period is a difficult era to discuss. Like I said, the fighting in the Conflict was ugly, wide scale, and messy, but it's hard to describe it as a full-scale war. It's more fitting to describe it as a sustained cross-country riot. The people actually doing the rioting don't entirely represent those staying peaceful but try explaining that to a cop that's been hit in the head with a brick. In this case, try explaining it to a soldier across from an Irregular that can drop an entire brick house on them. It was one of those moments in history where you had to pick a side or do your best to avoid the situation entirely, which was often unavoidable.

I rubbed the back of my neck as I thought of a way to answer Emma's question. "My memory starts a while after the official end of the Purification, but I wasn't a kid at that time, so I was probably alive then, but didn't make much of an impact during the Conflict."

"Makes sense," she responded by moving to one of the walls to launch an investigation of her own.

"How about you?" I asked following closely behind her, fascinated to see what her life was like during that time.

But Emma kept pacing along the walls, searching for the clues we had come to find. She gave no indication that she had heard my question, let alone provide me with an answer.

"How about you?" I repeated, unsure if she had heard me.

Again, she pressed on, without so much as a twitch of the head to acknowledge she had heard my question.

An uncomfortable silence hung in the air between us as we walked in the hangar, until finally she said, "I don't really like talking about that time period. Too many personal deaths."

"Understood," I replied even though I had no idea how to comprehend what she had just told me. I started to shuffle slightly away to give her space.

"You're a terrible therapist if you usually just leave it at that," she spun back towards me. Her voice didn't really match it, but her body language indicated she was trying to force a joke.

"Well, it got you to open up, didn't it?" I teased.

"Whatever," she tsked.

I thought back to our first meeting about how she mentioned her personalities worked and what she had just mentioned about personal deaths, then it hit me that she had never fully explained her lifetime or *lifetimes* and I never took a moment to ask, so I kind of just went with it.

"So how does the timeshare in your head work for you?" I asked.

She sighed, lifting her head up to look at me from behind her mask. "We might as well keep searching while I explain," she turned on her heels and headed to a different section.

"Like I said head trauma, spikes in my emotions, and death are the ways that trigger Angel to come out without me ceding control to her," she started. "In this cycle, I'm the dominant personality, so I can mostly take back the conn whenever I want to, but when my next death occurs, control switches back to Angel and she becomes the dominant personality."

"How does death switch the dominant personality?" I asked as we both started running our hands along the walls to see if there was some type of hidden switch that we could press or loose papers that would give us the information we came for.

"Have you ever played video games?" She questioned me in return.

"I'm familiar with them, but I can't exactly say I remember playing with them."

She shook her head without ever looking back at me. "Mid-Millennials," she huffed under her breath. "Well, when people used to play together sometimes you had to share controllers and if there weren't enough controllers you waited until someone else died in the game, then they gave the controller to you. So even if you're both playing with the same character and you can give tips from the side, that character takes on the personality and traits of the one in control."

I nodded, less so in understanding and more so in working through what she had just told me. "In this case the character would be your body I'm guessing?"

"Exactly."

"So, the next time you die that means …?" I let my question hang in there. If Angel was already super aggressive now while being the alter personality, I really didn't want to think about what she was like as the dominant.

"Exactly," her voice came out in a more somber tone from behind the mask.

"If that's the case, why wouldn't she just kill herself the first chance she gets when you switch, to take back permanent control?"

"Because I would just do the same in return. It would create internal chaos, benefitting neither of us," she turned away from me and started to search another wall, "Plus, dying isn't the most fun experience in the world."

"So, how'd you get your powers?" I asked, trying to change the subject.

She shrugged one shoulder. "Beats me. I didn't really discover them, or her until my first death. Wait a moment, I think I found something."

Emma was standing in front of a rusted steel door which looked out of place in the room. For one, it read *Authorized Personnel Only*. It wasn't big enough to serve as a hangar door because perhaps only a motorcycle would be able to fit through. It also didn't lead to the outside because we had entered through those doors earlier and from how the building was set up it would lead directly into another building which we had already searched and didn't find a corresponding door on the opposite side in that location.

"It's probably what we came for," I guessed.

Suddenly, a small creaking could be heard from above. I glanced up at the ceiling. A relic plane from the 1940s was hanging from the roof. I hadn't noticed it earlier, but I could see it slowly swaying back and forth as if something had bumped into it.

"Was there a draft in here?" I asked Emma.

She glanced in the direction I was looking and held her inflamed hand up to get a better look at the plane. "Perhaps."

Shrugging her shoulders, she turned back to the door. Emma twisted the handle and pushed the door open, revealing a set of stairs that led down into an unseen room.

I looked grimly down at the stairs. I've become accustomed to the tunnels in Peach City at this point, but since I was now fighting with Emma who could fly, a larger venue would've been preferable. I glanced again at the plane which had stopped moving, which only increased my suspicions of being watched. I shook my head to focus on the task at hand and descended down into the darkness with Emma.

"What exactly are we looking for again?" Emma questioned as we reached the bottom of the stairs.

"A code," I replied. "Though, I feel like they could've just texted him or delivered the information."

"No way," she interjected. "You never know the creeps that'll break into your room and spy on you."

"Touché," I replied before warning, "Keep your eyes peeled. This space is more cramped than I expected, so it's easier to grab one of us."

The ceiling in the room was probably seven feet tall, but definitely no higher than eight. The walkway we took was also decreasing in width, making the area more cramped the further along we traveled. Even with my night vision activated, I couldn't see much within the enclosed space. I absently ran my hand along one of the walls. It was stone from what I could tell, moist also. No wonder the room felt so damp.

The air also felt thin. I could hear it in Emma's breathing. The laborious breaths she was taking were even more pronounced from underneath her mask. Our environment was also starting to get to me. Every couple of steps I would find myself gasping for air, surprised by my own vastly depleting stamina. We needed to get the code quickly and escape. A possible prolonged fight wasn't going to do either of us any good if we weren't getting enough oxygen.

As we were walking, a consistent dripping could be heard, but it never sounded as if we were moving away or towards the noise. It just stayed, constant.

I held up my hand for Emma to stop. "Do you hear that?"

There wasn't enough room for me to fully turn around to see her response, plus she had her mask, but she replied, "Yeah, it sounds like a dripping water faucet, but the pitch isn't changing. It should be getting louder or fading away by now."

"Let's keep moving," I told her, lowering my voice to a whisper. "Spectre, what's happening?"

The Spectre didn't appear, but his voice was present. "A follower. Sticking to the shadows."

"Great," I muttered. "Keep me updated."

"Are you okay up there?" Emma asked. I could hear concern in her voice.

"Yeah, I'm good, just focused on making the plan to get us out of here," I peered back over my shoulder as much as I could to reassure her, and I caught a glimpse of a shadow scurrying along the ceiling. I paused, unsure as to whether it was a vermin or my imagination, caused from the shadows constantly changing with the light from Emma's hand.

I turned back around, my pace quickening. The dripping persisted never growing louder or lower in volume.

Finally, the path led to a circular room with royal blue lighting. A granite pedestal stood in the center of the room. On the pedestal, was a pneumatic tube that led somewhere beyond the ceiling. In the tube's entry point was a capsule with a message inside of it. I reached inside to retrieve the message.

Emma came around to stand beside me and look at the message as I lifted the lenses on my goggles to read it.

"Do these numbers look weird to you?" I pointed out to Emma.

"They're coordinates," she clarified. "See, longitude and latitude. I'm guessing the number below is like a pin number to confirm the transaction."

"I see," I said as I started trying to put what was on the message into memory.

"Watch Out!" The voice of the Spectre suddenly screamed. Spectre almost never raises his voice above a certain decimal threshold, so whenever he does, I know that things have gotten real.

Just as he screeched his warning to me, I felt something slimy run across the nape of my neck. I ran my hand across whatever was currently on my neck, and it appeared to be like some kind of saliva, but thicker. I peered at the ceiling and yet again there was something scurrying out of my line of view.

"Eww," I groaned as I examined the fluid. The fluid was very viscous and gooey, I rubbed it with my gloved fingers as panic suddenly struck me when I realized what the substance was. "We need to go. Now!"

"Okay. Open a portal," I could tell from her voice that she wasn't certain what was making me freak out all of a sudden, but she put her hand on my shoulder comfortingly and waited for me to open a portal.

I outstretched my hand to create a gateway for us to pass through. Then nothing happened.

Befuddled, I glanced down at my hand then lifted it back up to try again. This time a sickly-looking portal opened. Instead of the defined indigo brimmed portal that I was accustomed to, this one looked flimsy as if an elementary school kid were drawing a circle for the first time without a compass. The constant low humming was also gone, replaced with a sickly bubbling noise that you hear on television when a character has taken a laxative. Unsustainable, this portal failed and faded away.

"Umm, are you having performance issues?" Emma questioned as I tried and failed a third time.

"That joke is never funny," I growled at her. "I don't know what's happening. Can you just bust us out?"

"Sure, because that adds to us being stealthy," she retorted.

"Just get us out of here!"

"Okay, if you wish. Angel, Smash!"

In the middle of the switch though I saw what was perhaps a tongue, reach down and lick her in the same spot as my neck had been. The mask had switched to the frowning tragedy mask and the cloak took on more of a dark gray hue, indicating that Angel was at the helm. I couldn't tell how she was feeling, but from the way she was staring at me from behind her mask without speaking let me know that it wasn't anything positive.

Before I could open my mouth to explain the situation or more importantly appease her, the tongue shot down again and took the code from my hand. Then the figure slithered on the ceiling through the doorway we had come through.

I looked back at Angel who was still glaring at me, motionless. I offered a weak smile to cut through some of the tension. She turned her head to the doorway.

"You're on my list now," was all she said before she darted after the shadow.

I wasn't sure if she was talking about me or the slithering figure, but I'm pretty sure it wasn't going to end well for whomever she was referencing. I let out a deep breath and equipped my tonfas from my waistband and chased after the both of them.

Traversing the pathway back was pretty simple. Whatever it was crawling on the floor, no longer had reservations about being discovered, so the sounds of its scurrying were now detectable. Also, I was running behind a pissed off Irregular that was doing her best to try to roast the assailant.

As we all finally ascended the stairs, we were greeted at the site of a huge man with his arms folded leering down at us. I don't mean he was huge in terms of muscle or height; I mean he was huge in terms of he probably took 'all you can eat' a bit too literally. Not to body shame, but this guy was definitely skipping ab day.

"Halt!" He said in a booming voice. "You intruders must now face justice."

"Pray tell, who exactly is going to deliver this justice?" Angel asked lazily.

"None other than I, Walter Klump!" His voice seemed to have a mock air of authority as if he were reciting lines from a play. He jammed his thumb into his chest and gave a sly grin as if that gave him more credibility. The funny thing is that I think he truly believed we were supposed to be in awe of him.

"How do you plan on stopping us, Walter?" Angel tested him. We were a few steps away and I could sense her tensing up to pounce.

"You'll see," he sneered and pulled out a cigar and started chewing at the end of it. Walter began backing up from the door, which Angel and I took as an invitation to come out from the stairs.

As we both stepped out of the doorway, I was able to get a view of Walter. Other than his rotund belly, I could make out his handlebar mustache, which was admittedly pretty impressive, a security guard uniform with a tucked in white button up and black slacks, his belt was working overtime to keep that gut in. Watching him twiddle his cigar between his grubby fingers, gave me the impression that he was some kind of cartoon villain. I would say the situation was a little funny, if not for the six foot long gray spotted gecko behind him.

So, that must have been what was in the stairwell and path with us.

Its bulging lizard eyes watched the situation closely. The sopping pink tongue would come out from time to time in order to lick its face. I took a peek towards Angel and I'm not sure if humans could actually bristle, but she was coming very close as her mask stared craters into the creature.

Walter took notice of us peering at the enlarged lizard behind him and let out a hearty laugh. "Oh, allow me to introduce you to George. My partner in dishing out justice against thieving vermin such as yourself."

"We didn't really think you'd care about something going missing considering the fact that you're into human trafficking and all," I sniped at him.

"Losing such valuable information," he lifted the sheet of paper from George the lizard's mouth to show us. "And assets, is always hurtful. Don't take others' stuff."

"The robb'd that smiles steals something from the thief; he robs himself that spends a bootless grief." Angel quoted.

"Ooh, think of that yourself?" Walter teased.

"No, Othello," then Angel pressed off the ground and lunged toward him.

Unprepared for the sudden assault, Walter went down under the force of her attack. She began raining down hammer fists on him as he covered his face. His gecko companion soon darted into action, knocking Angel aside with a mad dash into her sternum.

"Well, what are you waiting for?" A scratching voice nearly brought me to my knees from the pain. I glanced up to see Barb standing on all fours dispassionately gazing at me.

"You're not running point on this one, the Spectre is," I chided it as I managed to regain my composure.

"I know. You're not ready yet," Barb turned its wire-thicketed head back at the scene in front of us before adding, "but you will be."

"What does that mean?" I was clutching my previously injured ribs. The numbed pain had subsided and was replaced with a sharp steady throbbing. I don't know what it is about Barb, but it seems to thrive off of pain and if I'm not the one delivering the punishment then Barb takes its pound of flesh from me. That's why Barb's presence tends to make me more aggressive, like an animal that's wounded, willing to do anything to escape its current predicament.

"You'll see, my prince," Barb responded, then moved forward to George the Gecko, and vanished.

The throbbing in my ribs stopped and I unclutched my hand from my side. I didn't like the tone that Barb spoke with. It usually mocks me like a school bully, but this time it seemed disinterested as if it were waiting for something. I expected Barb to be the first to jump in line for an opportunity to lead a mission, but I found its newfound apathy to be concerning. Whatever Barb was waiting for, I had no doubt it wasn't going to be doing me any favors.

I refocused on the fight happening before me. Angel was holding her own against her two opponents. She maintained her black flames low around her entire body, which served as a protective veil. She was using the same knife-brass knuckles combo weapon I had seen previously and whenever the gecko would get close, she would take a swipe at its soft skin. Security guard Walter seemed more like a director of the animal, never getting close enough to land or take a blow himself.

In the midst of all this action, I saw the paper with the codes sitting on the floor of the hangar. It would move every now and then, pushed by the gusts of wind that the squabble was producing.

Not being one to miss an opportunity, I bolted for the code, snatched it from the ground and fled the building. In retrospect, it may be considered kind of cowardly to leave Angel to fight alone, but I wouldn't have done it if I didn't believe she could handle herself.

Let's just call it a moment of trust.

I hadn't made it more than a couple yards before I felt something sticky wrap around one of my arms and yank me towards the ground. George the Gecko had noticed my escape and his animal instincts along with his enhanced size allowed him to catch up to me. As I lay on the ground, an explosion of brick and metal occurred as Angel hastily appeared from the hole in the wall that had previously been there. Walter arrogantly stepped through the void in the wall, and stood there with his hands on his hips, a proud grin spread on his face.

Still laying on the ground, I glanced at Angel who had landed beside me. From Walter's smug expression, I'm guessing he had managed to throw her out of the building.

The tragedy mask scowled back in my direction. "Thanks for the help back there. What a brave hero you are."

"I saw an opportunity and I took it," I rose to my feet, offering her my hand.

"Seems that lizard took it back," she begrudgingly took my hand and rose to her feet as well. "Why do we need to take the physical codes? Don't your swimming goggles allow you to take pictures or something?"

I stood there for a moment, baffled. I seriously hadn't taken the time to consider that I could've just snapped pics of the codes and then we could've both left. We still would've had to face the pair of guards, but we could've focus more on retreating rather than retrieving.

"You seriously didn't think of that?" I could hear the disgust in Angel's voice.

"A shame," The Spectre chided in from out of nowhere.

"Shut up!" I shouted back at him.

"Who are you telling to shut up?" Angel interrogated me. The flames around her grew, indicating that she must have thought my comments were aimed at her.

"Look at you two," Walter interjected, marching down from his perch on the hill above us. "Fighting amongst yourselves. You fail in comparison to the justice that my friend George and I represent," the enlarged gecko wrapped around him as he made this statement and Walter began rubbing it gently along its head.

Angel brushed the dirt from her cloak then gave her full attention to him. "I got your justice for you."

She took a step towards him, but Walter raised his hand. "Halt! Behold the power of justice as you see my true form."

Suddenly, a blinding fuchsia colored light appeared. Angel and I both raised our arms to shield our eyes. When the light disappeared, what was once Walter was now replaced, and I kid you not, by an honest to God magical girl. Her hair was now blue and fashioned into twin tails with navy blue ribbons. She wore a flowing mint crop top and skirt. The cigar that had once been in Walter's mouth was now a Witch's staff. Golden orbs of light surrounded her while she held a pose. A minacious smirk adorned her face.

And I swear I've never seen anything funnier in my life.

Angel and I looked at Magic Girl Walter, then back at each other a few times before we reacted. She began to shake from underneath her cloak as if she were trying to suppress something.

"Nope. I can't do it. Switch," the mask switched to the comedy mask, letting me know Emma was present. She took one look at the current situation and burst into a fit of laughter.

"Bahahaha. Are you serious? Did you just turn into a magical girl? Hahaha," she managed to speak between her spouts of giggles. "What are you five?"

I turned my head to the side. I was trying to suppress my snickering, but I just found the situation too funny.

Magic Girl Walter looked at the two of us with a confused look on her face. I'm guessing that was a new response and she didn't know how to process it. Even the gecko seemed unsure of how to react to our laughter.

"Why are you laughing?" She seethed. "This is serious! Prepare to face justice!"

Her voice was octaves higher than Walter's was in their original form. The look on her face was absolutely serious, but I kept picturing Walter in his security guard form, mustache and all, but I matched the new voice with the face, and it only made my chuckling worse.

"Please change back," I begged as I clutched my sides, dropping to my knees in laughter. My ribs were really hurting now, but the present circumstance was just too hilarious.

"Stop laughing!" She was really raging now as she clutched her question mark shaped staff.

"Hee-hee, I can't take her seriously," Emma said to me. Her words were barely intelligible now from all her giggling. "Can you be a dear and hand us the codes, sweetie?"

"I. Said. Stop. Laughing!" Magic Girl Walter had concentrated all of the orbs at the tip of her staff now and was floating from her original spot now. The staff was raised up and didn't take a genius to figure out what was about to happen next.

"Oh expletive," I cursed underneath my breath as the stored energy was sent rushing towards Emma and me. The orb crashed down, sending us flying a couple of yards yet again.

In retrospect, maybe we should've taken the situation a bit more seriously.

I crawled towards one of the trees to help me to my feet. "You good, Emma?"

"I'm fine," she grunted in reply with renewed focus. "We just need to get a quick glimpse of the coordinates and then we can retreat, right?"

"Basically."

She pulled out her dual butterfly swords and took a stance. "I think our powers were temporarily blocked by that lizard's saliva, but I still got some juice in me. How about you?"

I looked down at my tonfas and Desert Eagle. They both work better in tandem with my abilities, but I was thinking I could make do without for a while. I glanced back at Emma. "I can be pretty resourceful."

"Well then let's have some fun. I got dollar store Sailor Moon. You get the gecko," with that Emma pressed off and glided low towards Magic Girl Walter, who met her butterfly swords with the staff.

I pulled out my Desert Eagle and took a shooter's stance and pressed forward towards the lizard. I fired off two shots and pressed on, then let out another two shots to close the distance. I continued on like this until I was up close. Most of my shots were aimed at the limbs or tail in order to get the creature to scream in pain which would cause it to drop the letter. Finally, one of my shots had the intended goal and yet again the paper was sailing freely in the wind.

I felt a little bit of juice in me, so I opened a portal only big enough for my hand to fit through. It was still making that sickly noise, but it lasted long enough for me to snatch the paper and pull it back through. I quickly glanced at it and pressed a button on my goggles to record the numbers. The gecko let out a series of concerning clicks then dashed at me. I turned on my heels and started booking it away from all of the fighting.

"Emma, I got it. Let's go!" I shouted back at my companion.

"On my way!" She yelled back at me. I peeked over my shoulder to see her manage to singe the back of the gecko with a thin stream of flame. I've seen her call up much larger columns of flame, which told me the saliva was still having an effect on her, but at least we were both able to use our abilities in some capacity now.

Magic Girl Walter was right on our tails too, not wanting to risk us getting away. I was still running as fast as I could, but I'm not exactly built for cardio. When you can traverse long distances in almost no time, long distance sprinting isn't exactly at the top of the list of skills to master. Fortunately for us, Fort Gordon is about twenty minutes away from our intended destination and I was with someone that could fly.

"Catch me!" I yelled as I stopped and turned towards the oncoming wave behind me. The gecko was the closest and was gaining ground quickly. Emma was right on its heels so I had to trust that my plan would work.

As George the Gecko prepared to leap at me, I placed a portal right where his lead foot was going to be which caused the giant lizard to tumble over itself and crash into the ground. I raised both of my hands above my head and jumped. Emma, who still couldn't get much elevation in flight swooped by and grabbed me by the arms taking me away from our pursuers.

"I knew you'd catch me!" I exclaimed up to her.

"You're just lucky I'm not Angel," she looked down and responded. The comedy mask peered down at me, but somehow, I felt that the face behind it matched its expression.

We were about halfway to our intended destination when we were both struck by another orb of energy, which sent us crashing to the ground.

"If I fall one more time," Emma rumbled as she rose from the ground, brushing dirt from her cloak. Her aura increased, as did the intensity of the flames along with it.

"There has to be a better way to escape," I pondered to myself. I searched the nearby surroundings and the greenery around us indicated that we were at another golf course. Scanning the green, I stopped when I noticed an abandoned golf cart.

"Perfect," I felt more in my reserves, so I was able to open a normal size gateway and leapt through. It didn't take me as far as I would have hoped, but it got me close enough. I hopped behind the wheel and luckily the keys were left in the ignition, so I started the engine and started driving away.

"Well, isn't that fortuitous," Emma noted as she swooped down to fly beside me.

"Agreed," I answered. "Don't you think this new partnership is kind of jumping the shark a bit too early? I mean giant geckos, guys turning into magic girls, and now we're escaping in a golf cart. Sounds like the plot to a B-level, cheesy heist movie."

"Nonsense," she retorted. "If you establish the absurdity early on it gives you a lot more leeway in the future."

"Fair enough, but we still gotta do something about them," I referred to the security detail still in pursuit of us. "Even if they don't catch us, they're going to report to the higher-ups and the time and location will change."

Emma stared ahead of us then focused on our pursuers. "I got a plan. Head for the sand traps then stop."

I banked towards the upcoming sand traps and pressed the brakes as requested. Emma landed on the back of the golf cart and laid low. I could hear the flight of Magical Girl Walter as she was quickly approaching. Just when the golden light that had surrounded her earlier grew near, Emma rose up and whacked her with the driver club she pulled from the golf bag in the back with her.

The shot hit her flush on the forehead. I heard a sick crunching sound as the skull was undoubtedly fractured and this time, it was our opponent that was sent tumbling to the ground. When we walked over to check on our downed foe, Walter was back in his burly form, unconscious on the ground with a huge lump swelling up on his noggin.

The clicking sounds returned and so did George the Gecko. Seeing its handler laid out, caused the beast to start convulsing in a fit of rage and it ran at us with an untempered fury. I managed to withdraw my pistol and emptied the remainder of my clip into its gaping mouth. The shots had an effect and downed the beast. Then, who I thought was Emma walked over and yanked its tongue from its mouth. The saliva sprayed from its mouth, covering us in its viscous spit.

Angel turned around and walked past me back to the passenger side of the golf cart and took a seat not bothering to acknowledge me.

"I guess I have to clean this up," I pressed the comms on my goggles and placed a call. "Hey Toni, how long do you think it'll take to get a cleanup crew to Augusta? Uh-huh, right," I said in response to him over the phone. "Okay, it's on one of the courses. It's a Wario looking guy and a gecko corpse. I'll be sure to discuss it all with you when I get back. Thanks."

I made my way to the golf cart and slid into the driver's seat. I glimpsed over at Angel. She was as drenched in saliva as I was. Drool was dripping from her mask onto her folded arms. Using our powers to get back to our hotel was out of the question now. I opened my mouth to address the situation.

"Not a word," she warned before I could speak.

Mission completed, I nodded solemnly then slowly returned my focus to the wheel, put the vehicle in motion and drove off towards our hotel with Angel in absolute silence.

***

About thirty minutes had passed, but we were finally able to return to our hotel room, saliva free. I took my equipment off and tossed it aside onto one of the padded chairs.

"That could've gone better," I said to Emma, who had retaken control by the time we reached the hotel.

"What are you talking about? We got the top-secret information, beat the bad guys, and have one hell of a story to tell," she responded giddily.

"I guess you're right. It was pretty fu-" I started to say but was suddenly overcome with sharp pains all over my body, bringing me to the ground. I was having another attack. This one was odd though. Usually there are more warning signs than this and I can be better prepared for it.

"Barb?" I called out. Barb was unusually quiet today, but I always see it before the attacks happen. I thought that demon was the trigger, but maybe I was mistaken.

"You called me?" It replied lazily as it materialized before me.

"Why?" Was all I could manage as I fell to my side and began shaking violently. The seizures were starting to take effect.

"Devin!" Emma screamed and rushed to my side. "Devin! Who's Barb? What's happening?"

"You're being prepared," Barb replied while staring at Emma, then returned its crimson gaze on me. "This one is going to hurt, just like the truth I promised."

"What do I do?" Emma yelled, her eyes were wide with fear and surprise. I couldn't blame her. Only one other person had experienced the unseen ramifications that my dealings with the Underground had on me, and it nearly got them killed.

I weakly pointed to the front pocket of my travel bag. My pills were in there and if I could slip a few, I'd be able to manage until the morning. She let my finger guide her then she nodded and rushed over. I let my hand drop, or more accurately, I didn't have the strength to hold it up any more. I angled my head towards Barb and opened my eyes questioningly.

"Right," Barb affirmed, psychic connection and all, "Spectre and the boy wanted to hide this as long as possible, but if you want to beat the Southern Gent, you need to know the truth," with that, Barb walked out of my line of view. Just as Barb disappeared Emma kneeled down in front of me.

"What am I supposed to do now?" She held the two bottles in front of me, unsure of the next step.

I held my gaze on the bottle for the hallucinations and mouthed one. She uncorked the top and placed one pill in my mouth. She lifted my head and poured water to make sure it went down. While staring up at her, I tilted my head to the sleeping pills and again mouthed one. She nodded and repeated the process making sure the pill went down, same as the previous one. I looked up at her, thankfully. I couldn't manage a smile, but I nodded and closed my eyes, the pain receding.

"Don't worry," she reassured me in a lowered voice. "I'll be here when you wake up."

I fell asleep to the soothing feeling of Emma gently stroking my hair.

Chapter Seventeen

*L*eave the kid out of this!" The voice desperately cried out into the rain, "You've already won."

Standing across from him was Bennett in a trench coat. His face and features slightly less visible in the torrential downpour, but I could make out that it was him. He was holding a boy over a ledge. The boy was struggling to escape from his grasp, but his efforts were all for not. On closer examination, I could see the boy was wearing a rose red firetruck t-shirt and jeans. Looking at his face, I could confirm the boy was Sammy.

"My dearest hero, what you fail to understand is that I'm not here to simply beat you. I'm here to end you," Bennett replied, his voice oozing with southern charm as he dropped the boy.

"No!" The owner of the first voice yelled as he followed after Sammy.

He ran past the Southern Gent to the ledge, whose claymore gleamed as a lightning strike illuminated the night sky.

Then he leaped down to save the boy, his outstretched hand revealed that he was wearing a white and black coat with spiked gloves. Sammy was falling head first, but a portal opened before him, a hand reaching out to grasp him. They managed to safely avoid the first layer of barbed wire, but the coat was ripped along with the boy's jeans. There were several more layers of barbed wire though and the figure knew there was no way he could open enough portals quickly or far enough to save them both. So, he opened what he could and hoped for the best.

What comes next is the scream of a child followed by the horrid sound of barbed wire ripping away at the skin of its unfortunate victim. Blood trickled down a mangled *hand and silence followed. The boy's still gaze was wide and unblinking as he stared up towards the figure that attempted to save him as both bodies dangled from the last layer of barbed wire. The boy's reflection showed the figure huffing from the effort. A deeper look into the reflection shows the figure is wearing goggles, and even deeper, it revealed my face.*

I awoke startled, gasping for air as if I had just escaped the grasp of someone attempting to drown me.

"Easy, easy. I got you!" Emma held me in her firm grip as I twisted about wildly.

Finally, I stopped moving which caused me to start thinking. The dream and Barb's words were starting to sink in. Bennett and I were the two fighting on the rooftop that fateful night. I'm not sure what events led to that situation, but the conclusion was always the same and it had been haunting me for years. I let Sammy die that night.

Overwhelmed, I buried my head in Emma's lap, not wanting her to see the tears when they started flowing.

"No, no, no," I chanted to myself. "I'm sorry. I'm sorry."

Emma didn't say anything. She just kept stroking my hair and hummed to me. It didn't make the truth of my failure hurt any less, but it kept me from spiraling further into my sinkhole of sorrow.

We stayed that way until it was time to go. I injected myself with the nanites to repair my internal systems before heading out. They aren't perfect, but it beats opioids while maintaining the same feeling of floating.

We had to return to the clubhouse one last time, for the closing ceremony. As much as I wanted to speak with Vee one last time, I was in no condition to be around people at the moment. Emma did most of the speaking for us, bouncing around from one conversation to the next, steering potential pests away from me.

Captain Woods walked by, stopping when he caught a glimpse of me. He was wearing a similar outfit as the one he wore when he gave his speech. I met his gaze. He shared the same look of wanting to get out of here as soon as possible just like me. I pursed the corner of my mouth, it was the closest I was going to get to smiling, and then nodded my head in respect towards him. He returned the gesture and moved along, doing his best to avoid any further conversation.

"We can leave now. Just saying our final goodbyes," Emma was walking up to me, Jessica and Jerry close behind her.

"So sad to see you leave already doctor," Jessica whined and made a face. "I wish I had more time with you."

She came up to give me a hug, but Emma intercepted her. "The doctor isn't feeling well. I wouldn't advise touching him."

Jessica puckered her red lipstick covered lips and cooed, "Oooh, someone's very protective."

"There's a new play coming soon. I could always look for another lead," Emma warned. "There should be plenty of fresh blood out there."

Jessica urgently spun on her heels and grabbed Jerry by the wrist. "Come on Jerry. The good doctor isn't feeling well. We shouldn't be bothering him."

"Glad you understand. I'll be in touch," Emma said, proud of herself.

We headed for the Lamborghini when one last figure stepped into our path.

"My dearest Emma, how could you leave without saying goodbye?" Bennett questioned. His tall frame and broad shoulders blocked the sun behind him, which was beneficial to me, but intimidating at the same time.

I took a sharp breath at his sudden presence and clenched my fists. Emma again stepped in front of me and calmly put her hands behind her back to rest them on mine.

"You were so busy with all of your friends," she began, "but I knew a southern gent such as yourself would see a lady off."

"You honor me," Bennett replied and bowed before her. Then his eyebrows twitched as he seemed to notice me for the first time. "Aww Dr. Prince, you certainly gave the guests here a time to remember. Few people make such an impression their first time here."

I couldn't even manage my usual professional smile, but I tried anyway.

"Forgive my doctor. He's not feeling well today, and I want to get him back to his practice as soon as possible. I've *kidnapped* him long enough," I don't know if Bennett picked up on Emma's emphasis on the word, but if he did, he certainly didn't let it show.

"So sorry to hear that, but it was a pleasure meeting you," he extended his hand to me.

I hesitated for a moment but couldn't afford to draw suspicion so close to departing, so I reached out and took his hand.

A look of surprise flashed on Bennett's face. He looked from my hand to me and then tilted his head.

I raised an agitated eyebrow at him. "Is everything okay?"

He quickly took his hand from mine and massaged his wrist, "Yeah, everything is good. Hope to see you again," with that he walked off.

"That was weird," Emma commented as she tossed our bags into the car and plopped into the driver's seat.

"You're right, but at least we get to go home," I said as I sat and put my seatbelt on.

We were on the road for about twenty miles before either of us spoke.

"Do you want to talk about what happened?" Emma asked in a matter of fact tone, making it seem as if she weren't that interested either way.

I picked my head off the passenger's side window and turned to her. If we were going to work together, I couldn't put her or Angel at risk if I ended up having a mental breakdown in the middle of a fight.

"I'm schizophrenic," I sighed as I admitted the one secret dearer to me than even my own undercover identity.

Emma acknowledged me without speaking. She was going to let me say my piece and listen.

"I typically have three different beings that I see," I continued slowly, "but I'm not going to hear from them for the next couple of days."

"Is Barb one of them?"

"Yes," I confessed.

"What's that like?" She asked.

"Like last night," I shuddered before slumping back into my seat.

"Doesn't it get better? Can't you just take pills to keep them away?"

"It's not that simple," I answered.

"Even after all that pain?"

"If you could make Angel go away permanently, would you?" I asked, hoping that would help her see my point of view.

She turned to me with a sympathetic, yet pained look in her eyes. "No, I wouldn't. Thanks for telling me."

I nodded towards her and then returned my head back to its place on the window.

"Do you want me to drop you off back at your place?" Emma asked.

"No. There's someone I want to talk to first," I responded as I shut my eyes. "I'll tell you the address when we get closer to the city."

***

"You sure do sleep a lot, old man," I whispered to Dr. Green, lightly nudging him awake.

"That's because I don't have annoying pupils trying to wake me up," Dr. Green grumbled as he started gathering himself from the comfort of his slumber. "What brings you here, my boy?"

"You know I always visit you on the weekends," I reminded him as I presented him with some green tea, three teaspoons of honey, two teaspoons of sugar, and one drop of lemon, just the way he likes.

"I'm glad someone still has some respect for their elders," he griped as he tossed his covers aside and sat up to put on his brown slippers. When the sheets were gone, I could see that Dr. Green was wearing red and black checkered pajamas with an acorn colored night cap.

"The nurse told me you had a solid week so far."

"She doesn't know what she's talking about," he grumbled, making his way to the coffee table. "I always have solid weeks. Just slowing down that's all."

"Not too much, I hope. I still need you," I bantered back.

Dr. Green didn't laugh as I expected, so I peered at him to check if he was okay. Instead, I was met with a stoic gaze.

When he was sure that he had my full attention, he spoke. "You don't need me, Devin. You haven't needed me for years."

"Don't say that. I do-" I began but he raised his hand to stop me. I ceased speaking and looked away from him. In light of my dream, I couldn't bear the thought of losing someone else, especially Dr. Green. It'd be too much for my psyche to handle.

"Look at me Devin," he ordered and waited for me to meet his eyes before he spoke again. "I know it's hard, but I'm dying. There's no easy way to put it. It's probably further out than either of us should really worry about, but somewhere down the line the Reaper is gonna come knocking and I'll gladly welcome him. I've lived a full life and you've been there for a considerable portion of it."

He grasped my hand within his. I felt the wrinkles on his skin as his palms enclosed my hand, but it felt comforting, like holding your grandfather's hands.

"You've given me another shot at family. From client, to student, to son, and now you're almost like a father with how you take care of me," he paused to grip my hands. "But you're going to have to stand on your own two feet eventually. Others are starting to look to you as that beacon of hope in this city. I hear the whispers, read the dirt sheets. The Peach City Phantom and more importantly Dr. Devin Prince, is much bigger than this sick, demented old man. Understand?"

"I understand," I nodded grimly, "but what do you know about dirt sheets?" I asked, surprised that he even knew that terminology.

"Are you kidding me?" He retorted. "Dirt sheets were a thing before you were even a pup in this world?"

"Fair enough," I took out a deck of cards, shook it a bit and placed it on the table. "Rummy?"

"Of course, deal em out," he replied. "No chocolate this time?"

I took his favorite bar of chocolate out of my bag, held it up to present it to him, then slid it over.

"Alright, enough sappy talk. Why'd you come to visit?" He asked me as he started tearing into his treat and looking over his cards.

"The dream," I answered, "It was the most vivid it's ever been and the pain before it was unbearable."

He nodded once before taking a bite of the candy bar. "Tell me what happened."

I explained the details of the dream to him and then waited on his response.

He regarded me with my sober eyes. "So, you think this Bennett person killed Sammy? That's one of the figments, right?"

"Yeah, it is," I confirmed. "Does the timing make sense? I only remember using my powers this way for slightly over a year, but Sammy has always been with me."

Dr. Green leaned back in his chair and started rubbing his chin with one hand and examined the cards he held in the other. "You've told me before that it feels like the boy is hiding something as well as the ghost?"

"Spectre," I corrected gently.

"Spectre, who your current suit is based off of. It's possible that they were serving to repress the memory, but the *other* wanted to bring it to light, which could explain its aggression. The inner struggle currently going on inside you would make anyone go insane. Like I said, there was one like you before, but my internal calendar is off. I hate for you to suffer like this, but it looks like what you saw might be the truth," when he finished speaking, he laid down a club, winning this round and the game.

My shoulders sagged out of defeat in more than one sense of the word.

Dr. Green leaned on the table towards me and peered into my eyes. "But the question is what are you going to do now that you found out?"

I met his gaze and stood up, resolute in what I had to do. "I'm going to stop him, and the Underground."

"Good," Dr. Green encouraged me. "Then you should get to it."

"Then get to it I shall," I replied, repeating an old line to him that I used to say jokingly back when I was his student, and he would give me a task. We both got a good laugh out of that one as we played another round with me losing yet again.

I stood up from the table and headed to the exit. "Thanks for your help doc."

"I'm here to beat you anytime, my boy," he called out to my back as I walked out of the door.

"Thanks again," Nurse Gooding said to me when I passed by her in the hallway. "He really does well after a visit from you."

"Trust me, it's my pleasure," I said to her as I walked by. Then I took my phone out to make two calls, the first of which being Mr. Romani.

"Hey, Mr. Romani. Excuse the formality, but it's a business call. Can we meet in two days?" He responded back over the phone, confirming the time.

"Great, Centennial Park works for me," I continued after hearing his response. "What do you mean that's a weird location? Just meet me there," I told him. "Tuesday, at four o'clock. I know I'm usually working then, but I set my own hours if I don't have appointments. Bye Toni."

"Geez, he didn't have to make that so difficult," I said as I looked at my phone, annoyed.

Next, I surfed through my contacts until I found the exact number I was looking for. "Hey, what are you doing Tuesday at six?"

Chapter Eighteen

It was currently five till four on Tuesday and I was sitting on a bench in Centennial Park. The tepid afternoon sun was out, but thankfully the clouds and calm breeze more than made up for it. I was wearing a tan wool sweater over a white t-shirt, black jeans, and comfortable tennis shoes that I could reasonably walk or run in. A black skully sat atop of my head while I waited. My seat was in front of the sprinklers, so I could feel the refreshing mist peppering my face.

I had thankfully taken the past two days off from work and spent the time resting and recovering. No hallucinations, no patients, no Underground business, just me and my own thoughts. Admittedly, that last part was probably the hardest thing I've had to deal with in a long time. The weekend had taken its toll on me. I had made new enemies, not much in the ways of allies or friends, had a successful mission but got banged up in the process, and had a grave truth revealed to me.

The next two weeks were going to be rough. From what Toni had gathered from the information I passed along, the transfer of Irregulars was happening tomorrow night. I would've preferred more time to prepare, but crime is never convenient to the victims or those trying to prevent it. I was going to chat with Emma tomorrow to go over the details, but as for today I was dedicated to future preparations and strengthening current bonds.

I reclined back, crossing my legs and putting one arm on the top of the bench. I leaned my head back and began whistling. All of a sudden, in the middle of my tune, my vision became obscured. Panic set it in, and I was getting ready to spin and face my attacker, but then I took the time to feel what was blocking my vision. I sensed two small, soft hands over my eyes.

"Guess who," a childish voice giggled from behind me.

"Is that little Bella?" I guessed in a teasing voice.

"Hey, I'm not little," the voice complained as the hands removed themselves from my eyes.

Turning around, I found that it was indeed Mia Bella Romani, as cute as ever. Her red pigtails twirled in the air as she spun around to present herself to me. She was wearing her school uniform, a gray and blue plaid skirt and a white polo shirt with the school's gray stallion emblem embedded below the left shoulder, and black flat shoes with a ribbon on it.

"What are you doing here?" I asked as I peered over the bench at her.

"Daddy picked me up from school today," she pointed back to Toni, who was hustling a few yards back to catch up with her. Clearly, she ran off as soon as she thought she saw me, leaving her father woefully behind. "He said he had a surprise for me, and you're here!"

"You just left him?" I mockingly interrogated her.

"He said I could," she said, looking back from her father to me. "Can we play?"

"Well," I started nervously, kids are kind of a weak spot for me. I know that it only reinforces the behavior, but it's extremely hard to say no to them sometimes. "I really need to talk to your dad, but how about I buy you an ice cream cone?"

"Yay!" She beamed before twirling to her winded father, "Daddy, Uncle Prince said he's getting me ice cream."

Toni finally managed to trudge over to the two of us, wearing a full gray tracksuit. He put his hands on his knees, taking a moment to catch his breath.

"Mia," he managed to huff out, "What have I told you about extorting people?"

"That it only works when you negotiate from a position of strength," she answered matter of factly, a learned response from what I could tell.

I looked at Toni accusingly.

He gave an embarrassed smile and patted Mia on the head. "Oh, kids and their silly imaginations. No, the thing about extorting family."

"Oh, never extort family. You'll never know when they'll repay your kindness."

"Indeed," Toni nodded proud of her revised answer.

I frowned at the both of them and shook my head.

"Mia you can go play now," Toni said as he scooted Mia towards the play area. "I'll entertain your uncle for a while."

"Can I play in the sprinklers, papa?" She asked.

"Not in your school clothes."

"I have changing clothes underneath. Please," she prolonged the word as she pleaded with her father.

"I don't know," Toni thought aloud, "We don't have towels and your mother wouldn't want you coming home wet."

"I can open a way for you to get towels," I offered.

Filled with hope, Mia turned from me back to her dad, "See, please papa," she gave him a set of puppy dog eyes and reading the expression on Toni's face I knew he was going to cave.

"Okay," Toni conceded. "Try not to get too wet."

"Yay," Mia bounced up and down. She tossed her school clothes away, showing the pink and white polka dot bathing suit onesie she had underneath. She then ran off to join the other kids playing in the sprinklers.

"Go ahead and say it," Toni gave me a resigned look after picking up her discarded uniform.

"I don't know what you're talking about," I feigned ignorance. "But I do know she'll be running the entire family by the time she's eighteen."

"Please don't say that," he pleaded, "I don't want to think of my baby girl as a teenager. Her and Susan are going to clash, putting me in the middle of it. They both know I can't tell either of them no."

We both looked at Mia jumping up and splashing around as she continued to play in the sprinklers. What I wouldn't give to be that carefree. She had seen the monstrous side of people firsthand and was still battling her own internal demons, but she still chose to see the best in all of us. Yet here Toni and I were, about to discuss the worst that humanity has to offer and how we were going to deal with them.

"I'm pretty sure it'll work out," I encouraged him. "What are you going to do about her abilities?"

"I'm trying to convince Susan that if we don't foster her abilities and choose to repress them instead, Mia's going to rebel and seek help elsewhere," he sighed. "We need someone to train her, not on using the ability, but the how and why."

"How's that coming along? Got any candidates?" I asked.

"You."

My head snapped back in surprise. My job at times required me to help people see the best in themselves and draw that out, but I wasn't much in the way of a mentor. That would require more of a commitment than I was currently capable of.

The right side of my face scrunched up at the thought, but I didn't know how to let Toni down easy. "Toni, I don't know. I feel like there are much better options."

"I'm not asking you to make a decision today," he stated, unbothered by my uncertainty. "But I'm just throwing the idea out there. You should see how she is around the house, always running around with your goggles and messing up the trees by hitting them with those sticks of yours. You're her hero, so I think she would actually listen to you."

I blew out a huff of air. It was a lot to chew on, but thankfully I had time before I needed to give an answer of any kind. "Well, with everything going on now and her abilities she definitely needs a teacher. I'd hate to see what would happen if her powers got out of control. Give a kid a water gun and you'll just get wet, but give them a nuke…"

"And you get another Wyoming." Toni finished solemnly. "What did you need to discuss?"

"Underground as usual," I stated.

"How did your weekend vacation go?" He inquired.

"Great and terrible at the same time," I complained. "Did you find any information out about Hamilton Bennett?"

"Nothing good," he said while sliding me a manila folder. "Former IPF Alpha. He had free reign to go hunting Irregulars, no strings attached. A dangerous man."

My eyes widened in apprehension at the folder. I wasn't sure if I really wanted to read everything in the file. "So, are you a Cold War spy now?" I joked, trying to add levity to the situation.

Smirking, "I didn't want to risk getting hacked. Sue me. So, the transfer is tomorrow?"

"It is," I confirmed. "Abandoned train station. It should be routine unless Bennett gets involved."

"I wouldn't go counting your ducks before they hatch," Toni warned.

"It's chickens."

"Irrelevant," he dismissed my correction with a wave of his hand.

"Did you get anything out of the mall cop?" I asked.

I don't know whether he was amused at my joke or the interrogation process, but Toni gave a cruel smile.

"He gave us the entire communication apparatus," he replied. "Now they can't officially ship a single asset without us knowing about it until they make changes to the system. Apparently, guards are stationed for twenty four hour periods until the clients view them then leave after their shift without having to report back. So, your assault on them went unnoticed."

This managed to produce a smile out of me. This is what I had fought so hard for. An opportunity to shut the Underground down and now, right in the face of all this, it was up to Angelus and the Peach City Phantom to end their secret reign.

I took out a paper of my own and held it between my index and middle finger out at Toni. "My requests for the I.T. department," I clarified. "I'm going to need adjustments to my *sticks* after tomorrow and I also need another suit."

"Another suit?" He raised an eyebrow.

"It's nice to switch it up sometimes. Do you think it can get done within two weeks?"

"The weapons, probably within a week," he answered as he took the paper. "The suit, pushing it, but I'll see what they can do."

"Thanks Toni," I folded my arms and looked to the sky. It was a beautiful day, but around this time tomorrow I'd be somewhere beneath the surface fighting to free strangers from the throes of bondage. It would be the first time in a long time that I'd have to face the Southern Gent in combat and unlike with Sammy, I couldn't afford to fail.

"*Stai bene?* Are you okay Devin?" Toni asked me with a concerned look. He must have seen the worry on my face.

"I'll be honest with you Toni, I don't think I'm going to make it past these next two weeks," I admitted.

Toni nearly fell out of his seat as he spun to fully face me on the bench. "What are you talking about? You're going to be fine."

I hunched over and looked at my outspread hands. "Don't get me wrong, I have every intention to see this through. But even if we win, I don't know if I can mentally handle it anymore. This is killing me in more ways than one."

I felt a huge hand clasp my shoulder. I looked from my hands to see Toni giving me a sad smile. "We all make sacrifices for the things we believe are right," he paused to look up at Mia Bella who was still enjoying her time running around in the water. "And for the ones we love. We just have to fight as long as we can."

"I guess you're right," I leaned back on the bench trying to finally relax, "but nothing lasts forever," I looked up at the Olympic Rings statue in front of us. The black and red rings had been destroyed during the Conflict and the city never got around to fixing it. Yet the tattered monument remained, a reminder of a bygone era.

Toni followed my gaze until he stopped on the monument and pursed his lips solemnly. "I guess you're right."

He leaned back to join me, and we sat there in silent companionship, watching the kids run around in the sprinklers until it was time for the Romanis to leave.

***

"Okay, say goodbye to your uncle, Mia Bella," Toni told his daughter as they both prepared to leave.

"Bye Uncle Prince," she said and wrapped my legs in a hug, but while holding her left arm out making sure not to get her ice cream on me.

"Bye Mia Bella," I said. "Make sure to not give your parents any trouble."

"I won't," she replied before taking her father's hand as they prepared to leave.

"Always good seeing you, Devin," Toni extended his hand out to me.

"Same to you as well, Toni," we shook hands and the Romanis walked away, leaving me alone in the park.

I checked my watch to see the time. I had about ten minutes until I met my six o'clock, so I decided to get up and stretch for a bit.

As I stepped away from the bench onto the walkway, I was suddenly knocked over by a runner.

"Ouch," I groaned as I rubbed my right shoulder which I had landed on.

"Excuse you," an annoyed voice said from above. "What are you doing blocking the way?"

"Sorry, didn't expect anyone to be coming," I said as I rolled onto my bottom to face them. I couldn't initially make out the runner when I first looked up because the sunset was right behind them, but as I lifted a hand to shield my eyes, I was shocked to realize that I recognized them.

"Vee?" I gasped as I stared up at her.

She was wearing white running shoes with yellow lacing, canary yellow jogging pants, and a charcoal colored t-shirt. She must have been running for quite a bit because sweat was glistening off of her fair skin. A hand towel partially covered her face as she wiped it off, but I still managed to recognize her, mostly because of the short strawberry blonde hair and jade green eyes.

Vee looked down at me for a moment, confused that I called her by name. She must've still not have recognized me. She lowered the towel from her face and cocked her head to get a better look at me before blinking in recognition.

"Oh, Dr. Prince," she stated, still stunned.

"Devin," I stated, reaching up to her, "Mind giving me a hand?"

Her eyes darted around in embarrassment, realization of the current situation finally setting in. "Yes, yes. I'm sorry. I honestly didn't see you and the way I spoke, um, please forgive me."

"Of course. Simple mistake, I shouldn't have been in the way. Nice sleeve by the way," I noted the tattoos on her right arm as she helped pull me up from the ground.

Starting from her wrist, were the tips of lightning bolts that surrounded her arm and they all originated from a point on her upper bicep, but it was slightly obscured by her white running armband. I'm surprised I didn't notice it at the bar, but her dress did have one sleeve which covered most of her right arm, leaving the left arm completely exposed, so I wouldn't have seen it when we were sitting. Vee must've caught me taking notice because she quickly pulled her shirt sleeve down, covering her arm down to the elbow.

She gave me a timid grin and turned her body, so that she was fully facing me now. "Thanks. It's work related."

"The job you can't talk about?" I asked.

"Yes, but I rather not discuss work," she replied. "I thought the ball would be the last time I saw you. I thought we were at least going to get the chance to say goodbye on Sunday. What are you doing here?"

"Same here," I agreed. "I'm meeting someone at six, but I live in the city. How about you?"

"I live in the city too!" She exclaimed in surprise. Her eyes seemed to sparkle at the realization. "I usually take this route running when I get off of work."

"Looks like it's paying off," I intended this as a throwaway compliment, but surprisingly I got a blush out of her. Her cheeks flushed cherry red, and she ran a hand through her hair, glimpsing towards the ground.

"Thanks," she told me, still avoiding eye contact. "I'm not used to getting genuine compliments. Everyone at work is job first or absolute pigs, and I don't really frequent the night scene that much. But here I am worrying you about my troubles. How have you been?"

"I've been doing well," I lied, no point in opening up a conversation thread that would only lead to more lies. "I took two days off before I go back to the grind. I needed it after the craziness of the weekend."

"Oh," a voice playfully interjected into our conversation. "I'd love to hear all about this crazy weekend."

Vee and I both turned to see the newcomer. It just so happened to be my six o'clock, Sofia.

She was in a tan sweater that I'd lent her around the time we first met. The sleeves were longer than her arms, so her hands weren't visible as she balled the ends of the sleeves together. She also wore black jeans that matched her black beanie with a peach design stitched into it. I would say I was glad to see her, but she was wearing an unnatural smile that betrayed the look in her eyes which told me she wasn't in the best of moods, but she wasn't ready to unleash her full fury upon me, at least not yet.

"Hey Sofia. Is it six already?" I asked as I looked down at my watch. It was ten past six. Sofia wasn't one to be late, so she must've seen me chatting when she arrived and then decided to give me my own personal grace period which must've expired when she came over.

"Eleven past actually," she corrected me immediately while still maintaining a smile. Then, her gaze slowly tracked towards Vee and her eyes narrowed. "I was giving you time, but you seemed to be having such a great conversation, I couldn't help but come over."

As I expected. I sighed internally and did my best not to let it out. "At least I was here on time."

"More like bothered to show up. Do you know what it's like being alone in that empty space with no human contact?" She demanded.

"Actually, I do," I answered, rubbing the back of my neck nervously. This was starting to go a bit off the rails. "This is my friend Vee by the way," I said, trying to get off the hot seat.

I might've gotten more of a reaction out of her if I said the sky was blue. Sofia, with predatory eyes, looked Vee up and down then shrugged at her dismissively.

"Nice to meet you," An obvious lie. "Sorry that the doctor is holding you up. I'm pretty sure *you want to leave now though*."

It was very subtle in the way she phrased it, but I knew Sofia well enough to tell that she had just activated her abilities, the power of suggestion. My eyes widened in shock at her, but I did my best to hide my reaction from Vee.

When Vee, who had returned to the serious demeanor she had when we first met, heard Sofia's last words, she didn't react at first but then a slight shiver went through her. She glanced around confused by the sensation then looked back at Sofia and must've had some understanding of what happened because if looks could kill, I'd be on the stand as a witness to attempted murder.

"No. I'm fine, actually. *Devin* and I were discussing the wild weekend we had," she stated bitterly back to Sofia before aggressively posturing towards her.

While not an incorrect statement, I feel like she could've phrased that differently. This didn't seem like the situation that could afford to have any further misunderstandings.

Sofia shot a dirty glance at me over her shoulder. Yeah, definitely didn't need any more misunderstandings.

"And what is she to you?" Vee with folded arms looked at me, completely ignoring Sofia's presence.

"She's my assist-"

"We have a special relationship," Sofia interrupted, stepping protectively towards me.

Please stop, Sofia. I wished as I helplessly watched the situation play out before me.

"Right, a shame that you couldn't accompany him this weekend," Vee commented, also moving towards me, she pulled out a pen and wrote something down in my hand.

I glanced from my hand to Vee. From my limited interactions with her, it seemed out of character for her to be so bold, but I think she took Sofia's blatant disrespect as a challenge and was more than happy to oblige.

"Um, thanks," I said nervously, refusing to risk a glance in Sofia's direction.

"You still owe me a dance," Vee added intentionally. She gave Sofia a smug smirk and let her hand linger in mine for a moment longer than necessary before turning around and resuming her jog.

I immediately put my hands in my pockets. There were a bunch of different routes that I could take in the next few minutes to defuse this situation, but the deeper I thought about them I found each one less appealing than the previous.

Thinking about the situation, apparently Sofia's ability hadn't worked. Her charm was powerful, but only worked if the target was leaning towards the suggestion or had a weak will. In this case, it turned out not to be the case and she might've exposed herself.

Letting it sink in, I sighed and turned to Sofia. "What were you thinking using your powers in public like that, let alone on someone you just met?"

Sofia folded her arms, glancing away from me. "You're one to talk."

"That's different and you know it, Sofia," I defended myself.

She acknowledged my answer, yet shook her head, nonetheless. "She gave me bad vibes. I've seen tattoos like that before."

"Where?"

"The night I was kidnapped," she said reflectively. "A few of the guards had similar sleeves on their arms."

"That was over a year ago," I said trying to comfort her, "Plus, I don't think she'd be stupid enough to flaunt it like that."

She turned towards me, frowning. "And what do you know about her?"

"Enough," I muttered, "For now."

She whipped her hair aside and met my eyes. "How were you going to describe our relationship to her?"

"Look Sof," I exhaled.

"Don't 'look Sof' me," she scolded while jabbing a finger in my chest, her Argentinian accent became more pronounced. "I'm not just some lovesick puppy that works for you because you saved me. I've seen you at your lowest, more times than I can count, but I'm still standing here."

She paused as she started to tear up, yet I made no attempt to interrupt or comfort her. Whatever she had to say must've been brewing for some time, and I knew enough as a therapist that I needed to give her space to let it all out.

"You leave for five days and the most you can give me is 'I'll be out of the office for a few days' with no explanation after how you spoke to me," she continued. "I know what it was probably related to, and I can live with that, but then I see you chatting with some *chica* past the time that *you* wanted to meet. How am I supposed to react when you've been so dismissive of me the past week?"

I blinked, stunned at the hurt in Sofia's words. She was right about being there for me through my darkest times. In Augusta, that was the first taste Emma had of what my battles with the Underground and my own demons did to me, but usually it was Sofia whose lap my head occupied after battles. She also went out of her way to learn a bit about medicine in order to help treat and dress my wounds. It was nothing supernatural, but there's a spiritual kind of healing that even modern medicine can't help with. She was a tough woman, so I didn't really think my actions would've had this kind of an adverse effect on her, but looking at her now, I could see that was indeed the case.

"You're right," I conceded. "I'm sorry, Sof. I invited you because I wanted to tell you everything that's been going on. How about we go on the Ferris wheel, and I'll explain?"

She wiped the sleeve across her eyes and nodded. Looking up at me, "Also, you promise not to just treat me like love interest number one?"

I answered her question with a sly grin. "Number one? Of course not. I mean, that's pretty presumptuous of you. You're more like number two."

She lightly punched me in the shoulder and walked past me.

Calling back to me, "I hope you brought your wallet, 'cause you're paying for everything."

***

We sat across from each other in the Ferris wheel pods. The tension from earlier had dissipated, but I wanted to look Sofia in the eyes as I told my story of the crazy weekend. When I got done, she was laughing at my personal lowlight of the weekend.

"You got beat up by *la niñita*," she giggled in amusement. "I'm glad that you didn't get lizard juice all over this *suéter*, when you gave it to me."

"I think you mean, let you borrow," I corrected her.

She stuck her tongue out playfully at me and looked out of the pod window. The city seemed a bit smaller from up here, but the nightlife was still as vibrant as ever. The up-tempo beats of hip hop played around us as citizens walked around below, either clueless or negligent to the silent battle raging within the city. I wish that I could be in some of their shoes, maybe that way I could've been sitting next to and snuggling with the enchanting woman across from me instead of giving her a briefing.

"I'm glad you find humor in my suffering," I said sarcastically.

She didn't turn her gaze from the window, but her eyes flickered in my direction for a second. "I don't think any of this is funny," she said seriously, "but we have to laugh sometimes to keep from crying."

I tipped my head to her in acknowledgement and reclined back, closing my eyes.

"So, you're already going back out tomorrow?" Sofia asked, breaking me from my temporary respite. She regarded me with a look that was just as solemn as her tone.

"I am," I stated. There wasn't much inflection in my voice. I wanted Sofia to know that I wasn't going to be talked out of it. As much as I figured it could potentially cost me, it was something that needed to be done. Simple as that.

"Why?" She argued. "You know what it does to you, and you just got back?"

"I know," I sighed. I bent forward to look deep into her turquoise eyes. They seemed to ripple with worry as she knew I was about to validate her fears. "But I'm so close to a breakthrough with the Underground, and if I do, I can put down the goggles and coat. I can let Toni handle the rest and move on. I just have to do it two more times."

"You forgot that I work with you every day, see how passionate you are about helping people. I know you," she gave me a smile, but it didn't mask the sadness in her eyes as she reached a hand out to cusp my cheek. "You're going to see this through to the end, even if it corrupts or kills you. I just hope you're done before one of those days come."

I took her hand in mine without removing it from my face and nuzzled my cheek against it. "I'll do my best."

"That's all I can ask," she replied and this time her eyes warmed up as she smiled at me.

As our pod reached the apex of the Ferris wheel, the sky was suddenly filled with bright fluorescent explosions as fireworks shot off around us. Sofia pressed her hands on the window and stared in wonder out at the sparks falling down around us. Then Axel, the former Argentinian heartthrob and Sofia's favorite singer, played over the speaker in our pod.

She glanced back at me, raising a questioning eyebrow at me.

I shrugged. "Never know what you can get if you slip the right person a couple of bucks."

From our bet, Adkinson had donated 4.5 million dollars to an organization dedicated to combatting human trafficking. The other five hundred thousand, well you can say I took Toni's advice when it came to getting back in a lady's good graces.

"Scoot over," she said as she moved from her seat to sit next to me. She took hold of my left arm with both of hers, hugged it, and then rested her head on my shoulder. "This doesn't mean you're out of the doghouse though."

"I would expect nothing less," I replied and leaned into her, the two of us taking comfort in one another, not knowing if we would ever get the opportunity again once tomorrow came.

Chapter Nineteen

The next morning, I was awoken by the sounds of Mew's constant yowling. Since I hadn't been home for the entire weekend, he decided that it would be in my best interest if he slept in my bed at night, right next to my head, despite his perch being perfectly fine.

"Enough already," I moaned, forcing myself out of bed to slog towards the kitchen to pour him his breakfast.

Making my way back to my room, I caught a glimpse of a figure in the corner of my eye.

I stopped. "So, you're all back now?"

The figure was Sammy. He was standing in the doorway to the bathroom, watching me.

"So, you're finally awake now?" He said in response, mirroring my detached tone.

We stood there not speaking to one another. The awkwardness of the truth that I had recently discovered or from Sammy's perspective, the truth that he had been hiding stood there with us. Because of our shared mental connection, he knew that I had found his secret out.

"So, are we gonna talk about this?" I said, breaking the silence.

Sammy glanced away. Staring down with hands behind his back, he began dragging his foot in small circles on the tiled floor.

"Do we have to?" He asked, the childlike enthusiasm and confidence gone from his voice, replaced by a guilty nervousness.

I crossed my arms and gave him a stern look. "Considering the fact that it deals with both of our pasts and Bennett, I would say that we have to."

He shook his head, still not looking at me. "You never should've listened to Barb. You weren't ready for the truth of that night. Still aren't."

I let out a long breath and walked towards Sammy. I knelt down to his eye level and rested a hand on his shoulder. "Sammy, you died that night," I choked, "and it's my fault. Whatever happened that night, I couldn't save you Sammy, or whatever your real name was."

He looked up at me, then his eyes quickly darted away. Even now, I couldn't help but feel there was still something he wasn't telling me.

"We need to stop that monster," he said, ignoring my previous comments. "I don't think you can beat him with an unfocused mind."

"Then tell me!" I pleaded with him, becoming more animated. If anyone had seen me arguing with nothing like this, I probably would've been put in an institution. "You think going in not knowing how I failed you the first time is going to help. Please, there are lives at stake. I need you on point tonight."

Sammy finally met my eyes at the mention of the mission later in the day and the role that he was asked to play. It had been a while since he had run point, so he understood the earnestness of the situation. He nodded and stepped forward, reaching out both of his hands to touch the temples of my head. Before he could reach them though, his black eyes changed to a tinge of crimson and he dropped to the ground, convulsing. I had seen that reaction before. It was the one I would get whenever I would have my post-mission seizures, which could only mean one thing, Barb was nearby.

"Even now you withhold the truth, yet get rewarded nonetheless," the familiar ear-piercing voice echoed into the room as Barb prowled out of the bathroom, slowly pacing towards Sammy, who was crying out in pain now.

"Leave him alone Barb!" I demanded. My eyes darted frantically from the barbed wire abomination to my fallen, longest tenured aberration.

Barb's behavior was completely out of character the past week. Rarely, does two of my hallucinations interact with one another in my presence, and if they do, it's usually Sammy and the Spectre. They're only present when Barb is around in order to keep it from interfering with Underground related work, so that I'm not putting the hostages at further risk. Barb never went out of its way to converse with the other two and here it was, rendering Sammy helpless, which was a surprise because I always got the impression Sammy was the most dominant of the three.

Barb considered me with those malicious crimson eyes, placing one foot on Sammy's chest. I could see it pierce Sammy's skin, blood began streaming down, soaking the carpet below.

"After all the lies you still defend him," it looked down and scowled in Sammy's face. Blood, which served as Barb's saliva, dripped down onto the boy's face as he cowered below. "So lucky to have the love of our master. Our prince still isn't ready yet because of you."

"Get. Off. Now!" I barked at Barb, taking a defensive stance towards the monstrosity.

Barb regarded me with a grimace. "As you wish my prince, but our deal still stands. I delivered on my end, but you have yet to," it flicked its gaze back down to Sammy before turning around to prowl back into the bathroom. "I hope that weakling doesn't cause you to stumble yet again."

When Barb left my presence, by leaving the room, I rushed over to Sammy. "Sammy, Sammy. Are you okay?" I picked him up and carried him over to the bed.

His eyes reset to their natural black color, his breathing settled down after the harrowing experience.

"I'll make it," he nodded.

Relieved at his good health, I started stroking his hair. "What was that?"

His eyes focused on mine, his voice came out a bit raspy. "Communicating with Barb, it's made its influence stronger. Your link with me has weakened because of our recent fighting. Spectre's influence remains the same only because he's been running point so much recently, but other than that, Barb can almost come and go as it pleases."

The alarm on my phone started going off, alerting me that I would soon need to go into work. I looked at the time and back at Sammy. "Come on. We can talk about it in the car."

I quickly changed into my work attire, grabbed my glasses, and headed for the door, Sammy following close behind.

"What do you mean Barb's influence is growing?" I asked Sammy as I sat in the Stratus while it guided me to the office.

Sammy was in the passenger seat, drawing in a coloring book that I kept in the glove compartment. "You know the more you communicate with us, the more we influence you. Barb usually only comes out in spurts for whatever messed up purpose it has and bugs you, usually on missions. But now, it stays, and you talk to it, lending your ear. Thus, influence."

"But what does this have to do with Bennett and …" I paused.

"What you saw in your dream?" He finished for me.

"Yeah," I nodded. "You seem awfully fine for someone that's dead."

Sammy shrugged and continued working on his drawing. "The murder that happened that night was a long time ago. I've made peace with it. I just hope you get the chance to when the time occurs."

Something about the way he spoke was still cryptic. I took my attention away from the road to turn to Sammy. The early morning traffic rush of Peach City was still pretty chaotic even with automated driving, but I trusted the Stratus to get the job done.

"What aren't you telling me?" I questioned.

He closed his coloring book emphatically, the sound making a resounding thump as the pages slammed together. He placed his green crayon on the book calmly and regarded me with a patient look. "I don't know. I can only do what you allow me to do, and apparently your brain doesn't want me to tell you. Sometimes I think you forget that none of us are real."

Arrived at your destination. The GPS notified me, and sure enough I was parked outside of my office. When I looked back to the passenger's seat, Sammy was gone.

"I guess you're right," I muttered to myself as I gathered my belongings and exited the car to head into my office.

"Hey Sofia," I greeted her as I walked in the door. She was seated, so all I could see of her was that she was wearing a white shirt with a huge black tie designed for women around her neck, her usual rimmed glasses graced her eyes as her face lit up when I walked into the room.

"You came through the front door today," she pointed out while passing an envelope to me. "Bills as usual."

I took the unwanted mail from her and slipped it into my coat pocket. "Nice to know that life still goes on as usual. How's the slate looking for today?"

"All clear. Mr. Jenkins would have come today, but he canceled his appointment over the weekend," she reported. "Try not to look so down. He's a stubborn old man, but he'll come around eventually."

She must've noticed how my shoulders sagged at the mention of Mr. Jenkins's name. I knew he could be surly at times, but I couldn't help but feel that I was failing him. There were moments where I caught myself staring at my phone waiting for him to call, but there was nothing I could do but continue to wait.

"Thanks, Sof. I guess I'll be doing research for later then," I said and headed for my office door.

"I'll be here if you need me, fending off unannounced clients and organizing spreadsheets."

"What would I do without you?" I asked playfully.

"Probably be swamped with paperwork. Now go, I don't want any excuses about you having *performance issues* tonight," she answered with a teasing smile before returning to her work.

I shook my head in response and pushed my door open to enter the office.

I headed over to one of the huge bookshelves, opposite the door, in the room and ran my index finger along the spine of the books until finally, I located the proper text, Ryder Watson's *Guide to Irregular Abilities and Behavior*. Say what you will about the man, he knew about Irregulars surprisingly well, and I would study his book before I went out to fight the Irregular trafficking within the city. It didn't cover every Irregular that I've come across, but it's provided me with countless advantages and tips that I've used to take out opponents before, which is beneficial since I'm not always as skilled of a fighter as those I face.

Watson was a smart man, but unfortunately, I also had lingering suspicions about how he had gathered so much information. As the husk of Fort Gordon showed, the Purification wasn't solely about eradicating Irregulars as he made it seem. Experimentation and research had clearly been another goal, just less talked about. I shuddered at the thought but grabbed the book nonetheless and went to my desk to spend the next couple of hours researching potential abilities I might come across.

I found myself reclined in my chair facing the clock behind my desk. There was no other noise audible in the room except the consistent ticking of the hand as every second passed by. It's funny how time doesn't slow down or speed up, Einstein's postulations aside, but somehow every passing moment feels like an eternity when you're either bored or anticipating something. Right now, I was experiencing the latter, playing different scenarios in my head that I could face tonight and planning counters to every situation.

The ringing of my phone broke me from my stupor. I checked the caller ID, and saw it was from an unknown number. Usually, I don't answer the phone if I don't know the number. I'd wait to see if they left a message and then call back. It's a matter of principle, wouldn't want to waste my time talking to a scammer. This time though, I picked it up on the third ring.

"Hello?"

"Hey Dev," Emma responded. "I'm with our realtor now and he discovered the location of the coordinates for the perfect home. When do you want to meet to survey the house?"

She was doing a good job of going out of her way to keep the details coded, so I played along. "Oh, would you be able to tell him hello for me? I can make it in about thirty minutes. When does the viewing begin?"

"In an hour."

"Perfect. See you then."

"Ciao."

I swung my chair around to face the center of the room and pressed on the arm rests to propel myself to stand. I headed over to my closet to retrieve my gear.

I picked up my old bandana, a red and yellow color scheme, which made it seem like one had a row of colored razor sharp shark teeth when it was tied around the mouth. I hadn't worn it much since the first couple of outings. Originally, I thought it had a great intimidation factor while at the same time covering my face, but then I realized how ridiculous it looked. Also, since I usually fight stealth battles in areas of low visibility, it's hard to see the rest of my face. I still keep it as a memento though after all this time, a reminder of simpler times before I knew who were behind the kidnappings. I held up the bandana and gave it a wistful half-smile.

"About to head out?" A voice asked from behind me.

I turned to see Sofia peeking her head through the door, concern written all over her face.

"Yeah, soon," I said, slipping the bandana back into its box. "Are you going to be at my place later?"

"Oh my," she said covering her mouth in mock shock. "How forward of you, Doctor."

I rolled my eyes and went back to collecting my equipment. "I think you picked the wrong profession. Comedian better suits you."

She came over to me and placed a soothing hand on the back of my shoulder. "Lighten up. You know I'll be there. Just do me a favor and don't come back with too many scratches this time."

I stood up and stretched without turning around "Don't worry, I'm in two sets of good hands."

Sofia pursed her lips and raised an eyebrow. "Oh, that Emma girl," Sofia said Emma's name as if swallowing bitter medicine.

I swung my coat on and turned to face her, offering a reassuring smile. "She's not that bad. You two would probably get along. As for you and Angel, I'll just leave that alone. How do I look?"

"As stupid as ever," she replied. Sofia was holding my goggles, the final piece of my uniform. Stepping forward, she gently placed it over my eyes. Then offered me a look. "Just make sure you come back as you, Devin."

"I always try to," I grinned at her then opened a portal to the coordinates Emma sent me and walked through to meet her.

Chapter Twenty

C an I ask you a question?" I looked at Emma who was also already in full attire.

"What is it?" She asked, peering down towards the target location.

We were in the downtown region, perched atop the remains of the Hard Rock Cafe, the handle on the guitar was missing and the neon lights no longer lit up, another piece of the city lost to the Conflict. Our destination was the Peachtree Center Station. At one hundred twenty feet below the surface, it was the deepest underground station in Peach City. The environment wasn't going to be a problem for me because I was used to fighting in enclosed spaces, but Emma on the other hand was going to have her flying ability severely compromised. That might've been what was bothering her or the stakes of the upcoming battle, but either way I wanted to try to relax her before we headed in.

"What are the names of your masks? They're from theater, right?" I asked.

She turned towards me, her face covered by the silver comedy mask. Her hand reached behind her head, and she removed the disguise. "That's right. This one," she paused to examine the artifact in her hand, running her fingertips over the smooth polished surface while she spoke with me. "Represents Thalia, a goddess who presided over comedy among other responsibilities. She was a joyous figure in Greek mythology. The one Angel wears, represents Melpomene, a goddess of tragedy. She and her sister were both Muses, so Angel and I wear them to represent the different aspects of ourselves and pay homage to our theater roots."

"How does it switch back and forth between the two of you?"

"Who knows?" She replied with a shrug. "We both fight differently, so I think it's strangely in sync with us. A lazy explanation, but sometimes things don't always have clear answers."

"I know what you mean," I agreed solemnly. Given recent developments and my entire lack of undefined history, her answer hit more at home than she would have realized. "Is that why you two use different weapons?"

She nodded in affirmation. "Yes, I use my butterfly swords. I love the way they work in tandem, kind of like how Angel and you both work with me now. She loves using her BC-41 knife though. I tell her to upgrade to something less brutish, but in fairness my swords are centuries behind her."

"What about the daggers?" Having a partner was a new and so far, enjoyable experience, so I was genuinely interested in getting to know Emma better in order to improve team chemistry.

"Ahh those," she patted the sheathed daggers in her belt affectionately. "Our combo weapons. I like throwing and seeing them fly through the air, but she prefers stabbing. They're important to us both. How about you? Do you just use batons?"

"They're actually called tonfas," I pulled the Palladium coated weapons out for her to see. "They do look like batons, but it's a common mistake. I saw someone using them on TV and thought it would be fun to try. Who knew it would be my go-to all this time later?"

"Funny how time works," she turned back in the direction of the station, placing her mask back on. "Unfortunately, it's time to go."

"You're right, let's begin," I stood up and jumped off the ledge, falling into a portal below that brought me inside of the station, with Emma following close behind.

Peachtree Center Station used to be one of the busiest stations for this particular route. Like many of the older stations in Peach City, it had been abandoned for some time. The last official up and running train was sometime around 2041. The city figured it wasn't worth spending the money to continue maintaining such a beaten down rail system, so they found it best to invest in a new project, leaving the old station to the rats.

The interior of the station had an island platform, two tracks on opposite sides, running parallel to each other. The floor was made of gray tile. Surprisingly, it was still smooth as if someone were preserving it. The walls comprised of solid gneiss rock, a solid, darkened sand-colored stone that the city built around during the original construction of the station in the eighties. You could see places where the rock had been chipped away.

Underground stations were sanctuaries of protection during the fighting that took place overhead. They managed to hold, but fractures such as the ones I was looking at showed that it was never meant to be a shelter from such attacks. The station was still connected to the modified power grid, so it had electricity. The lights above the platform were spotty though. Around every other light was lit, making the visibility in the room dim, but still manageable. Deeper into the tunnels, there was an eerie red light that painted the tunnels. I wasn't sure whether to take that as an invitation, or a warning.

"So which way?" Emma asked, while pacing the platform back and forth, taking her time to examine the surroundings.

"Follow the coordinates," I replied and pressed the button on my goggles that would activate the GPS navigation for us to pick the right route.

My vision of the station was replaced with the tunnel network system, a series of yellow tracks that showed all the old pathways of the tunnels, and a blinking green dot that indicated our destination.

"This way," I said before hopping down to start walking down the tracks into the tunnel.

"Right behind you," Emma leapt onto the tracks and jogged to catch up, matching my pace. "Do you think we should be walking directly on the tracks though?"

"A train hasn't run down here in over ten years. I think we should be fine," I took a peek back over my shoulder to check on my unusually quiet companion. "Are you okay without having to fly?"

She was looking at the roof of the tunnels as we trudged along. Because of the mask, I couldn't gauge her reaction to see if she were examining out of curiosity or trepidation.

"Wouldn't be the first time," she called up to me. "I can always tag out with Angel. She loves the down and dirty fights the most."

"If you say so," I returned to navigating the different pathways until we came to a bend in our paths. I lifted a hand, halting Emma behind me. There would be no benefit to us getting caught in a hidden trap or ambush.

"See anything?" She asked, peering her head around me to check the route.

"No, but that's the problem," I said perplexed. The schematics of the subway system were telling me that we should've been a few yards away, but there was nothing out of the ordinary there, not even an abandoned railcar. "What do you think we should do?"

"Hmm," I could hear her pondering our next move. "Is waiting an option? That's what you're supposed to do when you're lost."

"I am not lost," I shot back.

"Men and their sense of direction, how it never changes," she sung aloud whimsically to no one in particular.

I growled at her then proceeded forward, no longer interested in being insulted.

After a few paces, I closed my eyes to see if my other senses would be able to pick anything up that my vision missed. A steady dripping was also present in the underpass. I would have considered it peaceful, if not for the near pitch black darkness and lack of life underneath. The sound of rats scurrying on the tracks could also be heard. Their squeaking echoed off the walls of the gneiss rock. The fact that the vermin were even present told me that their habitat hadn't been disturbed by people for a long time and there weren't too many if any were bothering them now.

Unfortunately for my sense of smell, the more detailed attention I gave to the aroma of my surroundings, the more it had to suffer. Something was definitely dead down here. Whether it was nearby or much further along the tracks, there was a definite scent of decay. I withdrew a black bandana with white flames from my pocket and tied it around my face, covering my identity and muffling the putrid smell that tainted my nostrils.

I looked back towards Emma, who was running her hands along the wall.

"Do you think that'll work again?" I asked.

"Give me a moment," she continued testing the walls until an audible click was heard. She turned her head back towards me. The silver smile on her mask spoke volumes without her even uttering a word.

"Okay, I get it," I turned the navigator off and joined her by her location on the wall. "I don't understand why I couldn't find it though."

"Sometimes the old ways are still more efficient than the new," she said smugly. "I think it's a door. We should try it."

Suddenly, we started to hear movement on the other side, the sound of shuffling and distorted voices. Emma and I retreated around the bend, then peaked our heads around in unison.

Another click could be heard before the door opened, and two men walked out. Fortunately, or unfortunately for us, depending on how the events of the night would follow, both men were recognizable.

The first figure to exit was a potbellied individual, wearing a custom-fitted midnight blue suit. I looked from his plump cheeks to his bald head. It was Chrome Dome himself, George Adkinson. He must've gotten over the whole golf fiasco because he had the smile of a man that just sealed the deal to a huge business venture.

Behind him, walked the hulking figure of a man. The broad shoulders and huge claymore strapped to his back gave me a pretty good idea of who it was, but it wasn't until I saw the orange ascot that I confirmed that it was Hamilton Bennett, the Southern Gent. Instead of a fancy suit, he wore the dark trench coat that I had seen him in before at the abandoned subway.

Bennett had his hand clasped on Chrome Dome's shoulder as they exited from the secret door. He too, looked pleased about what had occurred behind those walls.

"It was a pleasure doing business with you, my dear Hamilton," Adkinson spoke. "With this haul, I'll be able to put the assets to good use, getting back at that damn quack doctor being chief among them."

"Wow, you really pissed him off," Emma whispered up to me from our hiding spot.

"I'm guessing he won't take a fruit basket as an apology," I murmured back down to her. She giggled at my response before we both silently returned our focus to the two business men ahead of us.

"The pleasure is all mine, George," Bennett replied. "As a gentleman, I take it upon myself to treat clients with the utmost hospitality. The organization thanks you for your patronage."

I rolled my eyes at his pandering and self-aggrandizing. *I wonder if that's what I sound like when I talk to my clients.*

"I do appreciate it. You may want to do something about that smell though," Adkinson advised.

Bennett nonchalantly pulled out a pair of white gloves and began to casually put them on. "Forgive us. Unwanted guests get disposed of nearby, but since this station is defunct, the sanitation crew rarely stops by."

I've worked enough with Mr. Romani to understand what Bennett was talking about and whatever "sanitation crew" that got sent down here wasn't simply sweeping up dust.

Adkinson greedily rubbed his grubby hands together, looking around. "So, where are they?"

That was a great question.

Ever since we got here there was no indication of any other humans, let alone an entire group of terrified Irregulars. Maybe the coordinates were simply for the unofficial handshake and the prisoners were elsewhere. This would've been the first time I've encountered such a situation, showing that the Underground was starting to wise up and change their methods.

"Oh George, don't you worry about that," he grabbed the collar of his trench coat and uttered something into it, but at this distance I couldn't make out what.

"Um Devin," Sammy interjected from beside me, yanking on the tail of my coat.

"Not now Sammy," I brushed his hand aside.

"Um Devin," he tried again. "I really think you should look."

"Look at what?" I snapped, turning around to see what was so urgent. Then, I peered down the tunnel behind where he was standing. There was a faint light deep into the tunnel.

Could someone have been walking this way also? The more I looked, the light seemed to be getting closer at an abnormal rate and also much bigger. The sound of a deep rumbling in the tunnels could be heard as the light approached even faster. I could feel my insides vibrating from the bellowing echoes. My eyes widened in shock. No train should've been running down here. Yes, the station and tunnel systems still received power, but it was only for the lights, not nearly enough to have a full-scale train up and running.

"Are you okay up there?" Emma asked, concerned by my sudden conversation with myself. She shifted her body to look at me before growing frighteningly quiet.

She spun back around to dart away from the incoming train, but I grabbed her by the nape of her cloak. If I had let her continue running, Bennett and Adkinson would have seen her, and we couldn't afford to get caught now. The problem though, was that if we stayed in our current spot there wasn't enough room to get out of the way of the incoming locomotive.

"We can't stay here," her voice quivered to me as panic began to set in.

"I know. Just let me think," I searched the tunnel for any potential exits or places that I could open up a gateway for us, but no option was particularly appealing or plausible at the moment. If I teleported us out of the way there was no guarantee we would find the hostages if we came back to this spot once the train passed

"Come on, think faster," she whispered harshly, tugging on my coat sleeve to move forward. I guess she figured it would be best to take them head on, but I couldn't risk that without violating my core rule of missions, hostages come first.

"Roadrunner," a voice came from beside me. I glanced to see that Sammy had reappeared beside me. He was staring at the train, then peeked over his shoulder and repeated himself. "Roadrunner!"

I thought about what he was trying to suggest and frowned to myself. This plan was either going to work or the "sanitation crew" was going to be scraping Emma and me off the tracks.

I grabbed Emma and held her tightly next to me. I was going to have to use my ability on a larger scale than usual, while maintaining the portal for a sustained period. It would also require precision which is where the issue would lie. I typically use my ability to either transport myself or others from one location to another but creating a continuous and undisrupted portal to transport a vehicle of that mass would be challenging. I could either focus so much on precision that the portal wouldn't be big enough and we'd get squished, or I'd make the portal large enough, but cause the train to derail, potentially killing the hostages if they were on board.

I shielded Emma in my cloak, for as much good as that would do, extended my hand toward the train, and turned my head away from it. I wanted to visualize the path that I needed to send it on to keep it on the tracks as it banked around the corner. I also didn't want to perform a reenactment of deer in headlights as the train came bearing down.

The train continued its vast approach and when I judged it to be a few feet away based on the distance of the noise, I activated my power and opened a portal. Focusing on the tracks ahead and the specific way I needed to activate the exit portal, I opened my eyes to glare at the spot. I don't need to use my hands to summon a portal, but it does help me to get an idea of where I want to place the gateway while maintaining its stability.

I picked a spot and strained my eyes, as another portal opened mere inches from my face and the train continued through, its progress undeterred. When the caboose passed through the second portal, my shoulders sagged and I nearly felt myself collapse, but Emma caught me in her arms, supporting me after the exhausting effort.

"I got you," she said comfortingly. I felt a pat on the back as I rested my head on her shoulders. "That was pretty cool, but please don't do it again."

"I'll try to remember that the next time we're about to get steamrolled by a train," I groaned. My head felt like it was spinning, and I felt a wet stream running down from my eyes. I tenderly touched my cheeks and gazed at my fingers in order to investigate. In the little bit of light that we did have, I noticed that it wasn't tears or sweat leaking from my eyes. It was blood.

This had happened twice before, due to overuse of my ability. Regardless though, we were going to have to keep moving forward. I made a look of disgust at the liquid and wiped below my goggles to make sure that Emma didn't see it. If we were going to fight the Underground's thugs tonight, I couldn't afford to have her worrying about me before the hostages were freed.

"I'm fine now," I told her. I don't know if she believed me or not, but she looked me over and nodded. Emma helped me to my feet, and we peaked around the corner again, this time I used her weight to support me.

The train had stopped by the door. Adkinson and Bennett were talking but couldn't be heard over the sounds of the train. Eventually, Bennett placed a hand on Adkinson's back, extending his other hand out towards the train. Adkinson nodded with a grin before stepping onto the train, with Bennett following close behind.

"We need to get on that train," Emma stated, heading towards the train.

I moved with her. Whoever else was on the train would have their vision obscured and most likely wouldn't be able to see us as long as we stuck to the shadows.

"You're right," I agreed. "We should split up, board from opposite ends, meet in the middle."

"What?" Emma turned on me suddenly, lifting her mask to reveal her face. Her eyes were wide and even in the dim lighting I could clearly see the obvious concern in them. She furrowed her brow and walked back towards me. "What are you talking about? In your condition you'd never make it to the middle if we choose the wrong sides."

"Don't worry about me. If you go to the front, most likely you can stop the train, so I'd really be able to work my magic. We don't have that much time before it leaves," I looked away from the train and towards Emma, pulled my bandanna down and gave her a confident smile.

The train was slowly starting back up and beginning to pull away. If we didn't make our move now, we were going to be chasing it down, potentially losing the locomotive altogether.

She rolled her eyes then put her mask back on, but this time it was the Melpomene mask of tragedy. "Fine, but don't let that macho man crap get you killed."

"After you," I said as I held my hand up and created a portal for Angel. She shook her head in what I could only assume was annoyance and rushed through just as the train started really picking up steam.

"Good luck," I called after her when she disappeared. "Now for me."

I opened another portal and ran through as well. My destination was outside the door of the caboose. I still needed to compose myself after using so much power. As I braced myself against the door, I felt something wet drip onto my hand. I checked my cheeks again to see if it was from my eyes, but they were clear of blood. Checking my hand, revealed that it was simply water. The dripping continued and my hand started to become drenched.

"What?" I questioned aloud. The tunnels shouldn't have been leaking this bad unless they were flooded, but it hadn't rained in weeks and there wasn't any construction in the area that would affect the piping.

My head was soaked now, as well as the rest of my clothes. There was a real downpour now, so much so that the sound of the water droplets pounding on the train and ground was louder than the train itself. I looked up and the roof of the tunnel was gone. There was only rain falling down from the sky above, streaks of lightning racing through the clouds.

"What. In. The. Hell," I gaped upwards.

"Ah, so you've come to fail again?" A familiar southern accent mocked me.

"Who?" I asked trying to figure out what was happening around me. When I looked back down, the train was gone, and I was on a rooftop. Bennett was standing across from me, his longsword withdrawn. Rain continued pouring, the droplets splashed around us. Along with the booming thunder and racing wind, they played a symphony of chaos. The perfect tune as my battle with Bennett was about to begin. I withdrew my Desert Eagle and began taking a step forward, when suddenly I felt two small hands on my cheeks and yank my face down.

"Snap out of it!" I was staring Sammy right in the face. The rain had stopped, and I was no longer on a roof. I looked down to see that my foot was dangling over the edge of the train. I quickly scrambled towards the railing on the back of the train and placed my back on the door. If Sammy hadn't stopped me, I would've stepped straight off of the moving train. The train was moving at full speed now and if I would've fallen off, I could've broken my leg or worse.

"Sammy, what happened?" I was gasping for air as I tried to get a grasp of my surroundings.

"You were hallucinating," he was standing next to me now, looking at the tracks curiously.

"Hallucinating? That badly?" I asked bewildered.

Sammy nodded then looked up at me. "It's been a long time since you've had one that vivid. Are you sure you can do this?"

"That's what you're here to stop," I gave him a disapproving look. The purpose of the apparition that ran point was to make sure that I didn't fall down the rabbit hole of my own delusions. If I didn't know what reality I was dealing with then it put myself and innocents at risk.

"Don't worry, I'm on it," I could tell Sammy wanted me to believe in him, but after what Barb had done to him earlier, I didn't know if he was going to be up to the task. It wasn't too late to switch to the Spectre. He had been in charge a lot recently and I found the majority of missions went smoother with him but with the determined look in Sammy's eyes, I couldn't break his confidence like that. Our relationship probably wouldn't be able to recover. I gave him a nod of trust, took in a deep breath, raised my pistol, and grabbed the handle, now prepared to swing the door open to take on any potential threats.

Before I entered, I was welcomed to the sight of the back of a guard. There weren't many details that I could make out about the guard other than he was wearing a camo combat vest and fatigues with a dark hat sitting atop his head. I couldn't see much around him, but I could tell that he was the only guard in there. There were also chains extending to the silver poles that protruded out from the seats. I stood on the tips of my toes to see what was chained there and unfortunately saw *who* was chained there.

It was the back of a boy. He seemed big enough to be slightly older than Sammy, maybe a fresh teenager. The forest green shirt and black sweatpants he wore were in tatters. His head hung low, dreadlocks drooping in front of his face covered any other details that I would've been able to make out if he were able to turn around. His legs barely held him up as he sagged against the chains which meant they were biting into his wrist. Every now and then, he would quickly convulse, and the train would speed up or slow down.

That's when it hit me. This kid was operating the train. I wasn't sure if he was powering the train or manually willing it to run, but factoring in the weight, speed, and conditions of the track, the effort must've been putting a major strain on him.

He would've just started puberty and if the human body hadn't fully developed yet, no way were his powers fully fleshed out and matured. I had to save him now or there could be irreparable damage done to the boy, or worse.

"Keep it coming," I heard the guard sneer, his voice slightly muffled through the door, but I had made a tiny portal and put my ear to it. "You're going to make your new owner very happy. You may even get a reward."

I can't really pinpoint what it was, but something inside of me nearly broke. What pisses me off so much about the Underground, regardless of their reasoning is that they treat those they kidnap like no more than objects you find at a pawn shop, merely items that can be bought, sold, and auctioned off without a care in the world. They don't see us Irregulars as humans, so when I'm in the field I try to view the captors in the same way, just monsters that are taking away the freedom of others, which makes it easier to do what needed to be done.

What gives them the right?

This boy had a name, a story, friends or family somewhere that cared about him, and they took that away just to improve their status or make a quick buck. Not tonight.

My grip tightened around the Desert Eagle. Originally, I was planning on pistol whipping him on the back of the neck, rendering him unconscious, but he deserved so much worse. I took another deep breath, to quell the raging waters of my fury. Unchanneled anger leads to mistakes, and I couldn't afford that, not just for me, but for all of the prisoners' sakes.

This was going to require precision, but I needed a slight distraction to make it work.

"Hey kid, if you can hear me lift your head," I whispered into my small portal, while creating another miniature one next to his ear, which should've been blocked from view by his hair.

He lifted his head in surprise and tried to look around to find the sound but couldn't identify it. Then, as if realizing the situation, he lowered his head and nodded. Smart kid.

"Okay great. I don't know how your powers work, but if you think you can do something about the lights, I can get you out of here. If you dim them somehow, I'll get the chain off of you, but you can't move," I instructed him. "Keep your arms up and head down."

He nodded again and went still. The lights in the car began flickering like a temporary power surge. When they settled, it was dimmer than before. The chain blended in with the surroundings and was barely discernible from its position before.

"What do you think you're doing? Turn these lights back up. I don't care how tired you are. I'm not standing here in the dark with you," the guard stepped forward. I could see the keys hanging from his belt.

I reached my hand through the opening I created and took the keys. Next, I unlocked one end of the chain from the pole and held it through the opening, keeping the tautness steady. After that, I attached it to the bottom railing of the caboose where I was standing.

Now for the hard part.

"Do what he says kid, but sag to your right when you do it," I instructed again.

The lights were restored to their original luminosity and the boy slumped to the right as instructed. His hair covered his right hand, and I used the key to unlock that one.

"Get up!" The guard barked. He raised his rifle and pressed it to the boy's head. "Run this train right or there'll be trouble."

That was my cue. I pulled my bandana back up over my face and pressed the voice modulator on my goggles. I was going to hate the voice that came out next, but I needed to send a message tonight. I clamped the free end of the chain to the guard's ankle and yanked the door open.

"You already have trouble," my voice came out scratchy, just like a wildcat clawing its nails against a blackboard, just like it was dripping in pure malice and delighting in causing harm to others, just like Barb's.

The guard spun in astonishment and raised his rifle in a panic, but I didn't just have the element of surprise. I had the element of fear. When this voice is activated, the pupils emitted from the goggles turn into red, snake-like slits. My coat fluttered around me, making it appear as if I had no legs, but a body composed of darkness and white flames. At that moment, I embraced my moniker as the Peach City Phantom, the demon that the entire city suspected me of being.

The guard froze, petrified by the terror of seeing that demon before him. I used that time to grab him by the collar of his vest and then pitch him out of the widened portal that connected the chain to the rail outside of the train. His body flew from the portal located at the tail end of the train and landed with a sick thud on the tracks, but his leg was connected to the railing of the last car, attached by the train. After a few yards, the chain snapped taut and the guard proceeded to be dragged behind the moving train, his body thumping against the unforgiving rusted steel of the tracks. His screams of pain could be heard over the train, the pitch alternating from high to low as he impacted different points on the track.

I walked around to the front of the boy and knelt down to check on him. "Are you okay?" My voice reverberated throughout the car.

He looked up at me. When he saw my face, his eyes widened, and he recoiled back. I sighed internally. I've been getting that reaction since my first night putting on the suit, just a part of the price of doing business. I cut the Barb settings off and lowered my bandana.

"Sorry kid," I said, my voice back to normal. "What's your name?"

He looked back at me tentatively. He seemed distrustful of me, rightfully so, given my appearance at the moment. His eyes flashed from fear to a more defiant and resolute look, as if he realized that his emotions were showing.

"Marcus," he said confidently.

I flashed a grin. "Well Marcus, you're in luck. I'm getting you and the others out of here. I just need you to stop the train now."

He shook his head defiantly. "I can't. The man with the sword said he'll hurt my sister if I do. She doesn't have powers, but he took her too."

His head drooped to hide his expression from me, but I've seen that look enough times to tell it was because he was dealing with the shame of not being able to protect the ones you love.

I sighed and rested a hand on his shoulder. "Okay Marcus, keep driving, but slow it down. It'll cause them to come check on you and I can take them out. Got it?"

Determined, he nodded and rose up.

"Good," I said and turned to head to the next car. I instinctively put one hand behind me to protect him. "Stay behind me."

"Hey wait," he said. I turned to look at him. "You're the PCP guy, right?"

I turned my head and shook it exasperatedly. "Wrong guy. You should stay away from him though. Come on."

I opened the door to enter the next subway car. We entered into complete emptiness. Nothing, but the blue seats, silver railings, and advertisements for products or performers that had seen better days.

"Weird," I noted to myself.

There was indistinct radio chatter from somewhere in the cart. Marcus and I cautiously proceeded forward checking between the seats, so that we wouldn't be caught off guard by an opportunistic coward. We reached the location of the sound and it appeared that one of the guards dropped their walkie-talkies. I bent down to pick it up when the window next to my head was met with a resounding splat.

I jumped back to see an Underground agent's body plastered onto the window before slowly sliding off as the train kept progressing.

"*All units to the front four cars. Repeat. All units to the front four cars, aah,*" The radio screeched in my hand. It seemed that Angel was having a little too much fun and creating a raucous. Lucky for me, I thrive in chaos.

"Do me a favor Marcus, decrease the lights the closer we get," I requested.

I didn't need to turn around to see if he understood my message, because as requested, the lights began to dim in the current car we were in and were completely out in the caboose.

I withdrew my left tonfa and grabbed the door handle in my right hand. And so, we proceeded to the next car. This time there were three guards, all with their backs to us. They must've been entrusted with the rear but moved up as Angel's attacks intensified. This probably meant the hostages were in the car after this one or else they would've been further up. They were here to make sure no one escaped out the back. There was just one problem.

They weren't accounting for someone entering through the back.

I pulled up my bandana, smirking underneath. I quickly rushed the back guard and bashed him at the base of his neck. I had really gotten better at that over the past year because he dropped instantly, though the sound of his body dropping to the floor alerted his buddies.

They turned on me, weapons raised. It seems the Underground was making an effort to be more coordinated in their attire these days because all of them had the same camo gear with vests. It would make sense for them to upgrade security with my consistent interference and this being a crucial business transaction.

The one on the left was a dirty blonde with a crew cut, a toothpick in his mouth, and in need of a major shave. He bore a translucent leather gauntlet on either hand and balled them into fists. The guard on the right looked barely younger than me but had an annoying look of arrogance on his face that told me suffered from a superiority complex. He gripped a Bowie knife, pommel held forward, and took a defensive stance.

None of us moved for what felt like an eternity but it couldn't have been more than a couple of seconds.

"This is it for the welcome party?" I broke the silence with my Barb voice reactivated. "I should feel offended. Lights, please."

As I spoke, I grabbed and equipped my other tonfa. Marcus instead of dimming the lights, this time made them flicker. I stood there in the center of the car, both weapons equipped, and I tilted my head slowly at them. I was mimicking Barb's mannerisms currently and judging by the increased pace of breathing and steps they took back, I knew I was starting to get to them. Then a yell, accompanied by the sound of another body smacking into the train window disrupted their focus. They both visibly flinched away from the noise, and I took that as my cue.

With the flashing flights distorting my movements, I rushed in and smacked the younger guard on the bridge of the nose and followed with a tonfa-assisted uppercut. He was lifted from his feet and fell to the ground limp, his knife clattering from his grip. I turned to finish off the final guard, but he had already mentally recovered.

He swung at me with the gauntlets, but I stepped back, barely dodging his blows in such a confined space. Marcus hid in between the seats, watching my battle. The gauntlet guard smashed two of the handicapped seats, causing them to crumple around the gauntlets and reshape themselves into metallic like boxing gloves.

This man could use the gauntlets to help reshape an object. I had read about those that had the ability of matter manipulation. It came in different forms, but it seemed that this guy had to physically touch me in order for it to happen. I wasn't sure the extent of what he could manipulate or how, but I sure didn't want to find out the hard way.

He rushed me again, this time smashing more seats and poles as he tried to get to me. I heard Marcus yell as the seat he was hiding behind had its top smashed, exposing him. But the guard was too focused on me to grab Marcus, which is what I preferred.

I was continuing to get pushed back, parrying a blow every now and then when our distance was too close, but then I felt my retreat stopped by the cold metal door pressed to my back. The matter manipulator saw this as his opportunity and chose to bull rush me. I created a portal and jumped to the side, his charge continued unimpeded as he went through to the other side. I actually had no idea where I sent him, which probably wasn't the best for him because my random portal exits tend to spit things out of mid-air.

The flickering of the lights came to a stop, settling for a dim illumination that allowed me to see everything that was relevant, but still have some places to hide in the shadows. I stood up and brushed myself off, making my way over to Marcus.

"Are you okay, kid?" I asked, peering over the seat to check on him.

"Yes," he answered, grabbing onto my coat to pull himself up. "You sound scary, but you fight like a coward."

"Excuse me," I turned to leer at him. "This coming from the one hiding and screaming."

He sucked his teeth, turning away from me.

During our dispute over fighting tactics, the door connecting the car to ours opened up.

"You should be safe in here George," Bennett said, guiding Adkinson inside the car with us. "The guards will handle the interferen-" he looked up and saw me standing there with Marcus and a grimace came over his face.

"One second George," he patted Adkinson on the back and took his position in front of him. "One more interloper to deal with."

Chapter Twenty-One

I stood there frozen. This was the moment that I had longed for, and now the opportunity was right before me. If I could stop Bennett here and now, the Underground would be at a serious disadvantage. I only took one step towards him, and it was enough for me to realize I was terrified.

My right arm was shaking, so I tried to play it off as if I were tapping my thigh. There was probably a subway car full of people behind him that were depending on Angelus and me to get them out of there. If I dropped the ball here, they may not experience the taste of freedom ever again. I failed Sammy, but I could save these people.

At least, I hoped I could.

"I thought your presence was familiar," Bennett remarked coolly. "It's been so long since that night. I thought I retired you permanently, but I'll make sure to rectify that mistake."

Come on. Stop shaking. I thought to myself, trying to get it under control.

"I wonder what happened to the boy that night," he mocked in his thick southern accent. "Or at least his body."

He gave me a sick twisted grin and that did it for me. I found my courage and rushed him. Creating a portal, I jumped into it, exiting from behind him. My blades released from their tonfas, so that I could bring them down on his neck, finishing this for all of us.

Too bad Bennett had other ideas.

Bennett had me by the neck, holding me within his grip with one hand. He wasn't even looking at me as I was held there. He then slowly turned his head towards me wearing a mockingly disappointed expression on his face.

"Oh my dearest hero, did you really think that was going to work again? You must really be out of practice," he scolded me.

I dropped my weapons and gripped desperately at his thick, tree branchlike arms with my hands. They didn't even come close to grasping his arm by themselves. That's when my vision started to get blurry, the lights flashed but this time the figures were indiscernible. My breath became shorter as the air had no passageway to reach my lungs. I kicked futilely at him when I realized that my legs were alarmingly much shorter. Rain started pouring down and somehow, I seemed so much smaller, still stuck in Bennett's grasp.

We were back on that rooftop, rain pattering nonstop around us. I was hopelessly scared, knowing that I was going to die soon. Thunder boomed out above us and if I had the energy, I would have winced. My flailing slowly stopped, as I felt my body begin to go limp.

"Devin," a voice cried out faintly.

I looked up, to see a neon sign, a beautiful woman with curly mop hair, advertising some kind of beauty product. I guess there are worse things to see before one dies.

"Devin," the voice called out again, this time closer.

I didn't even get to land one blow and he was already going to beat me, wasn't fair if you ask me.

"Devin!" The voice shouted and jolted me from my fading consciousness. "Wake up and fight! Don't let anyone else die. Fight!" My eyes shot open, and I saw Sammy standing in the cart where Marcus was hiding.

"Fight!" Marcus screamed at the top of his lungs as Sammy faded away next to him.

Marcus's shouting caught Bennett's attention. His grip loosened as he looked the boy's way. This was as much of an opportunity as I was going to get. Brute force wasn't going to work, I needed a different tactic. One less honorable.

So, I decided to bite his hand.

The human jaw is much stronger than we give it credit for. If you tried to bite yourself right now, most likely you wouldn't even break skin. Subconsciously, your brain would never actually allow you to bite yourself with full force. But if you did, major damage. This is what Bennett experienced as I pulled down my bandana and found the energy to chomp down on his hand.

He let out a sharp curse and released me. I let out a huge gasp as I hit the ground. The coolness of air rushing into my lungs filled me with life, filled me with hope. I barely managed to extend my arms to prop myself up onto my hands.

That's when I started to fly. Bennett grabbed my coat and tossed me directly into the ceiling of the railcar. I landed with a thump and before I could even moan, he tossed me up yet again. I was able to groan this time when I felt another tug on my coat. He was going to launch me again, but as they say, "fool me once shame on you, fool me twice shame on me, but there sure as hell wouldn't be a third time."

This time he launched me, but instead of having my back broken by a third meeting with the ceiling, I created a wormhole above myself and flew through the roof. I landed on top of the train as it sped along. I lay there silent. The coolness of the steel on my face felt welcoming and I didn't want to disrupt my temporary reprieve.

"Are you just going to lie there?" Two small feet stood before me.

I already knew who it was, so I didn't bother looking. "I was planning on it. Seems like the best idea I've had all day."

"What about Bennett?"

"I never asked for this," I said, my voice came out more melancholy than I expected. "I'm just a therapist doing a terrible cosplay impression."

"Right now, you and Angelus are all those people got."

The knees bent and Sammy looked down at me. He had a look on his face that I'd never seen before, genuine disappointment. Usually, I got that attitude from the Spectre when I argued about going out to fight, but Spectre was an unfeeling ghost. Sammy was the part of my brain that had some idea of what it was like to be human, so he at least sympathized with my post-fight suffering. This was different though. I was on the verge of giving up. The consequences of that decision were going to affect a lot more people than just myself and we both knew it.

"Alright," I conceded. "I'm getting up."

I managed to get to my feet, but then immediately lost my balance. The train was speeding up for some reason. Luckily, we were above ground now. Otherwise, I would've been doing Bennett's job for him. I regained my footing and stood, looking at the passing landscape, blurring by in the night. Nothing was discernible at the speed in which we were going.

A *clank* on top of the car caught my attention. It was a longsword. Bennett was working his way to the top of the train to join me.

"Great," I groaned to myself. "As if I didn't have enough problems."

In the open, I had more options with my ability, but now he could also swing his claymore freely. If that sword, with Bennett's strength fueling it, connected with me, it would be over.

I couldn't let that happen, so I withdrew my Desert Eagle and charged at him while he was still climbing, releasing short bursts as I made my way over. It was tough finding my footing, but I at least managed to put one bullet through his hand, another grazing his arm. He yelped in pain and paused his ascent onto the roof. I stalked towards him and aimed for his head, my finger happily ready to pull back on the trigger.

That was when I felt three consecutive blunt forces impact my back, pushing me towards the top of the next subway car. My Desert Eagle dropped from my hand, tumbling somewhere unknown. I laid there stunned by the blows. I took in a breath and my back screamed in pain on the inhale. It felt like someone had smacked me in the spine with an aluminum baseball bat. I shifted my head while laying down, so that I could see where the attack had come from.

It was the young guard with the Bowie knife that I had dropped earlier. I thought he was down for the count, but such is life.

He stood there with a small black pistol raised, probably .22 caliber judging by how precise the impacts seemed to be.

"You can get up now. I know you're still alive," he had a haughty Australian accident and carried himself in the same arrogant fashion as before.

I accepted his invitation and got to work on the presently difficult task of regaining a vertical base. Not only did he pull off a masterful sneak attack, I also didn't have my tonfas or handgun on me, so I wasn't properly equipped for combat. He holstered his pistol and withdrew his knife, licking it in delight as he knew he currently had the advantage.

Ugh, he did the tongue thing. I thought in disgust.

"What's wrong mate, missing your fancy playthings?" He mocked.

"Actually, I am," I finally managed to stand and face him. I grabbed at my right arm with my left hand. I had landed hard on it, and the limb was currently throbbing to inform me of the pain.

"Too bad. I guess this is where you die then," he tossed his knife back and forth, taking steps back, so that I could join him on the moving platform.

I hopped over to him and let my arm hang loose. There was still feeling in it, but it hurt less to just let it sway. The Aussie caught his knife before taking a defensive posture.

I took my stance too, except mine involved kneeling and placing both hands on the smooth surface of the train. I raised my scarlet slit eyes to him and spoke.

"Do you know what an infinite loop is, mate?" I asked in a mock Australian accent.

"What?" Was all he could say before he fell through a portal beneath him and exited out from one above, sending him back into the one below.

I could feel the blood running from my eyes again, but I ignored it. Instead, I chose to smirk at the effectiveness of my favorite technique. "Crikey, works every time."

While I was admiring my work, a thought hit me. Bennett was climbing up onto the roof with me before I shot him, but I wasn't sure if he had gone back inside the train or not.

"Duck!" Sammy appeared to warn me.

When out in the field, I usually take what the Spectre or Sammy say as gospel, so I dropped down swiftly. I heard a powerful *whirring* of wind sweep past where my head had been. I looked back and saw Bennett standing over me, his claymore withdrawn. He had a look of someone that was tired of entertaining a fly and had decided to squash it, indefinitely.

Not taking the time to banter, I rolled through backwards and attempted a bicycle kick from the ground. I quickly found out that this wasn't a good idea because he caught my foot, spun me around towards him and with *one* hand swung the longsword down at me. I rolled out of the way, but with so much force that I nearly fell off the high speed train.

I barely managed to grasp on the edge with my left hand, but my body was still flapping to the side of the train below, completely at the mercy of the vehicle's unsteady acceleration and the corresponding wind resistance. I peered into the windows and found the reason why the train was currently running so unstable. Adkinson was standing over Marcus, kicking him, and at the rate his gums were flapping, I'm guessing he was berating the boy too.

I tapped into my simmering rage, placing both of my feet against the glass while the two of them couldn't see me. I took a quick glance up to find Bennett's head starting to loom closer to the edge as he made his way over to me.

I wasn't going to have a lot of opportunities to do this, but it was either get inside, go back up top to fight, or get knocked off the edge of a moving train. I turned my head to find that the train was nearing a tunnel to go back underground, so getting smashed like a fly on a windshield was also now on the table. *Delicious*.

The first option was definitely the best.

Bennett must've seen the tunnel coming up also because I could hear his boots pounding on the roof as he fled from the top of the train. This granted me a slight reprieve, but I had to get inside before him.

I braced myself and pushed off the glass. My body swung out from the train and as my lower half started its descent, I kicked into it, adding force. My shoes landed with a resounding thump that got both Adkinson's and Marcus's attention. The window only cracked though, a spider web design spreading throughout the glass.

I grimaced at the failed attempt. I could've just made a portal to get inside, but I knew that I was quickly reaching my reserves and couldn't afford to tap into them at the moment. Despite his wounds, Bennett was nowhere near defeated and I hadn't located or secured the hostages yet.

I braced myself one more time, my back filed a grievance at the effort. Thus, I told my back to take its grievance up with my behind and kicked off again, even more powerful than before. I let out a yell as I swung my legs back towards the glass and finally broke through.

Letting my momentum carry me into the train, I managed to clip Adkinson with my right foot, sending him tumbling to a seat behind him. I rose to my feet as fast as my ailing body would allow, which in my current condition wasn't very fast at all.

"Stop the train kid. We gotta go," I told Marcus after locating him. I grabbed Adkinson by his lapel and dragged him into the next car with me, hoping Marcus was following close behind.

As I expected, the next cart held the hostages. I entered to the sight of about a dozen men, women, and children chained down to the seats. Even with the ability to sit up, many of them cowered to the side of their seats or were curled up in them. Too many scared faces, all of them in need of help. Help that outside of breaking their chains, I didn't know if I could provide.

I threw Adkinson before me. He landed with a thump on his broad belly. The crowd collectively whimpered at the sudden action. Then a silence settled over them, as Adkinson had their full attention. This wasn't a scared silence on their part. It was the type of reticence that a predator adapts when it stumbles upon prey.

Bennett had shown Adkinson all of his "animals" for his zoo exhibit, strolling through casually. Knowing Adkinson, he probably made a comment or two, trying to rile them up to see the big bad tiger do something interesting. Well, Adkinson had just fallen into the enclosure and there was no longer any security to prevent him from finding out just what the tiger was capable of.

The captives leered at him. A mixture of fear, anger, and pure hatred. He tried to rise to his feet, but I put my knee in the small of his back, pinning him to the ground.

"Look at them, you prick," I said slowly, sadistically, drawing upon all of my conversations with Barb. I tried imitating all of its mannerisms and speech patterns into my words. "This is what your filthy money pays for, humans. People that try to live peaceful everyday lives, but now they're here, all because of you. Don't be such a poor host. Welcome them."

When I finished speaking, I drove his head into the floor. It bounced off of the ground, leaving him clearly dazed, but conscious. This gave me the time to get to work on the locks on the captives as the train started to decelerate. I pulled out the key that I seized from the guard earlier and began freeing the prisoners of their bonds. You would expect that a well-funded criminal organization wouldn't allow henchmen to have a universal key to all of the locks, but I wasn't complaining. Less work for me.

As the now free captives were released, they started to circle around Adkinson, like wolves going for the kill. He cowered, crawling away from the group as he regained his wits.

Just when they were going to give him exactly what he paid for, the door to the previous car opened and Bennett came through. He was carrying Marcus by the nape of his neck.

"Step away from him now!" His voice boomed with absolute authority through the car causing everyone to take notice.

One of the freed hostages, a male about mid-forties, decided to push his luck and rushed at Bennett. The man shot some type of blue energy beam out of his hands, which Bennett deftly flicked away with his claymore and then in a continued opposite motion, cleaved the poor soul's head clean off. Cries and choked back sobs filled the train. Bennett never fully swung his sword, with the lack of space in the train it would be near impossible without clanking it against something, which made the feat even more impressive, as sick as it was.

The head dropped to the floor and rolled towards the center. His brown eyes stared directly into mine, blinked and then I watched as the light faded from them, an image that I knew was going to stick with me forever. The body dropped down to its knees and stayed there. I nearly threw up, but just managed to keep the bile down.

Bennett placed one of his boots in the center of the chest and shoved it aside. "Anybody else want to try their hand?" He raised his head, challenging everyone in the vicinity.

No one moved an inch.

"Good," Bennett extended a hand towards his downed business partner. "Now George, come here."

Adkinson clambered up to his feet and scattered over to Bennett, making sure to avoid the severed head. He clutched Bennett's trench coat tightly and cowered behind him.

I looked from Bennett to the severed head to Adkinson, shocked over how casually Bennett just killed the man. As much as I hated using the terminology, from

Adkinson's perspective, Bennett just destroyed his "property" without barely a moment's hesitation.

Seeming to read my thoughts, Bennett cleared his throat and shrugged nonchalantly, "The transaction already went through. Consider what just happened as a recall of a faulty product."

The casualness in his statement made me think about Emma's reaction to Bennett's stories back at the ball in Augusta. This man had truly forsaken his humanity. His sole purpose was the task that the Underground had set before him. I clenched my fists, until I felt the tendons and bones in them start to pop.

"Why are you doing this?" I asked in a low, angry voice.

He met my gaze and considered me for a moment as if he had never given the topic much thought. "Well, if it were up to me, I would exterminate all of you vermin, but the higher ups decided that an Irregular in chains is much better than one roaming free. They're restricted by the laws of society, but we give them the opportunity to use their powers for a greater purpose."

I picked up a chain, presenting it to him in condemnation. "And what about these? I guess only the metaphorical restrictions exist in your holier-than-thou garbage."

He dismissed my argument with a wave of his hand. "You're stuck fighting battles, while we prepare for war."

"War with whom?"

"Who else?" He spread his hands, gesturing for me to look around. "The agency that's created a monopoly off of you abominations."

I sucked in a breath. He slowly smirked at my reaction and nodded. "Yes, the IPF."

Bennett had just confirmed my theory. The Underground was hoarding Irregulars in order to take on the Irregular Police Force. The IPF wasn't just some two-bit organization. They were nationwide, so that must've meant that the Underground indeed was operating at least on a state level right now with eyes on a much larger scale. This was so much bigger than me. Even if I beat Bennett, I wouldn't be able to stop the inevitable from happening, a full scale war.

I unclenched my fists, letting both of my arms dangle loosely. The past year had been a waste in trying to stop the Underground. I was arrogant to believe that simply two more missions would be the final nail in their coffin, especially when Bennett was merely an overseer, not even a top boss.

In the midst of my despair, I felt a slight tug on my coat. I looked slowly at the source of the pulling. It came from a small hand, a hand that was attached to a small arm, an arm attached to a small girl. She had two black puff balls sitting on her head, a faded pink skirt on with frills around the legs, and white shoes with pink ribbons on them. She couldn't have been any more than about five years old.

"Excuse me Mr. Hero, are you going to save us?" She asked in an adorable, innocent childlike manner, even though she must've been terrified. Her eyes met mine when she spoke, and she held my gaze as her eyes widened pleadingly.

I broke eye contact first. Gazing around the cabin, I saw the other captives with similar looks of pleading in them. I was their only hope at the moment, and they were depending on me to get them out of their current predicament.

Even if the Underground secretly had control of the entire country, I made a promise to myself that Peach City was under my protection. I thought back to the photo of Mia Bella that Toni shared with me and I knew what I had to do. These people weren't going to be subjected to someone else's war.

I bent down to pat the little girl on the head. "Yes, I'm going to save you. I need you to be brave for me and take everyone to the front of the train. There's going to be a mean looking lady with a mask making a frowny face, but she's actually really nice. She'll protect you. When everyone is safe tell her to come to me."

Hopefully Angel would be able to protect me, if she arrived in time.

She gave a grin, then turned on her heels and told the others to head to the front of the train. Bennett started to make his way towards them, but I stepped into his path.

He laughed. "You really want to do this? You should've stayed retired."

He lunged at me, but I moved behind a row of seats. I grabbed him by the sheath of his longsword and started running forward away from the fleeing people in the train. Bennett regained his balance and took hold of my head between his arm and shoulder, squeezing tightly. I landed a few blows to his abdomen, but I had the feeling they weren't doing much damage, like beating a brick house with a stick.

I remembered that my gloves had spikes on them, so instead of balling my fists in normal punches, I curled my fingers without closing them and started laying into him with back fists, the spikes driving into his armor, lightly piercing his abdomen. I knew my attacks were at least bothering him now because he roared in anger and hurled me into the window back first. I landed ribs first on the head of a seat. As something inside of me crunched, I could only pray that they were cracked and not broken.

My back took this as a sign to take an immediate leave of absence because I couldn't even sit up, let alone stand. I crawled away from Bennett, the effort causing sharp pains in my abdomen. The effort proved to be futile because simply enough, Bennett walked over to me, palmed the back of my head and slammed me face first into the window repeatedly. The glass received new cracks each time my head was introduced to it.

Luckily, my goggles protrude out, so they were receiving the brunt of the impact, but I was still in serious trouble. He dropped me and let me crawl away some more, a cat playing with its food. I drew in as much effort as I could and went for my ace in the hole. I produced a portal beneath his feet to initiate the Infinite Loop, but he jumped out of the way before it even opened fully. My lack of energy must've caused it to open too slowly.

"Your charlatan tricks will work no longer," he stalked towards me slowly. "It's Irregulars like you that make me feel the need to kill you all. Your actions cause others to believe, emulate you, and that's when all of the crazies come out. It's this path or suffer another Wyoming."

This time I crawled away more desperately. My vision looked like a kaleidoscope with my goggles cracked from the beating. I was leaving a trail of blood as I moved away from him. I couldn't see how much, but any blood loss is bad blood loss in my book.

I glanced up and caught a glimpse of Angel in the door window of the next car. This told me that at least the hostages were safe. I raised a finger to the sky then brought my fist down lightly on the ground. Finally, I gestured back at Bennett as I continued to move away from him. I don't know if she completely understood my message, but she nodded anyway.

I rolled onto my back and both sides of my body groaned in protest. Managing to prop myself up onto my elbows, I looked in Bennett's general direction. I couldn't see him clearly because of the damage done to my goggles, but I had an idea of where he was.

"What made you this way?" I asked. If my plan didn't work out and I was going to die, I at least wanted to know what could drive a man to such a state.

I didn't see it, but I could hear him sigh. "A story for another time," I heard the sound of his sword being unsheathed. "Unfortunately for you, I'm not the type of person to give you my backstory before killing you."

I heard him tense up and the air change around him as he drew back his sword to provide the finishing blow. "Wait!" I exclaimed, raising a hand to stop him.

"What is it?" I heard him ask devoid of emotion.

"Meep. Meep," I said in my best Roadrunner impersonation, even with the now broken voice modulator.

Confused, "What?"

And then Angel came bursting down on Bennett's head like an anvil from a portal that I had slowly opened on the ceiling of the railway car. Bennett was lying flat on the ground beneath her, either unconscious or disoriented from the sudden impact. All that was missing was the A.C.M.E. logo.

"Can't beat the classics," I breathed in relief and dropped back down on the ground, flipping the lenses on my goggles up so I could stare at the pretty lights.

"Is there some reason a little girl asked me if I was the angry lady?" Her mask looked towards my downed body.

"Maybe she overheard one of the guards," I responded in feigned ignorance. I really wasn't trying to draw Angel's ire at this exact moment.

She stood over me, peering down to check on my status. "You look like hell, but why do you sound like Carnage?"

"We are Carnage." I joked back towards her.

She shook her head and groaned in disgust as she helped me to a seat. Angel looked me up and down. I didn't know if she had a concerned expression because of the mask, but she was definitely taking notice of my battle scars.

"Emma is going to freak when she sees you," she stated.

"A lot of people are," I replied back between shallow breaths. My ribs were really hurting now and if one was broken, I could've possibly had a punctured lung. "The hostages, are they okay?"

The mask nodded in confirmation. "The train stopped moving, so I told them to get out and start heading down the tunnel towards the nearby platform. I told MyKey the location, so he should be notifying the Romani family."

"Thanks Angel. You did a really great job tonight." I turned my head to Adkinson who was trembling in the corner. "So, what do we do about Chrome Dome?"

"We could always kill him."

I shook my head. "Too easy. Plus, he looks like a groveler. Let the family interrogate him."

"Gladly," Angel made her way over to Adkinson and grabbed him by his collar, dragging him back towards us. On the way out of the train, she helped me to my feet and supported me as I walked to the exit with her.

A click followed by the sound of a pin hitting the ground caused us to stop in our tracks.

"Not so fast," a southern voice said from behind.

I flipped my lenses down and relied on Angel to turn us around. When she did, we both saw the sight of Bennett with a grenade in one hand, Marcus in the other.

My heart raced in realization that Bennett had tossed Marcus beside him when he first entered into the car with me and the hostages. Marcus never had the opportunity to escape with the others.

"Give me Adkinson, or I shove the grenade down the boy's throat," he warned.

"What do we do?" Angel whispered to me. "I can't fight him and support the two of you."

I tried to run different scenarios through my mind. My power was spent at the moment. There weren't going to be any more portals that I could rely on. If Angel fought Bennett, she wouldn't be able to use her flames without harming Marcus or me, causing it to be a hand-to-hand fight, which even with her enhanced strength might not have been enough to stop Bennett. If we chose to call what he was doing a bluff, I had no doubts that he would be true to his word and blow the boy up, leaving us with one option.

"Hand him over," I sighed.

"Seriously, what about interrogations?" She asked in frustration.

"Hostages first," I replied steadily. "We always put the hostages first."

She let out a low curse and tossed Adkinson over to Bennett, who let out a cry as he landed.

Bennett, from what I could tell from behind my broken lenses, looked down at Adkinson and then back at Angel. "Oh, you made this too easy."

He swooped down and picked up Adkinson then jumped off the train and all that could be heard was a loud boom.

"No," I said, "No, no, no."

I broke from Angel's grasp and immediately fell. I managed to get to my feet, then clumsily stumbled my way out of the train falling down to the damp dirt below. I was on all fours, searching around me. I didn't see Bennett or Adkinson, but what I did see was blood.

Lots of it.

It was splattered on the tunnel walls. The smell of iron was prevalent as scarlet liquid dripped down before me. There was some type of cloth, soaked in the blood a few feet away from me. I crawled over to it desperately and wiped the substance away. The original color was a forest green, same as the one Marcus was wearing. Except the hue was much darker now because of the blood.

"No!" I screamed at the top of my lungs, slamming my fists down on the concrete with the cloth still clenched in my hand. Bennett had done it. He had really killed the kid and I did nothing to save him. How was I going to explain to his sister that her brother was dead, that it was my fault?

I kept beating the ground until I felt two arms embrace me tightly.

"Relax, there's nothing there," Angel was holding me, preventing me from doing any further damage to my fists. "There's nothing there, just relax."

I stopped my thrashing and looked up at her. I lifted the lenses of my goggles to see her better. She had moved the Melpomene mask to the side, so that I could see her face. The lighting was poor where we were, but I could read that she was worried about me.

I turned from her back to the scene. I blinked. The blood was gone, no coloring of the walls, no smell of iron accompanying it. Angel must have broken me out from another one of my episodes. I was relieved that Marcus didn't get blown up, but he was still nowhere in sight. Bennett must have taken him along.

I gritted my teeth, frustrated not only because of my own failure, but also for having let Angel see me this way. I put my weight on the side of the car and used it to prop myself up.

"Come on," I said, resigned and started walking down the tunnel. "We need to check on the hostages."

Angel followed close behind me. Neither of us said a word as we trudged along to meet the hostages, who had stopped when they heard the explosion.

They were huddled together in small pockets of people, their expressions varying from numb shock to an overwhelming outpouring of emotion. Clutching my right arm, I limped into what was essentially the center of the group and looked around, observing all of those who had made it out.

That's when I felt a small tug on my pants this time. I focused on the person who was trying to get my attention. It was the little girl with the puffballs from before.

She looked up to me, a pained expression on her face. "Have you seen my brother?"

I visibly winced at her words, as if she had been the one to give me all of my current wounds. A sudden tightness occurred in my chest that had nothing to do with my injuries. I barely managed to stop myself from clutching at it.

"What's your brother's name?" I asked, even though I already suspected what came next.

"M...Marcus," she sobbed, "he said he would find me when the train stopped."

"Oh, did he now?" I said, "Don't worry he's alright."

She wiped a tear from her face and looked back up at me. "R...Really?"

"Yes, he's helping me stop the bad guys," I looked directly into her eyes and lied. "Marcus went to find out where he was hiding and he's going to tell me when to come and get him from their secret hideout."

She grinned at me, completely buying the tale I had spun. "Marcus is stopping the bad guys?"

"Yes, your brother is a hero," I patted her on the head. "He said he had a cute little sister, but never told me your name. Would you mind telling me?"

"Tina," she responded and then yawned, rubbing her eyes drowsily.

"I tell you what Tina. Come with me and don't worry about Marcus. Everything is going to be fine," I didn't know if that last part was a lie or not, but it was my job to worry about that, not hers.

She extended both arms up to me and leaned forward, silently requesting that I pick her up. I bent my knees to lower myself and scooped her with my left arm, supporting the child from underneath, so that she wouldn't fall.

Tina wrapped her arms around my neck and rested her head on my shoulder. Turning back to Angel, I gestured with my head that everyone should continue on. Thankfully, she did all of the talking and we all started walking together to the next platform, presumably to safety. Angel took up a position to my right. She was close enough to catch me if I stumbled but kept enough distance to respect my pride. She barked orders, from time to time making sure the group stayed together. The talking completely ceased, the further we progressed down the tracks.

The only noises in the tunnel were droplets of water splashing down around us, rats squealing as their habitat was being encroached upon, and the shuffling of the now freed captives behind us.

Chapter Twenty-Two

My God, kid! You look awful," Toni exclaimed as he saw me.

"Feel worse," I replied tersely. "Thanks for being here, personally."

"Of course, I know how important this is to you," he rested a hand on my shoulder then looked to Tina, sleeping on my shoulder.

"Her brother got taken," I felt the shame in each of those words as I confessed to Toni.

"You'll get him back," he said in a low, reassuring voice.

I shook my head and could feel my anxiety starting to bubble up. "And...and he chopped a man's head off, like it was nothing."

"Devin," he whispered so that only the two of us could hear. "Stop."

But I kept going, barely hearing his words as I continued to ramble. "It happened right in front of me. He charged so quickly and...and I didn't do anything. I couldn't. He's too strong, Toni. He's just too strong."

Toni grabbed my face in between his two palms. "Listen to me. Go home. Let me take care of this, but you need to leave here. Rest. Got it?"

Since my head was in his grasp, I had no choice but to meet his glare. My eyes darted away from him, and I simply nodded my head in understanding.

"Good. I'll take the girl," he reached for Tina, but I instinctively flinched away from him, putting my body in between them.

"Sorry Toni," I caught myself. After all that had happened, I was being overprotective. My paranoia was starting to get the best of me. "Here, you can take her."

I offered Tina over, but he declined with a wave of his hand. He gave me a slight grin. "You can take her. I trust you'll make the right decision about where to put her."

Though my heart wasn't totally into it, I gave him a small smirk in return. "Thanks Toni. That means a lot."

After waiting patiently for my conversation with Toni to end, Angel walked up to me.

"What are you going to do now?" Her tone indicated to me that she wanted me to head home as Toni had suggested.

Admittedly, it was a great idea. I looked at Tina, still resting in my arms. Her small breaths came rhythmically as she rested in her deep sleep. I knew I couldn't take her back to my life and the craziness that was going to result from the fallout of tonight. Comforting her was the best I could do for now, but I'd need to put her in the hands of someone that had experience with this, one that could give her the care that I couldn't until everything settled down.

I turned my attention to Toni, who was giving instructions to his workers around him. He brought with him a host of doctors, counselors, and general volunteers, some of whom were once in the same position as those they were currently assisting. He even had Leo leading a small security team, but Toni was wise enough to not have them flaunt their weapons or wear obvious combat attire. Most of the security detail wore casual clothing and you wouldn't be able to distinguish them from the other helpers, but I could tell by the way they carried themselves. They formed a perimeter, didn't speak too much to the victims, and their eyes searched around, scanning for every potential weak point in their surroundings. I regarded Angel again after the answer popped into my head.

"Would you ask Emma to drop me off somewhere?" I asked.

She gave a brief gesture of affirmation. "Where to?"

***

In time we eventually reached our destination.

"Are you sure about this?" Emma asked, nervously shifting from side to side as we waited outside on the doorsteps.

"Don't worry, we can trust them," I turned back to tell her. Tina squirmed in my arms and let out a tiny whine. I patted her on the back to calm her. "Shh. Go back to sleep, little one."

I knocked on the door to the home. Emma took a few steps back off the porch. Her mask still occupied her face, but she had it slightly adjusted so that her face was partially visible. Out of respect for the inhabitants of the home, she didn't want to give off the impression that we were robbing the place. For this same reason, my goggles and bandana were removed.

It was past eleven, but I hoped that they would answer the door. I knocked one more time and stepped back, bouncing Tina gently in my grasp to lull her back into a deeper doze.

"Who is it at this time of night?" A voice snapped on the other side of the door.

"It's me, Devin," I said in the most ingratiating fashion I could muster.

I heard three locks get removed and the door swung gently open.

"Devin, why are you here and my goodness what happened to you?" Susan Romani asked me as she stepped into the doorway. She adjusted her silk nightgown, while looking at the three of us on her porch, assessing the situation.

"I'm sorry Susan. I wouldn't have disturbed you if it weren't important, but this girl. I mean her brother...she just needs someplace to stay," I stammered as I began rambling off how to explain the situation. The more I tried to talk, the worse it got. "I tried Susan, I really did, but I couldn't. It's my fault."

"Give me the girl," she said quietly, but in a calming fashion, stepping towards me and extending her arms to receive Tina from me.

I nodded and carefully transferred Tina from the cradle of my left arm into Susan's caring hands. The girl snuggled up against the seasoned woman as if it were the most natural thing in the world, which let me know that I had made the right decision.

"Thanks Susan," I said, taking two steps away from the door.

"Come inside," she told me in the same quiet voice.

I clutched at my injured arm and shook my head nervously. "I...I can't. I let her down. I let them all down. Besides, I promised Sofia I would go back to my place tonight. I just need to go...away. I didn't want this."

"Come inside, Devin," Susan said, keeping her voice low, but it was sterner this time, letting me know that her words weren't a suggestion.

I stepped forward towards the door and Susan settled a hand on my cheek, letting me rest my head there as she looked me over. "You poor thing. Look at what they did to you. Sit on the couch and rest. I'll put this one to bed, then I'll call Sofia for you."

"Thank you," Was all I could manage to choke out as I removed my cheek from her hand and headed in.

Susan was the closest thing to a mother I had in my life. I was grateful for her hospitality to me even in spite of the fact she didn't particularly like that I had to be the one fighting the Underground and the fact that I was mostly a recluse. I turned down my fair share of invitations in the past, but if I made it through this, I'd start rethinking that.

She peered behind me to Emma. "You too, honey. Come inside."

Emma flinched in surprise and let out a gasp. She looked down, away from Susan before also giving her thanks and followed closely behind me.

While Susan took Tina upstairs, I removed my coat, tattered and covered in blood, then placed it in the dirty bin where they put heavily soiled attire, such as rain coats or muddy boots. Placing a sheet on the leather couch, I plopped down, releasing a much needed sigh of relief.

Emma took a position across from me on the couch opposite of the one I was laid up on. She sat silently, looking around nervously about the house as if preparing for someone to jump out and attack her. When she felt safe, she stared at me with a morose look in her eyes.

"Go ahead and ask," I rolled my eyes, reclining onto my back.

"Are you okay?" She asked.

The question that I had been hit with a lot tonight. I was far from okay, but I didn't feel like talking about it. I just wanted to repress what I had experienced and skip ahead to tomorrow.

"No, I'm not," I answered her, staring directly up at the ceiling. "A family is broken up because of my failure."

"It's not all on you. I was there with you too," she responded earnestly.

"Yeah, but at least you did your part. I just needed to stop Bennett and failed miserably."

"Well, maybe if Angel wasn't having too much fun, we could've made it to you sooner."

I shook my head and interlocked my fingers, resting my palms on my chest. "No. What happened in the tail end of the train is on me. I have to own that. I just need to focus on getting her brother back."

"*We* need to focus on getting her brother back," she corrected me.

I didn't answer her, just grunted and adjusted my body to relieve the pain.

"Look at me," she ordered.

The sternest in her voice caused me to flinch. I did my best to gaze at her without disturbing the delicate balance of rest and pain relief in which my body had achieved. I raised my eyebrows to let her know that she had my attention.

She gave a satisfied smirk and moved over to crouch in front of me, our faces only a few inches away.

"We're a team now," she started, "Angel and I didn't do a great job of having your back tonight, but that's not going to happen again. Now we can keep blaming ourselves or we can recover and figure out our strategy for next time. There's still one more shipment coming. We need to be prepared for it."

I looked into her eyes and pursed my lips. Marcus's words combined with my actions or more accurately inaction played through my mind.

"Do you think I'm a coward?" I whispered.

Her hazel eyes widened in surprise as if I were a child asking their parents if they loved them.

"No, of course not," she lightly gripped my hands in hers. "What would make you say that?"

"Marcus, the boy, he said I fight like a coward," I told her, "Then when Bennett was beating me, I just lay there. I just wanted to stay down, not fight anymore."

My eyelids drooped as I admitted my shame. I've had rough nights before, but tonight was the first time someone had died on my watch, let alone in front of me. I never had one taken away, either. Hostages come first. That was the first credo I made to myself when I started this. It kept me focused, centered on the task at hand. It was eating at me that I didn't uphold that standard and it ended up costing someone their head, and another their brother.

Emma gave my hand a quick squeeze of support. "But you went back down there and fought. Some advice from an old lady, no matter how good you are, how much experience you have, or how much you prepare, you never get it perfect every time. Plus, you're not a coward. You're possibly the only one in the city that gave a damn about us and was willing to do something. The city doesn't need you to be a brave hero, we just need you to be what you've been this entire time."

I closed my eyes and nodded to her in gratitude. Her words may not have been the deprecating ones I wanted, but it was exactly what I needed to hear. "You know I still don't remember saving you," I said while squeezing her hand back.

"Maybe if you walk through it with me, you'll remember."

I pursed my lips in thought then shook my head. "Not tonight, not after all that's happened."

She nodded in understanding, "I get it, but let's just say that if my muse that saved me shows up against Bennett next time, that Southern Gent doesn't stand a chance."

Emma glanced up to the stairs where Susan had gone up then focused back on me.

"Why'd you tell the girl her brother was helping us?" She whispered into my ear. "She's going to worry the longer he's gone and it's going to get harder to explain why he hasn't come back yet."

"The miserable have no other medicine, but only hope," I recited to her.

This caused her to beam. "You remembered?" I could feel the joy radiate off of her as I returned the lines from our first formal meeting we had in my office.

I turned away from her. Due to the lack of lights on in the house currently, she wouldn't be able to see me blush, but I still didn't want to risk it.

"We're going to get her brother back. I know we are," unexpectedly, her expression changed as if she just had an idea that she thought was brilliant. "I got it, let's make a pact."

"A pact?" I repeated, questioningly.

"Yes, be my brother!" She said excitedly.

"Um, I don't think it works like that."

"I know that, but if people can fall in love after one day, how come we can't become siblings after fighting together for about two weeks?"

"Really?" I questioned. "I think you've been reading too many plays?"

I turned my head back to her and my eyes widened in shock as they met hers. From her gaze, I could tell she was being deadly serious. There wasn't a hint of a joke or teasing in her attitude. She must've seen my reaction to her expression because she let out a long breath and set her jaw, determinedly.

"I told you before that I had three brothers, but I never had the greatest relationship with them. It was around the Great Depression when our mother left us and our father. Everything was fine before then, but I started taking on the lead roles, which sometimes involved romance. And since I was the youngest, they always wanted to *practice* at home." she paused, her eyes shifting away from me.

It was the look of someone starting to play back a traumatic experience that had previously been repressed. She spat the word practice like it was pure poison to her. Her body began to tremble as she froze. I held her hand gently and nodded soberly.

"Thanks," she said, wiping a tear away from her cheek before continuing. "I was in my late teens when the Depression got really bad, people stopped showing up to the shows. Who's going to waste money on a play when you can't even feed your kids? So, the income stopped coming. They had to get manual labor jobs and since I was a woman, I couldn't work. This meant I was an extra mouth to feed, so they decided to tell me we were doing a show in a faraway town. It was supposedly the only place with an interest, and income. My brothers, they took their last pound of flesh from me, and left me there, alone, hungry, and abandoned. I lasted as long as I could, but not long enough."

As she was speaking, her aura was steadily increasing. Her hazel pupils receded, replaced by a filmy glow in her eyes. The pearly, white flame that usually surrounds her in combat, had tinges of abyss black in it, the kind of black that draws you deeper as you stare into it.

"Emma," I said steadily. The flames were starting to singe me, but I didn't release her hand.

Her eyes snapped back to their normal hazel state, and she looked down at me in surprise. "I'm sorry," she finally noticed the minor damage her flames had done and started panicking. "No, please forgive me. I take it back, you don't have to do this. It was just a silly idea."

I gripped her hands and met her eyes, the corner of my mouth mustering up as much energy as I had to form a half-smile. "Emma, I'll do it."

Her pupils dilated and she threw her arms around my neck in a hug. "Oh, thank you, thank you, thank you!"

"Ouch," I groaned as my body sent me a pain report about how much it didn't appreciate the gesture of affection. "I regret this already."

"Oh sorry," she quickly released my neck then stood up. "Okay, we have to make this official for all three of us."

"Three of us?" I raised an eyebrow.

"Yes, Angel too," she confirmed. "She suggested it by the way."

"Somehow, I doubt that to be true," I replied dryly.

"Believe what you will, it matters not to me," she withdrew a dagger and took a step back, outstretched her arms to her sides, and tilted her head back.

When her head came back down, the penetrating gray eyes told me that Angel was now present.

"Let's get this over with," she sighed.

"That's what I figured," I muttered under my breath.

"What was that?"

"Nothing. I couldn't agree more."

She gave me a dirty glare before taking the dagger and slicing her right hand. Afterwards, she extended the weapon to me.

"What?" I exclaimed, eyeing the dagger. "Can't we just sign some papers?"

Her frown deepened and she jabbed the knife closer to me, waiting for me to take hold.

"Maybe I was mistaken. Can we just be friends? I was caught up in the emotion and after thinking about it I don't really see you in that, oof."

Angel had slammed the handle of the dagger into my chest, driving the breath out of me. I think she avoided my stomach on purpose, but I didn't want to test that theory.

"If you say one more joke, I'm putting the blade in you next time," she warned.

"Sorry," I tried to say normally, but I think it came out as a croak.

I took the dagger and shallowly sliced my right hand also. She then offered me her right palm. I propped myself as much as I could on the couch and took her hand. We shook on it and Angel left the room, leaving me to my pain and thoughts.

I reclined back into the couch, trying to get some rest. That's when I saw two glaring red eyes in the doorframe leading to the hallway across from me.

"I'm really not in the mood, Barb," I warned my aberration.

"Nor I," Barb came casually strolling out of the doorway. "I'm merely watching over you as usual."

"Is that what you call it?" I coughed and immediately my abdomen started throbbing at the sudden motion.

"Yes," Barb's eyes flicked to my abdomen then back to my face. "I've always tried watching over you. The one night I didn't, this happened," referencing my current condition.

I started to give a reply but stopped to seriously consider it. Usually, Barb's unwanted presence was the worst my schizophrenia got, but it hadn't shown up and I ended up consistently losing control tonight. I've hallucinated on missions before, but never to such a degree as tonight. Was Barb actually watching over me on missions?

I shook the thought from my head. That still didn't explain the pain I felt afterwards, but Barb oddly seemed downtrodden this time and it never directly caused the pain, just stood there mocking or talking to me.

I sighed inwardly. Sometimes I really hate what's going on in my brain.

Seemingly pleased with the effect its remark had on me Barb smiled, which looks like when a wolf bares its teeth, chilling. "Sleep my prince, there will be no nightmares tonight."

"Are you okay, Barb?" I asked, my tone serious, thrown off by Barb's behavior.

"No," it responded, "My little prince is in pain. No more talk, sleep now."

I welcomed the invitation as I closed my eyes. The throbbing of my body began to recede as I faded into the recesses of my consciousness into a deep sleep, and like Barb said there were no nightmares.

Chapter Twenty-Three

I woke up with my head resting on something soft. Actually, as I moved my head a bit, I noticed that it was two soft somethings. I fully opened my eyes and looked up to see the illuminated face of a goddess looking down on me. As my vision adjusted to the light, I realized that it was Sofia. She had my head resting in her lap. Even though we were in the midst of autumn, she had the fresh aroma of spring, a mixture of wild flowers and fruit filled my nose.

"*Buenos días,*" Sofia grinned seductively down at me. "We should do this more often."

"You'll get *zero* complaints from me," I replied happily. There aren't many better ways I can think of than waking up in the lap of someone you love. Suddenly, a small weight could be felt shifting on my chest and when I looked down to investigate, I found a furry ball of mass curled up on me.

"You brought Mew?" I tilted my head back to question her. "You know Susan hates cats."

"Special exception, besides I couldn't leave this little guy all alone," she reached down to pet my feline friend. Mew purred in pleasure, rubbing his head against her hand.

As I watched the cute display unfold, I saw that I was no longer in my gear from last night. Instead, I was in canary yellow and baby blue polka dot pajamas. Squinting down, I raised a suspicious eyebrow at Sofia.

She raised her hand to her mouth, failing to suppress a giggle. "Oh my Devin, what kind of girl do you think I am? Susan had the honor of doing this. Your suit is being washed. Speaking of which, I brought your work clothes for today."

"Someone's getting a raise," I sang playfully.

"I'll be vice president in no time. Ok, time to get up," she kissed me gently on the forehead, then patted my head, indicating that my stay in paradise had ended.

When I left the comfort of her lap, she pointed to where she had put my clothes before walking out of the room. From her footsteps, I could tell that Sofia was still standing outside of the door. She must've wished to talk, but still respect my privacy.

"You're taking this better than I expected," I spoke to her through the door as I gingerly began taking off the pajamas.

"Susan told me I was lucky that you came here first," the voice responded somberly. "What happened last night?"

"Ouch," I muttered to myself as I attempted to take the top off over my head. I was still majorly sore from the whoopin' I received last night. "Everything went off the rails, Sof. I'm not fighting rent-a-cops anymore. This guy's on a different level."

"Do you think you can beat him?" Her voice sounded closer, as if she were pressing against the door, the wooden barrier separating us, hardly seemed to make a difference.

I was putting on my dark brown slacks now, observing myself in the mirror. I had a few new scrapes and bruises on my face, nothing that would last forever.

I gingerly touched the scar over my left eye that I had received previously. *But some scars last longer than others.* I thought to myself before breaking myself from my trance.

"For the sake of those siblings and all of the potential future victims, I have to," I replied in a shaky tone to Sofia.

"You sound scared, Dev," she noted.

I was finished dressing now and I had my back pressed against the door as I spoke with her. "I...am. He was so casual about everything he did, but that wasn't the scary part. Most of the Underground are in it for the money, power, influence, or circumstance, but he's different. Whatever his reason is, it defines him. His will seemed greater than mine. It's like what he does is his sole mission in life, while I just put on my suit as a hobby. That's what's scary."

"You do always come off as you hate this life," she quietly reminded me.

"I despise it," I admitted, sliding down onto the floor. "The things I see, what they do to these people is inhumane. The only thing I find enjoyable is successfully getting everyone home...but if I can't even do that, what's the point?"

"The point is, you're at least doing something about it, fighting back," her voice seemed to match the same location as mine as if she slid down on her side of the door as well.

"Are you sure you're not the therapist?" I asked jokingly.

"No thank you. I don't want to deal with the clients you have," she laughed. Then in a quieter tone, "Hey Dev?"

"Yeah, Sof?"

"Even though I can't go into battle with you, you know I got your back, right?"

I stood up and opened the door. "Yeah, I know," I offered my hand to help her to her feet and we embraced. I felt her warmth radiating to me, making everything in those few moments feel right. If I survived this, maybe I could finally start to move forward with us. We held each other like that for a moment before my phone started ringing.

We broke the hug and stepped back from each other, smiling.

"I'll be waiting in the car," she brushed off her skirt then headed down the stairs.

I nodded in confirmation and went to answer my phone. It was a number that I recognized, but I wasn't sure why they were calling me.

"Yes?"

"Are you still in the house?" Angel asked me.

"I am. Did you need something?"

"I'm stuck. I need you to get me," she reported.

"What do you mean you're stuck?" I asked, confused.

"Just come outside to the forest," then the phone clicked.

"Those two are going to be the death of me," I growled to myself before going outside.

I walked to the forest, wondering how my newfound sibling got stuck. I would expect this of Emma, but not Angel. She always seemed to be the more responsible of the two. My steps became more cautious the deeper I stepped into the Redwoods. I knew the Romani bear was somewhere in here, but I wasn't exactly sure where. I was currently intruding on its territory and in my condition, I didn't know if I could trust my ability to get me out of there.

"Up here!" I heard a shout from above me in the trees.

It was Angel. She was up in the Redwoods, perched on one of the branches. The Romani bear was standing on its hind legs, its front two paws pushing the tree, bellowing at her from below. The bear was a grizzly, and it made the bear from *The Revenant* look like Winnie the Pooh.

I gaped up at her. "How'd you get up there?" I whispered sharply to her, trying not to draw the bear's attention.

"Something weird's been happening to me, just get me down," she barked.

"Why don't you just fly down?" I asked.

"Only Emma can fly. I hate heights," she responded angrily.

"Why not change back?"

"Do you think if I could, I would've done it by now?"

"Fair point," I extended my hand to create a portal beneath her. "Just drop down."

She let go of the branch and fell through the gateway, and out of another one I created next to me. The bear clawed cluelessly at the Redwood, wondering where its potential morning breakfast had gone off to.

"Thanks," Angel said as she regarded me. "I think we shouldn't have done the blood oath. Things have been weird since I woke up."

"What do you mean weird?" I asked.

"Weird like-" she unexpectedly poofed away. Poof may not be the most accurate term, but it was almost as if she had been summoned. There was a weird misty energy around her that collapsed in upon her and the next second she was gone.

"Hmm," I said surprised, then started to walk off.

"This," I leapt back in fright as Angel reappeared beside me.

"Did you just teleport?" I asked.

"Ever since I woke up, and I haven't been able to change back yet."

"Do you want to talk to Toni about it?" I suggested. "I'm pretty sure one of his people can help you."

She shook her head indignantly. "I don't want any help from the mafia. I have my own people that I can talk-" she suddenly disappeared again.

I waited for a couple of moments, puzzled, before I looked to see the bear back on all fours, very still, leering at me hungrily.

"Nice weather we're having, huh?"

The bear roared back in response.

"As I thought," I took that as my cue to leave and walked backwards into a portal behind me, never taking my attention away from it.

I appeared back at the mansion, said goodbye to Susan, and thanked her again for everything she did last night. She assured me that Tina would be in good hands and sent me on my way.

"So, who's on the schedule for today?" I asked Sofia as I hopped in the passenger's seat of my Stratus. Given my sorry state, she decided that she would sit behind the wheel today.

"Stan," she replied with a giggle as she activated the auto-drive to pull out of the driveway.

I groaned loudly. "Of all days, it would be him."

"Don't worry," she struggled to contain her laughter. "I'm pretty sure it'll be fine."

She continued giggling as we made our way through morning traffic on the way to the office.

***

"So, by my theory the Peach City Phantom is actually a ghost with Irregular abilities or an Irregular with ghost abilities," my patient Stan droned on in my office. I was doing my best to listen, but I gave up after about five minutes.

Stan was somewhere in his early thirties. His curly, sand colored hair flopped back and forth as he talked to me. The round spectacles that magnified his eyes creeped me out at times when he actually took the time to meet my gaze. He was wearing a zebra-patterned jacket with matching sweatpants which I think was supposed to be an homage to my alter ego's color scheme.

My rates are usually by the hour, but for him I charged by the minute. You see Stan was obsessed with heroes, and since there hadn't been a lot of vigilante activities since the end of the Purification, my enterprise is what he's become fixated on. It's odd too, because he functions fine in everyday society, but his friends recommended him to me.

Initially, I figured Stan should get new friends, but after numerous sessions with him, I can finally understand their plight. Out of respect to Dr. Green, I refuse to turn away a client until after I have conducted at least five sessions with them. Stan was one of the clients that put that code to the test. This was our fourth meeting.

"First reports about him came around a year and a half ago. Suddenly though, he goes off the radar for two months before reappearing. What explains that time between appearances? Could it be that he was simply a novice, merely trying his hand in the superhero business until he realized he needed intense training?" He adjusted his round spectacles as he continued.

More like, I didn't feel like dressing in that ridiculous outfit only to get punched in the face. I thought to myself as I propped my head up in my right hand, trying to maintain consciousness as his dissertation continued. For my personal sanity, I found it was best to treat Stan like commercials on the radio, unless something catches my interest or is important, I typically just ignore it.

"Or it could be that it was supposed to be a onetime mission? Someone else had to convince him to come back and he begrudgingly accepted the offer."

I raised my eyebrows at this hypothesis. That was the exact reason for the long hiatus between my return. Leave it to Stan to provide at least a few nuggets during each session. It was beneficial that he talked to me about these things because I had the opportunity to throw him off the trail if he ever got dangerously close to the truth.

"I like your first theory, Stan," I repositioned myself in my seat now that he had at least garnered some of my attention. "There hasn't been a non-IPF Irregular fighting crime in nearly two decades."

"That's where you're wrong," he pushed his glasses up on his nose and handed me a stack of papers.

Yes, he brings notes to his own sessions.

"What are these?" I asked, receiving the pages. Annoyance tinged the edges of my voice.

"Well, I was doing research when I ran upon that," he pointed down at the files.

I started shuffling through the pages, until I ran across a picture. It was a cloaked figure. They had aviator goggles, with a *Matrix* style solid black long coat, and leather gloves. The figure also had a detective's bowler hat. In other words, it looked a lot like the Spectre.

"Where'd you get this from?" I held the picture up to him.

"Dark web," he shrugged. "A lot of the old rumor boards, history books, and information pre-Conflict is heavily redacted or erased, but you can find anything if you look hard enough."

"When is this?"

"The message board I took it from was dated 2040."

2040, huh. My memory started somewhere around 2042, which would put me in my late teenage years. It was possible the photo was around the time Sammy died. Which would make sense that the traumatic experience, especially around my age at the time would cause me to repress everything that had happened. It would also explain my aversion to wanting to fight and the current motivation for my costume design.

"Good work Stan," I congratulated him. "This is some impressive stuff."

"I do my best. If anyone's going to expose the Peach City Phantom, it's going to be me," his voice had gotten progressively nasally as the session advanced. He pulled out a bottle from his coat, stuck it in his nose then breathed. Liquid started dripping from his nose in a very gross fashion. I was going to have to have someone else clean that, maybe Sofia if I ever needed to get back at her for something. I grabbed hold off my box of tissues and offered it to him, with a disapproving look on my face.

"Thanks, Dr. Prince," he blew his nose, the tissues barely doing their job, but still managed to prevent any more leakage from getting on my couch. "So, what notes did you write down?"

"Oh, these," I scrambled to cover my clipboard. I was coloring on one of the pages of the coloring books that I leave out for Sammy. I was halfway done with the picture by the time Stan had said anything of interest. "They're personal notes for future reference."

"Oh, nice. Okay, so for the next part, I wanted to talk about the symbolic reference his name has to the old comic and present different costume ideas that would help distinguish him from such comparisons."

I groaned inwardly and went back to coloring. The session lasted another hour and fifteen minutes, and I felt every second of it.

"Thanks again, Dr. Prince," Stan said as he rose to leave. "I'll be sure to schedule another appointment when it's convenient."

"No rush, Stan. I really need time to process this before the next meeting," I called back to him.

He waved before leaving the room. As soon as the door closed, my forehead dropped to the cool surface of my desk. Per usual, Stan exhausted all of my patience. Before I could close my eyes to sleep, the intercom buzzed with Sofia on the other end.

"You have a walk-in appointment today," she notified me.

I pushed the button on the intercom and switched it to the phone. "Today of all days?"

"Don't worry," she comforted me. "He's actually quite charming."

"Those are the craziest ones." I replied dryly. "I'll meet him at the door."

I popped a few pain pills and headache medicine then stood up. My body was not even close to being in top condition. Susan had wrapped up my abdomen to the best of her ability and Sofia's charm skills in combination with the pills at least did a good job at making it manageable.

I reached my door and opened it up to a sight that made me audibly catch my breath. Bennett was leaning over the desk, giving Sofia a gentlemanly smile. He was working his full southern charm as the two were engaged in conversation, even going so far as to stroke her hand tenderly. A bandage was wrapped around where I had shot his hand the previous night.

"Hey Sofia, what's going on here?" I strained to keep my voice professional and my hands from wrapping around Bennett's throat. I felt my eye twitch as I tried to keep a neutral face.

"Oh, Boss. Hamilton here was telling me a lovely story about when he was a boy," she said in response, none the wiser. She was smiling freely until she saw my face, her smile became much more reserved after that. Sofia knew me long enough to tell the difference when I was being paranoid and when I knew there was immediate danger. This was a case of the latter.

"Dr. Prince, you have this lovely lady refer to you as Boss. How unsightly," he turned his elegant grin towards me.

"One must establish boundaries," I said with a smile that was bordering on too obviously forced, like an agitated child on picture day. "Good to see you again Bennett. To what do I owe the pleasure?"

"A simple conversation. I figured since you're one of the most renowned therapists in Peach City, you would be able to help me," he replied.

"Of course, step in and have a seat," I stepped aside from the doorway and lifted a hand, welcoming him inside. I gave Sofia a look of warning. She nodded in response. A look of unease spread across her face. I nodded back then followed Bennett inside and took a seat in my chair.

Bennett was wearing a burgundy Victorian suit jacket, to go along with brown dress pants and shoes, orange ascot as always situated perfectly below his neck. He took his wheat straw skimmer hat off, the type that you'd see old plantation owners wear in the Old South and rested it on his lap after crossing his legs comfortably in the chair across from me.

"Are you okay, Doctor?" He asked me.

"Fine, why do you ask?"

"You seem stiff, and you have bruises on your face. Also..."Bennett flicked his gaze to the table.

I turned to see what he was referencing. My pain pills were on the table. I forgot to put them back in the drawer after Sofia had called me.

"Oh, it's nothing. I got jumped by a couple of thugs on the way home at night earlier this week," I lied smoothly, "but luckily an IPF agent was nearby and scared them off. I didn't lose anything valuable except a little bit of my pride."

"Unfortunate. The city really is falling apart," he said, the barest traces of empathy in his voice.

"Yes, it has seen better times, but what can you do?"

"Not sit on our behinds and do nothing," something in his eyes that told me he was referencing something specific.

I didn't want to question him on the matter, so I pushed my glasses from the bridge of my nose and reached for my notebook. "So, what did you wish to discuss?"

"Morality," he stated.

"I think a priest may be a better reference guide on that topic than me."

He shrugged. "Possibly, but I'm beyond that now."

"How so?"

"In my line of work, Dr. Prince, I'm required to perform certain acts," he answered.

Though, I already knew the answer I asked, "What kind of acts?"

"Murder among many others," he said so casually that you would have thought he was talking about killing mosquitoes that got in his house.

I widened my eyes in mock surprise and let out a breath. "Wow, really embracing the doctor-patient privilege. You do know there are limits to that?"

He shot me an annoyed look as if he were thinking about committing one of those 'certain acts' on me. "Please don't patronize me, doctor."

"Okay," I gulped. "So, do these acts bother you?"

"At this point, no," he hesitated briefly, "It's been a long time since death has affected me in that way."

"Is it when you lost someone close?" I asked him carefully. I didn't want to risk sending him into a rage, but this was a perfect opportunity to get inside Bennett's brain and pick around because it seemed like brute force wasn't going to be the way to beat him.

He pursed his lips then folded his arms. "At this point, I'm afraid we've all lost someone close."

I nodded with him somberly. As much as I hated agreeing with him, he was right. "Is that what drives your current *objective,* I guess for lack of a better word?"

"Objective," he repeated thoughtfully, "At this point it's probably my life's mission, but I can't dispute that phrasing. Yes, I would say that."

"Was it during the Conflict?" I asked.

"No."

"Purification?"

"No."

"Oh really? That's what most of my clients deal with. Are they at least the one responsible for your ascot? I see that you always wear it."

Bennett touched the orange ascot below his neck affectionately, his fingers playing over it gently as the beginnings of a small smile touched his lips. Quickly though, he seemed to break himself out of the trance and frowned back up at me.

"I don't wish to discuss it," he snapped back in a cautioning tone.

"Okay, we don't have to talk about it," I raised the fingers on my free hand to him in a sign of concession. "What about morality do you wish to discuss?"

"If even the worst of actions can ever be truly justified," he said, looking away from me disinterestedly.

"Is that for one person to decide?"

"Maybe, maybe not," he focused back on me and asked in a deadly low voice, "Tell me doctor, if I snapped that pretty assistant of yours neck, how would you feel?"

I noticeably gripped my notepad tightly, the wood began to fracture as I glared daggers back into him.

"Easy, easy." he raised his hands up in mock surrender. "I would never harm such a beautiful woman, without reason anyway."

"Don't do it," a voice warned me. I spun my neck to see the direction from where it was coming from. When I found the speaker, it turned out to be the head of the poor captive that was decapitated last night. His neck had traces of tendons and muscle where it had been severed from the body. It looked ghastly pale but had a normal look on its face as if it weren't missing its entire lower extremities. "He's just trying to get a rise out of you. Look at what he did to me."

I recoiled back from the head in alarm and tried to refocus on Bennett.

"Is your schizophrenia flaring up, Devin?" Bennett asked mockingly, a cruel smile spread across his face.

I froze in shock. Only seven people knew of my secret identity as the Peach City Phantom, but as of last Sunday only three people knew that I dealt with schizophrenia, Dr. Green, Sofia, and Emma/Angel in that order. I know that none of them would spout that off as simple gossip, especially not to this guy. I had a few incidents that caused my condition to be recorded down as public information, but I thought those were sealed off since I was still a minor at the time.

I fixed my glasses and tried not to give him a dirty look. Bennett was definitely trying to push my buttons. The fact that he was here definitely meant he suspected that I was at least more than Emma's personal therapist. I couldn't slip now, or Marcus could be lost forever.

"I'm doing fine, Hamilton. And I do wish that you wouldn't refer to my condition so casually as if we were friends. It's also of no concern to you," I said sternly, but evenly so as not to provoke him, the way a parent teaches a child a lesson on right and wrong without blowing up at them.

He grimaced at me calling him by his first name but recovered quickly. "Well after the events of last weekend, you became quite the superstar. More eyes are on you now than you expect."

"Curiosity killed the cat," I said calmly. There was no pretense in my voice that my previous statement wasn't a threat, so I just let it hang out there in the open.

Bennett was the first to break the silence. "Indeed, it did," he grinned. "You never answered my question doctor. If you lost someone you loved, would you not feel compelled to act, to bring the one who wronged you to their knees?"

I closed my eyes then let a breath out of my nose. "I would probably want revenge, but I'm afraid I lack the ability to get said revenge. After all, I'm only a therapist."

Bennett seemed disappointed by my answer as if it were an open invitation but acknowledged it with a gesture of his head. "I guess that was kind of what I was expecting. Good talk, Devin. We should do this again sometime," he grabbed his belongings, withdrew a few bills and tossed them on the floor, before heading to the door. "That should cover my time."

"Hamilton!" I barked at him. He froze instantly, his hand grasping the door knob. "Do you ever hurt kids?" I gave him a serious look as he stood there.

It was his turn to let out a sigh as he waited at the door. "Some things are better left undisclosed in certain company," with that he turned and walked out of the office.

I waited a few seconds, until I figured he left the entire building and slammed my fist down on my desk in frustration. He was right here, in my office and if he knew who I was then he was mocking me. That arrogant bastard threatened Sofia to my face. I wasn't going to let that stand. Next time, I saw him would be the last.

"That's more like it, my prince," Barb cooed as it prowled from around my desk to sit on its hind legs next to me.

"What do you want?" I sniped at Barb.

"The same as you," Barb shot an evil look at the door then turned to Sammy's desk, "and him."

I spun in my chair to see the head was still there, observing the two of us silently.

"And how can you help?" I questioned.

"By embracing me," Barb answered simply. "You're going to have to tap fully into that part inside you that birthed me. Just like you did yesterday."

I shivered at the mention of the events of the prior evening. I hadn't used Barb's voice on a mission in months and it creeped me out just thinking back to what all of the people I helped free saw yesterday.

Just then, my office door opened, and Sofia hurriedly walked in. "Are you okay, Devin?"

"Think about my words," Barb's voice loomed as it disappeared from view.

I looked at the table and the head was gone too. I spun around to Sofia and shook my head. "No, not even close, but I will be once I get out of here."

I started gathering my belongings to head out for the day.

"Will you at least tell me who that was?" She asked.

"He's the one that left me worse than how you found me yesterday?"

She gasped, "What did he want?"

"I don't know," I turned around and put both of my hands gently on her shoulder, "But can you do me a favor? Stay at the Romani's until all of this is over."

"Devin, I don't know what's going on, but you can at least-"

"Please," I begged her, grabbing her arms in my distress. Gently, I rubbed them reassuringly, more for myself than for her. "Just promise me you'll stay there. Tell Toni, that I requested it personally."

She raised a hand and placed it on my cheek. "I'll pack a bag and head over tonight."

I smiled in response. "Thank you, Sofia. Take the car also, you'll be safer."

She smiled back, gave me a peck on the cheek then turned to leave.

I let out a long sigh. The entire day had been long and eventful, I was looking forward to going home and getting some more rest until Emma and I figured out when the next drop would be.

I had all my belongings packed when I suddenly got a phone call. I checked the number and saw that it was from Dr. Green's nursing home.

"Hello," I answered.

"Hey, Dr. Prince. It's Nurse Gooding."

"Hey nurse, is everything alright?"

"It's Dr. Green," she said, hesitation in her voice. "He got lost again today. We found him out by the gardens. He's in his room now, but would you be able to stop by and check on him?"

"Of course, nurse. I'll be there soon," I hung up the phone and looked at the belongings in my hands. I sighed before placing everything back on the table. If Dr. Green was having a bad day, then I would be there for him, just as he had done for me so many years ago.

Chapter Twenty-Four

I gave it a few minutes before I created a gateway to the nursing home, so as not to raise suspicion about the brevity of my arrival, but still managed to get there in a relatively short amount of time. I stepped through the other side into the public restroom of the home. I've visited enough times to know that it was rarely used, so the likelihood that anyone would see me was slim.

The first thing that hit me was the pungent smell of urine. I nearly started to tear up at how strong it was. One of the many reasons most people don't use this restroom, old timers, just like children, forgetting to flush the toilet. I covered my nose, prodded the yellow wooden door open with my foot, and pressed the button on the back of the wall that flushes the toilet, should the sensor fail, which in this case it definitely did.

"Disgusting," I turned out of the stall and made my way to the exit, out of the urine scented restroom into the mothball scented home.

I rushed down to Dr. Green's door and knocked before peeking my head in. Nurse Gooding was sitting there humming to Dr. Green when I peered into the room. She gave me a sad smile, but still waved me into the room.

Dr. Green was holding Nurse Gooding's hand and breathing calmly. I've seen him get lost before and it was a scary sight, not just because of the potential danger he was to himself at times, but this was the man that seemed to have all the answers when I was younger. It seemed unfair for his mind to start going so soon already.

"Hey Doc," I greeted him with a grin. I kept my voice low and smooth, so as not to make him anymore excitable. "I heard you gave everyone quite the scare just to get Nurse Gooding here to sing to you, ever the player."

He gave a quick chuckle. "I've been a player since before you were in diapers, my boy."

I gave the nurse a warm look. "I can take it from here. Thank you so much."

Nurse Gooding stood up and gave me a slight bow. "It's my pleasure," she turned to my bedridden mentor, "You're lucky to have such a caring young man, please don't give him any trouble."

He waved his hand in a playfully dismissive manner. "How else am I going to get any fun around here?"

She smirked at the good doctor then headed out the door, shutting it gently behind her.

"So how are you doing?" I said, my tone more serious.

He frowned and looked away from me. "I thought I was back home."

I pulled up the chair that Nurse Gooding had previously occupied, spun it backwards and sat down in it, facing the bed. "I thought you said you had the perfect system in place now, so that you'd remember where you were?"

"I thought I told you not to sit in a chair like that," he complained, not in a bitter way though, just in the manner that a parent scolds a child about a minor bad habit.

I rolled my eyes at him. "I never do it when I'm with clients if that makes you feel better. I usually take your prim and proper posture," I straightened up back in the seat, imitating how he used to sit back during our sessions.

"I see your sense of sarcasm hasn't disappeared," he sighed before looking in the direction of the door, but I could tell he wasn't seeing the door. "It's not always where Devin, it's when. Sometimes I don't know if I'm talking to you as your therapist, teacher, or your pity patient."

"It's the same as it's always been," I reached to grab his frail hand. "We're talking as friends."

He looked down at my hand then slowly back at me and grinned. "Thank you, my boy. Can you do me a favor?"

"Anything Doc," I responded readily.

"Would you be the one to speak at my funeral?" He said resolutely.

I gasped, not even bothering to control my reaction as he had taught me so many years ago. "What are you talking about Dr. Green? You still have plenty of time," I rose from my seat and started shuffling quickly through his notes on his condition that were situated on one of his bookshelves. "You have years left. The symptoms are still manageable, we just have to get the conditions right, that's all."

The elderly man began chuckling as he witnessed me in my panic. "Devin, it's alright. I'm not dying tomorrow, but when it does happen, and it will. No amount of furniture moving will prevent it. I never had a family of my own and you're my closest friend. Can you promise me you'll do it?"

"I...I don't like discussing this," I tried not to gaze in his direction.

"Devin, promise me?" I could feel his gaze locked on me as I shifted around anxiously. Of course, I couldn't turn down his request, but imagine looking at your oldest friend in both senses of the word and imagining what you would say about them when they're gone. I didn't want to start throwing dirt on him before he even breathed his last breath.

"I'll do it," I twitched my lips but couldn't manage to smile. I went back to sit by his bedside, placing my hands on the bed.

"Thank you, my boy. It means the world to me," he smiled, patting my hand. After observing me closer, his eyes widened. "What happened to you?"

"Where should I begin?" I sighed before taking the time to explain to him all of the events that had occurred since we last met.

"Wooh boy," he whistled. "Sounds like you had a doozy of a week. When are you going back out?"

I shrugged. "I'm not sure when the date for the next transaction is and I can't make a move on Bennett in my condition unless I want you speaking at my funeral."

"You got to save the boy, Devin," he implored me quietly.

"I know," I looked in the corner of the room and saw Sammy standing there silently, watching our exchange. "I will."

"Is it the little aberration?" He questioned, noticing my far away gaze.

"Yeah."

"How's he doing?" Dr. Green asked sincerely.

"We've been better," I replied somberly. "I'm afraid history is repeating itself."

"What did I tell you about being afraid?" He asked strongly.

"It's natural, but overcoming it is the only way we can be brave, which is unnatural," I recited back to him.

"That's right, my supernatural hero," he leaned over to thump the back of his fist against my chest. "As long as that thing keeps beating, you keep living, keep fighting. This city needs you."

"Everyone keeps telling me that, but no one else is stepping up," I folded my arms, brooding.

"From what you tell me, you've inspired at least one to act so far," he noted.

I pursed my lips but didn't respond. I always hated when he was right. It always made it seem like he could read the parts of my mind that are roped off to my conscious self.

"See. Right again," he cheesed at me, childish glee in his features.

"Always one to do a celebration dance," I rose from my chair and poured him a glass of water before sitting back down.

"Oh Devin, when did you get here?" Dr. Green glanced at me in surprise, as if I had just entered the room.

I felt something tug at my heart. I had only turned my back for a couple of seconds, yet he had already reset. I wanted to scream or punch something in anger, but I suppressed it and instead gave him my best professional smile.

"I just got here, Doc," I offered him the glass of water.

He took the glass from me gratefully, his two hands shaking as they grasped it, but not spilling a single drop. "Thank you. It's good to see you nonetheless, my boy. Did I get lost again today?"

"No, you did great today," I lied, while preventing my lips from visibly trembling. "You were just about to go to sleep."

"Other than your visits, it's what I look forward to most," he whimmed.

"I bet you do, Doc," I gave a half-hearted laugh while pulling the covers over him, making sure that he was comfortable. "I'll leave you to your dreams then, doc.

"Devin, wait," he stopped me as I stood.

"Yes?"

"Can you stay with me until I fall asleep?" He requested. "I'd enjoy the company."

"Of course," I said, turning the chair around to sit properly and face him.

"Can you sing that song you'd always used to sing when you were younger?" He asked. "You know the one by Of Mice and Men."

"It was Of Monsters and Men, and it's been sometime since I've actually sung."

"Oh, please. Grant an old man's request?" He made puppy eyes at me, which for his age somehow came off as adorable in an elderly way rather than creepy.

"Alright, you win," I held his hand and started singing *Your Bones*, in a low voice to him. The song turned into a lullaby as my mentor started to fade away peacefully to sleep. The deeper I got into the song, I didn't bother suppressing the tears anymore and wept freely until I finished.

When he was completely out, I stood up and placed the chair back at the table.

"I'll come talk to you tomorrow, doc," I patted my friend's head then turned to wipe the rest of my tears away before creating a portal to leave. "I promise."

***

After leaving the home, I stepped out of the portal near the North Buckhead area of Atlanta in Peach City. I was in front of the main location of the Romani's I.T.

department as I liked to call them, an eight-story clay brick warehouse that served as a laboratory. The decor caused it to stand out significantly in the affluent neighborhood, yet it managed not to draw too much attention. I could see the lights flashing inside through the windows. The crew must've been still working on different technology.

Hopefully, the recovery team had managed to gather my belongings after my run-in with Bennett. All of my weapons had been dropped during the fight and I was definitely going to need them before the next as well as the improvements I requested.

I took out my bandanna and wrapped it around my face, then pulled out a pair of sunglasses to protect my identity. Before I could even ring the bell, the large sliding entrance door opened.

"The P.C.P., to what do we owe the pleasure?" A short teenager with glasses poked his head from behind the door.

"Hey Chester," I greeted the cornrowed teen before me. "Do you have my belongings?"

"Yeah, come in," he stepped aside, allowing me inside the lab.

"Is he in today?" I asked as I walked into the giant building, placing my hands in my pocket as I examined the lab. There hadn't been many changes since the last time I had been here.

There were robotic exoskeletons displayed upon the walls. The head of the lab was a real robot fanatic and had prepared if there ever came a day where he needed to step inside one of them. I've been trying to convince him for the past six months to aid me, but he has a complex when it comes to stepping out into public and he also doesn't want to work with someone whose identity he was unsure of, which was fair in my opinion.

The workbenches were occupied with other workers of various ages and backgrounds, all intently tinkering with a weapon, piece of tech, or article of clothing that they could find a way to improve. Sparks flew from some stations, while shouting and arguing erupted at others. It was like your typical auto shop, just operating at a much larger level.

"No, he's out," Chester turned to me, his white lab coat fluttering as he did. "Your gear is over here. You should really be more careful, this stuff is expensive. We did have time to make those adjustments to the weapons though."

"And what about the suit?" I asked.

Chester paused and looked at me in slight irritation, hands in his pockets. "That won't be done for some time."

"Really?" I raised an eyebrow, not masking my disappointment.

"What you're asking for is...complicated," he replied annoyed, continuing to walk towards my gear as he spoke. "We would need exact readings to speed up the process, but you refuse to stay long enough to provide it for us. Other than that, we could've had it done already."

"Okay, I get it," Geez, kids these days really took their science projects seriously. "Thanks for the adjustments though."

"Child's play, my dude," he smiled back over his shoulder. "Just don't lose it again."

"Hey Chester," I called before he left.

"Something important?"

"Yeah, tell him the time is much closer than he thinks," I instructed Chester.

He looked at me, twisted his mouth, and gave me a tilt of the head in acknowledgment. "Will do. Do your thing P," with that, the second in command of the lab spun on his heels and walked to one of the stations to break up an argument.

I collected my tonfas off of the steel tabletop, checking to see if the improvements had been added, as Chester stated, they had been. I gave a devilish grin, thinking of all the fun things I could do with my new toys, but shook the thought from my head and pocketed them. Lastly, I picked up my Desert Eagle. I was surprised they found it since I had dropped the pistol when I was on top of the train, but Toni's cleanup crew was, if nothing very thorough.

I looked at the lab one last time then portaled out to a local convenience store. I picked up Dr. Green's favorite chocolate bar and some tea for when I would go to see him tomorrow. Maybe he'd be able to help me with the photo Stan showed me earlier. If not, at least I'd be able to keep my promise and chat with him as he crunched down on the bar of candy.

Chapter Twenty-Five

D r. Green never did get to eat that chocolate bar and I couldn't keep my promise. I knew something was wrong as soon as I entered the nursing home that morning. It was almost like a scene you'd see in a movie. An ambulance was stationed outside the building. As I walked in, everything appeared to go in slow motion even though everyone was in a rush. The staff was running in different directions, avoiding me by inches even though it seemed as if they didn't see me. Elderly patients that lived there stood huddled in the corner, some with hands over their mouth, shaking their heads in shock. But the moment I knew, was when I met eyes with Nurse Gooding.

When she saw me, her eyes immediately flew away from mine, dropping to the desk. The candy bar and tea in my hand, nearly dropped to the floor. I forced myself to walk over to her, to have her quash my fears, but I knew.

"Nurse Gooding, please," I started. I could feel my voice starting to crack. "Please, don't tell me," I searched her face for any kind of hope but found none.

"I'm sorry Devin, but..." she stopped, fighting back tears just like me. "But, when I checked on him this morning, he wasn't responding."

"I just spoke to him yesterday," I could feel myself starting to become hysterical. "He had one bad day. I checked his records, and he wasn't supposed to go this early. I promised him…" My voice trailed off as the heartache started to take over. I felt like falling onto the floor and curling up, but I clutched the desk to keep myself on my feet.

"We never know how these things progress, Devin," she started to reach out her hand to comfort me but saw my increasingly erratic expression and thought better of it. "He went peacefully though. That's all we can ask for sometimes."

My eyes darted towards her, a glare settling across my face. Nurse Gooding flinched in response to my sudden change in temperament.

"I'm sorry," I sighed in apology. "This is so sudden. Would I be able to see him?"

She pursed her lips, a pained look overcame her face. "Are you sure?"

"Yes."

"You know the way to his room," she directed me.

I made my way past the EMTs and explained to them that I was 'first of kin' and wanted to see the body before they took him away. They gave each other a questioning look before nodding back at me somberly. When I entered the room, I saw Dr. Green's body lying there peacefully, just the way I had left him yesterday. His tan stocking cap, drooped to the left side of his face, covering his cheek. His hands were above the covers, lying parallel to his sides. I noticed one of his pillows was missing, must've been from when the EMTs started adjusting the room after finding him.

I took my work coat off and placed it on the chair as I pulled it up to him.

"Did you already know?" I desperately asked his body when I sat down. "Why didn't you tell somebody? We could have gotten you some help, took you to another home."

I stood back up and began pacing frantically at the foot of his bed. I was trying to think of all of the signs that I could've missed, what could've been done.

"Why? Why'd I have to lose you now?" My voice trailed off as I spoke into the empty room. Everything felt unnaturally still, like Dr. Green was the life force that had made the atmosphere pop, but now there was none of that present.

I perched back in the chair next to the bed. "Please, talk to me," I whispered. "Just one more time," I waited for an answer, but of course there was nothing.

"Answer me!" I started knocking against my head. If there were ever a time where I wanted to talk to someone that wasn't there, this was it. After more silence, my voice finally broke, "Why won't you answer me?"

"You know it doesn't work like that," there was Sammy, standing next to me, overlooking the body. His bleak expression matched mine.

"I wish it did," I turned to him. My vision was now blurry due to the tears. "He was my only friend before I became what I am today, and I couldn't save him."

"No one could," Sammy put a small hand on my back, rubbing it gently as he did his best not to comfort or console, but just be there for me. "Sometimes you can't fight Mother Nature."

I gripped Dr. Green's hand, it was cold, stiff, rigor mortis had settled in. I leaned towards him and whispered in his ear. "You said you look forward to the dreams. I hope you sleep well, my friend."

"He was a good man," Sammy commented. "He always treated us like we actually existed. May he rest easy."

I rested my forehead on the back of Dr. Green's limp hand. I just sat there and wept. I remained that way until the EMTs came back in the room, requesting that they take the body now. I stood up and bent over him, placing a kiss on his forehead. "Goodbye Mo. Thanks for everything."

I collected my coat and made my way out of the room, lightly brushing past the paramedics as they brought the gurney in to take my deceased mentor's body away.

I pulled out my cell phone and dialed the office.

"Hello, Dr. Prince's office," Sofia answered the phone in her usual cheerful tone.

It was probably the first piece of warmth I felt all day. I hated having to bring her mood down, but I needed to tell her that I wasn't coming in today.

"Hey Sof," I couldn't keep the melancholy out of my voice, so I just pressed on. "You can have the day off."

"Devin, what's wrong?" I could hear the worry in her voice.

"It's Dr. Green," I paused to gather the words. "He passed away."

"Oh no," she gasped. "Are you home? I can come over."

"No, I'm still at the nursing home," I considered her offer for a second, but then shook my head. "Thanks Sofia, but not today. I just want to be alone right now."

"Entiendo," there was the slightest hint of disappointment in her voice. I did my best to ignore it as she disconnected from the other end of the line.

I let out a deep sigh as I placed my phone into my pocket. As much as I probably needed Sofia to accompany me, I doubted that it would be in my best interest to be around people right now. I went into the restroom, then used my ability to make a way home.

***

When I stepped into my apartment, I headed straight for my bed. It was going to be a lie in bed with the curtains drawn kind of day. Before I could plop down face first into my pillow, I saw a box sitting there. My senses immediately jumped into action.

Only Sofia had a key to my apartment and since she always gets to the office before me, I knew that she hadn't been the one to place the package here. No one should've had access to the apartment except for me, not even Mew, who was staying at the Romani's. I gingerly stalked over to the bed, checking to see if the intruder was still in the apartment.

I finally reached the box and found that there was no name of the sender. It was just a plain brown box with tape around it. I pulled my bronze apartment key from my pocket and punctured a hole in the tape, ripping it away. I slowly opened the package and saw an envelope situated on top of a pillow.

This wasn't a usual dollar store letter either. It was the kind that was used to write formal messages, there was embroidery addressed to me and a cherry red seal placed there.

I wasn't in any particular mood for an invite, but I opened the letter, nonetheless. It read:

My Dearest Devin,

I hope you recover well in your time of grief. It is unfortunate to hear that you lost someone so close to you. Just know that the good doctor passed on with full dignity and a fighting spirit. I wanted to give you a memento to remember him by. From a business standpoint, you being Peach City's Phantom disappoints me, but on a personal note, I truly relish the fact that it's you. I hadn't confirmed it was you until you mentioned children and visited your mentor. As I said during our talk, some things are better left undisclosed in certain company. Maybe now you can give my question a proper response.

Yours Truly,

Hamilton Bennett

Time froze for me. I stared at the letter, reread it, followed the logic of the wording, but it still wasn't registering. The shock wouldn't allow me to move from where I was situated. Slothlike, I slowly peered from the letter to the box. The pillow, *Dr. Green's pillow*, was stationed there as the final piece to the puzzle. I felt my eyes slowly widen in recognition, my nostrils began to flare, and eyebrows began twitching. When I saw the pillow again everything finally registered.

Bennett somehow knew who I was. But that wasn't what made me feel ill. The pillow in the box along with his words about Dr. Green's final moments could only mean one thing.

Dr. Green hadn't died due to natural causes, he had been murdered.

I tossed the letter aside and tore the pillow from the box, staring at it. Then the second wave of nausea hit me. Bennett must have murdered Dr. Green because of me. My mentor had died simply because I checked up on him yesterday. I rushed to the bathroom and immediately began vomiting into the toilet, hurling up all the painful emotions and bitter truths.

When there was nothing left to eject, I just began screaming. Not a scream of fear or surprise, but a constant cacophony of rage and hysteria. Luckily, the walls are reinforced so that the neighbors wouldn't hear me, but I'm pretty sure even those have their limits. I stayed that way, yelling until I had nothing left and lay on the cold tiles of the floor, motionless, looking out the door.

Barb slowly came strolling into the room. The rage in its eyes matched my own from a few minutes ago. "Are you going to just lay there?"

I eyed it fiercely as it stood over me. "Not in the mood, Barb."

"I'm sure nor was your mentor when Bennett killed him," Barb responded simply, there was no sarcasm or bitterness in its voice, just a statement.

"What do you want?" I asked. To some extent it was almost as if I was asking myself.

"To do what should've been done to that monster the first time we saw him," Barb walked up to me, leaned its tiger-like head to my ear, and whispered lustily, "Kill him."

I glanced up into those scarlet eyes. It was an odd sensation. The majority of the time, I barely wished to recognize Barb's presence, but the fact that this construct was a product of me, had to mean it couldn't be all bad. My eyes flicked over behind Barb, it was the severed head from the train. It merely stared at me and said nothing.

No more. I thought. Bennett couldn't be allowed to do this anymore. Stopping him wasn't enough, I had to end him, permanently. I gazed back at Barb and uttered the words it had been longing for its entire existence.

"Barb, you're on point," I said as coldly as the tile-floor my head rested upon.

Barb's mouth widened, revealing rows of barbed wire teeth, all tainted with crimson blood. "As you wish, my prince."

***

"Are you sure you want to do this?" Toni Romani asked as I spoke with him outside the door leading to the cell of one of the guards who had survived the train episode. He took a cigar out of his velvet pinstripe coat pocket and lit it with a lighter engraved with the family symbol.

I had given him the cliff notes version of what had transpired this morning and asked if I could come down to the interrogation black site, which was surrounded by trees out in the middle of nowhere of northern Georgia, so that I could get information. He agreed, but only on the condition that he met me there personally.

"You do it all the time," I responded, getting my tools together. I was in full attire now my coat had been stitched back together, my steampunk goggles replaced with a more advanced pair, and I was using my original bandana again. It gave it a nice touch of intimidation that I was currently going for.

He raised his head from the lighter, flicking it closed with a twist of his wrist. "Torture is different than combat. You either have to lack basic empathy or enjoy it on some level to get the answers you want."

"Don't worry Mr. Romani," I addressed him formally since we were in the field as I pulled the red and yellow, fang designed bandana over my mouth and pressed the voice modulator on the goggles, changing my voice to the high-pitched fear-inducing sound of Barb's. "On some level I am going to enjoy this."

I opened the door to find a bed, the kind you would see in a hospital, in the center of the room, positioned facing away from the door. An IV was attached to the patient, lying in the bed. They were currently out cold, the chemical goodness of morphine providing them with a peaceful slumber. It was the Aussie that I had put in my Infinite Loop. He had managed to survive once the attack ended. Mr. Romani said he landed on the tracks then had the wherewithal to immediately roll onto a soft bed of grass, which diluted the impact of the blow, but the fall had still left him immobile.

I walked over to the IV and yanked it from his arm. He woke up instantly, clutching at the location of the needle that had previously been there.

"Wakey, wakey," I sang to him menacingly.

His eyes widened in terror, the moment he heard my voice. I made sure to stay out of his line of sight, increasing his anxiety.

"No, no," he panted. "I gave him all the information he asked for."

"Well, you're talking to me now," I released the blades from my tonfas. The metallic sound of their unsheathing echoed in the tiny metal room.

"Please, just wait. We can negotiate," he pleaded, trying to turn his head to see me, but the gesture was futile. His body was mostly strapped down by leather belts.

"No. No negotiating. Just answers, understand," I placed the edge of one blade against his neck. He grew still, letting me know that I had his attention, and he would give me every answer I wanted.

"What do you want?" He let out tenderly, not trying to move his jaw too much, so that he wouldn't puncture his own throat.

"Bennett, where is his hiding hole?" I demanded.

"Uh, he moves constantly," the Aussie stammered, "He came in a couple weeks back because of the trouble you were causing."

I pressed the blades deeper into his neck but made sure not to puncture his jugular. "Excuse me?" I found his framing of my dealings with the Underground to be rather distasteful.

"Sorry, sorry. The bosses thought you were a problem, so they sent him in. He's like an overseer. Makes sure things get done, then reports back. They give him free reign to deal with the situation anyway he sees fit."

"Go on," I urged him.

"Right, he has different safe houses. I wouldn't know where to find him. That would be the clientele."

"Clientele?" I pressed.

"The people who buy the products?" He clarified.

"You mean the people that buy *people* into slavery," I whispered scathingly into his ear.

"Look dude, we just do what we have to so we can get by," even in the dim room, I could still make out the beads of sweat dripping down his head now. "They give me the money and I do what they ask. I'm just a hired hand, it's nothing personal."

"Tell that to the guy who got his head chopped off," I looked up to see the head on the scared guard's chest, glancing towards his previous captor with a detached look that lacked any sympathy. "Or the sister who had her brother snatched away from her. And you lay here and tell me it's not personal."

I straightened up my arm, forming an L with it, fist up, elbow down. Then I brought it down straight into his chest, puncturing him with my blades. He let out a scream that I knew could be heard in other cells.

"Wait!" He yelled. "I told you the truth. You don't have to do this. It wasn't personal, I swear."

I lowered my voice and hissed into his ear, "Oh, that's where you're wrong. While I thank you for not lying to me, this is most definitely personal."

His screams continued until he passed out from the pain when I was done with him.

Afterwards, I ripped the white tee from his unconscious body. He was going to need another one anyway after the mess that was made. I wiped my blades down with it as I strolled out of the cell. The shirt was now soaked in his blood, when I found my weapon to be satisfactorily cleaned, I discarded the rag to the floor.

Toni simply watched my casual display as I closed the cell door behind him. He didn't say a word, but I could tell from his eyes that he was disappointed, if not in my actions, then at least by my nonchalant reaction to them.

"Go ahead and say what you're thinking," I spoke first.

He dropped his cigar and stamped it out with shoes that probably cost more than a month's worth of rent for me. "This is a bad road you're about to go down. You should go home. Grieve before you decide what you're going to do next."

"Sitting on my hands, is what got me here in the first place," I gripped my weapons and squinted towards Toni. "Now is the time to act. I'm not waiting for Bennett to kill anyone else."

Toni sighed deeply before putting his hands in his pockets. He glanced off into the distance then spoke. "I saw the tail end of the train."

I tensed up at the mention of the caboose of the train. I hadn't given it much thought since then, about what happened to that guard. I lowered my head and grunted in acknowledgement.

"Only a leg was attached when the train stopped," he lowered his voice, "Devin, his remains were all over the tracks. Don't take this alter ego thing to heart. You're still human, not a demon."

He walked over to put a hand on my shoulder. I glanced up at him then looked back down. Barb was prowling in circles, patiently observing the exchange.

"You speak as if you haven't got as much blood on your hands either," I regretted saying those words the instant they left my mouth.

His hand tightened at the mention of his previous mafia duties. I turned to him, expecting anger in his eyes, but only found regret. "Devin, you and I are not the same person, nor do I wish us to be."

His words and demeanor didn't come as a scolding, but a gentle warning. Toni really didn't want me to continue on this path, but just like stopping the Underground, I was resigned to see this through.

"Thanks Toni, but I'm a big boy now," I stepped back, his hand slid down to fall back by his side as I moved back, away from his reach. "Take care of Sofia and Mew for me."

"Devin please," He reached out again, but I stepped back through a portal, on the way to my next unsuspecting victim.

***

I watched Chrome Dome walk around shirtless inside of his penthouse, a rather putrid sight to behold. He had just gotten out of the Jacuzzi, which I mercifully didn't have a view of from where I was perched. This was Midtown and it was starting to reach the late evening. The sun was beginning to hide behind some of the taller skyscrapers. Traffic was decreasing as the post-work rush was wrapping up.

I had traveled throughout the city seeking criminals or other shady figures that would've had potential dealings with Adkinson in the past. I stuck mostly to the shadows while questioning them because I hated going out in the daytime like this.

After roughing up a few individuals, I ended up with the address to Bennett's location. There were a few guards stationed outside the room and on the roof, but I had no intentions of dealing with them currently. I was merely scoping out the building as I waited for it to become darker, which would help with the plan of interrogation that I had for Adkinson.

The penthouse had a wide balcony, with room enough for a pool. Soft looking, pearl couches encircled a wooden table. The inside of the penthouse had glass serving as the walls. They were probably bulletproof given who was in the room. No way after what happened to him, would Adkinson risk being so thoroughly exposed to danger. I suspected the only reason he had the curtains open was because he thought that Bennett had broken me enough that I wouldn't come after him. Well, he was in for a big surprise.

"Are you going to let him off the hook?" Barb asked me. The barbed wire feline was clinging to the side of the building, similar to that of a lizard. It stared up at me in anticipation, pure delight in its eyes.

"Wasn't planning on it," I responded, focusing back on my mark.

"I can smell your bloodlust, but you have reservations," Barb noted.

I shook my head but didn't turn back to Barb. "Adkinson is the type of guy that if he meets an unfortunate end, there'll be too many eyes looking his way. It would have to be a pure accident with witnesses or a clear and obvious suicide. I can't cause the former without me, or my ability being seen, and I'm not skilled enough to do the latter without foul play being suspected. For most people I could, but not at this scale."

"You'll let him get off easy?" Barb spat. I could sense the hate and disgust emanating from Barb in Adkinson's direction. Throughout the course of the day, I had begun to lose track of which emotions were purely mine. We shared the same sentiment about most of the people we had to deal with today, so it was easy for our thoughts to blend.

"No, but I will be smart about it," I answered calmly.

Adkinson finally closed the curtains to his space, so I took that as my cue and jumped from my perch on the tower and into a portal below.

I came out near the breaker within the suite. I was inside previously, scouting the place before I could head back out. There was a monitor with security camera footage from the building, but there were no cameras in the room.

I reached into the box and cut the power.

"Wait, where are the lights?" I could hear Adkinson cry out in the now darkened suite. "Damn, safehouses. They would give me the cheap one."

A small flame danced in the darkness some feet away from where I was. Adkinson was wisely lighting candles to give the place some visibility. I pulled out my tonfas and unsheathed them, moving as swiftly as I could while maintaining silence. The floors were granite tile, so I didn't have to worry about creaking floorboards.

Continuing to move stealthily, I was finally in position behind Adkinson. He was bending over to light another candle on a coffee table in front of a mirror. When he stood back up, Adkinson caught a glimpse of me in the mirror, a pair of scarlet feline eyes glaring at him with the faintest trace of fangs visible below. He yelped in surprise, dropping the matches to the floor. When he stood back up and turned around, I was gone, vanishing into a portal behind me.

"Just the shadows," he murmured to himself. "Old age finally getting to me."

"It seems to have gotten to your head years ago," I whispered sweetly into his ear.

He let out a scream again and fell to the floor. He started scrabbling back to get away but ended up bumping right into me as I reappeared from behind him.

"Hey George," I bent down to look at him, the fangs of my bandana bearing down intensely on him. "We need to talk."

"It can't be, Hamilton dealt with you," he muttered to me, "You got beat. I saw it."

"Yes," I droned in annoyance. "No need to rub it in my face. Besides, his first mistake was not killing me. His second, is going to get him killed."

"What was his second?" Adkinson asked me, confused.

"Wouldn't you like to know?" I was going to snag him by the shirt, but remembered he wasn't wearing one. All he wore was a plain white towel, and no one wanted to see that.

So instead, I chose a different method. I withdrew my Desert Eagle and nonchalantly started loading it in front of him, making sure to be slow and deliberate, so that I appeared as if I had no reservations about putting a bullet in him.

"Wh...Why do you have that?" He stammered again, his eyes darting to the gun nervously.

"I think you know why George. Get up," I gestured with the pistol, and he rose accordingly. "Now, I'm going to ask a few questions and make a few demands. Then maybe, just maybe, you walk out of here alive. If not, well," I tapped the gun to my head. "I think you know what's next. Understood?"

He nodded quickly. I think I even heard a gulp.

"Bennett, where is he hiding?" I asked.

"I don't know," Adkinson replied hurriedly.

I sighed in disappointment, walked over to the kitchen, pulled out a dish towel then wrapped it around the barrel. Adkinson leaned forward to see what I was doing, until I shot in his direction. The bullet intentionally whizzed past his head and into the marble wall next to him. He ducked down, covering his head, and slid to the floor.

"Wrong answer, George," I admonished him. "This test isn't multiple-choice, it's free-response. You *will* give me detailed answers. Let's try again. Where's Bennett?" I trained my gun on his forehead.

"Wait, wait. I really don't know," I tsked and slid back the top of the gun. Adkinson raised his hands at the clicking sound. "He doesn't stay in one spot often. I only know where he'll be when we have a meeting or appointment for pick up."

"That's better. Now, when is the next appointment?"

"It hasn't been set yet. He advised me to lay low for a while until he took care of you."

I tapped my gun against my chin, pensively. That would make sense. However you look at it, the train wasn't a rousing success for either side. I had lost two people, while Adkinson lost his entire shipment with Bennett as the handler. From a professional standpoint, while he did hand the hostages in good order to Adkinson by the time the transaction was complete, it's bad business to lose a client's assets before they even got to take them home.

"What do you think we should do?" I looked at Barb who was crouched beside me.

"We? About what?" Adkinson questioned me, squinting perplexed.

I shot the muzzled pistol in his general direction without taking my focus off of Barb. That earned me a scared whimper in response. "Only speak when spoken to."

"Ask about the boy," Barb crooned, "Then ask of Bennett's ability. Finally, set the next meeting time."

"Good idea," I looked back to Adkinson who was staring at me dumbfounded. "Don't tell me you don't talk to yourself sometimes?"

"Uh, don't we all," he raised his hand in an 'I guess' gesture and smiled pitifully.

"Now where is the boy, the one with the dreadlocks? And before you say I don't know," Interrupting him because he was opening his mouth too quickly to answer, "I saw him get dragged out of there along with you, so don't lie."

"I, uh, Bennett took him. Said he'd hold onto him and put him to use. He'll be a part of the next shipment."

"Shipment of what?" My voice dropped to a deadly tone, it was the same tone Barb used when it had Sammy under its thorny foot. "Do you even hear yourself? These are innocent people that you treat like trading cards, or I guess in your case business *assets*."

"You don't get it do you. The Purification made Irregular trash, like you free game. You think this stops at me? Something is brewing and those with the most *assets* in our back pocket will be in the best position to weather that storm," Adkinson sneered back at me. This was the first time that he had shown some spine since I got here, like he was confident of something. It made me nervous.

"What's coming?" I walked over and slammed the handle of the pistol by the side of his head, but I didn't get the intimidated reaction I expected. Instead, he gave me a cruel smile.

"Wouldn't you like to know," he mocked, "You won't be around for it much longer anyway. Bennett is going to kill you. I'll enjoy watching your legacy burn in Hell with you!"

His comments made me realize why he was so confident. I'm not sure how Bennett tracked my movements, but if he had that ability, then Bennett could have been on his way now and the longer we talked, the greater the chance he would arrive. I would need to change tactics to reestablish the natural order.

"Listen here you fat prick," I slammed his head against the wall with one hand then pressed into his cheek with the blade from one of my tonfas. "I'll make sure both of you are waiting down there for me before I join you, but I have people to save right now. Isn't Bennett an Irregular, why do you treat him like he's on par with you?"

Chrome Dome took the bait. He whimpered as the cold obsidian blade drew blood yet grinned at my mention of Bennett. "You truly know nothing. Bennett wasn't born an Irregular he's an Enhanced."

I blinked. I had heard of the term before but couldn't recall the meaning. I turned towards Barb to piece things together.

"Enhanced, usually IPF trash." Barb relayed to me.

My expression dropped in exasperation. "Thank you, Barb."

"I'm not the one being interrogated," it lazily replied back.

"Um, are you okay?" Adkinson asked. From his perspective, I probably appeared to be talking to the air beside me.

I stiffened my arm, which in turn pressed my weapon even more firm into his throat.

"Not now, I'm thinking. Enhanced, huh?" I thought to myself until it hit me.

Barb was right. Enhanced was a term coined by the IPF during the Purification, a classification for some of their agents. In reality, an Enhanced is no different from an Irregular, just a human with special abilities. But where the definition of an Irregular applies to someone that either was born or acquired their powers accidentally, an Enhanced was an IPF agent that essentially got to cherry pick their abilities from a pool of powers for combat purposes. They took a page out of the 'fight fire with fire' catalog, but the danger of an Enhanced is that their fire is designed to burn significantly fiercer than their Irregular counterparts.

Their power is impressive, and in a world where superheroes don't exist anymore, you can tell the difference between a trained warrior with years of expertise, honing, mastering their craft, and a common thug that uses their abilities because no one can stop them. The attention to detail is missing.

I mean I've been doing this for a year and I'm still no better than a novice when it comes down to pure hand to hand combat. I had only fought the IPF once and now that I think about it, there was a good chance that Captain Woods was an Enhanced along with his lightning user lieutenant. Knowing that Bennett wasn't just a Normie, gave me slight comfort in explaining our skill gap, but not knowing his ability was unsettling.

After pondering everything over, I finally gave Adkinson my full attention. "What's his ability?"

"Not telling you," Adkinson spat back at me. He was really getting bold now. So, I held him in place with one arm then used my free hand to serenely shoot him in the kneecap.

He began to let out a yelp of pain, but I put my blade parallel into his mouth, the edges touching the corners of his lips. "Ahh, ahh, ahh," I warned him. "Scream now and you'll never speak again."

Tears welled in his eyes as he nodded in understanding. Barb purred in pleasure, watching the portly man squirm beneath my blade.

"What. Is. His. Ability?" I made sure to emphasize each word, so that he knew I was no longer playing games with him.

"He...he's a tracker," he panted between labored breaths. "Using your ability tells him where you are when he focuses on a particular person. He just needs skin to skin contact first."

It made sense now. When I first shook Bennett's hand, I had my gloves on, so he had no clue that I was using my ability at Fort Gordon. It wasn't until I left the clubhouse that we had shaken our uncovered hands. That's how Bennett had known to come to my office. I go in and out of my office using portals like someone living on the top floor of a high-rise apartment uses the elevator. From his letter, he couldn't have confirmed exactly that it was me making portals into the office, but once I visited Dr. Green after getting back, it wouldn't have taken a detective to make the connection.

So, it *was* my fault Dr. Green died.

If only I had gone anywhere else except straight to the nursing home using my ability or if I hadn't let Sofia keep my car, Dr. Green would've still been alive. I felt that pain thumping where my heart was. It hurt.

I raised the pistol to my chest, clutching at the spot where I felt the throbbing. I probably would've thrown up if Barb didn't prod me back to reality, which is troubling in of itself.

"We must press on then leave my prince," Barb spurred me on.

Nodding in response, "Right," I lowered my gun and eyeballed Adkinson, "Okay George, last thing. I need you to set up the next shipment and deliver a message for me."

"You think he'll listen to me? Ah, my knee," Adkinson was looking really pale now, sweat was clinging to him and his breathing was becoming more ragged as time progressed. "He'll know it's a trap."

"I guess you're right, but I do recall you being hell-bent on getting back at a particular doctor. I'm pretty sure he would believe you wanting to get back at me."

Adkinson looked sickly again and this time it had nothing to do with the constant rate at which he was losing his life force.

"How did you know about that?"

"The walls have ears George," I grinned knowingly at him. "The quicker you agree, the quicker I can leave," glancing down at his bleeding leg, "and then you can get that looked at."

"Okay, I'll do it," I released the pressure of my tonfa from him, letting him drop to the floor. I turned and began walking away. "You can't hide from him. Bennett's going to kill you and I'm going to enjoy it. You can't change anything, all of those people will be mine!"

Adkinson was screaming his lungs out as I departed. I mostly ignored him, but his line about not changing anything got to me. He was right. I temporarily maimed him, but he could simply get a cane and cover up the reasoning. He'd probably say that his knees couldn't handle the weight anymore. I had seen the real George Adkinson when I was in his hotel room. He was an ugly man, and I wanted the entire city to see it too.

I paused and turned around slowly before strolling back towards him. Releasing my blades yet again, my arms swung loosely by my sides as I got closer.

"Wait, what are you doing?" He raised his hands in pleading fashion, begging me to stop my march towards him.

"Do you have a favorite Tarantino movie, George?" I asked him, no different than how you would ask a stranger that you were getting to know.

Confusion set in over his face again, "What?"

"I'm sorry George, that's not the one I was thinking of, but good guess," I pulled his head closer to me and began carving into his face, the initials that would let the city know who had paid him a visit, letters that would turn attention to my activities, the initials that would be my first public declaration of my existence, P.C.P.

I'm pretty sure guards burst in, wondering what was wrong after hearing all of the screams, but I was long gone by then. I was back where I started, on my perch overlooking the penthouse. I can't say I was proud about what I did, but it was time to start bringing what was happening in this city to the light. Time to stop the monsters that go bump in the night.

"We know our enemy's ability and how we can get him to come to us. Should we go after him now?" Barb questioned me, sticking from the same spot where it had been earlier.

Thinking back to my vision and the billboard, I gestured at Barb that it wasn't the time yet. "I still need to do one thing before our reunion is ready. And I know just the person that has the answers."

Chapter Twenty-Six

Respect is an overused word in society, but the meaning has been significantly devalued. Regardless of who I'm dealing with, I do my best to afford them the respect they deserve, especially if I'm entering their house, but I was having a terrible day, so I wasn't in the mood to uphold such pleasantries.

I walked straight through a portal into one of MyKey's holdings, past the guard who was stationed behind the door. He stood there flabbergasted at my brazen entrance. Usually, I take the time to knock and I'm almost never in my full attire.

Although my suit usually matched the dress code for this particular establishment, it was easy for me to stand out. It was probably the absolute authority with which I walked in, or the blood on my person. The only people that had ever seen me in my full attire were the victims that I rescued or the guards who I knocked upside the head, most of whom never saw the light of day once the Romanis were done with them. Other than that I was mostly a rumor, but today I was slowly proving to the public that indeed this city's boogeyman is real.

The patrons of the establishment looked at me in shock as I strolled the halls looking for MyKey. Some stepped back away from me, others fled. They must've thought that I had finally changed my agenda and decided to go after him and his operation. That wasn't the case, but I wasn't going to waste time explaining the situation.

The twists in the hallways were familiar, seeing as I had been here before. It was the same building where he held his illegal fights. The cages were up ahead, the loud sounds of the crowd cheering on the competitors were easily distinguishable.

When I turned to find the cages, MyKey was there in his best Mad Max cosplay. He was facing me when I walked in. Someone, probably one of his employees, was whispering in his ear. MyKey nodded before dismissing him. A hush fell over the entire arena as he came over to meet me.

"Well, Mr. Phantom," he greeted me. Not surprised, but clearly displeased with my intrusion, "What cause brings you here to scare my clients away and disturb the peace?"

"I need information," I stated. MyKey slightly flinched but did a good job of not showing it to the rest of the crowd, as I spoke to him. My voice modulator was still on, so they were hearing the same voice that had plagued me so many nights.

"A simple phone call or appointment, couldn't do?" He recovered nicely, eyeing me rather pointedly, "Or a knock?"

I glanced at the crowd as he spoke to me. Every member of the arena had their eyes glued to the exchange. This is what I meant by respect. MyKey was probably more essential to the economy and workings of Peach City than even the mayor, just with less publicity. The people of the city knew he wasn't one to be casually dismissed or taken lightly. Considering the fact that I strolled in so brazenly and that we weren't exactly friends, my intrusion could be interpreted as a declaration of war, a metaphorical tossing of a white glove to the ground.

Despite our current environment, MyKey wasn't one to escalate a situation to physical confrontation, but he couldn't afford to let me walk all over him. Even though words couldn't describe the mood I was in, enough training as a therapist taught me that I needed to get a grip and channel it for now. Plus, MyKey may not have been my friend, but he had certainly been an ally over the past year.

I stopped scanning the crowd to peer back at him. "Forgive me," I tilted my head slightly, deferring to the host of the establishment, but not deep enough to convey submission, "I need to speak with you. It's urgent."

He smiled gracefully in return. Dipping his head also, matching the exact depth in which I tipped my head to him. "How urgent are we talking?"

"Deadly," I said matter of factly.

Whispers spread through the crowd, wild speculation on what I could have needed MyKey for. You see our relationship is an informal one at best and since I had just given him reverence publicly, no matter how minor, his stock had risen from a hard to reach itch to nearly untouchable and he knew it.

"Well, why didn't you say so?" He spun to the crowd, outstretching his arms. Elevating his voice as he addressed them, shouting, "What is with the gloomy faces? The guest of honor, none other than the Peach City Phantom, has graced us with his presence!" He made sure to say my name as loudly as possible, so that no one in attendance would have any doubt of who I was, "Enjoy the festivities! We still need another challenger for the champ," he clapped twice, and everything went back to normal as if I had never visited.

Dropping his voice, he walked past me, "Follow me."

And so I did, all the way to a tiny meeting room. There were only two tan folding chairs in the room and a tall floor lamp in the corner, lighting the room.

He extended his hand out, offering me a seat before taking his own across from me, crossing his legs comfortably. He watched me closely as I sat.

"I thought tonight was finally the night that you would declare me as your enemy," he said, the first time either of us had openly acknowledged the potential clash between us.

"Not tonight," denying his fears, but confirming our underlying tension, "I only have one enemy I'm focused on right now."

"Hamilton Bennett," he whistled. "Judging from your demeanor, I'm guessing it's personal now?"

I glared at the dark wall behind him. "We've moved beyond personal. We're in blood feud territory now."

He pursed his lips then took off his spiked shoulder pads, setting it to the concrete beside him. "What do you need?"

I leaned forward, my arms resting on my knees. "I need a location."

He raised an eyebrow at my request. "I think you would find a GPS or map more suitable."

I glared at him, a growl started up deep in my throat.

"Sorry, sorry," he raised his hands at me in a placating fashion. "Force of habit. Do you have anything for me to go on?"

I leaned back in my chair, thinking back to the vision or hallucination, don't know what to call it sometimes, I saw when I was in Bennett's grasp. I relayed to MyKey all the details I could recall from the billboard and the surroundings on top of the building we were on.

He rose a hand to stroke his chin, pensively. "Not a lot to go on, but I'll try. When do you need it?"

"Now."

His eyes lifted in surprise. "That serious, huh?"

"I told you, deadly."

"You seriously overestimate my abilities," he glanced back at me in an annoyed manner.

I folded my arms to match his demeanor. "Do I?"

"Okay, I can do it," he relented. "I'll need you to close your eyes, though."

"Seriously?"

Matching my tone from earlier, "Deadly."

"Alright," I closed my eyes, waiting for him to notify me when he was finished.

I was expecting him to make a phone call or something similar to that, but I felt the air beginning to swirl around me. A shiver went through my spine as the temperature in the room cooled considerably. I knew MyKey was still in his seat, but I felt movement around me as if the shadows themselves were swirling to surround me. The last I heard was a wailing in the room before everything abruptly went silent.

"Okay, you can open them now," he notified me. I opened my eyes to see him meeting me with a confident grin. "I got what you're looking for."

"Was the whole Halloween routine necessary?" I asked.

He raised another eyebrow at me. "Coming from the one whose voice sounds like they've put nails inside of a blender."

"Point taken. Where is it?"

"Bankhead. The abandoned Wellington Project Homes, also known as *Personas non Grata*. That place is devoid of anything valuable. Why would you need to go there?"

Knowing the information I did now, I rose to my feet slowly. "I'm not sure yet, but I will."

MyKey rose with me, picking up his shoulder pads and placing them back on. "Well, I hope you find what you're looking for," gazing upon me seriously, "but don't get yourself killed when you do."

"It's not my life you should be worried about," I replied, turning my back to him to open a gateway to the location he had given me. "Thanks MyKey."

"Farewell Phantom," he said back as I passed through.

Coming out on the other side, in front of the Wellington Homes. MyKey was right about it being a *Persona non Grata* for those wanting to visit. Broken glass from the windows and general debris was everywhere. Graffiti with gang paraphernalia marked the walls, I'm pretty sure this place was currently a trap house of some kind. Ladies of the night patrolled their territory in front of the building, while the homeless assumed the walk of those who hadn't had their faculties together in years.

It's funny how we often assume that everyone here is responsible for their current lot in life, but all it takes is one bad day and you're pushing a buggy down the street with your belongings in it. Look at me, I was experiencing the worst day of my life and it brought me here.

I moved towards the building but felt something grab my arm. I looked down to see Sammy tugging restlessly at my wrist, his heels digging into the ground.

"Don't go!" He pleaded desperately.

"Release him, boy," Barb came roaming towards us. "You know this is how it was always meant to play out."

Sammy shook his head desperately, "No, not here. Don't go."

"Why shouldn't I?" I looked down at him, confused.

"You just can't," he cried, refusing to answer my question.

"Barb is correct," The Spectre appeared, floating from behind me to face Sammy. "The truth has been hidden long enough."

"What is this, a conference call?" I screamed out into the open. A man pushed his buggy past me, giving me a puzzled look then shook his head as he moved along. Shows how crazy I must have looked if even I couldn't fit in here. "What is going on?"

"Tell him," Barb demanded of Sammy.

"No, I'm not going back here. Not ever again," with that, Sammy ran away, fading into the night. I guess I couldn't blame him. He had died here, so many years ago. The both of us having to relive that moment was probably too much for him to bear, but he was a hallucination, not a ghost, so his reaction was still odd to me.

I glared at Spectre looking for answers.

"It is not my burden to unload," he responded. "The boy will come around, but if not…"

He trailed off, leaving an unspoken warning to me. "If not, what?"

"You'll never know what he's hiding," Barb finished for him, lurking towards the homes. "Come, my prince. It is time to confirm your genesis."

"My genesis?" I repeated aloud, following after him. The three of us moved up the stairs to the roof. When we arrived, I knew this was the place. Everything about the rooftop looked familiar, from the texture of the solid concrete below my feet to the billboard on the west side of the building overlooking us. The face of the woman was no longer visible, it had faded from years of decay and neglect.

"Over here," Barb called to me. It was at the edge of the roof. The same edge that I leapt off of in my nightmares. The edge that Sammy was dropped from and where he died. I hesitated, but slowly made my way over. The Spectre followed close behind me, not speaking.

When I reached Barb, we all looked down. The alleyway below was empty, just clotheslines and a dumpster.

"Are you ready?" The Spectre finally spoke.

I looked at him contemplatively, taking my goggles off to gaze upon him clearly. The Spectre did not get along with Barb, so for him to be in lock step with it gave me slight comfort. If even my two darkest aberrations could get along then that meant I might've had a chance against Bennett, but I wouldn't be able to do it tonight with my emotions in flux the way they were, and I wasn't going to be able to do it in a straight up fight. I was going to need an advantage.

I shook my head at Spectre. "I need to make preparations," I looked back at Barb, who was staring at me intently, waiting for my answer, waiting to start the hunt. "Plus, there's something missing."

Peering into the abyss of the alley below, where a boy fell, and blood was shed. Tomorrow, I would return the favor in kind.

Chapter Twenty-Seven

I can see why people warn you about holding grudges. Plotting revenge takes an exorbitant amount of time and energy, both of which I was in short supply of. Preparing for tonight's festivities took the entire previous evening and all of my morning, bleeding into the early afternoon. I slept on a dusty bed overnight that probably should've been quarantined along with the rest of the building. I wasn't concerned about Bennett coming after me at the time, if he wanted me then he would've interrupted my meeting with Chrome Dome yesterday, raided MyKey's operation and if he remembered the Wellington Projects, then he could've paid a visit there also, which led me to believe he was looking forward to our next meeting and wanted me to stew in my grief.

I spent most of that time working, setting as many traps as I could think of and implementing every trick in my arsenal. I guess I know how Wile e. Coyote felt now.

I had finally returned to my office. There were still last minute items I wanted to gather and check on before the battle began. Stumbling out from my portal exit, I bumped my knee into my desk.

I let out a word that you shouldn't say in front of your mother and kicked the desk in frustration. Usually, I'm much smoother entering my office, but the lack of sleep combined with the emotional torrent swirling around inside of me was hampering my efficiency.

I tossed my goggles onto the desk and laid down on the couch, resting an arm on my forehead, thinking about how I got here. I just wanted to save one eight year old girl and now I was being tasked with trying to take down a criminal organization that had more money than I would ever see in my life, influence that most likely affected local governments if not also at the state and federal levels. Even if I overcame Bennett tonight, they would keep throwing people at me until I eventually fell too.

I sighed, resigned to my eventual fate, but I couldn't worry about that now. I rolled off of the couch to get to my feet, too tired to get myself up properly. A resounding thump echoed as I landed on my knees rather than my feet. At that moment, the door to my office opened and Sofia came running in.

From her attire, I could tell that she wasn't here working. In fact, she looked more suited to go jogging. Sofia had on gray sweatpants, a black cardigan with a hoodie, and brown running shoes. She had a disheveled look about her. It was telling that she was wearing her hair down. I actually liked it like that, but she clearly hadn't brushed it as strands of it, frayed out from her scalp.

"Devin, where have you been?" She rushed over to me as I propped myself back onto my feet. "I stopped by your place last night, but you didn't show up."

"I told you to stay with the Romanis, Sofia," I chided her.

"I know you said you didn't want visitors, but you weren't answering your phone," she responded defiantly, "I had to call Toni and he told me that you weren't acting like yourself."

"I'm fine," I said dismissively walking past her to my desk, picking up my goggles in the process.

"No. You're not doing fine. Where were you, and why is there so much blood on you?"

"Not mine," I replied without missing a beat.

"You didn't answer my question," her accent was starting to become more apparent, the further agitated she became.

"I don't need to check in with you about my whereabouts, Sofia. I think you're misunderstanding the nature of our relationship and -"

I never finished my sentence because Sofia stepped forward and in one motion slapped me, hard. I stood there stunned. Slowly reaching up to touch my stinging cheeks, I looked at my hand, confused on how I should feel about the blow, but with everything that happened in the past two days, I could only settle on one emotion, anger.

I frowned at my hand then glared at Sofia, whose fury matched my own. Clearly, I had crossed a line and she sure as hell was going to make it known.

"You promised you wouldn't treat me like that," she seethed in a very low voice, her Argentinian accent was thick now. "There's nothing that I misunderstand about our relationship. You've made it pretty clear where I stand," she was staring daggers into me, cutting much deeper than Bennett's claymore ever could.

We stood there in tense silence, glaring at each other until I finally relented with a tired breath. I didn't have time to pick any more fights. I walked past her towards my storage closet.

"Where are you going?" She said, clearly not pleased with me just brushing her off.

"To kill Bennett," I stated quietly, but there was definite weight to my words.

"You couldn't beat him last time. What makes you think you can now?" She asked as I could hear her voice get closer as she approached me from behind.

I flinched at her words as if she had just verbally slapped me, just as she had done earlier. That was the thought running through my head at the current moment. I honestly didn't know what was different, but I had to believe I could beat him, or I might as well burn all of my gear right now and give up.

"The truth can hurt," Barb appeared inside the closet door as I opened it. "You should tell her what the difference is now."

"I'm not telling her that," I responded tersely.

"Tell me what?" Sofia asked.

"I'm not talking to you," I replied before starting to dig through the ammo for my pistol.

"Send her away. Distractions will get you killed," The Spectre offered me that piece of advice as he hovered above Barb.

"I'm glad you two are friends now, but you both know the rule about speaking in public," I scolded them as I deposited bullets into the clip for my Desert Eagle.

"Are you talking to *them*?" She asked me. The anger had left her voice, replaced with pure concern as she witnessed me in the midst of a conversation with my hallucinations.

I turned to her with a sad look and grunted in confirmation.

"Which ones?" She asked.

Other than Dr. Green, Sofia was the only one that I had described my hallucinations to in depth. Now she was the only one left, so I understood what she was asking me. Acknowledging the Spectre would've been fine, but Barb was a different story. I turned to Barb and bit my lip. No way was she going to let me out without raising a fuss if I told her, but I also didn't want to lie to her.

"Sof," I replied quietly.

"You see *it* don't you?" She pressed, trying to confirm her suspicions.

"Sofia, please just go," I knew she wouldn't leave that easy, but a small sliver of me wanted to believe she would hear the pleading in my voice and respect my wishes.

"Devin don't go. It's going to get you killed," she knelt down beside me, placing both of her hands on my shoulders so that she had my full attention. "You've never trusted it before, why now?"

"Things are different now, I feel," I paused, "alone," referencing my current circumstances.

She shook her head furiously. "That's not true. You have the Romanis, your new sidekick. You have *me*," tears were flowing from her eyes, Sofia's desperation to get me to stay was on par with my earnestness to make her leave.

I could hardly look at her now. Everything she said was true, but I didn't want to accept it. Logic was shrouded by the thick veil of rage that enveloped me.

"I need to do this, just support me by going back to the Romanis."

"Please, don't go! The way you are now, you're going to get yourself killed tonight," she looked away briefly, then met my eyes with a deep intensity that I had never felt from her before.

"I love you."

I lost my breath. Staring into her turquoise eyes, I could see that there was no greater truth that existed between us. We had playfully said it to one another before and there are multiple variations of love that you can have for someone or something, but this was perhaps the purest form that she was expressing to me. Despite my reservations about being in a relationship with her, I felt the exact same way and we both knew it.

The problem is that using those words isn't a cure all potion. The timing in which she expressed her feelings were usually reserved for the climax of a movie, but this was real life. Love couldn't bring back the dead, or in this moment, heal the searing sensation in my heart. I knew what I had to do, but I also knew that I wouldn't be able to put the toothpaste back in the tube on this one.

I gently placed a hand on her cheek with a pained smile on my face and simply uttered in a quiet voice, "Go."

She looked away from me quickly, clenching her eyes, fighting back the tears that I caused. I knew that I had just broken my best friend's heart, and with it my own.

I stood up to get the rest of my gear to leave. I didn't need this on my mind before squaring off with Bennett. Before I could take two steps, I heard her call out to me.

"You don't want to leave."

I halted my trot and looked around in confusion. I was in my office, but I didn't really remember why. The work day would've been over by now. I peered at my attire, for some reason I was in my fighting gear.

Was I going somewhere? I thought to myself.

I wasn't really in the mood to leave. My office is cozy at this time of the day. I could've stayed longer if I wanted to. I saw that Sofia was in the room with me, but why was she on the floor? Her eyes looked puffy, like she had been crying for some reason. Maybe I had been comforting her. I couldn't leave now seeing her like this.

I wondered why she wasn't looking at me. She avoided direct eye contact as I cocked my head to get a better look at her. She was biting her lip as if something were greatly troubling her.

Weird.

I took my attention away from her and looked at my hands. There was blood on them. Why did I feel like I just came back from somewhere important? Even though I wanted to stay, I still felt there was something I desperately needed to do. I saw Barb staring deliberately at me.

"Break the bond," it said in an even voice.

My gaze turned to Sofia again. Her face was going through different expressions, in a very shifty manner, like she was hiding something. Like she was guilty of something.

I glanced back to Barb, who nodded steadily, and then glared back at Sofia. She winced when my gaze fell upon her. She knew that I recognized what she had just done. She had used her charm ability in order to get me to stay.

Because of my condition, the one concrete promise between us was that she could never use her ability on me without my explicit consent. For the both of us, this was non-negotiable, and she had just broken it when I had my back turned.

The embers of my rage became a tempest of fury as I thought about the betrayal of trust.

"Devin, wait," Sofia quickly rose to her feet, outstretching her arms to appease me as she approached gingerly. "I didn't mean to. I got caught up in the heat of my emotions…"

"You promised," I said between clenched teeth. It was my turn to remind her of the vow she made.

"I'm sorry," she cried to me desperately, reaching a hand up to my cheek. I stepped back away from it, turning my back on her.

My head felt like someone was driving a stake through it, with the splitting pain that began. I was trying to recall the exact moment she had charmed me. The thing about her ability is that it makes your memory fuzzy, a temporary malaise settles over you as you acquiesce to the effect. It takes a very strong mind to not be affected by it. The only other way her ability wouldn't fully activate is if the command didn't match the person's desires as in the case of Vee earlier.

I didn't have the former, so I needed to remind myself of what was real. Which was forcing me to relive everything that had happened the past few days, every bruise, every heartache, every mistake that got someone killed. I felt like my insides were melting from the agony of it all. I was driven to a knee, clutching my sides.

"Get up. Focus," Barb called to me.

"Rise," The Spectre followed after Barb.

"Are you okay?" Sofia asked in concern.

I clutched my ears. It was just all too loud, so many voices, and none of them my own.

I felt a hand grab my shoulder.

In a fury, I spun on them without thinking and grabbed them by the base of the neck, pressing them against the wall. It was Sofia. She was looking at me with worried eyes, but she was calm. She spoke to me in a soothing voice, without having to use her powers.

"It's okay," she whispered while calmly holding my face in between her palms, but I could still feel them shaking. "Just breathe, just breathe. Come back to me, *mi amor*."

I felt my breath become steadier. I tried to focus on just her voice, but then I saw the severed head again in my periphery.

"You letting people off the hook is what got me here in the first place," he observed.

"Ignore him, my prince," Barb said to me.

"Focus on the task at hand," Spectre wailed in his voice.

I closed my eyes, wincing from the pain within me. It was just too loud again. I felt the surge of everything that was welling up in me, the fire was now an eruption that could no longer be quelled. I launched my free fist out, smashing into what was in front of it. I heard a sick cracking noise as if something had just snapped that wasn't meant too.

Then, I remembered that I had Sofia in my grasp. *God no.* From the sound that I heard, I could only pray that I hadn't just killed her.

My eyes snapped open in a panic. There was a hole in front of me, where one of my bookshelves had been. Dark blue flames flickered around the new opening, dancing with newfound energy as it had finally been released. I was confused by the sight. Flame abilities weren't something I had in my repertoire. How I managed to pull that off was beyond my reasoning.

I then looked towards Sofia. I had just missed her head by centimeters. When my eyes met hers, I saw something in them that I've never seen from her before, absolute terror. She thought that I was actually going to kill her and considering the fact that I had swung blindly it was a real possibility that I could've. When she caught the recognition on my face, the fear flickered away as if it had not even been there, but I knew that it was going to stick with me for a long time.

"I'm sorry," I said, immediately releasing her, "Go."

"Wait, I-" she started.

"Go now!" I screamed at her.

She cowered away from me and slinked away to the door, timidly giving me one last glance from the half-opened door before closing it behind her, leaving me to my demons.

I stared at the hole in the wall. That could've been Sofia, decapitated by my rage. I felt disgusted with myself. I was really starting to lose control. Bennett may have been the stimulus for my mood, but he wasn't responsible for my actions. I had chosen to torture that prisoner, to disfigure Adkinson. Their screams and whimpers gave me a sense of power that I hadn't felt since Bennett stole that away from me on the train. He wasn't the one that brushed Toni off, stormed MyKey's place, or perhaps ended my friendship with Sofia.

My phone started buzzing in my pocket. I withdrew it from my pocket quickly and looked at the caller id, it was Mr. Jenkins. Taking the phone, I chucked it at the wall. The device didn't break but I heard a loud smack before it plopped to the ground with a thud. I was in no mood to deal with Mr. Jenkins temperament today. If I saw him right now, I might've actually killed him.

I sat on the floor of my closet and reclined back. I was planning on waiting at the apartments before my showdown with Bennett, but it was my confrontation with Sofia that had truly taken a chunk out of me. I was twirling in the toilet bowl of turmoil that had been partly of my own doing. I was in need of a lifeline, but I don't know if I would've taken it given the opportunity.

Barb came up to me and simply laid it's head on my chest. This time I didn't feel the pain from its touch, but what I did feel was a bitter cold. The kind of cold that has nothing to do with the temperature, but when the fire inside of you is extinguished and you feel nothing. I lay there like that for what had to be at least an hour before I heard a knock on the door to the inside of the closet.

"Well, I guess this is what rock bottom looks like," a bemused voice spoke to my downed body.

I rolled my eyes in annoyance because I knew how this particular exchange was going to end. "How'd you find me?"

I sat up to look at Emma who was leaning against the door, one foot up resting against the doorframe. She was in her gray battle cloak, both hands covered within the robe.

"Sofia gave me a call. Said I should check up on you before you go and do something stupid," she leaned her head back to look at the new hole in the wall. "Judging from the change of decor, I'm guessing I'm already too late."

I turned away from her, gritting my teeth in frustration. I had no idea to what extent Sofia had told her about what happened, but Emma was no idiot. She easily could've figured out what went down in the office, I mean she was the first person to actually work out what my true identity was all by herself.

"Since when have you two been pen pals?" I asked, nonchalantly.

"Angel and her exchanged numbers when you were down for the count at the mansion."

I winced at her phrasing of my condition at the time. "What time is it?"

She turned over her shoulders to read the clock behind my desk, that wasn't visible to me. "About six. Are you ready to head out?"

"You're not coming with me," I replied back, rising to my feet and regathering my gear. I started with my tonfas, sheathing the blades and placing them in my waistband carefully.

"What are you talking about?" She took her hands out from her cloak, revealing the Thalia mask that was hidden underneath. "I came prepared."

"You're not coming, nor are you stopping me," next, I grabbed my polished Desert Eagle, holstering it into position and getting an extra clip to go with me.

"Oh, come on," she whined. "You can't sideline me now. Every mission has been a success so far."

I felt the anger well back up inside of me. Ever since I met Emma and Angel, I've had some of the most fun in my battle against the Underground and I was truly grateful for their support in the field, but I also couldn't stop thinking about all the unnecessary danger that I had been placed in because of them, the chaos that we had created, and the carnage brought upon us. I thought of the man now missing a head, the sister now missing a brother. We had differing definitions of the word successful, and I was definitely not in the mood to let that comment slide.

"Successful, huh?" I questioned her. "Is that what you call it? Is getting on the IPF's radar what you would call successful? Is getting a child kidnapped successful to you? How about beheading?" All of the emotion was pouring out of me now, the grief, bitterness, the anguish. It was too much to bear, so it continued to flow. "In a year, I hadn't lost one hostage, not one, but I meet you and I've already lost two. I went to that stupid party with you, now Bennett knows my identity and God knows who else he's going to tell. He killed my mentor because he knew who I was!"

I was seething now. My nails were digging into the palms of my hands as I had them balled up so tight.

Emma folded her arms, glancing away as I verbally tore into her. From her perspective, she was probably just trying to cheer me up, but Emma's casual attitude had finally gotten to me and right now I truly wished that I had never run into her, regardless of if I saved her or not.

"We're a team now," she spoke in a soft voice, not looking at me. "Siblings, remember?"

"Right now, I need you to be a stranger," I placed my gloves on deliberately and pulled my red and yellow, shark teeth bandana from its shelf. I had had it with all the talking and arguments, it was time to do what needed to be done.

I walked to the exit from the closet, but Emma stepped in my way to block my path. Neither of us spoke, but we both glared at each other, waiting to see who would back down first. I easily could've just made a portal to get by her, but this was a matter of pride. If I acquiesced to her, I might as well have handed Bennett my cloak and goggles, then bow down to him in submission, begging for leniency.

Emma saw the resolve in my face, but still did not move. Instead, she retreated within herself bringing out Angel to take her place. I admit, a part of me wanted to take a step back on the spot, but I firmly held my ground.

A thought hit me, I could use this opportunity to my advantage.

"Angel, you would understand better than anyone," I pleaded with her while she stared at me unmoving. "What if someone tried to hurt Emma? You would burn the world down to get to them."

A grimace flashed across her face for a split second, like a bad memory had crawled its way to the surface and she was swatting it back down. I had just struck the right chord.

I pressed on. "Dr. Green meant the world to me, so let me avenge him."

Without making a sound, Angel nodded and simply stepped out of my way, turning perpendicular to the door, similar to opening a gate to release the animals. She didn't look at me as I was passing her, but I felt a sudden yanking on my coat pocket. I looked back at her inquisically. Maybe she had changed her mind.

She side eyed me then in a warning tone said, "Fools rush in where angels fear to tread."

"What does that mean?" I asked her, squinting my eyebrows.

"It means don't die, Edgelord." she started heading towards the door but called back to me one more time without turning around. "Emma would never forgive you, nor would I."

With that, she left the room and now all of the distractions were out of the way. I peered towards the goggles I had placed on my desk earlier. Their presence seemed heavier, a burden that I was never prepared to bear, but was asked to carry anyway. I went over and picked them up. Stopping to examine my reflection in their lenses, I noticed that I looked awful. My eyes were completely bloodshot, red veins ran to my emerald eyes. My pupils were near fully dilated, like I was some kind of mad man. I touched the scar above my left eye, the first of many. It made me think of how many other scars I was going to get tonight and which one of them could be my last.

With a sigh, I put the last piece of my attire on, snapping the goggles into place then headed towards the window. I opened them up and crouched on the frame, looking out over the city. It was a cloudy night. An overcast had settled over the sky and there were possible thunderstorms later, a fitting metaphor for how I was feeling inside right now.

Correspondingly, there wasn't much traffic below, so I would be fine when I descended out the window. I turned back to my office to be greeted by the sight of Sammy standing in the middle of it alone. He was watching me with a grim expression on his face, a look that seemed so much older than anything the boy should've been able to manage.

"We can't beat him there," he warned me. "We won't get a second chance this time."

"So we make the most of it this time," I responded, nodding towards him reassuringly. I wasn't sure if I believed it or not, but now wasn't the time to debate that.

I pulled my bandana over my mouth, obscuring my face, turned back to the city and dove out the window, descending down into a portal below that would take me to the Wellington Homes and the biggest if not final fight of my life. I dismissed all of the previous thoughts, arguments, and doubts from my head, but held onto the pain, held onto that rage. My mind was clear now because there was killing to be done.

Chapter Twenty-Eight

Rarely do I fully let loose in a fight, but circumstances had changed. With Barb consistently in my head and the anguish that I had been dealing with the past couple days, there was only one thing on my mind. Bennett died, *tonight*. If anyone else got in my way, well, they'd have to join him in the grave.

I knew with his ability he'd know how to find me, so he'd also recognize when I was directly challenging him. I made constant miniature portals, as not to expend too much energy, within the drab room that I was currently in. No way he wouldn't see the extensive use of my abilities as a request for his presence. This also meant that I was sacrificing the element of surprise of ignorance to his ability, but at this point I didn't care. When I figured that my power usage was sufficient, I pulled out a wooden chair and sat in it backwards, facing towards the splintered door in front of me.

Maybe twenty minutes later, I heard a jiggling of the door knob. In the moment, time seemed to slow down. The air I breathed became thicker and I tensed up like a cat about to pounce upon its prey. As the door swung open, it revealed the man that killed my mentor. Hamilton Bennett stood there in the doorway, Claymore sheathed behind his back. His customary brown trench coat was traded in for a blood red one, which I found to be fitting of the circumstances. Of course, he also had that stupid orange ascot. A smarmy smirk donned his face as he looked down his nose at me.

"I was wondering how long it would take you to figure it out. The good doctor had to die for your lack of intuition," he needled me.

Don't let him rile you up. You do this all the time. I cautioned myself.

I flared my nostrils and tightened my grip on the chair. I couldn't take him in a pure hand-to-hand fight, so I had to keep my wits about me.

"Barb, status report," I muttered under my breath.

"Others lurking, maybe eight," Barb appeared beside me and reported the details of my environment. Barb laid down beside me, its red eyes looking just as intently at Bennett as I was behind my goggles. At that moment it would have appeared as if a tiger and his handler were one, ready to strike together at a moment's notice.

"What's wrong? No welcome for me," Bennett asked, still trying to antagonize me.

"Why don't you tell all of your friends to join the party?" I responded, my voice devoid of emotion, my eyes never leaving him nor blinking.

He sighed as the smug smirk disappeared from his face. His eyes had a slightly disappointed look in them. Resignedly, he lifted his hand and snapped twice. Immediately, teams of two crashed through the four windows into the room dressed in black and crimson paramilitary garb, all with weapons trained on me.

I didn't flinch.

I looked around lazily regarding my situation, similar to how Mew would do at home. "All of this for me?"

"No expense was spared for the Peach City Phantom," Bennett spread his hands out in acknowledgement. "A coward like you may have escaped me for all of these years, but I never let a target get away. You *heroes* never learn that innocents suffer because of your actions."

"Does this include the innocents you help kidnap for the Underground?" I spat back.

"The Underground, is that what they call us?" He chuckled before shrugging his shoulders in admission. "An unfortunate occurrence for a better cause. I spent years with the IPF trying to stamp out ants like you. First, it's you and your little sidekick. Then, I'm setting my sights on something bigger. General Watson and the IPF are next. They accomplished their goals, but he's like a hungry animal that doesn't know when to stop eating. An army is needed to take them down."

"Any means necessary then?" I questioned. "Even killing a child."

"It's not my fault if you couldn't save him," Bennett sneered. We were both talking about that night where our paths first crossed. The night he killed Sammy. The night he destroyed my sanity.

"*Kill him. Kill him now, my prince,*" Barb hissed in contempt.

I nodded and slowly stood up from my chair, but kept my left hand gripped to the top.

"One of us dies here," I told him simply. It wasn't intended as a threat. It was a simple truth that both of us openly recognized. Either him or I took our last breath tonight.

"I couldn't agree more," he smiled in reply.

The corners of my lips rose, but what was on my face was not a smile.

The next part isn't for the faint of heart.

I tightened my grip on the wooden chair and while spinning to gain momentum launched it at the nearest thug. The chair crashed into them and launched the goon into the nearest wall. Their body landed with a loud thud, and they slumped to the floor. Then all hell broke loose.

Bennett's lackies were taken by surprise, but they soon showed that they were well-trained professionals. Those with guns stepped forth and kneeled to let loose repeated short bursts with their assault rifles, while those with melee weapons stepped back and readied themselves to attack on the reload.

The problem with being trained for every situation is that you can't possibly train for every situation. That's why guerilla tactics are so popular. At some point, a genius recognized that maybe we shouldn't walk in a straight line, give a live musical performance, and be target practice for the enemy. This genius was an agent of chaos, and for tonight so was I.

I wasn't just waiting in a broken down apartment so that I could be riddled with bullets, so I introduced the gunman behind me to my Infinite Loop. They began falling repeatedly through portals above and below. Creating another portal, I jumped in and retrieved a wooden stake more fitting for medieval times. Then I created one more portal above me and pushed it vertically three-fourths of the way through, closing the gateway behind it. The entry point of the stake was in between my Infinite Loop, so the gunman became impaled on the stake as they fell through the portal. Blood slowly trickled down the wood as their body spasmed lifelessly on the stake.

Seven to go.

I withdrew my tonfas and immediately unsheathed the blades, no kiddie gloves today. Jumping through the gateway used to receive the stake, I reentered the room right behind one of the gunmen. I drove a blade through the back of their skull, his blood stained the obsidian blade as it protruded through the front of their noggin.

Six.

I spun yet again and threw them through a portal I created in front of me. The body smacked into the third gunman, knocking them to the ground. The wooden floorboards creaked as they both landed. I jumped in after the body I threw and then came down upon the third shooter as they attempted to gather themselves. I savagely smashed the front edge of my tonfa into their head repeatedly. The sickening sound of the dark metal blades along with the palladium sticks filled the room.

Five.

In my blind rage, the final gunman had time to train their weapon upon me. I noticed it on the edge of my peripheries through the live scan of the room through my goggles. Fortunately, they were slightly shaken by my display of barbarism, so their gunfire was a bit scattered. Some of the bullets hit their mark on me, but my coat had been relined with Kevlar, so none of the gunfire pierced my suit.

I turned to them and reached out my hand. I grabbed them by the back of their neck through a portal I created behind them and dragged them backwards, except this time I changed the exit point to be out of the same window they had arrived in.

Four. All in a matter of seconds.

"Yes, kill them all," Barb lustily encouraged me. It was taking euphoric pleasure in my actions. I was becoming what Barb had always wanted me to be, cold and ruthless.

I stood up with both of my weapons equipped and looked at the other three fighters, challenging someone to step to me. Bennett stood in the same spot in the doorway, not making a move to help any of his underlings.

The three other thugs looked at each other questioningly, unsure of who would make the next move. I regarded them while they silently debated amongst themselves. These fighters didn't wear masks like the gunman. I guess it would affect their fighting ability since they were close range fighters. There were two men and one woman. They all had short crew cut hair and each of them sported a different type of tattoo on their neck. The woman had a Cobra snake entangling from one side of her neck to the other. The other guys sported a bear and a tortoise ink, respectively.

"Poison type, rager, and a tank," I muttered to myself as I analyzed my next move.

Bear tattoo revealed two Freddy Kreuger styled claw gloves and charged at me. I initially brought my sticks up to block, but quickly realized he would probably break both of the blades along with my arms. So, I stepped aside and parried his blow which came crashing down and smashed the wooden chair I had used earlier to bits. The gloves indicated he wasn't a pure polymorpher, but the tattoos must mean that they were all potentially totem bearers. They were probably born with these abilities but adorning the symbol or representation of your totem would multiply your strength and other than a brand there is no greater permanent symbol a person can have on their body than a tattoo.

He started swinging his paws (no pun intended) at me in succession and I continuously bobbed and weaved out of the way. Eventually, I noticed that I was being cornered. Again, I'm not a hand-to-hand specialist. The gunmen were easy to handle because I had the element of surprise and portals are much easier to use at a distance, but when pressed, it can be tricky to use them effectively without leaving myself open. From my experience, gunmen are usually one-dimensional and typically not Irregulars. Otherwise, they'd most likely use their abilities.

As I was still on the defensive, my goggles indicated an incoming projectile. As Queen Cobra spat her venom at me, I ducked to avoid the shot but left myself open to an uppercut to the gut from my current opponent. The blow lifted me off of my feet and I landed uncomfortably on my back. Before I could completely gather my wits, I caught a glimpse of him standing over me to deliver a double-fisted sledgehammer blow. I rolled out of the way only to find myself on the receiving end of a kick to the stomach from Tortoise. These three clearly worked together often and it showed. They were efficient in their coordination. Mr. Bear left openings for Queen Cobra to secretly launch her venom and vice versa. I'm pretty sure Tortoise took the majority of blows, so attacking him head on would be foolish. I had to devise a plan, quickly.

I groaned as I recovered from the successive shots to my ribs. No way they weren't fractured again after all of the recent damage they'd taken lately. I crawled a couple of feet but stopped from exhaustion. Mr. Bear walked up to investigate my current condition. When he got close enough, I created a portal beneath his feet and we both fell through the floor to the room beneath us. Fortunately, I knew I was positioned over a bed, while Mr. Bear was positioned over a rounded nightstand.

He broke through the nightstand. Blood oozed through his uniform from the splinters that pierced his back and torso as he tryingly got to his feet. I rolled off of the bed, swiftly picking up one of the bigger splintered pieces of wood to begin stabbing him between the ribs. Mr. Bear let out a roar mixed with pain and defiance. He then began churning his legs as we were closely entangled in the tight quarters. I don't know where he was getting his strength from, but I felt myself getting pushed back as he continued pressing forward. Looking over my shoulder, I noticed that we were headed for a window. He was going to either push me out and die from his wounds or he was coming down with me. Either way, Mr. Bear wanted his last act to be my demise.

I desperately continued stabbing him with the wooden fragment. We were edging ever closer to the opening and if he didn't drop in time, I had a first class ticket out the window.

Good thing that I came well equipped. I released the stake and reached for my holster. I whipped out my .44 Desert Eagle and put one shot into his brain. He began slowing down, but his momentum was still enough to have us both careen out of the window if I didn't do something. So, I made a gateway behind me in which he pushed me through as I completely entered, I closed it before he could also come through. When I reappeared from the opposite direction of the window, all I could hear was the sound of him crashing through the glass before I could turn around.

Three more.

That battle was more exhausting than I expected, and I still needed to kill that bastard Bennett. Playtime was over.

I could hear the creaking of footsteps and distorted voices above me, probably wondering what was going on below them, with one pair of steps sounding decisively louder than the other. I focused upon the lighter steps and created a portal underneath. Queen Cobra fell through the ceiling of the current room and bounced as she hit the floor, hard. I didn't give her much time to recover. I ran over to where she landed and grabbed her by both legs.

I'm not particularly strong. Angelus in both of her forms is much stronger than me and I wouldn't be able to pull off what I was about to attempt on the recently departed Mr. Bear or Tortoise. But anger and adrenaline can give us all powers we never thought we had.

So with all my might, letting out a cry of effort and twisting around with both of her legs in my hands, I was able to lift and slam her through the table in the room. The air immediately left her body and she struggled to collect her breath. I methodically stalked over and looked down upon her. Her eyes were glossed over and there was blood beginning to pool from the back of her head due to the impact with the table. My goggles gave a warning that a projectile was incoming. I leaned to my right to avoid the venom as her jaws disgustingly unhinged in order to spit at me. She still had fight in her yet, and this was her last ditch effort.

"Choke on this," I said evenly and punctured her mouth from below her jawline with my blade. Queen Cobra instantly started convulsing.

I kept her pinned until the convulsing ceased and her breathing stopped. I looked into her eyes as the life in the snake slit eyes began to fade and returned to the circular form of a human.

Two.

I caught quick glimpses of myself in the broken pieces of glass that plastered the floor. The reflections showed my face, coat, and hands all covered in blood. The liquid life force was dripping from my goggles. I attempted to wipe them away, but the mess on my hands only smeared them. I looked at my tonfas on the ground. The color had changed from its normal metallic silver to a dark hue of red. I choked back a sob of disgust. This was murder, through and through. There were plenty of chances to stop, but I was enjoying myself too much. Bennett was the only one that absolutely had to go, but the rest, while probably still aligned with chaotic evil, were just pawns doing their duty, no matter how despicable it was.

"This is not the time to dwell on morality," Barb rested its head on my lap, comforting me. "We are too far on this path. Continue and do what needs to be done." Though resolute, there was genuine regret in its voice. This was the first time that I've heard Barb speak so saddened about killing, the joy and pleasure from before now departed.

I tilted my head in acknowledgement. After closing Queen Cobra's eyelids, I rose to my feet, walking deliberately over to pick up my tonfas. I let out a deep sigh, tired from what I had gone through but resolved to see this through.

I ran towards the bed and jumped on top, the corresponding force propelled me upwards into a portal above me where my goggles detected the heat signature of

Tortoise. I rose up out of the gateway and held my tonfas beneath his chin, front up and blades down. For a second, I paused to look into his eyes. In your last moments, your eyes can reveal all of the emotions you're going through. I saw him cycle through surprise to fear and then finally a sad acceptance, but it's the fear that I knew would stick with me because I know he saw the same thing that I had just seen, a demon. Finally, I double tapped the triggers and blew his brains out with the shots I had installed into my weapons.

One.

Landing on my feet, I turned towards Bennett. Stalking slowly over to him, I withdrew my Desert Eagle from its holster and put three bullets into the goon I had slugged with the chair earlier, never taking my eyes off of the Southern Gent.

Zero. Just Bennett left.

Bennett stood planted at the doorway. He regarded me for a second before looking at the mess left from my chaotic rampage. A hint of disapproval tinged his eyes for a moment before he looked back at me, and his face hardened. He had finally gotten angry. I doubt any of those I had slain were particularly close with Bennett, evidenced by his complete lack of effort to try to intercede on their behalf, but those were still men and women under his command, and he had just led them to be slaughtered like animals. He now knew what it felt like to be directly responsible for someone else's death and would have to live with that. Fortunately for him, I didn't intend for that to be long.

Bennett let out a deep breath through his nose. "Demon indeed. You live up to your secondary name."

I didn't respond, just kept staring intently at him.

"At least I have the decency not to kill those I take, just those in the way," he looked again at the bodies in the room, "Though misguided, I at least thought you were an honorable man, but you are no better than a barbarian."

I bared my teeth towards him from underneath my bandana, but yet again the expression on my face was far from a smile.

"Not here," I gestured with my head upwards to the roof, "There."

Creating a doorway behind me, I paced backwards through it and waited for Bennett to join me.

"How poetic," he drawled as he stepped through. "It is just like that night."

We were up on the roof of my original failure, letting Sammy die. It was night time and the skies were overcast, the light of the moon obscured by the clouds. I glanced down to where he had dropped Sammy all those years ago. There were still traces of barbed wire below, but I added some more during my preparations. This is where I intended for Bennett to also meet his end, screaming, followed by the sound of barbed wire tearing into flesh.

"Tonight, it ends," Barb stated as its presence lurked behind me.

"Exactly," with that I rushed towards Bennett, both of my obsidian tonfa blades unsheathed and hanging by my sides.

Bennett withdrew his Claymore and took up a defensive stance.

A loud clanging echoed through the night sky as our weapons met. I was well inside of the range of his sword, so I wasn't in danger of a killing strike, but he still managed to deftly deflect my attacks, a clear sign of the experience and skills he had acquired from years of combat. The impacts from my tonfas were landing with considerably more power than they did on the train. Whatever slight power boost, I had gained since that night couldn't simply be explained by adrenaline, but I wasn't in a position to complain at the moment.

Realizing I wasn't having as much impact as I had hoped for, I backed out of his range and assumed a defensive posture, raising my tonfas parallel to one another in a cross guard.

"What happened to you?" I shouted towards him. "What made you throw away your humanity?"

I was in a position to understand him now. Dr. Green's death had caused a precipitous decline in my mental stability and empathy. It was a catalyst that drove me to the acts that I had committed to get to this point, standing across from Bennett. Something equally bad if not worse must've occurred to him in order for him to be committed to his path for all this time.

"What happened?" He repeated back to me, gritting his teeth, "You Irregular filth happened, Wyoming happened. This miserable society toasts the state as if it were a national monument, but they don't toast the people. Those that died because scum like you walk around unchecked."

"Who'd you lose?" I asked him genuinely. I couldn't help but go into therapist mode. It was the most compassion I had felt the past three days and he was clearly holding on to a pain that had existed for decades now.

His jaw clenched as his grip tightened around his sword. He was clearly debating whether or not he should tell me. I waited, neither taking my eyes off of him nor relaxing. Every muscle in my body remained wound up, ready to pounce or evade if necessary.

Bennett let out a low stabilizing breath. "Like you said, you're a doctor not a priest. You're not getting a confession out of me today."

With that, it was his turn to charge. Luckily, I was anticipating it so when he closed the distance, I created a portal in front of him, but he spun around it with the grace a man his size shouldn't have possessed and continued his charge unperturbed. He lifted his longsword and brought it down to cleave me in half. I knew blocking his attack head on would be futile, so I parried with my right, then in the same motion spun to attack him with my left in a backfist style attack. I felt my blades connect with his coat, the ripping of the leather nearly caught my weapon, but I managed to tug it free.

He turned around, unphased by the cut, dragging his claymore towards me as he prepared for his next charge. I decided not to wait and take the fight to him, running into a portal that appeared from his left, but he blocked me, holding his weapon with one hand. Then, I backed into a portal and attacked from his right, the same process playing out.

"When will you learn?" He mocked. "All these years later and you still fall into the same patterns. You're also much weaker than before."

I could feel my eye twitch in frustration, so I stepped back to consider his comments. The same patterns, what could he mean. Every time I accessed a portal, he knew exactly where it would appear from, marking me with a complete disadvantage because my element of surprise had been entirely neutralized. I decided to pocket my right tonfa then pulled out my .44 from its holster with its new and final clip. I opened a doorway to my front, then three others triangulating around Bennett.

I shot into the portal before me and the bullet came from behind the Southern Gent, nailing him in the shoulder. He stumbled forward from the impact, but he stabilized himself by digging the point of his weapon into the ground.

So, that was the drawback to his ability.

He knew when and where I was going to use my ability, but he had no way to determine how I was going to use my ability if I had multiple portals open. I grinned in delight at this knowledge, preparing to press my advantage. I fired three more bullets into the gateway before me, but instead of having them hit him directly from the exit points around him, they flitted through the manipulated gateways, gaining momentum and speed each time they went back and forth, trapping Bennett inside. When I had determined they're power was sufficient, I changed the angles of their exit trajectories by turning the portals slightly towards Bennett, which caused all three of the bullets to tear into his torso.

He let out a cry of pain and was driven to a knee. I pressed the attack by jumping into the portal in front of me and came out from the one behind and attempted to pistol whip him in the skull, but he managed to slightly lean to his left causing the blow to land on his shoulder. My hand recoiled from the blow, throwing me off balance, giving him the time to drive a sledgehammer fist into my gut.

The air was removed from my body as I gasped from the attack, an audible crack came from somewhere inside and after all of the damage they had taken the past few weeks, I knew that my ribs had finally been broken. It drove my feet off the ground, but I didn't land on my back. Instead, I shuffled back a few paces, clutching at my stomach in clear pain. It felt like my insides were being stabbed every time I inhaled too much but my stomach was also straining against constrictions on exhales.

Bennett took a moment to gather himself as he rose from the ground. He stood and turned towards me, a spiteful glare on his face. "I'm going to put you down like the rabid dog you are. Then, I'm going after your sidekick. When I'm done with them, I think I'll talk to that secretary of yours."

My grip tightened on both of my weapons. I felt the fire inside of me swelling again as he spoke. His taunts of Dr. Green, though distasteful, could be put aside. The dead feel no pain, but threatening Emma and especially Sofia was crossing a threshold that I wouldn't let him get away with. Despite recent events, those two were family and he wasn't laying a single finger on them.

"Maybe, I'll take her to the higher-ups," he continued, "I'm pretty sure they could find effective uses for a pretty lady like her."

The flames were swelling up and I could feel the temperature of my body rapidly rising.

"Or better yet, I'll make her my personal plaything," his grin was sadistic as he spoke about Sofia in such an unbecoming manner. "With you out of the way, she'll need a shoulder to cry on. Those will be my shoulders as I make sure that she cries from the pleasure every night."

"Enough!" I erupted into a primal scream. That was the insult that did it, the one that set me off, and the one that caused the flames to erupt.

Stunned from the sudden emittance of fire, Bennett jumped back, raising his weapon in defense. I glanced at my hands in surprise. I was enveloped in a dark midnight blue blaze. It was almost as if the aura was projecting from my body. I had seen this before, from Angelus. I don't know how this had suddenly happened, but Angel was experiencing teleportation like abilities similar in nature to my own. I couldn't pinpoint how this could've happened, but I didn't have the time to process it. Bennett had crossed the line, and I was going to make sure he never had the chance to do it again.

Racing towards him, at a speed beyond what I was normally capable of, I fired two shots at him. He deflected the first one, but the second managed to smack into his thigh, throwing off his balance.

"Die!" I yelled and brought my left tonfa across his chest, tearing his shirt, revealing the brown military vest below. I pressed him with a combination of bladed attacks and pistol whips, all of the previous pain numbed by my wrath, forcing him to be driven back or risk being burned by my flames.

Finally, I had placed him in the exact location I had prepared the night before. The roof collapsed under his weight, and I jumped in after him, planting my feet on his stomach which helped worsen the impact of his landing. I rolled off of him as we landed, bringing myself up to my feet and blasting him with sheathed blows from my weapon. I wanted to make sure he felt every last blow as I was in full blown berserker mode now.

Punch after punch, more bruises painted his face and the pleasure of what I was doing drove me into an ecstatic rush, the flames increased after each blow. This started as revenge, but the enjoyment that I derived from this was euphoric. I dropped my pistol to grab him by the collar, yanking the orange ascot, his pride and joy, from his neck in the process.

"You wanted to get my thoughts on morality?" I screeched in my altered voice, "Well, I finally have an answer for you." I raised my tonfa, releasing the blade again to deliver the blow that would end this nightmare.

Then the rain began. I looked up to the sky, a streak of lightning raced through the clouds. The fire around me died as I stared up into the cloudy night. Even though I was in the midst of battle, the raindrops falling around me seemed oddly peaceful, but when I looked back down at Bennett, I seemed smaller for some reason.

"Not again," I said in disbelief as I realized I was hallucinating, just like I did back in the subway. I began stumbling back and forth, grasping at things around me, trying to settle myself.

"What's real? What's real?" I chanted to myself. I ended up picking up the ascot as I clutched my head to try to regain my stability. I saw Sammy standing stoically before me in the hallway exiting the room. "Help me," I begged him as my meltdown continued.

"I told you, we can't beat him here," he responded, before disappearing suddenly, with my head getting smashed into what happened to be a mirror, not a hallway, in front of me. My panic had given Bennett time to recover, and did he ever use it.

He was enraged now. "How dare you?" He seethed, stalking towards me. Bennett already held a physical advantage, but now he seemed to loom over me like a boogeyman, the same one that had haunted me throughout all these years.

"How dare you touch that?" Referencing the ascot, I had clutched in my hand. I was blinded by the blood which was dripping into my eyes and the cracks in my goggles from being smashed into the mirror. "You wanted a confession," he said grasping me by the back of my head, "I'll give you one."

Apparently, his idea of a confession was to plow my head into the mirror repeatedly. Each impact produced a resounding crack as the broken glass tore into my face, my bandanna fell off during the process. When Bennett found my punishment sufficient or maybe when he just got bored, he pulled me away from the mirror and easily tossed me aside. My body bounced with a resounding thump, landing a considerable distance from my original position. The numbing of my pain quickly faded away, and the physical agony returned in full force, with interest.

Breathing normally, was beyond me now. I had to take quick sharp breaths in order to avoid disturbing my ribs. I caught a glimpse of Bennett admiring his work, overlooking my blood slowly dripping down the fractured mirror. Casually turning to me, he picked his Claymore up in the process.

"You want to know who gifted me my ascot, and what made me who I am today?" He asked before kicking my legs out from under as I attempted to stand. "My little sister. It was the last thing she gave me before she went to Wyoming."

My eyes widened in realization and terror. That's what he meant by the people of Wyoming. The population of Wyoming had never been the largest in the country, but it was still a devastating amount of people that had died. We saw them as only a number the more time had passed, but for Bennett this was personal.

He pulled a hunting knife from his belt and jammed it through my right hand. I let out a howl of pain as the blade pierced my skin, sinking into the floor to pin me in place. I tried to pull it out, but it was in there deep and I couldn't get leverage from my current position. Satisfied with my predicament, Bennett picked up his ascot then strolled back to the bed and sat down. Hunching over to consider me, before continuing.

"She was a freelance reporter, believed journalism was one of the principles of freedom. There were reports of strange activity going on out there. Most of us dismissed it as normal government testing, but not her. She wanted to get the scoop, said she would be the first one to get the scoop of the century, and did she ever," he paused, looking far away, past me and everything in the room to a past that was no longer there. He sighed before pressing the palms of his hands against his knees to prop himself up.

It was the most tired I had seen Bennett since meeting him, the bone deep kind of tiredness that comes from years of working towards a singular goal. The kind of quest that requires you to abandon all distractions and commit solely to the task at hand, regardless of the personal cost. He was near his end, but I was an unforeseen annoyance that he needed to quell first. There wasn't much in the way of talk that I could do to bring him back. He was already too far gone.

"What was her name?" I asked as he approached slowly towards me. I was still desperately fidgeting with the knife to detach myself from the floor.

"It doesn't matter to you now," he said morosely, "Villain monologue time is over," Bennett pulled the knife out by its hilt with the ease of me pulling a toothpick out of butter. The pain in my hand resurfaced as it started throbbing from where the knife was removed, blood oozing from the wound onto the floor.

I tried to scramble away, but Bennett grabbed me by my coat, held me in front of him, and charged through the wall into the next room. I was hanging in his grasp limply now. My vision became blurry as I faded in and out of consciousness. I had just enough energy left to make a portal where I had dropped my gun, I grabbed it with my left hand and weakly raised it to his gut, pulling back the trigger twice.

He smiled at me as he was either unphased or couldn't feel the bullets hit his armor. Snatching the gun from me, he pressed my trusty Desert Eagle to my temple and pulled the trigger to end me once and for all.

The gun mercifully clicked empty.

He tried a couple of more times before bitterly discarding the gun across the room. I gave him a triumphant smirk as I hung within his grasp. If I were going to die, it wouldn't be with my own weapon. I couldn't deny the slight enjoyment I got from the minor inconvenience.

Bennett scowled, tossing me to the ground again. This time he pulled out his claymore and rushed towards me with it, dragging it low before he would sweep it down on my head. I quickly remembered that I had holstered my other tonfa. There was no time to avoid the blow, so I fumbled to pull it out with my damaged hand, before raising it up, bracing with my left hand to support my defense.

When the longsword came down my tonfa snapped, along with my right arm. I cried out, immediately dropping the weapon to cradle my fractured limb. I was also in shock. My tonfas were custom made and designed to be durable, but Bennett's claymore had just cut through them as if they were papier-mâché. There was no sensation in my arm. The only reason I knew it was there was because I was holding onto it with my left hand which had a sprained wrist. Not only had Bennett broken me physically, but he had also shattered my identity along with my spirit.

I sat up and scooted away from him, knowing that it was over now. All of my weapons were either empty or broken and I didn't have any further tricks up my sleeve. I could feel my eyes starting to bleed as I reached my limit.

The problem with the way pushing your limits is portrayed, is that it lies to you about how easy it is, and the lack of repercussions. It seems like as long as you don't give up and believe in yourself, any physical limit can be easily surpassed. If you drive a car and the engine is smoking, you wouldn't keep driving it on the basis that your car should be able to exceed its limits because you believe it can. Same with the human body, I wouldn't squat a max of two hundred pounds then believe I can do four hundred pounds on my next rep without consequences. The goal is achievable, but I would have to get there in increments, a couple dozen pounds at a time and also give my body plenty of time to make it sustainable.

The fire within me and the physical boost from earlier had drained me completely. Every movement I made felt exponentially slower and my attacks lacked the same kick from before. In other words, my body at its own normal skill level couldn't match how my brain was still processing everything that had happened before, making me clumsy and rendering me useless like a baby fawn.

It didn't matter now at this point. I had no fight left in me. Bennett had done his part to render me physically damaged and my ill-timed hallucination had left me mentally undone.

I backed through a portal I made, returning to the roof. The rain continued to pour overhead, and I just lay there as it fell down on me. As weird as it sounds, it felt peaceful. My head rested on the concrete and the cold rain pattering around me played a rhythmic lullaby, guiding me to the sweet reprieve of death.

"I'm sorry, my prince," I tilted my head in the direction of the noise to find Barb, standing on all fours in front of me. "I couldn't protect you. I promised I would protect you."

I began army crawling towards Barb. In my last moments, I didn't expect it would be the last thing I would see. My vision continued to blur as I got closer. Its voice also seemed different, the screeching sound that I had become accustomed to was replaced with a soothing, motherlike voice. It made me want to come closer, to rest in the comfort of the sound. My vision continued to blur, and I swore Barb changed from its feline-esque state to a woman. The body was still made entirely of barbed wire, but the spikes weren't present, and I wasn't hurt as I lay my head in her lap.

"It's okay, my little prince. Just rest here, it's alright," she said to me in a nurturing manner.

I wanted to believe Barb. I wanted to stay there in her embrace and forget everything that had happened, but Bennett had other ideas.

He came through my portal which I hadn't managed to close in time. I felt the goggles get snatched from my face. He dropped and stomped them beneath his boots, crushing my signature piece of equipment along with the remaining hope in me.

"No more hiding Devin. You're a relic of a bygone era. It's time to kill the past and move on."

I felt my coat get ripped off, revealing the Kevlar lined black shirt I wore below. Bennett playfully moved his sword along the trails of my shirt, easily tearing it, along with some of the flesh on my back. I couldn't see the blood, but I knew it was there, being washed away by the downpour.

"Seems like I did damage you all those years ago," referencing the scars I had along my back. They had been with me since I could remember. I always had them covered up because of the gruesomeness of their appearance. This is where the pain usually originates from when I had my post-mission seizures.

He grabbed me by the throat and carried me to the edge of the roof. I just hung there loosely in his grasp, the rest of his talking seemed distant as he positioned me over the edge.

"This is so familiar. Did you do all of this for me?" He asked, observing the barbed wire that were fashioned similar to clotheslines below. I had so desperately wanted this to be the way he died, but it seemed I was going to sleep eternally in the bed that I had prepared.

In my vision, I saw the Spectre standing behind him. I wanted to reach out for help but had no more strength to do so. The Spectre looked at me desperately. It was the only show of emotion I had seen from him since he started appearing. It was also the first time I ever saw his face, or at least what was meant to be his face. Below his cowl and behind the shadows was a skull. Golden eyes peaked out from within the sockets.

"No, you've already won," he wasn't speaking to me, but to Bennett who couldn't hear him. I moved my eyes to see Sammy who was standing next to Bennett.

"I told you we couldn't beat him here," he reminded me, before turning towards the Spectre. "Even he couldn't."

"What are you talking about?" I croaked at him.

"At least have the decency to listen to me," Bennett responded before releasing me from his grasp, leaving me to fall to the barbed wire death trap below.

I saw Sammy, peering down at me as I fell, regarding my current predicament with somber eyes.

"At least in the end, we were all together again," he said sadly, disappearing along with my vision as I closed my eyes to meet my fate. I doubted I had any energy left to scream, but I knew there would still be the twisted sound of barbed wire tearing into my flesh.

Chapter Twenty-Nine

I was met with a familiar scene as I lost consciousness during my fall. I was rewatching the scene that I had seemed to be replaying my entire life. Except this time, I wasn't a neutral observer. I was in the same position before I had fallen, within the grasp of Bennett.

"Leave the kid out of this," the voice standing across from us desperately cried out into the rain, "you've already won," I looked to see that it was the Spectre, or at least what the Spectre had been when he was alive, in full attire and his face still mostly veiled.

I looked down to see my feet dangling over the same ledge. I struggled to escape from his grasp, the legs of my jeans swung back and forth as I kicked at him desperately. I could see my rose red firetruck shirt as it got soaked in the rain.

"Oh my dearest hero, what you fail to understand is that I'm not here to simply beat you. I'm here to end you," Bennett replied, his voice oozing with southern charm as he dropped me.

"No!" The Spectre yelled as he rushed after me.

He ran past the Southern Gent, whose claymore gleamed as a lightning strike illuminated the night.

After he leapt down to save me, his outstretched hand revealed that he was wearing a white and black coat with spiked gloves. I was falling head first, but a portal opened before him, and the hand reached out to grasp me. We managed to safely avoid the first layer of barbed wire, but the coat was torn along with my jeans. There were several more layers of barbed wire though and the Spectre knew there was no way he could open enough portals quickly or far enough to save us both. So, he opened what he could and hoped for the best.

He managed to open a portal at each layer to save me, but the tradeoff was that he couldn't save himself. I screamed as I witnessed him fall through each layer, the wire taking each pound of flesh from him as I managed to pass safely through. The sound of it ripping away at him, along with the straining of the wire as it snapped from its holdings was sickening. He was getting tangled now and there was another layer beneath, but if I fell at the speed that I was going, the impact would've killed me, barbed wire or not.

The Spectre created a portal to get closer and just managed to grab me by the collar of my shirt, but my back collided with the bottom netting of barbed wire below. Our momentum stopped as I felt the barbed points pierce into my back. Everything went silent and as I stared up with a wide gaze, I saw the Spectre hanging there holding me. The wires were digging into him, causing his blood to drip onto me, some of it trickled into my mouth as I gawked up at the scene.

"I'm sorry kid," he apologized in a somber voice. "I wish I could've saved you. I'm sorry for the future burden you have to bear. Please forget me, forget this, and live a normal life."

With that he opened one more portal which deposited me gently to the ground and the life faded from his eyes, silence followed. I lay on the ground in such shearing pain that I couldn't move. It felt like I was having a seizure. I couldn't stop shaking from the chills of the rain and the mess that was now back.

After some time of me just shivering there, a woman came by. She had a silver rain coat, with the hood pulled over her head, so I couldn't see her face. I was hurting too bad to focus on her anyway.

"Oh you poor thing," she rushed over to me with concern in her voice. "My God, what happened to your back?" She looked up at the scene above and gasped, covering her mouth before focusing back on me.

"I'm going to get you out of here," she said, scooping me into her arms. The motion was effortless as she carried me away. Looking down towards me with a smile, "It's going to be okay, my little prince. I'm Barbara. Don't worry, I'm going to protect you from here on. No matter the cost."

With the pain becoming too much to bear, I faded back into the darkness with the gentle sound of her voice lulling me to sleep.

***

I slowly awoke to a dark room. A single ray of light peeked through the blinds into where I was stationed. I turned my head to the window and my body instantly let me know that movement of any kind would be met with resistance. On the bright side, this let me know that I was still alive.

How it was possible was a question to me. Bennett and I were the only people in the vicinity of the roof, and nothing was there to stop the impact of me crashing through the barbed wire to the concrete below. I felt a slight weight shift near my leg. I did my best to gingerly peek towards it without my body sending another status report on my broken condition.

I was met with the sight of Emma sleeping near my legs. Her arms were folded on the bed beside me with her head resting on top of them. She looked at peace, her brunette hair covered most of her face as she slumbered.

"She's rarely left your side since you've been here," a voice came from beside me. I slightly tilted my head to the left to see Sofia sitting in a chair next to me.

She gently smiled at me when I looked at her, but from the bags beneath her eyes and the way her body sagged against the chair, she seemed fatigued. I'm not sure how long I was out, but I was pretty sure she had spent a considerable amount of time watching over me as well.

I opened my mouth to speak, but felt my throat constrict which caused me to cough, the convulsions resulted in the pain from my abdomen to reemerge. Sofia rested a hand lightly on my chest and shook her head politely, advising me that I shouldn't attempt to speak.

"It's Wednesday. You've been out for four days," she took it upon herself to inform me of all the going-ons that had occurred since I was in my coma. "I don't know how she saved you, but her other," referencing Angel, "brought you to me that night. I thought you were dead. There was so much blood."

Sofia paused as her voice cracked. Pushing back a sob, she looked away from me. "You weren't moving. I called Toni and told him your condition. You would've thought he was bringing the entire Red Cross with him. He managed to keep your identity a secret though. Something to do with an illusionist and a mind wiper, both of whom you saved before. I thought I was calling him to organize your funeral," she regarded me with a troubled look that still managed to convey an 'I told you so' message to me.

I took a moment to think over everything she had told me. Angel had managed to grab me before I plummeted to my death. Toni not only gave me the best medical attention he could afford, but still managed to protect my identity, and both Sofia and Emma stayed by my side after I drove them away with psychotic fits of rage. Tears streamed down my cheeks as the depth of my bonds became clear to me.

Most of us look for those relationships that are thicker than blood. Some of us try to compile as many friends as possible, but never fully feel close to anyone despite the quantity of those so-called companions. Others try to limit the number of friends to the bare minimum, but still end up keeping those people at a distance because of a lack of trust in people.

But it's those pure friendships, the ones that are with you in spite of everything you've done or what you've gone through. The way I like to think of it is, if you were robbing a bank and you needed to fill three slots, who's coming with you. Whatever the outcome, you're in it together through and through. I smiled as the tears continued to run down my cheeks because I knew that I had filled those three spots.

I turned to Sofia and indicated with my head towards the water. She nodded in response but pulled out a yellow pill and dropped it into the water. The pill diffused into a yellow filmy substance that clouded the water. She lifted the cup and held it towards me. I raised an eyebrow, but she returned serve with a look of her own. The look of a mother giving her sick child medicine despite their protests. No wasn't going to be taken for an answer.

"*Bebe,*" she instructed.

I sipped the water as she held it for me. It tasted about as nasty as it looked, a chalky sensation that still managed to clear my throat and granted me the ability of speech.

When I finished, I rested my head back on my pillow. "I'm sorry," It was an apology for the way I spoke to her and nearly killing her, but it was also a 'thank you' for everything she had done and staying by my side like always.

"You're welcome," she replied, never a hint of satisfaction of being right entered into her voice.

I looked away from her. I couldn't stand what I had done to her, but we were going to need to firmly draw the line between us now or risk falling into the same cycle as before.

"You know I love you, Sofia," I spoke towards the window. I felt her hand tense up on my chest then slowly remove itself as she responded.

"I know," she answered, peering towards the nightstand by the bed.

"But you know we can't go back to what we were," I continued to the window.

"I know," she replied to the nightstand.

"But maybe one day," I said to the window.

"Maybe one day," she repeated to the nightstand. "I'll leave the two of you alone, but you're going back to sleep afterwards."

"Yes, ma'am," I replied as cheerfully as I could muster. With that she stood up and quietly left the room. I angled my head to Emma down by my feet. "You can stop pretending to sleep now."

"Ugh," Emma groaned as she peeked at me from out of her arms. "How'd you know I woke up?"

"You moved too much when I was speaking," I enlightened her. "It was as if you were trying to remember to suppress all of your reactions when you heard us."

"Leave it to a therapist to read body language," she sighed to herself. Emma got up then occupied the seat Sofia had recently vacated in order so that I didn't have to raise my voice. How considerate.

"How'd Angel save me?" I asked.

"Well, remember after we made the oath, the next morning how she kept teleporting at random. We talked to MyKey, and he got us a suppressant, which worked thankfully because it was getting out of control and Angel was becoming more unbearable than usual. She can manage it in spurts, so she managed to catch you before you fell into the wires below."

"But how'd she know where I was?"

"Tracker," Emma presented the tracker to me as she spoke. "She planted it in your coat before you left. That's why she's the smart one between us."

I chuckled lightly. The pain didn't hurt as much because of the yellow pill, so I was able to manage. She had gotten me again. I gotta admit she was resourceful. Then something about Emma's story hit me. I hadn't had time to digest Angel's sudden disappearing acts with all that was going on, but now that I had no choice but to lie here and think about it, she did start teleporting after we did the blood oath. And in the dream, or actually it may have been a memory, that I had just experienced, the Spectre's blood had gotten into my system, so maybe my power could somehow be transferred to another by blood.

Could the mixing of blood also have given me some access to her abilities, and is that what General Watson discovered during the Purification to create his Enhanced troops? That was another can of worms entirely, but the reveal of where each of my aberrations had come from was finally starting to sink in.

I was Sammy or Sammy was me, however I wanted to phrase it. The Spectre was my predecessor all those years ago and Barb, Barb wasn't what I thought it was, or more accurately, it wasn't who I thought *she* was.

"You okay Devin," Emma asked, breaking me from my train of thought.

"Yeah, I'm good. Just seeing things a bit more clearly now," I answered. "Would I be able to speak to Angel for a bit? I want to thank her."

"Of course, she would be happy to see you," Emma closed her eyes and took a few patient breaths and when she reopened them, her eyes had changed to gray and the bubbling smile turned into the usual scowl, letting me know that Angel was present.

"Hey sis," I welcomed her as the change was completed.

She recoiled slightly at my friendly greeting. I think she was taken aback considering how our last exchange ended.

She sucked her teeth as she realized my comment had caused her to react in such a manner. "You look terrible, but at least you're alive."

"I heard it's you that I should thank for that," I replied gratefully.

"You got lucky I gained a new power."

I'm guessing that was the closest I was going to get to a 'you're welcome' from her, so I just grinned and accepted it. She lifted her arm to remove her now longer strands of hair from her face, revealing that her arm had been recently bandaged.

"What happened?" I asked, bringing attention to the wound.

She looked at her wrapped arm as if it were a birthmark that had been with her for her entire life. "Don't worry about it. How are you feeling?"

"Like I almost got killed," I responded dryly.

She smirked at me from her chair. "Sounds about right."

I pensively looked at her, thinking of one of the many questions that I had since I woke up. "How do you control it?"

She squinted at my question but didn't look at me. "Control what?" I could tell that she understood the meaning of the question, but she was clearly trying to avoid talking about it. Therapist skills activate, yet again.

"The flames. The anger," I clarified. "I was going toe to toe with Bennett. I even had him for a moment. I don't know how else to describe it other than …"

"Ecstasy," she finished for me.

"Right," I nodded once in confirmation. "It burned, so much on the inside. I thought my blood was boiling, but when I let it out, I couldn't control it. I almost hurt Sofia because of it," I became quiet after my confession, waiting for her response.

Angel inhaled a breath through her nose then let it out patiently. "Do you know why you're not constantly falling through portals every time you walk, when you sit down, or go to sleep?"

I started to shake my head to answer her, but she continued on, not interested in hearing my answer. "It's because you draw your power from elsewhere. With my abilities, you were accessing a power that you weren't familiar with, a power that didn't belong to you, but one that you must now make your own. It's the same reason I couldn't stop myself from teleporting after we sealed our bond. The power didn't belong to me."

"But how does Emma manage it?" I asked.

"Her flames don't come from anger, it's something much more...pure. Something that maybe you can access one day," she replied.

"And you?"

She waited before answering, turning her head slightly towards me, to indicate that she had heard the question, but was not in any rush to answer. She rubbed her temple before looking up to respond, "My anger is my sole purpose for being. The burning sensation you felt, it fuels me, drives me. I've been down the path that you were just thrown from. I got revenge for Emma on her brothers, each one of them," Angel took time to pause, letting out a sigh before she continued. "I've done many terrible things when I've had control, so I know how you feel, but however you decide to make the flames your own, it won't be with your rage."

"How do you know?"

"Emma and I have lived many lifetimes, and there's always someone like you in each one," she rose from her seat, brushing off her darkened cloak.

"And what's that?"

"People call you heroes. Claiming it's because you're special, blessed by the gods themselves, or even the second coming. But it's none of those reasons," she folded her arms and shook her head to emphasize her point. "It's because you're the only person to give a damn, and actually willing to do something about it."

She headed towards the door, looking back before she left the room. "The mob boss wishes to speak with you. Be brief and go back to sleep."

"Wait," I called to her.

"What is it?"

"Thanks for staying by my side."

She flinched again at the compliment and tsked. "It's not like I could've left you alone. I mean, Emma would've been upset."

"You're such a tsundere," I told her trying to keep the joking expression from my face.

"A what?" She cocked her head to the side in confusion.

"Don't worry about it. It's a compliment." *Technically.*

She frowned in suspicion back towards me. "Like I said, be brief and go to sleep."

I smiled at her in affirmation and waited for Toni to enter the room. My patron came bursting into the room as if he had just gotten permission to come in to see his newly born child.

"*Mio ragazzo,*" he rushed to me, holding my face in the palms of his hands. "I'm so glad you're well."

"If you keep disturbing me, I'm pretty sure it won't stay that way for long," I complained as he held my head up from its rest position, straining my neck.

"*Perdonami,*" he apologized, dropping my head back onto the pillow. I grunted my displeasure at the lack of gentleness being displayed to my already damaged body. "I called in every medical favor I owned. We didn't think you'd make it. Your medical report looked like a thesis statement I heard you doctors have to write."

"Dissertation," I corrected, but I couldn't help but enjoy the exchange. This was the Toni I had known for over the past year, and I wasn't going to complain to the man who had continuously done right by me. "Thanks for helping, Toni. I know it must've been a pain taking care of me and still running the business."

"Nonsense," Toni waved a hand dismissively. "When Susan saw you, she nearly had a heart attack. Thank the Lord Mia Bella hadn't seen you. I don't think she would've recovered from that. I had no choice but to save you or I wouldn't have been able to come home to a happy house. You're family, Devin. That's not going to change."

He dug into his pocket and withdrew my ring. The family sigil still visible even in the lack of light. Tenderly, he lifted my hand and slid the jewelry onto my ring finger. He patted my hand with a joyful grin then stood up. "The gear you asked for is at my place whenever you're ready but get plenty of rest. You earned it."

After Toni departed, I was finally left in the room alone. For the first time, I took the chance to observe my surroundings. The bed was covered in white linen sheets. The room still darkened, with only the single ray of sun truly breaking through the veil of darkness. There were candles around me, lavender scented. I thought of how I must've looked to the others laying there, still and unmoving. An outsider would've thought it was a wake for a fallen friend. I wonder how it must've felt for them, not knowing if I would breathe my last breath as they sat there helplessly.

I glanced back to the door and caught a glimpse of a small figure sitting in the chair beside me. I did my best to angle my head towards the figure to find it was the boy who had been with me my entire life. It was Sammy, or I guess after my mini-revelation, it was me.

"Welcome back to the world of the living?" He watched me with intense eyes, eyes that didn't match the youthfulness of his face. His clothes also weren't torn anymore. The rose red firetruck shirt and jeans were perfectly fine as if they were new. Something about the way he carried himself felt different as if he were complete now, whole once again.

"Me, Devin?" I asked him.

He raised a hand, stopping me and shaking his head. "Whoever I was, died that night, plus I've gotten used to Sammy now."

"Sammy," I recited. "Why didn't you tell me all this time?"

"Would you have believed me?"

I took a second to consider. I would've liked to believe that I could've been open minded about it, but I knew I probably would've dismissed it as his childish pranks or just a byproduct of my condition. "No, I guess you're right," I admitted.

"It's okay," He swayed side to side in the chair, humming as he spoke. "I kept it from you anyway. I was afraid for us. I didn't want...want us to remember that night."

"I can see why," I said, thinking back to the memory. Everything that I thought I knew about myself had been incomplete. The fear of falling from that night, the pain of the barbed wire eating into my back, the uncontrollable shaking, and the two others who had played an instrumental role in my life, it all had a purpose. "Where are the others?"

Sammy frowned. "The Spectre is recovering, and Barb has gone dormant. I can't feel its presence."

"Her," I urged him.

"Her," he nodded back. "So what do we do now?"

I raised a shoulder up as far as I could. The effort was as much of a shrug as I could manage. "I'm beat Sammy. I know Toni got all the king's horses and all the king's men, but I don't know if he can put me back together again."

"I'm pretty sure the drugs they're giving you and the Irregular healers could have you out of here by tomorrow if they wanted to," he replied assuringly.

I shook my head slowly at him. "That's not what I mean. I damaged a lot of relationships over the past few days. It's a testament to the kind of people standing outside that door that they were still here for me. Bennett has me at a psychological and physical disadvantage. He's killed people in my life that have protected me since I was your age. I gave him my best shot and it wasn't nearly enough. Even if I get out of this bed by tomorrow, I doubt I can overcome that."

"You're missing something though," he told me.

"What's that?"

"It's true that we have friends in our life that are far greater than we deserve, but it's also a testament to the kind of person *you* are that they chose to stick around despite what happened. Also, you may have given it *your* best shot, but not the best shot at your disposal. You walked to the mound but refused to throw everything in your repertoire."

"Angelus?" I asked, knowing the answer.

"Yes, if a cute girl is willing to fight for you, don't turn her down." he chastised me.

"Dude, in case you missed it, that's our sister now," I returned the attitude.

"You just had to go and make it weird," he hopped out of the chair. "Well, at least I have a family again."

With that last comment, Sammy entered into me. It's a difficult sensation to explain. It was almost as if a ghost walked into my body to possess me, but in this case, it was merely a piece of me that had returned. I felt something well up in my chest, like I too had just been made whole.

"Again?" I repeated to myself as I felt my eyelids start to become heavier. What had he meant by that? I didn't take too much time to ruminate over his statement because soon I faded back into a deep dreamless sleep.

***

I didn't end up getting out of bed the next day. Due to Sofia's insistence, I was forced to stay another night.

The day was a mix of medical professionals coming in to tell me how much pain I was in as if I didn't know, swallowing bitter concoctions to heal, and muscle massages to combat the atrophy that had set in. Emma spent the time giving me briefings of what had occurred while I was in my coma.

She called MyKey to get a feel for the city and if the Underground was making anymore moves. Apparently, the powers that be were doing their best to make me a pariah. Adkinson had tattled to the IPF about what I had done to him. In fairness, he actually had a good case. I quite literally carved my initials into his face. It was going to be hard to claim plausible deniability on that one. Considering the fact that my first encounter with the IPF was less than cordial, the organization was more than happy to officially label me a criminal.

It also seemed that Adkinson had taken my demands to heart. He had set up the final shipment for Saturday, only two days away. I wasn't in any kind of mood to go back out into the fray. I was hoping that Toni would be able to call down the Family to handle the business, but he said his hands were tied since Adkinson was such a major player in the city. Emma never asked me directly if I would be going out to stop the transaction, but every time I looked into her eyes, I could see her silently pleading with me to join her.

The look had stuck with me for the duration of my stay before I was finally able to get released the following day. I was going to have to give her an answer tonight, but I put those thoughts on the back burner. There was another pressing matter that I was on the way to tending to.

Chapter Thirty

Mr. Jenkins had called two more times since I had launched my phone into the wall. Sofia told him that I had been in a terrible accident and that I would meet with him as soon as I could. She informed me that it was urgent and when I was able to leave, I should give him a call back. I figured that if he took the time to call twice more, I could at least afford him the decency of meeting face to face.

I was currently en route to the address he had given me when we began our sessions. I ask every client to provide a home address, so that I can do an in home session in the event they would find it more suitable. Sofia was in the driver's seat as I was deemed unfit to be behind the wheel, despite the car having an autodrive function. If my medical practice was a Fortune 500 company, she would've definitely been Vice President by now with just the work she had done over the past week alone.

"We're here," I felt her prodding me awake.

Lifting my head from the passenger's window, I felt the sun's rays beaming down. I must've dozed off during the drive. It was late morning when we left the facility, so guessing from the sun's position it must've been noon. The house was a ways out. It made sense since there wasn't much farmland in the center of Peach City.

"Do you want me to go with you?" Sofia asked. There was a slight look of concern in her eyes. She knew as well as me how ornery Mr. Jenkins could be when he was in a mood.

"No, I should be fine," it would've been helpful to have her by my side, but this was a task that I needed to face myself. Mr. Jenkins probably wouldn't respond well to being tag-teamed in his own home. I put my sunglasses on since I still needed to get reacclimated to the sunlight. Leaning back through the window to talk to Sofia, I told her, "Go have yourself some free time. I'll call you when I'm finished."

"Good luck boss," she replied with a tired grin before pulling out of the gravel driveway, the road crunched beneath the wheels of the car as she drove away.

I turned back around to look at the Jenkins estate. I could see why he would want to live so far away from civilization. The only noise out here came from nature. The birds sang to each other in the tall Georgia pines. The cows in their pens moved about carefree, eating grass as they lounged in the sun. I even heard running water coming from a stream that led to a small pond he had built.

In front of me was his home. Nothing special, but it did seem welcoming despite the man who lived in it. It was a log cabin that appeared to have been built purely with manual labor. Two rocking chairs were staged on the porch along with other decorations that clearly must've come from his late wife. Mr. Jenkins had hardly ever worn a different outfit whenever we had met up, so I knew he wasn't responsible for the colorful decorations in front of the house. Lawn gnomes, flamingos, and even some windmills. It warmed my heart to see such color in his domain, but if Mary Beth was responsible for the ornamentation that meant Mr. Jenkins hadn't made any adjustments to his lawn in over two decades.

I approached the porch, stepping up carefully on the wooden stairs. Walking was another adjustment that I needed to become familiar with again and I didn't feel like taking a tumble so soon after being medically cleared. I took a quick breath to get my confidence back then rapped on his door a few times.

"Hello, Mr. Jenkins," I called past the door. "It's me, Dr. Prince. Sofia told me you called me, so I came to see you."

There was no movement or any discernible sound that I could make out from the other side of the door. I knocked a few more times and patiently waited.

"Hello," I called out again, but still no answer. I don't know what possessed me to do this, but I tried turning the doorknob. It was unlocked and the door swung slowly open with a slight push. I peered inside, calling out once more before stepping in.

Technically, I wasn't breaking and entering since the door was unlocked. I could also probably avoid trespassing concerns since I was his therapist and was here on official business. I could always claim I was concerned when he didn't answer the door, so I did the only responsible thing and went in to check on him.

I entered the room and the first thing I noticed was how much was lacking compared to the outside.

There wasn't much in the way of color in the house. It seemed as basic as you could make a home. There was a hallway that possessed two bedrooms and a bathroom. I quickly glanced at the master bedroom to see if he was in there but didn't enter any of the other rooms when I didn't find him there. That would've been a bit too much snooping and something told me that he wasn't inside at the moment. I was making my way past the kitchen when I noticed the dining room. The table was set, but that was the weird part.

It was set for four.

Four plates, four glasses, four sets of cutlery, but still what was more unsettling was that there were three picture frames on the table. There was also a shotgun in the one seat where there was no picture frame. My mind immediately thought to what this could've meant moving forward.

I moved closer to analyze the pictures. In the seat that was across from the head of the table was the picture of who must've been his wife. I had never seen Mary Beth before, but glancing at her now, I could see why he gave everything up for her to become a farmer. The picture of her was probably taken after they had their children, but the woman in the frame still maintained the look of someone that held onto her youth in spite of growing more seasoned. There were streaks of silver in her long black hair, a sign of maturity not age, and she possessed a smile that managed to touch me even through the photo.

Next, I looked at the two pictures across from each other, Eli and Zacheriah. From what Mr. Jenkins had told me, Eli was the older of the two. Both of them had short brown hair, but Eli was more muscular and defined, like he was an athlete or accustomed to helping his dad on the farm. Zacheriah had more of a mischievous look about him, like he was the one that constantly got into trouble. Every picture had the Jenkins family smiling and at that moment I realized why it was so hard to reach him. He had something that I never had, something most people spend their entire lives searching for but struggle to ever find and obtain, people he genuinely loved to come home to.

He had lost this, each and every last one of them. Simply telling him that they would want him to move on wasn't the point. To him, what was the point of moving on, what was the point of living if there was nobody to do it with or for? He wouldn't be able to move forward until he was able to find that again. Lee Jenkins wasn't a young man anymore, he was simply an old man waiting to die.

I placed the picture of his wife down and headed to the barn. It was the only other place I could imagine him being. If he weren't there, I would probably just spam his phone with calls. I headed to the barn, your typical red wooden structure, but it was huge. He must've spent a significant amount of time back in the day building this. I heard a dog barking in the distance. I turned to the noise to find a golden retriever trotting over towards me. I'm not much of a dog person, but I did give his head a good rub and a few platitudes before he ran off.

I entered the barn door and knocked to alert anyone of my entrance. A gunshot rang out from within, causing me to I jump back. When I slowly put my head back into the barn, I saw that a hole had been produced near where I was standing.

"State your business or leave," a stern voice warned from within. "Next one won't miss."

"It's a pleasure to see you too, Mr. Jenkins," I greeted him sarcastically as I walked into the barn, presenting my hands to him, so that he knew I was harmless.

"Doc? What are you doing here?" He looked me up and down, shaking his head disapprovingly. "That accident must've been terrible. You look like you got run over by a bus, then it backed over you jus' for good measure."

He wasn't wrong. My right arm was still in a cast brace. The medical team had healed most of the damage, but they didn't want me doing too much activity with it over the next twenty-four hours. I was also wearing navy blue sweat pants and a gray tee shirt perhaps a size too big, courtesy of Toni. I wasn't exactly a sign of sterling health.

"Yeah, something like that," I replied to him, bemused at the current situation. The plaid attire wearing gentleman still had his rifle trained on me, making no clear effort to remove it. "So, is this how you treat all your guests or am I just special?"

He looked down the bridge of his nose at the gun, then smacked his lips in apology. "My bad, most of my guests don't trespass," he gestured to one of the bales of hay across from him. "Have a seat. You must've come all this way for a reason."

"Yeah, I did," I said, taking a seat across from him.

When I got a good look at Mr. Jenkins, I was taken aback by his appearance. My longtime patient didn't seem sick in the typical sense of the word, but he did look haggard as if whatever it was that was eating away at him had finally taken too big of a bite. His eyes were sunken into his face, his clothes seemed to be hanging off of him, a sign that he may not have been getting enough nutrition. What was really telling was how his shoulders sagged. His head, which was usually held up defiantly, just drooped. He looked like a defeated man.

"I saw the inside of your house," I spoke carefully, leaving the comment in the air, but making sure not to have any judgment or perceived malice in my voice.

Mr. Jenkins grimaced, realizing that I had seen his dining room and the implication the table setup gave off. "You had no right to break into my house. I should call the cops on you."

"You're right. I'm sorry," I apologized. "I knocked, but when I didn't hear any noise, I got concerned and entered, but that's still no excuse for me intruding into your home."

He nodded righteously at me as one of his hogs, a thick coffee brown pig, trotted up to him and stood by his side. He began absentmindedly rubbing its neck as he glared at me.

"I also wanted to apologize to you as your therapist. I let you down," he squinted his eyes at me as I continued. "I was insensitive to your situation. I asked you to move on from a situation, from people, that meant the world to you. I assumed that I would know what they would want you to do, but I see how wrong I was now. I also didn't keep my word to you. I didn't have my accident until after your first phone call. I had just lost someone that meant a lot to me, so I ignored it. I hope you can forgive me."

During the course of my apology, his expression softened. The menacing scowl that had marked his lips had deformed into a sympathetic frown. His eyebrows rose in place as his eyes lost their hostility and were replaced with something more empathetic. He glanced towards the barn door, still rubbing his hog, then nodded twice which I figured was him granting me forgiveness. "Who'd you lose?"

With melancholy, I pursed my lips, having been forced to confront the reality that Dr. Green was truly gone, and I'd have to start talking about him in the past tense. "Someone that helped me when I didn't even know how to help myself. He was a mentor, father...friend."

My eyes sunk to the hay covered ground beneath me. The pain of his death was different now. I was no longer filled with uncontrollable rage from the shock of it. I was just numb about how immutable it was. There was nothing I could do to change his fate, and it hurt knowing I couldn't see his joking smile or listen to the sound of his voice anymore.

"I guess we all lose someone eventually," Mr. Jenkins responded, giving his best shot at consoling me. Right then, it was easy for us to connect. We were two grown men grieving and were the only ones that could comfort the other at the moment.

"I don't want you to go through with whatever you had planned, Lee," I told him in a quiet voice while clasping my hands together and twiddling my thumbs. "I didn't know your family or how you lost them, but I do know they wouldn't want someone to find you with your blood on the ceiling."

He looked down at the hog, pensively. "You're probably right," he sighed. "Mary Beth hated a messy house. She'd have my hide if she saw what it would have left the dining room like." He stopped and paused, looking off into the distance somewhere that only he could see.

"Lee?" I asked after a few moments.

"This is where we had the argument," he stated simply.

"Which argument?" I asked.

"With my Beth," he returned his gaze to meet mine, a regretful look on his face, "We both knew the IPF was coming. 'Not our boys' she told me. She wanted to send the boys away, but I insisted that we'd only make it worse if they knew the boys were out. I told her they'd come back or just wait. I said the boys would be fine, either way we'd protect them. But when the IPF came, we panicked and hid them at the last second. There was a secret doorway to hide in the walls of the house. I built it in case we got attacked during the Conflict, so that's where they hid. They were fine, but we were just so nervous. You don't know what it's like to have your kids, something so precious that you held in your hands the first day they came into this world and have people threaten them."

He paused. His hands trembled as he looked at them, memories of when they were babies possibly flashing through his head. I didn't dare interrupt him. This was the first time that he had begun to walk me through what happened to his family. I simply picked up and rubbed the belly of the little piglet that had come over to see what its fellow swine was up to.

Mr. Jenkins lowered his hands, taking slow breaths to steady himself before pressing on. "Beth attacked them with the frying pan. 'Fore I could even make a move, one of them blasted her with some kind of energy gun. I held her as she died. She made me promise to protect the boys and I couldn't even do that. Zacheriah was the hot-headed one, too idealistic. Too naive for his own good, but that's what made him the sweetest boy I knew. I told him not to go, but he loved us deeply. Said he would've done the same if it had been me instead of his ma. I sent Eli with him. He always looked after his brother. I figured after they knocked a couple of heads, he'd be able to convince him to come home, but…"

He didn't finish his sentence, pulling out a white handkerchief to wipe at a tear streaming down his cheek. "I know at the heart of it, it's not my fault, but I can't help but feel responsible."

Unfortunately, that was another thing that I could sympathize with him about. I knew at the end of the day, responsibility for Dr. Green's murder lay at the feet of Bennett, but if there was even one thing that I could've changed that day, would it have saved him?

That was a question I had been wrestling with for a few days, but Mr. Jenkins had been struggling with it for over twenty years.

I stood up to sit next to him. I didn't put my arm around him or hold his hand. No way would his pride allow for it, but I did just sit there with him. He unfolded his arms and started rubbing his overalls, his body casually opening up as I sat with him.

"I don't know what to tell you, honestly," I admitted. "What happened to your family was evil and you shouldn't replace what you had with them, but what if you could find something else?"

He considered me for a moment, "Like what?"

I gently placed the piglet down to think. That was the million dollar question. Mr. Jenkins wasn't a man in need of someone to take care of him, but something he needed to take care of. The animals had sufficed for a time, but that had run its course. I mean, I love Mew as much as if he were an actual person, but if I lost everyone in my life, I don't think he could solely replace those bonds. Pensively, I started rubbing my chin, watching as the piglet ran to the bigger hog. It nuzzled up to it, with the bigger hog lying down and the piglet joining it.

I think that's when it hit me, but there were a lot of moving pieces required for it to work. It would require sacrifice that I still wasn't in the mental headspace to make yet, but I wanted to save my client, and keep a promise.

"Can you give me three days, Lee?" I asked, turning to him to let him know how serious I was.

"Three days?" He mimed, taking off his hat and rubbing at his bald scalp. "It's not unreasonable, but why three specifically?"

"You just gotta trust me on this one," I said to him, firmly holding his gaze.

He gave me a quizzical look, but ultimately relented. "I guess I can hold out till then, but you better not be taking me to a nursing home or I'm taking everyone out with me."

"Trust me Lee, a nursing home is the last place I want to go right now. Deal?" I extended my hand toward him.

"Deal," he grunted back, giving my hand a tight alpha squeeze.

"So, how about I help you out around here for a bit?" I offered cheerfully.

He raised an eyebrow before responding, "And what do you know about physical labor? I don't see how you get out much when you're hiding behind that desk all day."

"Oh Mr. Jenkins, I wouldn't doubt my physical ability. It might surprise you."

"Whatever you say," he shook his head in disbelief. "Well, first thing you can do is put those hogs back in their pen. After, you can get started on repairing that hole in my barn. Hammer, nails, and wood are over there."

It was my turn to raise an eyebrow. "You mean the one that you placed there?"

"You offered to help," he pointed out.

"Indeed, I did," I conceded before going to herd the mama hog and piglet back to their pens. "Indeed, I did."

I spent the next four hours helping Mr. Jenkins around the barn before Sofia came to pick me up. She was clearly displeased about the amount of work I had done when I had just gotten medically cleared but didn't grill me about it too much. On the ride back, I placed a phone call. I wish I had more time, but after my chat with Mr. Jenkins, I needed to speak with them tonight. I told them to meet me back at my apartment and we could discuss matters there.

I got dropped off at my apartment about two hours later. I was in no condition to use my powers, plus Bennett would've known that I wasn't dead if I had, so Sofia ended up taking the Stratus afterwards to ensure that I wouldn't go out anymore. I thanked her for everything before she left, and I told her to thank the Romanis when she arrived back at their house.

Slowly, I took my keys out of my pocket to unlock the door to my apartment, but it was already open. I figure my guest had let themselves in, even though they didn't have a key.

"I'm glad you made yourself comfortable," I walked in to find Emma grubbing on a bag of chips while lounging on my couch.

"I'm family, remember," she said innocently enough as she continued munching. "How'd your therapy session go?"

"Technically, it wasn't my session," I replied before locking the door and placing my keys on the table. I went to the kitchen to get a glass of water, so that I could take my pain pills on time. "It went surprisingly well though. I asked for three days to try to get him on the right path."

"Three days, huh?" She paused her chewing to mull over my deadline, then shrugged, "What does that have to do with what we talked about?"

I walked to the couch and plopped down next to her. "It means that I'm in for tomorrow."

Emma's hazel eyes lit up and she tossed the bag aside, spilling chips on the floor. She flung her arms around my neck to give me an exuberant hug. Her grip was tight, combined with my recent injuries and farm hand work, my body ached from the display of excitement.

"Let go of me," I tapped on her shoulder to release me. "Also, you know you're picking those up."

"Inconsequential," she said dismissively, "What changed your mind?"

"I want to save my client and keep a promise," I gave her a tired look though, "but I don't know if I have it in me right now. I didn't just lose a fight, Bennett exposed me, made me second guess myself. I'm going to be there for you, but I don't know how much help I'll be."

She cocked her head to the side, curiously. "What do you mean he made you question yourself?"

"His purpose," I said. The word held much more weight than it usually did. "Mine used to be so crystal clear. It was the reason that even after all the beatings, I was still able to get everyone home. It was why I could get back up, but after the train, after Dr. Green, after...the rooftop. Bennett's not in this for the money or power, he wants Irregulars either eradicated or in Underground control and his reasoning is resolute, unshakeable."

Emma pursed her lips while I was talking, taking the time to nod or emote with her face to indicate she was actively listening. When I finished, she stared up at my ceiling until a slow smirk spread across her face. Emma jumped up from the couch then spun around facing me again as if she were giving a performance.

"It's not that you lost your purpose," she stated, poking my nose playfully. "Your constant success just made you forget it somewhere along the line."

"What do you mean?" I stared up at her.

"From how you talk, everything always seemed to come up all sevens for you. Your alter ego never truly struggled until Bennett came along. Instead of him simply being a poor match for you, he ended up being the worst possible match with a purpose, a true purpose, which made you question if his crusade was more righteous than yours."

I squinted at her line of reasoning. It was true that other than my first night as the Peach City Phantom, most of my missions had been unquestionable successes and as time went on, it became more of a chore than a voluntary crusade. When I faced the Southern Gent, I realized what would happen if I didn't match his resolve. Emma had made a compelling point, so I motioned with my hand for her to continue.

"So," she dragged the word out, "you just need to rediscover your purpose, and all you need to do is remember."

Remember. I thought to myself. That had been my biggest issue for the longest and now I was being asked to recollect once more in order to defeat my greatest foe. I leaned back on my couch and pointed at Emma to sit in the chair across from me. I'm guessing it was time for me to be on the other side of the therapist chair for once.

"Well, if you're asking me why I started doing this, it's not overly complicated." I began. "I just wanted to save the little girl of what I was considering to be a friend."

"Are you talking about the Romani girl?" She asked for clarification.

"Yes," I confirmed. "You see I started my practice in the city about two years ago and the first four months it was just me, no Sophia, not much of a clientele, not really a lot of friends or associates. I would visit Mr. Romani's bar maybe once or twice a week. The name was different back then and I only had a faint idea about his side businesses and the Family at large, but I had heard it was a nice lowkey spot a guy could visit if he just wanted to relax. At first, he mostly left me alone, but when a person grows from a casual customer to a regular, you take time to get acquainted. Get it?" I asked, turning to her from my position on the couch.

"Yeah, it's similar to how I got familiar with Russ," she answered.

"So, Mr. Romani would come up to me from time to time, casual conversation, nothing special," I continued, "That was until he found out I was a therapist. Then he wouldn't stop talking my head off about his issues. I didn't complain because he wouldn't charge me for my orders."

"You ate and drank for free?" Emma raised an eyebrow at me suspiciously.

I smiled back, "Yep. He's a businessman and when he would come to me with his issues, he'd say that I was on the clock, so I ate free. I still tipped kindly, since I wasn't paying a tab. The waiters and waitresses obviously enjoyed this arrangement and word got back to Susan, who had a chat with me for the first time. She told me about how much she respected that because some of the other regulars have similar arrangements, but never tip. After that, there wasn't another place I'd rather spend my free nights at. Everything was going well, until that night."

"The night she was kidnapped?" Emma asked.

I nodded towards her grimly. "Yeah, Toni was on a warpath. I didn't really know what the issue was, but I stayed clear out of his way, until he came up to my booth and sat down. He cleared the entire bar but told me to stay. Honestly, I thought he had an issue with me, but he was asking me questions about justice and karma, not exactly my fields of expertise. I didn't quite understand at the time, but after we finished chatting Susan came up and explained the situation. Their daughter had gone missing earlier that day. The city had always had a weird string of kidnappings, but since most of the people taken were confirmed Irregulars, most people didn't do a thing or even raise questions about them. Mia Bella had just come into her powers, and I don't think the ones that took her knew who her parents were. I'm still not sure to this day why I did it, but I asked to see a photo of her and when I saw an innocent little redhead with pigtails smiling, it stuck with me. That's how it started."

"Then what?" Emma asked on the edge of her seat. My story had gotten her more engaged than she normally was. Her playfulness was subdued, filled with an interest in my alter's origins.

I sighed in exasperation. I usually never go into detail about the first time I decided to play hero. It's a combination of embarrassment, but also some moments that stick with me to this day. Everything changed for me that night, putting me in the situation that I'm in today. I like to look forward, but I guess just like the importance of remembering who Devin Prince truly was, I also needed to remember what the Peach City Phantom truly stood for in order to overcome my demons.

"Well, if you insist. I guess I'll just go from there."

Chapter Thirty-One

I left the bar soon after my talk with Susan. I couldn't get the face of their daughter out of my mind. I couldn't imagine the terror they were going through right now. Who would want to snatch such a sweet looking kid? The kidnappings had only increased in the city over the past few months and still no one did anything. I would've loved to help, but there wasn't really much I could do, except leave it in the hands of the professionals.

"But there is something you can do," a dark voice interrupted my thoughts.

"No, not you again," I stopped in my tracks and glowered at the ghost-like shadow behind me. "I told you to stop bugging me."

"I am you," The Spectre replied in his wailing voice.

"A part of me," I corrected. "There's a huge distinction."

Disregarding my dismissal of him, the Spectre floated alongside me. "It matters not. You can save the child."

"Using my powers is against the law, regardless of my reasoning. Especially since I'm not registered," I reminded him. "I'll have a hard time explaining to the IPF that the ghost produced by my schizophrenia told me to dress up and play vigilante for a night."

"They are ill-equipped to catch you."

"Ha, that's a good one," I stopped to laugh out loud in the middle of the street. Two teenagers that probably shouldn't have been out this late gave me cautionary looks then walked as far around me as possible without entering the street. "How many Irregulars have said that before? Do you understand what Purification means? I'm a no name therapist in the biggest city in the south. They wouldn't have a problem putting a bullet in my brain and going about their way."

"In and out. That is what your ability provides," The Spectre pressed.

"Well, I'm definitely not calling it that," I chuckled. "You're wasting your time."

The Spectre flew in front of me, impeding my path. "You know what will happen to that girl."

The smirk disappeared from my face, replaced by a scowl. I did know what was about to happen. If nobody found the girl within the next forty-eight hours, she was as good as gone and if she wasn't dead, I didn't want to even imagine the worse.

"You know he's right," I turned to see the new speaker that had joined us, Sammy. He was standing beside me, rubbing his hairless chin while nodding at the Spectre.

"You too?" I asked incredulously, "Why won't the both of you leave me alone?"

I opened my eyes to see an elderly woman clutching her purse a little bit tighter, while hurriedly moving past me.

"Nut," she grumbled back at me as she continued on her way.

"Great, my sterling reputation is getting ruined," the girl's face flashed in my head once more and again I couldn't drive the image out. I had never met her before, but to Toni and Susan she wasn't some face on a flyer, that was their daughter.

If there was even one thing I could do to help, why would I not? "Okay, I'll do it," I conceded.

"Yes!" Sammy shouted in joy, jumping and pumping his fists into the air.

"But," I said to temper his outburst, "I wouldn't even know where to start. I don't have a person behind a computer screen or a secret information network."

"But you've heard of someone that does," The Spectre added.

I winced at his comment. I knew who he was suggesting and was entirely dead set against it. The person he was hinting at had a less than admirable reputation. "That person is only a rumor."

"You know that not to be true," he chastised me. "Find him."

"Okay, okay," I raised my hands to placate the aberration. "It's just that I have to make a couple of outfit changes."

"Outfit changes?" Sammy asked.

"Yes, I can't go gallivanting around in my work suit," I sighed, picking up the pace to my apartment. I needed to make an outfit change before I could find out more info about the missing child.

***

"I look ridiculous," I complained to the Spectre and Sammy as I waited outside of the door to the trailer, a beat up little white building. The lights were on, so I figured someone was inside, but I couldn't be too sure.

"I think you look pretty cool," Sammy replied affectionately.

"That's because you picked it out and you had him help you," I gestured with my thumb towards the Spectre. "I don't know why I listened to the two people that never change outfits."

"I fail to see the problem," Spectre commented from the base of the stairs.

"You would," I rolled my eyes. "I look like I'm about to go on a flashing spree."

I was donning a bowler hat that a noir era detective would wear, a trench coat that was way too big for me, but I got it for a discount in an abnormally cold winter. I also had tinted glasses to help hide my face even though it was the dead of night. My hands were placed in my pockets while I tucked my head into the collar of the trench coat as if I were a turtle.

"What's flashing?" Sammy asked curiously.

"You know what, nevermind. What is taking so long?" I banged on the door again. I had been standing outside for twenty minutes and was starting to get ticked off at the lack of courtesy. "I knew this was a bad idea."

I turned to start walking back down the stairs when the door suddenly opened.

"Yoo-hoo," a voice sung from behind me. "Did you need something, sir?"

I scowled back over my shoulder to see a tattooed man with a rainbow colored spike mohawk. He wore a royal blue tie to go with his white vest and dress pants. I'm not sure what he was going for, but it wasn't working for me. "About time. What took you so long?"

"Oh, I fell asleep," he mimed. "You know how that is, don't you? Come inside."

I grumbled a curse to myself and made my way into the dingy trailer. My host offered out his hand towards the black metal folding chair on the opposite side of his desk and made his way to his spinning chair.

"What can I help you with?" He asked, leaning forward on the desktop to fix his name tag, it read: *MyKey*.

I pushed down the vomit I felt welling up and looked past MyKey at the monitors behind him. There must've been a hidden camera somewhere on the door because it showed the spot where I was standing previously. Glancing at his desk, I noticed there was a cup of coffee with the smoke steaming from the mug. It had to have been freshly poured, ten minutes max. He was definitely lying to me about sleeping and had probably been watching me the entire time. I looked from the coffee to the cameras and glared at him.

Noticing my intense stare from behind my glasses, he smiled placatingly. "Oh, you got me. When you walked up to the doorsteps, I thought you were undercover when I saw you talking to someone. I mean seriously, you look like the mascot for a neighborhood safety watch meeting."

I couldn't really argue with him on that point, so I just sighed and slowly took a seat.

"Great, now that we have the pleasantries out of the way, what can I do for you McGruff?"

I bit back my first response about what he could do and focused on why I was here. "I heard that you're good at finding things," I said, leaning forward and looking around the office. I have no idea why, maybe I wanted to look like I was checking for bugs, but why would he bug his own office?

He made a confused face at my seemingly shifty behavior. "You could say that, but it's more like I'm good at knowing where things are. What are you looking for?"

"A girl," I spoke in a hushed tone.

"I'm not in that kind of business, yet," he paused to write a note down. Sliding it over to me, "This is the best dating website I know of. There's also virtual reality these days. It's about as good as the real thing."

"Not that type of girl," I interrupted him, tearing the note up. "I'm looking for a little girl."

Before I realized the implication of what I had just said, his expression immediately switched from amused to astonished disgust.

"No, no, no," I pleaded, raising my hands at him to stop his train of thought on the matter. "I mean she got kidnapped. I'm trying to help her."

"Oh," he said in relief. "You should have said so sooner, you almost got blasted with my under the desk shotgun. You gotta be clear about these kinds of things."

"I see your point," I said rubbing my face, relieved the miscommunication had been cleared up. "Why would you tell me you have a shotgun under your desk?"

"Maybe I like you," he replied, interlacing his fingers and staring into my eyes.

The corner of my mouth twitched, I didn't know whether I was touched or disgusted. "Um, thanks. So, you know about the kidnappings, right?"

He whistled while reclining back in his chair, placing his feet on his desk, green crocs adorned his feet. Yeah, it was probably disgust that I felt.

"I'm aware, but the way the city acts, you would think everything is fine and dandy. Why are *you* looking though?" He asked intently.

I shrugged my shoulders nonchalantly. "Favor for a friend."

MyKey's face shifted to a more serious expression, his voice dropping. "Can I tell you something? What you're talking about doing isn't as simple as dog sitting for your buddy. If you're not going to take it seriously then you'd be best served leaving now and forgetting about me, your friend, and the girl. It'll help you sleep better at night. Understand?"

I stared back at him, pursing my lips in consideration of his words. This was the first time the eccentric host had shown some semblance of urgency. He was probably right. If I walked into wherever I was going half-cocked, then I was just going to end up getting myself killed and potentially a few hostages also. I squinted back at him and nodded. Playtime was over, this was my reality at the moment.

"I understand," I affirmed to him. "What do you know?"

The playful grin returned to his face as he took a sip of his coffee. Reaching into one of his drawers, he withdrew some papers and tossed them purposefully onto the desk.

"There," he said pointing to the papers. "From what I know, there's a lot of unusual activity in these three locations. I'm still working on mapping the underground tunnel system."

"To find hostages?" I asked curiously.

"Um no," he answered, his eyes shifting away from me. "For more profitable endeavors."

"Right," I responded, giving him a flat look, "What are the other two options?"

"You also have this abandoned plantation, with a huge mansion, and there's also possibly the port system."

"If I were a kidnapper, where would I hide them?" I muttered to myself, gazing at the pictures, trying to use my therapist skills to put myself in the mindset of a human trafficker.

"I don't like boats," Sammy commented as he peered over my shoulders to look at the cargo ships.

"You've never even been on a ship," I snapped back at him.

"Excuse me?" MyKey cocked his head to the side, unsure of how to interpret my seemingly random outburst.

"Sorry, I was thinking out loud," I shot Sammy a dirty look before focusing back on the cargo ship.

Containers lined the deck of the ship. Whoever was behind this could easily hide the hostages here. It was a possibility, but I wouldn't take a ship from central Peach City, especially at night. It's not a direct port city and if anyone with enough clout to have the ships stopped decided to do so, the cargo would be easily discovered. So, I could scratch that from the list of possibilities.

"Abandoned tunnels, you say?" I glanced back up to MyKey.

"Yes, here's a partial map I've managed to draw so far." he handed me a large map that many a cartographer would be proud of.

The map had lines perfectly drawn to scale, intersections, labels, symbols for every possible hazard or impediment. The only problem was that it was merely a fraction of the entire railway system. I recalled the map of the entire MARTA system and realized I'd only end up getting lost once I diverged from where his map ended.

"A waste of time and energy," Spectre advised from over my shoulder.

He was right, there was no way I could cover that type of ground by myself without draining my ability, which I hadn't used in months. So, that left only the plantation. The pearl mansion looked old and rundown. Dirty green vines clung to the walls as did cobwebs. The windows were surprisingly unharmed, other than a serious need for a deep cleansing. It appeared more like a haunted house attraction than an actual place someone used to live.

I could check this and have the cavalry check the tunnels, just in case.

"Here," I said pointing to the house. "That's where I'm going to check. Would you be able to send your people to the tunnels?"

"My people," he cackled, tossing his head back in the midst of his amusement, "I run my businesses from a small trailer in an abandoned construction site. Do you really think I have an army of assets that I can flood the entire tunnel system with? Also Stranger Danger, I don't take orders from you."

"But there are innocent people that could be down there," I protested. "It's the right thing to do."

"I don't know what you do in your day job, but moral currency doesn't pay the bills. Though it's probably going to end poorly for you, I commend your decision to help those people, but I have no incentive to help you further than this," he folded his arms casually and reclined back in his chair.

I scowled towards him, but I guess my anger wasn't purely reserved for him. This was probably the mindset of the majority of the citizens which allowed for these atrocities to continue. Before tonight, I was a part of that same hive mentality and the realization sickened me. I reached into my trench coat and withdrew a band of tens, flipping them onto the desk towards MyKey.

"Is that sufficient for you?" I growled.

He casually picked the stack up and shifted through the bills before pocketing them. He smirked to himself, but it left his face when he faced me again. "While I thank you for the donation, like I said I don't have an army to send in the tunnels. I can place a few calls if you would like though."

"You mean I just paid you so that you could be a pay phone?" I frowned.

"Lighten up," he said in a teasing voice. "This is the first step on a long journey of friendship."

"Absolutely not," I shook my head, shooting his hopes down immediately.

"Partnership?"

"No."

He pursed his lips and tapped his chin. "Loose acquaintances?"

I didn't say anything but grunted in approval. Then, I took a pen off of his desk and wrote down Mr. Romani's personal number on one of the pieces of paper I had ripped earlier and slid it to him.

"Great," he said, picking it up from the desk. "Who does this belong to?"

"Someone that will give you all the incentive in the world to help," I told him. "Tell him to check both locations, but I advise you to use your best professional voice because he might remove your tongue from your mouth with the mood he's in."

With that, I stood up from my seat, satisfied with the information I had received. I started heading for the door when MyKey called out to me.

"Are you going dressed like that?"

My first instinct was to ask 'what was wrong with the way I'm dressed' but I didn't really have much of a leg to stand on in this department. I glanced down at myself. These weren't really the best clothes to accomplish what I was hoping for, even though my plan was a simple snatch and grab.

"What did you have in mind?" I asked sincerely, holding the side of my trench coat disconcertedly.

A wide grin spread across his face. He relished in the fact that the fish had just taken his bait. "I'm glad you asked."

Spinning out from his chair, MyKey went to the trailer wall opposite the window and turned a wrench clockwise. The trailer wall made a whirring sound and then slid to the left, revealing a wall behind it that held clothing and different attire.

"Welcome to MyKey's Galleria," he delightfully presented the wall as if it were a prize on *The Price is Right*. "What can I interest you in? We have attire for athletics, stealth, business, and even the most intimate of situations."

I glanced at the wall and felt that I had stumbled into a spy movie and party store. He was right about having different outfits for different occasions. Starting from the left were the more professional decor. Suits, belts, ties, and briefcases hung on the wall, prim and proper, waiting to be taken. Not what I needed, but I made note of it.

I continued along to the right and saw different costumes that were probably best suited for Halloween and as I traveled to the far right, I realized what he meant by the most intimate of situations. Let's just say that his wall was like shopping at Spencer's. Great place to find cool attire, but if you have children with you, or a very high standard of decency, you should probably avoid the back for the best shopping experience.

I felt the blood flush from my cheeks as I refocused on the center of the wall. *What would best suit me?* I looked at the Spectre who simply floated there awaiting my decision. I gave him a once over and shrugged my shoulders.

"I'll take the coat, gloves, bandanna, and aviator goggles," I notified MyKey of my selections.

"Aww, an excellent selection," he said in his best used cars salesman voice. "I must advise you though that the proper term for these are steampunk goggles."

"Whatever, as long as they don't have spikes on them," I focused back on the jacket. It looked very familiar. "Where'd you get the coat from?"

He gave a quizzical look at the black and white coat then shrugged. "Beats me. I got it from someone that picked it up a few years ago. They called it a relic or something like that."

"If you say so," I turned to leave once again.

"Of course, now will you be requiring weapons?" He asked, clearly urging me to give him more money.

I rolled my eyes behind my shades. I don't know how, but he knew he had me over a barrel, so there was no point in arguing with him. If I kidnapped someone, there's no way I wouldn't have a weapon of some kind to not only maintain control over them, but also make sure no one could take them away from me. As nauseous as it was to think about, you have to protect your investments.

"Show me what you have," I placed my head in my hand. This was already becoming more tedious than I had hoped for.

"One sec," MyKey slid the wall back to its original position, waited for an audible click, and then turned the same wrench counterclockwise. This time the wall slid to the right, revealing a vast assortment of weapons.

I scanned the wall for something suitable, but then I scrunched my face in surprise as I realized that I couldn't find what I had hoped for.

"Seriously?" I voiced my displeasure as I glanced at him.

"Do you not find them to your liking?" He asked, slightly disappointed.

"Where are the guns?" I turned back to the wall. There were mostly melee weapons on the wall. The only things that could be used at a distance were a bow and arrow, plus a slingshot. I wasn't a hunter, so unless I wanted to make a fool of myself, those were off the table.

"Guns are a business too big for me right now," MyKey admitted, he gestured in a 'what can you do' manner. "You know since the Conflict and Purification ended, only law enforcement agencies are allowed to carry guns unless you're a registered bodyguard for a V.I.P."

"But you have a shotgun," I pointed out.

"And thus, I have an advantage."

Fair point. I thought to myself, looking over the weapons again. There were a lot of bladed weapons, but I wanted to steer clear away from them. If I could avoid bloodshed that would be for the best. I kept looking until two dual baton-like weapons hanging on the wall caught my eye.

"Those," I pointed at my selection.

MyKey gave me a confused look, raising an eyebrow. "Really? Do you even know how to use them?"

I shrugged. "Does it matter if I'm paying you for them?"

"I suppose not, but why those?"

"I saw it on TV once, thought it looked cool."

"Right," he said, dragging the word out. He must've really thought I was about to get myself killed because he took two more weapons off the wall. "Tell you what, I'll throw in these two daggers and utility belt for free and you can be on your way."

"Thanks," I said dryly. "How much do you want?"

"You can give me the real stack of money you're hiding and we're square."

A shocked look came over my face, but he simply smiled and didn't clarify how he knew I was hiding a bigger roll of bills. I took the roll of fifties from my pocket and placed it in his hand. "Square?"

"Square," he responded, sealing the deal. "Be aware of the power dampening chains that they use. If they get them around you, it's probably over."

"Thanks," I smirked back at him. "I'll make a note of that."

"Don't get yourself killed, McGruff," he said, returning my smirk.

"No promises," I replied, retrieving my new pair of bamboo tonfas from the wall before heading out.

***

"Wait, wait, wait." Emma abruptly interrupted my story. "You were being serious about getting your signature weapons because you saw them on TV and thought it looked cool?"

"Yes," I replied, perturbed at being cut off. "Not everyone received their powers or weapons from a god or prophecy. Now can I tell the story, or do you have any other questions?"

"No, I'm good," she put a hand to her mouth, failing to hide her giggles. "You can continue."

I placed my head back on the couch and looked to the ceiling. "Great now as I was saying…"

*** *** ***

After receiving the address to the plantation from MyKey, I made my way to the location using my ability. It felt weird using my power after such a long time of inactivity. I was hoping that I could simply get in and get out without over exerting myself. I had come out of my portal and settled into a tall oak tree.

"It's scary out here," Sammy commented in the tree beside me.

"Rest easy, child," Spectre said to ease Sammy's fears.

"I'm not doing this with the two of you," I chided the both of them. "One or the other, not both. I don't need the distraction."

"You can take it Specky," Sammy conceded shyly. "It's too creepy for me."

The Spectre did what I assumed passed for a nod and Sammy disappeared from view.

"Now keep silent and don't distract me," I ordered him, looking at my surroundings. Sammy was right about the place being unsettling.

The land was barren, and nobody moved about, at least no one that I could see. A fog was settling over the night, limiting visibility which I was grateful for, but if the assailants I was up against had night vision I was out of luck. The only light in the house seemed to come from candles or flashlights. I guess not having electricity would help keep them off the grid. The yard didn't have much in the way of scenery other than one shack, which could've possibly been an outhouse. I was tempted to ignore it, but there was a guard posted outside.

"It can't be that easy," I commented to myself before crawling to the end of the branch to go through a portal I created. I didn't want to risk hopping out of the tree and falling to the ground if my portal didn't hold.

I stepped out behind the shack, fixing my hat which kept almost falling off when I moved too suddenly. The shack was a beat up old wooden construction. Somehow it was the lone building out here that had withstood all of the years, but the wood would've definitely given you splinters if you ran your hand across its outer walls.

I peeked inside the window behind the shack and saw a small figure huddled on the floor. They were covered in a blanket or rags. A long steel chain ran from what I was guessing where their foot would be to the doorknob. It was too dark inside to make out any other features.

"Psst, can you hear me?" I whispered.

No movement.

"Great," I muttered to myself. I could get inside easy enough, but the chain would be the difficult part. I had no tools and I never attempted using my portal to cut something off before. I could possibly sever their leg or distort reality if I weren't careful. I wasn't too sure of the full extent of my powers yet, honestly. I was going to have to find a way to get the keys from the guard.

I searched the ground for something that I could use as a distraction, until I came across a small pebble. "This'll do."

I chucked a pebble towards one of the pine trees, deeper into the forest behind the shack. The small rock smacked off of a tree and bounced away.

"Huh," it caught the guard's attention, and he cautiously made his way to the tree line. I waited till he was almost in the trees before stealthily creeping up behind him and withdrawing one of the tonfas and whacking him across the base of the neck. Instead of crumpling in an unconscious heap, the guard let out a cry of pain and angrily turned towards me.

"That usually works on television," I commented disappointedly before grabbing the shaft of the weapon which was supposed to guard my arms and bashed the guard on the bridge of the nose which did the trick.

I quickly searched his person for keys, which I found on his right side. I dragged the body into the forest before running back to the little hut.

"Hey, can you hear me?" I called inside, while finding the right key for the lock to the door. "The guard is sleeping. You can come out now."

Still no response as I opened the door. I immediately got to work on the end of the chain attached to the door. "We really need to go. Come on."

There was a slight shift which notified me that they were at least alive. I went to the other end of the chain once I finished and released those as well. "Okay, let's go Mia Bella."

I removed the covers to find a long-haired brunette underneath. She was a young woman, maybe late teens, or early twenties, not who I was looking for.

Of course I couldn't get a simple win.

I turned to leave the shack since she was free, only to be met at the doorway by the Spectre. "I did my job. Get out of the way."

"You're a doctor," he commented.

"I'll be a dead man if I have to drag her out of here," I griped back.

"Help her."

I let out an exasperated breath then turned around to check on the unresponsive woman.

I examined the lady for a bit when I came back in. She still wasn't responding properly to my words. She just lay there, dirty and beaten. Strands of her hair were stuck together by clumps of mud. Honestly, the cloak that was around her was cleaner than her clothes which were torn. But it was the eyes that disturbed me. She looked far gone, as if I were merely staring at a carcass whose host had left a long time ago.

"Can you hear me?" I asked her, waving my hand in front of her face, but still nothing. "This is bad, maybe I should-"

"Behind you!" The Spectre shouted in warning.

I fumbled for the tonfas and raised them just in time as the guard I had knocked out earlier attempted to return the favor but instead brought down a knife towards my face. I managed to deflect most of the blow, but he still managed to cut the left side of my face above my eye and slightly below it. Blood trickled down over my aviators, impairing my vision.

When I recovered, I saw him withdraw a Desert Eagle pistol from his hip and prepare to fire. I quickly raised the tonfa in my right to smack at the weapon. The pistol let off a shot and the woman behind me twitched in response, the first sign that told me she understood what was happening around her. I definitely had to get her out of here now.

I swung wildly with one of the batons and missed completely, but it threw off his aim. I dropped my other stick and wrestled at his gun. We stood there battling for control of the gun when another shot went off. Panic set in as I reached for my gut. I thought for sure I had been shot, but it was the guard who stumbled back, falling onto the ground in pain, before passing out from blood loss.

I stood there shocked for a moment. I could still hear him rasping for air, while unconscious but if he stayed like that without any medical attention he would surely die. I never killed anybody before, and I certainly didn't want this to be the first time. I went to put pressure on the wound, but I heard noises coming from the house. Somebody must have heard the gunfire and was coming to check. I looked from the guard to the unresponsive girl and made a choice. I picked up his Desert Eagle pistol before I went back to grab the girl. She didn't put up much of a fight as I picked her up onto her feet. I opened a portal and rushed us through.

We came out on the opposite side of the property, but closer to the house. I peeked around as two guards fled from the compound towards the shack. After they were a comfortable distance away, I glanced back at the young lady. She was actually looking at me now as if my existence registered to her for the first time. I noticed she was staring at the blood trickling down my face. I touched the wound gingerly. The goggles had held up, so I was able to keep my vision, but the scar might last for a while.

Giving her my attention, "What's your name?"

She shook her head at me and cowered into herself. She might've been too far gone already, but the least I could do was make sure she was safe.

I bent down and slowly reached towards her. "Hey, I'm not going to hurt you," I said in a low voice, making sure to maintain eye contact with her. I finally reached the young woman's hair and started removing the mud which loosened her strands.

"It's alright you're free now. Can you take these? I don't really have room for them now," I handed her the two daggers and put the Desert Eagle in the spot they had previously occupied. Then I wrapped the cloak comfortably around her. "There's somebody that I'm looking for. It's a redheaded little girl. Have you seen her?"

The young woman looked towards me and there was a sign of a spark in her eyes again. She glanced to the house then back at me but didn't speak.

"Please, it's my friends' daughter. They really miss her, and I would like to meet her too. I'm not going to hurt her."

The woman's eyes widened as if she were about to cry. She slowly pointed towards the top of the house. I made a look of confusion at first, but then I think I understood. "They keep her upstairs?"

The woman nodded back confidently at me, a small smile crept on her face.

"Great. Thanks for your help," I grinned in gratitude before brushing a hand over her cheek. "You should smile more. It's very pretty."

Then I rushed to the entrance of the house. Before I reached the door, I heard a voice that didn't sound of this world.

"My little prince has found himself a princess," a scratchy voice spoke from behind me. I looked slowly over my shoulder and saw two glowing scarlet eyes within the fog. They looked upon me with pure malice. It didn't get any closer or further, but just stayed there, floating in the mist. I turned back to the door, instinctively rushing inside and locking the door behind me.

"Spectre, what was that?" I huffed to him, my back against the door.

"Uncertain," he said, floating towards the stairs. "But concerning."

"You don't say," I muttered sarcastically, scanning the house for any leftover guards.

I saw two flashlights overhead scanning the top floor. Neither flashlight headed into a room, but simply moved about the top floor. I looked to Spectre for advice, but when I saw him floating up the stairs an idea hit me. I opened a portal to my right and stepped through. When I came out on the other side it was within what appeared to be the master bedroom at the end of the hall.

I quickly searched the room, but found nothing special of note in the room, only the basics. A bed with old white sheets draping off the edges, sat in the middle of the room. The closets were open, so I didn't need to bother checking them. I was making my way to head through to the next room when I saw the same scarlet eyes as before within the darkness of the closet.

"Embrace me, my prince. Don't be afraid," its voice was one of the worst things I'd ever heard in my life. I covered my ears, desperately trying to block out the noise.

"Go away, go away," I chanted to myself. I didn't think it was real, but I definitely didn't want to find out if it was.

"Press on," The Spectre advised from my side.

He didn't have to tell me twice as I rushed to the opposite wall and ran through a gateway I created into the next room. It was much the same as I ran into different rooms until I stumbled upon a room with a small girl sitting on a bed. I nearly fell on my face trying to stop my momentum.

She was a redhead with pigtails, wearing a cute frilly pink dress and had the kind of shoes that you strap on instead of tie. I looked to her arms which were chained to the wooden bedpost behind her.

That's when I got angry.

It took really sick people to want to do this to another human being, let alone a child. This girl was innocent. I know Toni had probably done some suspect things in his line of work, but did the child have to be punished for that?

I rushed over to her and used the key I had obtained from the guard earlier and released the chains from the bedposts.

"Are you Mia Bella?" I wanted to confirm before I took the handcuffs off of her.

"Uh-huh," she confirmed in a high-pitched voice. Mia Bella leaned away from me as I approached.

"Hey, hey. It's okay," I said as I tried to calm her worries. "Your dad sent me to get you."

"Your Papa's friend?" She peeked sheepishly at me with deep green eyes that looked as if they were searching for truth in my face before I could even answer.

"Yes, I eat at his restaurant all the time," I told her.

"Okay," she offered her hand towards me hesitantly. I undid the last manacle from her wrist and faced her again.

"Okay, let's get you home," I turned to go, opening up a portal away from us. When I started walking towards the gateway, I felt a slight tug on my coat. I look down to find Mia Bella holding my coat while still sitting on the bed.

"What about the others?" Her voice rose as she was confused about our immediate exit. I tilted my head towards her, returning her bewilderment. I thought for sure she would be ready to leave, but it somehow seemed that everyone I rescued was more morally centered than me.

"You want me to get the others?" I asked. "That'll be kinda hard with me having to watch you. Your dad's guys are on the way. They'll be able to save them."

"But...but they have mommies and daddies too," she replied, releasing her verbal arrow to shoot me in the heart. I hated to admit it, but she was right. The same feeling that I felt when I saw her chained to the bed shouldn't have been reserved for just her. I should've felt it for every other person here that had been taken against their will, not knowing if they would experience the bliss of freedom ever again.

"Okay," I sighed. Patting her on the head, "Where are the others?"

"Downstairs," she answered, "They said I got my own room since I was special."

"They didn't hurt you, did they?" I asked looking over her face seriously.

She shook her head, which dropped a huge weight off of my chest.

"No, but they're scary. They said they would hurt us if we tried to run away."

"Well, I'll tell you what," I removed my goggles, revealing my full face to her. Next, I placed them gently over her face and glanced into them as I rubbed her temples in slow circular motions. "When you put these special goggles on, they make you brave. I'm not going to let anyone hurt you. Are you ready to help now?"

She nodded excitedly in anticipation. A smile spread over her face revealing that she had just recently lost a tooth. I made a promise to myself then and there that I would get this girl home safely, so that the tooth fairy would give her another dollar once she lost the next one.

"Okay, hop on," I turned around so that Mia Bella could hop on my back. I felt her petite arms clutch tightly at my neck as I stood up. I probably wasn't going to be able to use my weapons, so it would be all ability from here. I pulled up my yellow and red fanged bandana for the first time then tiptoed out of the room peeking my head through the door to check for guards.

The two from earlier had still not returned. It was only the two flashlights from earlier. Both of them finally appeared with their backs to us, talking at the top of the stairways. Both had on black shirts with cargo pants and army combat boots. They were very lax for two people guarding prisoners, even though they seemed like professionals. The upside was that neither of them knew we were here, and their buddies hadn't reappeared yet.

"Do you wanna see something cool?" I whispered over my shoulder to Mia Bella.

"Mhmm," I could feel her shifting in expectation after I asked.

I hadn't done this before, but I daydreamed about it in one of my more mundane therapy sessions recently. A portal opened below the two guards, and they fell through, but they came out above where they landed only to drop in the portal below. The larger guard dropped his flashlight which knocked over a lit candle as the two were still stuck in my trap.

Mia Bella giggled at the display as the two guards screamed in surprise and fear as they continuously fell through the portals without landing. I even let out a chuckle because it was much funnier than I had even imagined.

I might need to name this someday. I thought to myself while descending down the stairs.

Say what you will about fancy houses, but basements always seem to be creepy no matter the circumstance. The first thing I noticed was that I really couldn't notice anything. The room was completely dark, not even a flashlight or candle in the distance to guide me. Mia Bella's grip tightened around my neck, and I could hear a soft whimper emanating from her. I patted her hands gently to comfort her then started walking blindly into the basement as I hoped my eyes would slowly start to adjust to the darkness.

I felt around with my right hand while continuing down the walkway. I felt cold steel which may have been from shelves in the basement, but I couldn't be too sure. I paused in my tracks because I had seen too many movies to know how this ended.

"Where do I go?" I muttered aloud. I could only make out vague shapes down here and I found the lack of sound to be unnerving.

"This way," the scratchy voice returned along with the eyes. I instinctively took two steps back as my heart started racing. I had to remind myself to breathe as the red feline pupils glared at me unblinking. "Trust me, Devin. Free them."

I don't know what disturbed me more, the fact that the sinister voice called me by my name or that it actually wanted to help. Hesitantly, I made my way towards the voice. Its glare never seemed to get closer or further, but the glow provided me with some lighting as I made my way further.

I could see cages in the distance now. Shadowy bodies were huddled together, clinging to one another. If I had a chance to see clearly, it would've been possible for me to look at their faces, but I'm pretty sure it would've been no different from the expressions that Mia Bella and the girl in the shack had earlier.

There was a shuffling noise in the distance as if something were scurrying across the floor. I really hoped it was a rat or other small creature.

"Beware, another is here," The Spectre's voice warned. His advice proved valuable last time, so I knelt down to let Mia Bella off of my back. I told her that we were going to proceed on foot and that she should stay close. She walked behind me, clutching tightly to my coat as we pressed on.

The scurrying continued and something brushed past my left leg. I moved Mia Bella to my right, shielding her with my coat. Withdrawing the Desert Eagle, I began walking backward, aiming into the darkness for whatever may come bursting out. Then, a hand shot out and grabbed my leg. I jumped in fright, accidentally letting off a shot. Whimpers spread through the basement in response to the discharged weapon. I turned to where my leg had been grabbed.

"*Ayudame por favor,*" a voice sobbed. Another string of Spanish spewed from what happened to be the voice of a woman in a cage beside me. I didn't really understand much of what she was saying, but I knelt down to look at her, holding Mia Bella closely to my side as I did.

"Hey, I'm here to help you," I spoke the words unnaturally slow and felt very American at the moment, but I couldn't risk a misunderstanding. I took the ring of keys out and held it before her. "This key makes you go free. Um, fuera."

"*Qué?*" The feminine voice responded. I knew I really should've paid attention in those Spanish classes during my undergrad.

"Key, open door," I inserted the key into the lock and opened the door to hammer home my point. "Free *todos. Entiendo?*"

"That's not how you ask someone if they understand, in Spanish," Mia Bella commented on my lack of fluentness. "You told her that you understand, not asking if she understands."

"As long as she knows to get everyone out. It'll be fine," I turned towards Mia Bella as I responded when all of a sudden, I was yanked backwards by the collar of my coat.

I reached desperately for my collar as I was dragged on the dusty floor. The air was getting cut off from my lungs as I was being choked by my own attire. The bowler hat came off when I managed to turn on to my stomach to face my attacker. I didn't get a good look at them because I was propelled forward towards the basement wall in front of me. Before smacking into the wall and breaking my neck, I opened up a portal and flew through, landing uncomfortably at the same spot where I had been launched from.

A deep groan escaped from my chest as I managed to crane my neck up to look at my attacker. The first thing I noticed was their jaw, in the darkness they seemed to gleam and every tooth that I could make out appeared to be razor sharp. His skin was scaly, but not discolored as one would expect of a scaly shark jawed Irregular.

"Another one for the collection," he bellowed in a deep basso voice.

"Hey JabberJaw, can we discuss this?" I pleaded with him as I scooted away towards the entrance without turning my back to the guard, holding my hand up in hopes of pacifying him.

"Was that an attempt at a joke?" He demanded as he walked menacingly towards me, his silhouette becoming more defined as the distance between us shortened.

"Just making friendly conversation," I managed to say timidly, before I caught wind of something off.

The closer I got to the basement entrance, the more I could detect what the scent was. It smelled of smoke. I managed to sneak a quick peek at the entrance and saw that the lights were flickering, as if the flames were already in the midst of their dance for the incineration ritual. I knew that I was kinda responsible for the candle getting knocked over, but I didn't think it would set the whole house on fire. The more time I spent fighting would prevent the captives escaping. JabberJaw was blocking the one and only exit, and if he didn't stop them, the maturing fire would claim all of us.

"Wait," I shouted to him, raising both hands to emphasize the seriousness of the situation. "The house is burning down. You gotta let us go or we're all going to die."

"Your jokes are getting progressively less funny. Do you really think that's going to work?" He loomed over me now. A freakish smile crept onto his face.

Too much was rushing through my head in order to think clearly. I didn't know how I could beat this guy and save the hostages at the same time. I was going to die down here. A nobody that tried to do the right thing. *This is what I get for listening to the voices in my head.*

"Don't worry, when you wake up there'll be a nice piece of jewelry waiting for you." he said as he raised his fist, preparing to bring the mallet sized fist down on my head.

I raised my hand in a futile effort to shield my face. I began to close my eyes, preparing for the loud smack that would render me unconscious and then it came.

But not how I expected. A large boom came from upstairs, rattling the entire house. JabberJaw paused and looked to the ceiling stunned by the noise. During his brief hesitation, one of the steel cages went flying through the air, flattening the perp against the entrance adjacent to the wall.

"Holy expletive!" I shouted in surprise. I promised Sammy I would do my best not to curse as much, so we settled for this.

I lowered my arm to see who had launched the steel projectile. Mia Bella stood there, hand outstretched and panting. I looked from her to the cage, so that's what she meant by special. Mia Bella's eyes rolled into the back of her head before she fainted. I managed to rush over and catch her before she hit the ground.

"I got you," I comforted the weakened child as I held her in my arms.

Another thunderous sound came from somewhere upstairs, and the ceiling above came crashing down, blocking the exit to the basement. I stood up and turned around. All of those that had been taken were freed now. They huddled as one, looking to me for what to do next.

"Lead them," The Spectre appeared, hovering next to me.

I glanced from him to the gathered crowd. I wasn't sure why it had to be me, but I was going to get them all out of here, whatever the cost. Nodding my head in understanding, I opened a portal beside me.

"Everyone inside," I called out to them, standing beside the portal to usher them away. The exit point should've led outside of the home into the fog outside. I waited until the last person made it through then looked back once more into the darkness of the basement and was met with the sight of the scarlet eyes staring back at me. I shuddered at the sensation of its gaze, so I rushed into the portal as quickly as I could, fleeing from its presence.

I didn't exactly come out where I expected though. Maybe I was too frazzled or maybe it was because I wasn't too accustomed to using my powers to this degree. Mia Bella, resting in my arms, and I were inside the house beside the front door. The inside of the house was engulfed in flames with the second floor collapsing above us.

I saw the two guards that were within my portal earlier laying on the ground, burning. I covered Mia Bella's eyes even though she was still spaced out from the earlier effort.

Was I responsible for this? I knew what they had done was terrible, but I don't know if they truly deserved to die like that. I went to exit the house but turned back one more time and I could've sworn that the fire surrounding them was black with tinges of white surrounding them, but it could've been a trick of the smoke. I turned back and exited out the front door and down the stairs with Mia Bella clutching at my neck with both of her arms as I carried her gently in front of me.

That's when I heard the cocking of a pistol behind me.

"Don't you move," a voice spoke with absolute authority. I froze in place, not daring to even turn around. "Put the girl down."

"She's tired," I said calmly. "I don't think she can walk."

A gunshot fired off. I felt the bullet zip past my ear, causing me to flinch.

"I won't tell you again," the voice became deadly quiet letting me know that the matter wasn't up for negotiation. "Put my daughter down."

My eyes lit up as I finally recognized the voice. Mr. Romani was behind me. That MyKey character actually came through. I still needed to be careful though. I'm pretty sure in his current state Mr. Romani wasn't going to wait for me to give him a full explanation of the situation.

I looked down calmly at Mia Bella. She was still holding me closely, nuzzling her head against my chest. After everything that had occurred, no surprise that she was terrified and exhausted from the whole ordeal.

"It's going to be okay," I whispered to her in a soft voice. "Your daddy is here for you. I'm going to put you down now."

I knelt down and gently placed the girl onto her feet and stood back up, holding my hands high. She stood beside me, holding onto my coat, not making any effort to move towards her father.

"It's okay, my sweetie. Papa is here," Mr. Romani's voice gingerly called to his daughter. "I'm here to take you home."

She looked back up towards me. I nodded my head once at her reassuringly and she let go of my coat. "Thank you," she said in a quiet voice and made her way over to her father.

When I'm guessing she was back by his side, he spoke to me again. "Tell me why I shouldn't shoot you here and now?"

"Because you know me," I hoped this didn't get me shot, but I pulled the bandana down from my face and slowly turned to face him.

"Prince?" Mr. Romani looked at me with a look of absolute shock but didn't lower the gun. He must've been doing the mental calculations in order to better understand the situation. When all of a sudden Mia Bella pulled at his pants leg.

"Don't shoot him," she begged her father. "He saved us Papa."

This must've been what finally clicked for him. Romani uncocked his gun and pocketed the pistol, looked around to observe the situation then picked Mia Bella up with one arm. After surveying the scene, he glanced back at me, a look of gratitude on his face. His eyes began welling up in tears as Mia Bella rested her head on his shoulder. "I won't forget this, Prince. Also, I don't think you'd mind if my people take the three guards you incapacitated out here. I wish to speak with them."

"That's fine with me," I capitulated, nervously rubbing my arm. As father and daughter left, a thought hit me. I didn't take out three guards outside. He must've meant to include the two from inside.

I started walking away when all of a sudden, my body became wracked with pain. Convulsions started coursing from my back to my limbs, bringing me to my knees. My skin felt like someone was piercing into it, digging into my flesh but there was no blood. I started to panic, unsure of what was happening, but I was in a full scale mental breakdown now.

"Well done, my prince," the eyes came from the fog, revealing a feline-like creature whose body was completely made of barbed wire. It prowled towards me, baring its teeth. "I knew you could do it."

"What do you want?" I managed to eke out.

"To protect you, of course," the figure started to circle me as if I were prey. "Relax, everything is going to be okay."

A hand suddenly touched my face and I completely freaked out. I spun towards the hand and grabbed at whoever was touching me. It so happened to be a beautiful young woman, who had long hair covering half of her face. "Who are you? Are you real?" I grabbed at her shirt crazed, unsure of my surroundings.

From her eyes, she was clearly terrified by my raving, but stroked at my head calmly, speaking to me in Spanish. I had no idea what she was saying but all of a sudden, I felt very sleepy. My vision began to fade as I listened to her lovely voice. I caught one more sight of the barbed wire feline and then faded to sleep.

***

"And that's how it went down. Take those off," I scolded Emma who was wearing my glasses as I concluded my tale.

"Wow," she said while holding my glasses, casually chewing on the earpiece. "I thought the part after you got me out of the shack was more epic. No wonder you don't like telling that story. It sounds like the Romani girl was the real hero of that tale."

"She's the hero that the city doesn't know about," I admitted and looked back up at my ceiling. Then I sat up abruptly from the couch, staring at Emma. "Wait, what do you mean after I got you out of the shack?"

A knowing grin spread across Emma's face, her eyebrows rose, and a look came across her face telling me to think harder. I always wondered about the girl from the shack afterwards. She simply vanished, not even one of Toni's crews mentioned her, but the flames. *Could it be?*

"That was you?" I asked dumbfounded.

She reached into her pockets and withdrew two daggers, pressing them into my hand. I looked them over and upon closer inspection realized that they were the same ones MyKey had given me, and that I had passed along to her that night. She had held onto these this entire time. Her eyes welled up as they met my own. "Indeed it is, my muse, my brother."

We embraced immediately, holding each other as our reunion was truly complete now. Emma may not have been the person I intended to save that night, but she was the first person I had ever rescued. I could only imagine what this moment meant to her. Sometimes we drift through life, living from moment to moment, never stopping to consider the impact that you have on people and that they have on you.

I remembered now, why I go out as my other self. It's because of the chains that imprisoned those people that night, them placing their hopes of freedom in me, and the joy I felt when I managed to get them out. Bennett stood in direct opposition of that and in order to keep good on my promise I would have to face him one more time.

After some time, we finally broke the hug, smiling at each other as we did.

"What now?" She asked me expectantly.

I smirked knowingly. "Now, we get my toys back. I'm going to need a lift."

Chapter Thirty-Two

When you said you wanted a lift, I didn't think it would be to a place where you could walk through the front door. Why are we up here? And why don't you just poof your way in?" Emma asked me on the second floor of the Romani estate.

"It's because Susan doesn't know that my toys are in Mia's room. Also, it's rude to just 'poof' into someone's room and take their belongings without permission," I responded as I knocked on the bedroom window.

We both waited silently until the window curtains began to be disturbed. The face of a sleepy child appeared as the curtains were fully withdrawn to reveal Mia Bella. She must've been in bed but hadn't fallen asleep yet. Otherwise, I probably would've had to 'poof' into the room.

Mia Bella had a glazed over look as she peered out the window. I waved to her from outside the window to get her attention. She rubbed at her eyes wearily to focus, but when she recognized me, a joyful smile spread across her face and she started bouncing in place, fumbling to get the window open.

I turned to Emma. "You can hang out here for a bit. She's not a total fan of strangers."

Emma gave me a nod of understanding then flew up to the roof. "Call me when you're done."

I turned back to the window when Mia Bella had finally opened it.

"Uncle Prince!" She cried out to me, spreading her arms for a hug.

"Shhh," I whispered, putting my finger to my mouth before returning her embrace. "We gotta be quiet. We don't want to wake your mother."

She nodded to me, mimicking my gesture. "Shhh."

"Great," I entered the room carefully and suddenly something pounced on me. I almost let out a shriek of surprise, but I felt a wet sensation on my cheek. It was Mew. He was licking me as if I were a part of his litter.

"He says he missed you," Mia Bella said in a low pitched voice as she tried to keep quiet.

"Get off of me, Mew," I brushed him aside as I was able to sit upright again. I picked him up and looked into his face affectionately. "I missed you too buddy. Wait," I turned to Mia Bella stunned, "You said he *says* he missed me."

"Uh-huh," she came bounding over towards us, her pink bunny pajamas flapping back and forth as she approached. "He also said he wants to go back home because Momma won't let him roam around the house and the bear won't let him hunt in the forest."

I looked back at Mew and gave him a suspicious glance. He meowed in my face and then wriggled out of my grasp, flicking his tail across my nose before returning to lay at Mia Bella's side.

"I told you that's not nice to say, Mr. Mew," Mia Bella scolded Mew before caressing his chin which elicited an instant purring from him.

I was really confused over this entire situation, but I had to put it aside for now, "Mia would you be able to do something for me?"

"Do what?" She asked innocently, still petting Mew lovingly.

"Your dad said that he had a present for me. Would you know where that is?" She looked at her ceiling as she mulled over the answer before giving me a confident thumbs up. "Great, can you get that for me? I'm going to need it."

"When?" She cried out reflexively. I was caught off guard by the suddenness of her question. She must've seen my reaction because a downtrodden look came over her face. "I heard Momma and Papa talking about you when they thought they were alone. Papa said he thought you were dead when he saw you. Momma was crying. Momma never cries."

Mia Bella's voice trailed off, her eyes glued to the floor. Maybe this is what people meant when they told me I wasn't alone. To the majority of the city, I was nameless, faceless, no better than a rumor, but to a few I was a partner, friend, and uncle.

My actions or lack thereof as the Peach City Phantom had consequences, and when I took a beating like I did at the hands of Bennett, those few had to bear the burden of worrying about my health.

"Don't worry Bella," I sighed, calling her by the name I do when I'm being serious with her. I scooted across the floor to pat her head. "I'm better now. Plus, I have someone watching my back now."

"But I don't want you to go," she whined, looking up at me. Her eyes were misty as if she were barely holding back the tears of her fear for my fate as she clutched my arm tightly.

"Bella, do you remember what you told me before we went to the basement to save the others?" She stared at me then nodded somberly. "Right, well I need to reunite those people and make good on a promise. So, can you find my present?"

She wiped her face before rushing out of the room to find my equipment. I sighed as I stared at the door. Why did someone so young have to be tasked with helping to carry my burden?

I looked to the bed for the first time since I entered the room. There was a small lump underneath the covers. It was little Tina. She was fast asleep in Mia Bella's bed. The covers rose and fell in tune with her breathing.

I approached quietly, so as not to disturb the sleeping girl. I couldn't help but feel a tinge of guilt being in the same room as her. Not only had I lied about her brother, but I also had wasted precious time by being in a coma for a few days, an unfortunate result of my prolonged temper tantrum.

I knelt beside the bed and wished I could tell her that I had already found Marcus, but I could only tell her what was on my heart.

"Hey Tina. How've you been? I know I said your brother was helping me, but that's not true. I couldn't protect him, and he got taken because of me," I paused to take a breath. "I got a sister recently. You could say that she kinda adopted me. She gets on my nerves a lot, she's childish, and can be really mean, but she has a sweet side. I'd miss her if she got taken away from me and I know that if she's even as half as amazing as you then Marcus misses you twice as much. I'm going to make it right. I promised that I'd bring him back and Mew as my witness you'll see him tomorrow. Whatever it takes."

I rose from beside the bed in time to see Mia Bella walking in with the suit and weapons I had asked for. She came in almost immediately after I finished speaking with Tina, as if she were listening in to my conversation.

"Here's your stuff," she presented the attire to me. "Your costume looks weird now."

"Oh, don't worry," I said, lifting the suit up to examine it over. "I'm pretty sure it'll fit just fine. One more thing. I need my old toys also."

"Why?" She asked curiously.

"The meanie who beat me up, broke my new ones," I told her in mock sadness.

"He broke your toys?" Her mouth gaped open in pure shock as if the concept of breaking someone else's toys was unfathomable, a sin that couldn't be forgiven. She put her hands on her hips, pouting. "Wait here," she ordered me before stomping off to the compartment where she kept my old weapons.

"Here," she said defiantly, holding out my old bamboo tonfas.

I took them from her and even though the weapons had been slightly modified, they seemed to fit perfectly in my hands, just like they had over a year ago. I flexed my grip on the handles to test out the sturdiness, just fine. I looked up to Mia Bella and smirked.

"Thanks. Can I have my goggles too?" I held out my hand to collect my old aviators.

"One second. Kneel down," I did as my adopted niece asked as she revealed the steampunk goggles that she was hiding behind her back. She put the goggles gently on to my face and pulled them down over my eyes. She rubbed my temples gently in a circular motion while I knelt there. "These special goggles make you brave."

A large lump formed in my throat, and I couldn't speak. I just nodded and closed my eyes tightly, so the tears wouldn't start flowing. Sometimes I really don't deserve the people in my life. She stepped back when she finished, and I rose from my knee.

"Take care Mia Bella," I said as I started climbing back out the window with all of my belongings. "I'll see you tomorrow."

Hopefully.

"Bye Uncle Prince," she smiled innocently. "See you tomorrow. Tell your sister I said hi."

"Will do. Now go back to bed. See ya Mew."

My cat simply licked its forepaw then turned its head away from me and went to sleep.

"Typical," with that, I closed the window behind me, and she shut the curtains.

"She's so sweet," a voice remarked next to me.

"I thought you were waiting on the roof," I gave side-eyed her as she sat next to me.

She shrugged her shoulders lightly. "It was boring up there. How could you say I was annoying?"

"I never called you annoying, and I don't care how old you are, eavesdropping is still frowned upon."

"Coming from the person that eavesdrops for a living," she folded her arms and leaned back, pouting against the rooftop.

"You are such a child sometimes. Here," I said, holding out the package that Mia Bella had grabbed for me.

"What is this?" She looked at the gift with hesitation as she peered closer at the contents.

"It's for you," I said casually, trying to hold back my smile.

"I thought you were coming for new gear," she picked up the suit and held it up for examination.

"I never said it was for me," I turned to look at her. "Your cloak was pretty impractical. There were singes on it from your flames, but this is fireproof. Also, since you fly but Angel doesn't, I didn't want her to have something that hangs so loosely. Plus, it still changes colors when the two of you....ack," I was cut off as Emma threw her arms around my neck.

"Thank you! Thank you! Thank you!" She exclaimed, squeezing tightly.

"People are trying to sleep," I complained as she continued impeding my air flow. "Some are also still in recovery."

"Thou doth protest too much," she dismissed my complaints as she finally released me after a few more precious moments. "I wanna try it on already, and Angel is going to love the present you got for her."

"Hopefully," I muttered as I watched her spin around with the suit. She seemed to be moving to the rhythm of some unheard melody. I enjoyed these little moments. After all of the hell that I'd been through the past few days, it was nice to have some degree of levity. It's moments like these that don't give you something to fight against, but something worth fighting for.

Maybe now we had a chance to win.

Emma finally finished her best ballroom impersonation with the attire and collapsed down beside me.

"Tomorrow's going to be fun," she sang before resting her head on my lap. "Don't worry Devin. We're going to get the kid back. We're going to get them all back."

I was initially taken aback, unsure of how to respond to the display of affection and trust. The sensation of someone resting their head on my knees was a foreign concept. It felt weird, but it also...tickled. I could feel her hair through my clothing, and I stifled a giggle at the feeling.

After some hesitation, I slowly stroked her head. It was a cool night. The nighttime fall breeze felt great from atop the roof and a full moon illuminated the night sky. Even though sleeping on a rooftop was going to be killer on my neck, I was in no rush to leave. For the first time in a long time, I felt truly relaxed. In less than twenty-four hours, the both of us were going to put our lives one the line again and there was no way to tell what the outcome would be. I guess this is what they call the calm before the storm.

Emma didn't stir from her position. In fact, she became more still as time progressed, her breathing slowed, and she seemed lighter as she began dozing off to sleep.

"Thanks for adopting me, sis," I whispered in her ear as I continued to stroke her hair.

"If you hurt her, I'll kill you," a different voice came from Emma's body in a tone so low that I barely registered the words.

"Angel?"

But there was no response, just the sound of the young woman in my lap breathing as she slept. There wasn't going to be any leaving tonight. I leaned back against the rooftop, resigned to my situation. After a few minutes I started to drift off too, hoping that I would be able to keep my promise, no matter the outcome.

Chapter Thirty-Three

I told Angel it would fit perfectly, but she didn't believe me," Emma said, twirling around in position to show off her new attire. The outfit I had designed for her matched my recently torn cloak in terms of aesthetic.

In Emma's current state, the primary color was white, but with black flame designs around the legs and arms. It brought to mind the pattern of a zebra. Instead of a cloak, the base of the uniform was fitted with a jacket option and hoodie attached to the back of the shirt, so it appeared she had a mini coat, similar in style to mine. She was also gifted with a Thalia comedy mask that was white, but also had the black flames around the edges of the mask.

"No need to show off," I commented as I examined myself in the mirror of my apartment.

Emma flew us back in the morning, so that we could go over last minute plans and arrangements. My old attire felt completely different now. I had gotten a little too hi-tech recently and now with just my bamboo tonfas, aviators, and simple black coat, I felt a bit naked. Not like my advanced weaponry and armor had done me much good in the fight prior, but it would've made me feel much better.

"Don't hate," she responded sharply. "Are you going to wear the hat?"

"Absolutely not," I answered immediately and went towards her. "Are you sure MyKey is right about this? Why is the transfer happening during the middle of the day?"

"Has he ever been wrong before?" She shrugged. "Plus, with you presumed dead, why would it even matter? It's just two rich guys meeting during the middle of the day. I heard where it's happening is shut off, so no prying eyes will be there."

"Except ours," I said, snapping on my goggles.

"Except ours," Emma replied with a sly grin, putting on her mask. "Ready?"

"Ready," I nodded and reached out my hand. Emma took hold of me and began flying us to the location of the drop.

If you're not a child, being carried can be a bit demeaning. Being carried while flying can be terrifying. I could feel the air resistance pushing against me as Emma continued picking up speed as she sailed through the sky. Everyone below looked so small as we flew overhead. If anyone spotted the two of us, they would either assume we were IPF or that Emma was kidnapping me, and in that case, we probably would've gotten shot down.

We couldn't drive because our attire would've most likely gotten us pulled over. Weird outfits were all the rage in Peach City, but unfortunately, we would be fitting descriptions.

Teleporting to our destination would've been more efficient, but with Angel's newfound powers being unreliable and me keeping the fact that I was alive a secret until the proper time, this was the quickest and most conspicuous option left.

She eventually landed at our destination, making sure not to drop me on arrival. From what I could tell, we were at a private airfield. Perched from the rooftop, I could see the runway stretching for hundreds of yards, waiting for takeoffs and arrivals.

This was totally out of character for the Underground. First, it was the middle of the day. Granted, this may be how the transfers went down, but I just happened to know where they held the captives after hand. Second, this was a wide open airspace. If a passerby with any kind of decency, saw what was going down it would compromise the entire operation. My presumed death couldn't have possibly put them in such a careless state. Human trafficking was still a crime, Irregular or not.

"This doesn't feel right," I voiced my concern to Emma as I surveyed the surroundings. There were no signs of anybody, let alone a full blown criminal operation.

"Maybe Adkinson's going on a vacation," she offered as she stared out at the horizon. "Lord knows after the crying he did to the media and IPF after you carved his face like a pumpkin, he probably needs one."

"Not one of my finest moments," I replied with genuine regret. Each person has their own set of lines that they shouldn't cross. Not because of some worldwide moral code that's implanted into our DNA, but because once you start crossing into previously taboo frontiers, there's no telling if you can come back, at least not the same anyway.

"He had it coming," she responded, turning to me soberly, arms folded, "But you're past that now."

I wasn't sure if it were a statement or question, but I decided it would be best to acknowledge and not answer. There was a mission to complete and for now I had to put moral dilemmas aside.

"Angel knows the plan, right?" I asked.

"Yeah," she confirmed. "I fly in, distract the guards and Bennett. You sneak around, get the hostages to a safe place with your ability then we handle Bennett. Remember not to get involved until the hostages are clear and we should be good."

I grimaced at the mention of me not taking part in the initial fighting. From what I've seen, the two of them could probably handle themselves, but if things hit the fan, I wasn't sure if I would be able to stay out of it, potentially putting the captives in danger.

Being dead sucks.

"I'll stay out of it as much as I can," I conceded, turning back to face her. "Quick, get down," I said as I caught a glimpse of what was behind her. I grabbed and guided her to sprawl down flat onto the roof beside me as we both looked over the edge at the incoming company.

Two separate cars were driving up to the airplane hangar where we were. One was a black minivan with heavily tinted windows, most likely the car with the hostages.

The other car was a silver Jaguar, speeding along quickly, clearly taking advantage of the lack of traffic laws in the current area. Bennett, maybe?

We waited there for five more minutes. I was waiting for another car to come. One that would be able to carry the cargo away, but it never arrived. Bennett wasn't one that would appreciate tardiness and I'm pretty sure Chrome Dome would be in a hurry for the deal to go down and get back to one of his many residences.

"Let's check the inside," I whispered to Emma and moved towards the latch on the roof that would lead us into the hangar, with her close in tow.

"It's been a pleasure doing business with you George," I heard Bennett's booming southern voice before I could even see him. Emma and I were on the walkway near the top of the hangar. We moved silently in order to get a better view of the proceedings occurring below us.

"I'm just glad all of this is over," Adkinson replied to Bennett hurriedly. Half of his face was bandaged, covering the scars I had given him nearly a week prior. He had a slick silver business suit to match the Jaguar he drove, and I also noticed he had a cane, probably due to the fact that I put a round into his kneecap. Other than that, he looked like his usual pretentious self.

"Me as well, my friend," Bennett wore a black trench coat, but somehow it seemed to match the business meeting that he was currently conducting. He stepped around to the back of the van and opened the door. "Everybody out!"

The unwilling passengers spilled out of the van as they were all chained together. Bennett ushered them towards Adkinson, an ambivalent expression over his face, business as usual.

"I hope you find them to your liking, George?" Bennett asked as he presented the cargo.

There were five in all. Two women of a more youthful age, an elderly man who seemed absolutely defeated, another youthful man of athletic build with no hair, and finally Marcus. They had him muzzled and he wore the most chains of all of them, ankles, waist, and wrist.

Adkinson looked over his new collection, pacing back and forth before them. He stopped to creepily brush his hand through the hair of one of the women. I caught a glimpse of Emma shudder before he moved on, but I didn't acknowledge it to her. Adkinson kept moving before stopping at Marcus.

"You," the bald geezer bent over to get in the boy's face. "You're the reason I have this," he angrily pointed to the bandaging on his face.

Marcus didn't respond and I couldn't get a great look of his face from up here, but I think he was glaring back at Adkinson, which Chrome Dome did not appreciate. Adkinson stepped back and backhanded him right across the face.

"I'm going to have fun with you. I'll work you to the bone until you rot away," he sneered at Marcus. "You'll never see your sister again. Unless I find her of course. Then the two of you can be reunited. I'll give it some time, but then she'll be my sweet little girl."

This drew a reaction as Marcus. He bucked against the chains to get at Adkinson, who jumped back in fright. Marcus strained desperately against the restraints until Bennett hit him with the pommel of his claymore, knocking the boy unconscious.

"Pick him up," Bennett directed in an annoyed tone to the athletic looking hostage, who capitulated immediately and scooped up Marcus's unconscious body from the ground and returned to his place in line.

I felt my grip tighten on the bar handle of the walkway but had to remind myself to breathe. We couldn't lose the element of surprise so soon. Emma looked at me with concern, but with the same tinge of anger that I felt. I gave her a thumbs up to let her know I was in control. She nodded knowingly and we both returned our attention below.

"Honestly, did you really need to rile him up like that?" Bennett questioned, rubbing his face in irritation.

"Some people need to know their place. You understand, right Hamilton?" Adkinson turned his nose to Bennett. It seemed like an innocent enough question on the surface, but there was something about Adkinson's tone and the look he gave Bennett that made it seem as if it were a boss reminding his underling of the natural order of things.

Bennett gave him a very terse nod then turned to the hostages. "All of you, on the plane now," he directed them. "May our paths not cross for a while George."

"Maybe if I need the sister to keep that animal tamed, I'll come calling again," Adkinson said before walking behind his cargo to join them on the plane.

I looked at Bennett who was staring daggers into Adkinson's back and it may have been for just a second or a trick of the light, but I thought Bennett tightened his hands into a fist as if he had regrets about the entire situation, but it quickly passed as he straightened up his ascot and headed back to the van to leave.

"We gotta go n-" I started, but Emma had already beat me to the punch.

She leapt into action and unleashed a column of flames in front of the would be passengers, blocking the entrance to the plane. After that, she sent a spiral of flame towards the minivan and Jaguar, blowing both of them to smithereens, destroying any means of escape as she landed gracefully in front of Bennett who had to roll out of the way to avoid the explosion.

"You're going out of business Hamilton, and you must go," she told Bennett, pointing towards him.

I cringed at her attempt at banter. I didn't understand how she could so easily quip with me but was downright awful at it when it came to fighting opponents.

"Oh dear," Bennett said in mock concern as he stood and brushed himself off. He held out his hand in a stop gesture, in the direction of Adkinson and the now increasingly animated hostages. "Look who came to avenge the fallen. I see you're matching the color scheme, how fitting. Nice of you to show up now, but where were you when he died?"

As much as I hate Bennett, I had to give it to the man. He had mastered the art of banter. Even though Emma knew I was alive, his remarks still had the intended effect on her as she immediately became incensed. Her aura began rising to intense levels, so much so that I could feel the heat from where I was standing on the balcony. The eye sockets within her mask glimmered with white flames.

She lunged at him, withdrawing her butterfly swords from their sheaths. Bennett met her blades with his own. Sparks emanated from their clash. I was surprised that there were no other guards present to help Bennett, but with him distracted I took that as my cue to start heading towards the hostages.

The clanking of steel echoed in the hangar as their duel progressed. While I continued making my way to ground level, I could see Emma struggling with Bennett's power every time she came in for a direct blow, but on the other hand, Bennett had no answer for her speed. She would stick and move, coming in for a power attack with her swords before leaping back when her attacks were blocked. At distance, Emma stuck to using projectiles. A combination of her flames and daggers flew in Bennett's direction.

He managed to either dodge or parry her flames due to his ability granting him knowledge of when she would use it, but I had informed her of this beforehand. So after her flames missed their mark, a dagger came flying in afterwards usually hitting its mark.

They didn't land any crippling blows, but the cumulative effects of the strikes seemed to be slowing him down and her constant movement was beginning to throw the larger man off balance.

I had just arrived on the ground floor. The column of flames that impeded entrance unto the plane earlier had died down, so Adkinson was herding the rest of his passengers onboard with the assistance of a revolver to ensure none of them got any thoughts on straying too far. I needed to hurry before the plane took off, so I knelt low and began stealth running to the plane, never stopping to look back at the fight.

Emma must've seen me because pillars of flame between me and the fight rose up as I ran to board the bone white private jet. I arrived at the steps and stopped. My advantage would be gone if I didn't handle this correctly. If Adkinson shot at me, it would get Bennett's attention, so would using my powers. Once I got on board, I would have to rush and disarm him without using my powers, having a round fired, or getting a hostage hurt.

Just another day at the office.

I took out my bamboo tonfas, said a quick prayer to the Man upstairs, and crept up into the airplane. I hid behind a blue cushioned seat once I entered. Adkinson was holding a glass of wine and watching the hostages gather together in their seats, adjusting the chains to the chair posts and armrests so that no one moved around too much when the plane took off.

This was my chance. I held one of the tonfas out and crept low. One of the hostages, an auburn haired woman that Adkinson had pervertedly touched earlier, saw me and her eyes widened in shock. She shrunk back away from my direction in fear.

I signaled for her to stay quiet and that I was here to help. She visibly became relieved as she took a deep breath, and her eyes began welling up with hope. I didn't know if I would be able to come through and validate that hope, but it was all I could offer at the moment. I pulled my new white bandana over my face and proceeded towards Adkinson.

"All of you sit still. The flight won't be too long, but if any of you need me to keep you company, especially you ladies. I'll be happy to oblige," Adkinson said between sips of wine. He was in a really celebratory mood right now, but he was going to have one hell of a headache when he woke up.

But why not have a little fun first?

"Can you keep me company Georgie?" I whispered mere centimeters from his ear. He spun around quickly, surprised by the sudden voice behind him, but when he saw my face or at least what the attire on my face represented his expression changed to dismay and he stumbled back, dropping the gun.

"No, no. It can't be. You're dead," Adkinson spilled his wine onto his suit as he fell backwards and started clambering away from me. "Get away from me. Get away! Help, Hel-"

I silenced him with a swift whack to the forehead, leaving him in a lying heap. I started to search his pockets for the keys. I knew he had it on him somewhere if only Bennett was guarding them.

"They're not in his pockets," the auburn haired woman spoke up. She had a rather irritated look about her whenever she peered at Adkinson. I couldn't blame her.

"Where'd he put them then?"

With a disgusted glance, she turned to the other woman who mirrored her expression of repulsion and shook her head. Auburn hair glared back at Adkinson and pointed. My gaze followed the direction of her finger and my face soured beneath my bandana as if I had just eaten a lemon whole.

"Seriously?" I looked back at her. She simply nodded and covered her mouth as if she were about to barf.

Let's just say I was able to secure the keys and I wasn't the only one on the plane who was currently taking pills.

Once I recovered the keys and thought of burning my hands afterwards, I took the chains off of each of the prisoners. The women and elderly man looked at me with gratitude. The bald younger guy didn't so much as blink. I looked him over quickly to check on his mental state, but he seemed gone. Not how so many victims are when they lose hope, but more in the way that a catatonic patient just stares out into nothingness. The lights are on and someone's in the house, but there's no way of reaching them. I made a quick note of his condition before turning to Marcus who was just beginning to stir.

"Marcus, are you okay buddy?" I asked, placing my hand gently on his shoulder and gave him a mild shake. "Come on. We gotta get you outta here."

"PCP guy?" He moaned, finally starting to come to.

"I told you not to call me that," I admonished him as I looked out the windows. "Let's get you up. Do you think you can walk?"

"Yeah, I just got knocked out or something. Why do you look so different?" As things began registering again his eyes dilated in worry once he saw Adkinson's body on the ground and stared back at me. He clutched at my coat. "Where's Tina? What happened to her? I told her I would be back, but that prick took me," he gave Adkinson's unconscious head a sharp kick, that would probably add a few more minutes to his midday *siesta*.

"Tina's fine. She's in the best hands I know of," I didn't bother telling him not to worry. He had every right to. The last thing he remembered of his sister was that they were kidnapped together before he was taken away again. He had no way of knowing her situation.

His breathing steadied a bit, and he was able to focus on the current situation. "Thanks man. I guess you're not a coward after all."

"The day is still young," I responded with mirth in my voice. Step one in fulfilling my promise was complete. Now I had to get them out of here. "Alright everybody, we gotta get off this plane before baldy here wakes up and starts screaming."

Suddenly, the private jet jolted as if something had battered against it. The hostages let out cries of panic as the slamming occurred again. I went to the window to see Emma in Bennett's grasp. Her flames were flickering, as if the kindles of her fire were dying out. I thought back to what Angel had told me. Emma's power didn't come from anger, but something different. Bennett must've driven her to burning herself out.

Bennett said some words to her as he had her pinned to the ground. She struggled fiercely, but it was useless. He was just too big, leaving her with zero leverage. The sockets in her mask had been fractured, revealing her eyes within. As she continued squirming, Emma looked into the plane windows and our gazes met. Her eyes were desperate and wild before they locked to mine. A sad resolve filled them as she shook her head at me. It was a plea not to get involved. The plan was that my powers would be used to get the hostages and myself to a safe place before I came back to help.

As our eyes still locked, Bennett picked up his Claymore which had been by his side and raised it high. I don't think I even remembered to breathe as my heart began pounding in my chest at the sight. I pressed my hand helplessly against the glass as the scene started to unfold. He plunged the longsword towards her heart. A strike that would take away another person precious to me. Emma closed her eyes, resigned to her fate as Bennett dealt the blow. Blood splattered, staining the concrete as the blade sunk into its mark.

Then Bennett fell over, blood pouring from his side.

I lowered my hand as I closed two portals. One that had appeared over Emma's chest and the other that had appeared to Bennett's left where the blade exited. His ability may have given him the ability to detect powers, but I waited until the last possible second to open my portals and once his arm was already in motion, there was no way he could stop it in time.

Emma opened her eyes in surprise. She put her hands to her torso, checking for wounds then looked at Bennett before peering towards me. She gave me a nod of gratitude before collapsing back onto the concrete in relief.

I let out a sigh, knowing that she was okay. The nightmare was finally over, until it wasn't.

I now understood why Bennett held his hand out in the stop gesture earlier after Emma had attacked him. He had brought insurance. Apparently, he didn't want to show his hand too early.

You see, the catatonic captive became responsive right after I used my ability. It seemed that was the spark that he needed to awaken. He stood up mechanically, grabbed me and then launched me out of the jet. I tumbled down the stairs, hitting each one on the way down.

I hit the concrete hard, driving the breath out of me for the moment. The sleeper agent began strolling down the stairs slowly towards me. Emma saw what was happening and began to get up, but Bennett had risen to his knees and struck her with a fist to the chin. Her head bounced against the concrete, and she lay there, uncomfortably still.

"Em-" I turned to crawl to her, but the Underground's planted agent picked me up by my coat and flung me closer to Bennett than my fallen comrade. I bounced against the gravel before I looked up at Bennett who was on his feet looming over me now.

"How many times do I have to kill you?" He asked in sheer frustration. His stance seemed unsteady as he held his side to slow down the bleeding. "Not only do you consistently get in my way, but you come back with a stupid new outfit every time."

"Maybe you're secretly in a coma and instead of killing me you have to try something else in order to escape this purgatory." I joked as I tried to prop myself back on all fours.

Bennett paused in his tracks, a confused expression spread over his face as he became lost in thought.

My goodness, he actually might've bought it. Before I could make a move though, the sleeper agent pinned me to the ground and looked at Bennett awaiting orders.

Bennett escaped his thoughts and gave me a disapproving smile. "Clever, but childish," he walked to the agent restraining me and held out his hand. The agent, it turned out wasn't a human, at least in the traditional sense of the word. He opened his stomach, a hatch door located on his torso, and produced a gauge and tray of medicine for Bennett. The android's insides, from what I could see in my position, were a blend of whirring gears and wires.

Bennett took the ointment from the tray to clean the wound and stop the bleeding. He talked to me calmly as he dressed the wound.

"Out of all the Irregulars and people I've hunted down. I happen to enjoy you the most," he winced as he applied a different ointment to the wound and wiped away at the blood. "You may be the only one of them that qualifies as good or at least consistent, which means so much more in my book. I'm surprised that you look as young as you do Devin. After all these years, shouldn't you be older?"

"You can say that you're good at killing the person behind the mask, but you suck at killing me," I huffed from beneath the weight of the android on me.

Bennett stopped to raise a questioning eyebrow.

There was really no point in keeping it a secret, so I just went for it. "Let's just say you dropped me from that roof twice before. There won't be a third time."

After a moment, his eyes lit up with recognition and he let out a low whistle. "*You're* the kid. I thought for sure both of you died," he let out a hearty chuckle at the situation before wrapping the gauge around his wound. "Full circle indeed. We truly have been doing this dance for years."

"The web of our life is of a mingled yarn, good and ill together," I recited.

"How poetic," he said before taking hold of his claymore. "You were right about one thing though, there won't be a third time. This time, I'm just going to put your head on my mantle."

He swept his longsword up into the air. The steel gleamed as the sunlight reflected off of it. Before he brought it down, he spun and brought it to his face in a defensive gesture, just in time as black flames shot towards him. When he lowered the blade, I could see that the fringes of his trench coat were singed. Standing before him in all her glory was, *Angelus Mortis*.

I thought Emma's aura was impressive, but that didn't hold a candle to what I was witnessing now. Angel's aura was so huge that I thought it would engulf the light surrounding us.

The sheer intensity of the atmosphere surrounding her was mesmerizing. It continued spreading from behind her as if it had a life of its own, but she was in total control. Even Bennett took a vigilant step backwards.

Angel stepped forward revealing that the costume worked as intended. The primary color of the outfit had changed to black, this time with white flames. The arms became studded, giving her a punk rock vibe. The coat shortened into a leather jacket with a hood as well. Her mask had reformed during the transformation. The Melpomene tragedy mask usually had the look of sorrow, but now it seemed to be glaring in the direction of Bennett.

"Step away from him now," she demanded as she slowly started pacing towards us. Her steps left black flames as footprints behind her.

"Just because you've had a costume change doesn't mean-" Bennett began, but was cut off by a raging midnight-colored fireball which he blocked with his claymore, but the force of the inferno drove him back a few inches.

"I will not repeat myself," Angel emphasized each word slowly as she continued to us. The eye sockets of her mask burned intensely as she got closer.

Bennett turned to the android and gestured with his head for it to get Angel. The bot released me and proceeded to attack. Angel met him head on and drove a fist through the side of his head, gears spilled from the wound, but the android persisted on.

At this Bennett turned to leave, but with my restraints now gone, I was able to use my powers to portal in front of him.

Withdrawing my tonfas as I spoke, "No more running Bennett. You're not going to hurt any more people as long as I breathe."

"Well, I guess that won't be for much longer," he said, while taking a stance with his claymore. "But I'll be more than happy to oblige you until then."

Before I engaged with him, I thought back to my conversation with Mr. Jenkins. Maybe there was one last chance I could reach Bennett. "I get it," I called out. "You lost your sister, and no one can replace that, but maybe there's another way to go about this. You don't have to destroy other families to get your revenge. You can walk away from this, start over."

He paused at my attempt to show him empathy. A pained expression came over his face, but he shook his head slowly and refocused on me. "I'm sorry doctor, but I'm past that now. This is how I choose to play this out."

"So be it," I said in genuine disappointment.

We walked to each other patiently and then exchanged blows with our weapons. With my tonfas, now bamboo instead of Palladium metal, I couldn't afford to take his blade head on as much anymore. I did my best to impersonate Emma, by parrying the blows at the last possible minute and effectively choosing when to counterstrike. With the density difference being significant between the two materials, I was much faster with my strikes, but they also packed less of a punch. The Law of Equivalent Exchange, working its way into real life.

Luckily for me though, the puncture wound in Bennett's side slowed him down considerably and also gave me an easy target, but Bennett wasn't a stupid man. His reach was much larger than mine, so the stance he took would've forced me to lunge to reach the wound, risking a slash from the sword or a blow from one of his thundering fists if I wanted to land an attack of my own.

I pressed my luck one too many times and nearly got beheaded by the longsword, but when I ducked, it opened me up to a surging uppercut that would've made any boxing purist proud. This time I wasn't lifted from my feet, but simply crumpled as my legs transformed into jelly. I lay on the ground with the world spinning, my sense of direction gone.

Bennett picked me up by the collar of my shirt. He was speaking to me, but it sounded like gibberish in my current condition. A moment later, I fell to the ground as Bennett was knocked aside by Angel when she charged him with her shoulder.

"E.I., handle this situation!" Bennett called to the android. He was clearly hurting as he stumbled in a rush to the private jet. "Start the plane!"

The door closed behind him, and the engine soon started running as the plane began its takeoff procedure. I lifted my hand to make a portal to get on, but my senses were still scrambled. The hostages were still aboard. If that plane got too far away, I didn't know if I would be able to get to it in time. I would have failed, again.

I turned over on my belly, willing my arms to push myself from the ground. They strained from the effort, my arms shook the higher I elevated myself from the concrete. I felt a hand on my shoulder, which assisted me to my feet. The world spun for a bit as I staggered to my feet, but Angel was there to steady me.

"Ah, you do care," I joked to her as I finally was able to stand on my own. "I'm starting to enjoy the thought of you being my knight in shining armor."

"Don't get used to it. You're still on my list," her mask glared at me as she spoke.

"What? How?" I asked her, perplexed.

"Emma told me what a tsundere is," she didn't explain any further. She didn't have to. I fell silent and innocently glanced away from her. She made a gesture with her head, which I assumed was her rolling her eyes, before she spoke again. "We gotta get on that plane."

"Agreed," I rubbed my temple as I looked at the plane. There was a consistent throbbing pain and merely standing made me feel nauseous. I probably had a concussion, which I was not a fan of, but such is life. I looked at the android as it walked towards us with half of its head missing. "But we need to take out the terminator first."

"It's pretty weak, by my standards at least," her mask glanced towards me before she amended her statement. "Not a lot of offense, but it can damn sure take a punch. Suggestions?"

"Use your new toy?" I suggested from behind her. "I'll support you."

Angel looked down and pulled out the midnight black brass knuckles that I had Toni's men design for her. She placed her fingers in their proper place then held a fist up to her face before turning to me.

"Now give it power," I advised quietly.

She bent her head down and the aura around her died out completely. Other than the engine of the plane, there was a long silence. That was until a whooshing gust of wind blew from the brass knuckles and a blade made purely of her fire protruded out parallel to her fist, opposite her thumb. The blade hummed with power as she stood there. I saw her flex her hands a few times then looked at E.I.

She took off in a dead sprint at the android. I opened a portal in front of her that led her behind the android, who was completely exposed. She cleanly sliced its left arm off then proceeded to sweep for the legs, but the droid jumped and punched her. Its right fist knocked her off balance. With its attention off of me, I ran forward and launched an assault on the missing piece of its head with my bamboo weapon.

The attack dented its already fractured skull even further. If the android actually had a brain, its contents would've been gushing out. The humanoid machine shook as it turned to me, clearly, we were doing serious damage on the machine, but it still kept ticking. We needed to finish it off before we could go to the plane though, which was starting to proceed down the runway. We wouldn't want a haywire machine going around and attacking citizens at random.

When E.I. faced me, it raised its remaining arm to grab me, but after a swift strike, I saw its head topple to the ground. Electricity sparked from the mechanizations neck and its remaining eye blanked rapidly before it finally lay still. Angel lowered the brass knuckles, her flames receding back into her as the blade faded away. She nonchalantly stepped over the body to stand beside me to admire her work.

"Ready to end this?" I asked.

"Yeah, let's get this over with," she said, turning to the plane, whose wheels were now leaving the ground.

I placed a hand on her shoulder and dropped us straight down through a portal. We landed on the other side in the cockpit of the plane. It was a bit smaller than the movies make them appear, but I guess they didn't need the extra space since it was a private jet.

The pilot turned to us in confusion at first. Terror spread over his face when he realized that two complete strangers dressed in steampunk cosplay had just dropped into his sanctuary from out of the blue.

"Sorry for the intrusion, but the docket said there were supposed to be two more passengers," I commented before heading for the door. "We'll just seat ourselves."

The pilot just stared at us in silent shock as we made our way to the main cabin. When I opened the door, I was met with the sound of two consecutive shots firing off. I shielded Angel behind me as I scrambled behind the door for protection. Some of the control panels were damaged by the rounds. The pilot let out cries of fright as he ducked away from the gunshots.

I wanted to create another passageway into the cabin, but Bennett would see me no matter which way I chose. Exiting out of the cockpit door wasn't an option, we would be open to gunfire and we couldn't stay because if he chose to walk in, Bennett's sheer size would put us at a disadvantage in the enclosed space.

I looked towards Angel. "Do you think you can teleport into the cabin?"

She glanced down at her hands and her mask looked back at me. "I think so. It's still not completely stable though."

"Don't worry, if you fall out of the plane, I'll catch you," I shot her a teasing smile as I pulled down my bandana.

"Knowing when to tell a joke is almost as important as the joke itself," she stood up and suddenly disappeared. Not a big cloud of wind or particle residue this time, but a simple blink and you miss it kind of disappearance. I heard a commotion back in the main cabin.

Peering around the cockpit door, I could see that Angel had appeared behind him. Bennett was turned around to face her.

"Enough!" He bellowed. "I'm killing you both. I'll put your heads right next to each other on spikes once I'm done."

He charged Angel, grabbing her at the waist and tackling her to the ground. The power difference between Emma and Angel was palpable now. Where Emma would have gotten swallowed up by his sheer size and pummeled, Angel managed to at least keep him at a slight distance with one of her arms. She was still fighting with a handicap though. She couldn't use her flames on the plane without risking puncturing a window or the hull and causing the cabin to depressurize. They wrestled on the ground and the four actual hostages huddled together, away from the skirmish. Adkinson was handcuffed to a chair, still unconscious.

I moved into the cabin to help but got knocked aside by an absent swing of a backfist by Bennett. I looked at the two struggling and then all of a sudden, they disappeared together. I heard their commotion behind me, but this time Angel was on top. I wasn't sure if she meant for it to happen like that, but she had the leverage now. My ally rained down blows on Bennett, causing his head to snap back after each successful hit. She even managed to stab him with one of her daggers, embedding the bleed into his armor.

She was winning, but the only drawback was that she had teleported right next to where he had dropped the revolver when she first arrived. Bennett picked up the revolver and let off three shots. Angel managed to avoid each one, but from how they were positioned, the trajectory of the bullets had caused them to strike the pilot. The plane started shaking in midair as the only person who knew how to keep it aflight slumped over. The control panel was making all sorts of disturbing sounds also, just to tell us we were about to crash.

I looked back to Angel and Bennett who were now both teleporting all over the place in the plane. "You have to control it Angel!" I yelled to her as they continued fighting.

They teleported one more time, with Bennett on top this time. He smashed one of his fists into her mask, fracturing it right down the middle. I could see Angel's eye clearly now. There was a look in it that I had never seen in it before, fear. Her single eye met mine and then they were both gone from the plane.

There was no sign of them anywhere on the plane. I ran up and down the aisle, checking for them but they were nowhere to be found. When I realized where they could be, my heart stopped. She must've teleported out of the plane. They were falling to their deaths below.

It would've been simple enough to just go after her, but there was no one to fly the plane. It was going to crash into some urban area, which would kill the captives on the plane and the innocents below. I was going to have to trust that Angel could get herself out of the situation, but then I thought back to our conversation in the woods. She said that she couldn't fly and when she was teleporting, she was unable to change back with Emma. Even in death, Bennett was going to take someone from me.

I started hyperventilating as I knew I was faced with a difficult choice. Someone was going to have to die, and it was going to be my decision.

"Maybe it doesn't have to be that way," Sammy said from beside me.

"Sammy," I called to him in relief. "What are you doing here?"

"I'm a part of you, remember," he said confidently before walking to the hostages. "Now think quickly, so you can go save her. You can't fly a plane, but there may be someone that can."

I looked from Sammy to the hostages, slowly until I got to Marcus. My eyes instantly lit up with hope. He had driven the train that night or at least propelled it forward. If his powers were what I believed them to be, there was a chance he could somehow land the plan. I nodded to Sammy in gratitude before rushing to Marcus.

"Marcus, you with me kid?" I shook him as I knelt by his side. Marcus was in shock along with the others. His eyes were wide, staring at nothing in particular, but his mind was probably playing out a million different scenarios of how we were about to die. I could sympathize with the feeling, but today wasn't the day where we met our end. "Kid, I need you to listen."

I lifted my goggles from my face, the lower portion of my face still covered by my bandana. I sandwiched his cheeks into my palms, so that he had no choice but to look directly into my eyes. When we locked gazes, I could see him start to settle down. The frantic look in his eyes had faded, and even though the rhythm of his breathing was still erratic, he was completely focused on me now.

"What are we going to do?" He asked me, taking time to gather air between each of his words. "He shot the pilot. The plane is gonna crash."

"That's correct," I said matter of factly. I didn't need Marcus to fly the plane and land cleanly after a smooth descent. I just needed him to not hit buildings when the plane went down. "And I need you to crash land it?"

"What? I can't fly a plane," Marcus looked at me in bewilderment. He tried to turn his head away from mine, but I kept his face steady in my hands and my eyes on him.

"You moved that train," I said calmly, but in a hurry. Angel was falling to the ground as I spoke, and every wasted second was one less I had to get her. "I don't know how your powers work, but your sister is waiting for you to come back as her hero. My sister has been waiting for me to act like a hero since we met. I have to save her, but I can't unless you land this plane. Can I trust you?"

Marcus stared at me in silence before looking away and biting his lip. Then he glared back at me assuredly and nodded. "Yeah, I got it."

"Good," I said standing up. "Try to land on a large strip of land and don't hit any buildings."

I turned to pick up my tonfas before heading out, when Adkinson started to come to.

"What...what's happening?" He asked groggily as he started looking around the cabin. He began tugging his arm against the handcuffs. "Why am I chained up like this? Who did this? When I find out-"

I knocked him upside the head, sending him back to sleep. He was probably going to have serious brain damage eventually, but you only live once. "Sorry George, but you probably aren't gonna be of much help right now."

I placed my aviators back on my eyes before turning to Marcus. I gave him a thumbs up and descended through a portal beneath my feet and suddenly I was free-falling from thousands of feet above the ground.

Chapter Thirty-Four

It's funny. I feel like I've been falling for most of my life. After getting dropped from that rooftop all those years ago, here I was on the opposite end, diving to rescue someone close to me that was descending to their own potential demise. The difference now was that I didn't feel scared anymore. I was falling backwards through the sky, with my arms and legs outspread, the air pushing against my body. With everything that had occurred the past couple weeks, I thought I would be feeling fear and apprehension, but now I only felt one thing.

Serenity.

My purpose was clear, and the promise nearly fulfilled. I knew that Marcus could land the plane. It wasn't so much that I trusted in his ability, but more so that I trusted in his desire to be reunited with his sister. Even though Angel and I weren't as close as my relationship with Emma, they were still one, and both of them were family. I took a deep sigh and let it all go, clearing my mind to the task ahead before twirling my body to face the ground below and put my arms and legs together in a dive to increase my acceleration in order to catch them.

I saw the two of them tumbling in the air below. Bennett had his claymore with him, but it was merely something to grasp because he wasn't able to stop his rotation as he fell. Angel wasn't faring much better. She let off spurts of fire every few seconds to slow herself, but without producing a steady jet of flames she wouldn't be able to completely stop her perilous plunge.

I willed myself to go faster. The air slapped at my face as I leaned into my dive with everything I had. I didn't have enough time to focus on creating one portal at a far enough range to grab her, so I had to shorten the distance in intervals. Portals appeared before me as I sped through into each one, closing the gap between Angel and me. After I exited the fourth portal, I was close enough to reach out to her.

Angel looked up at me through her fractured mask and stretched her hand out. The space between us felt painfully insurmountable and the time to reach her seemed like an eternity. Our fingertips brushed by each other, but we couldn't secure a grip.

Angel sent one more rush of her flames from her feet, stopping her momentum long enough to propel her back up into me. I was able to seize her by the wrist and with her acceleration going in the opposite direction of my own, I was hauled up with her before we started falling together again.

"I got you!" I shouted above the rush of the wind. I wasn't sure if she heard my words, but they were more for me than her anyway.

Her mask turned in my direction and I could see one of her gray eyes peeking out at me. There was another look in them that I had never seen before. It seemed to be smiling back at me and given our current predicament, that was not easy to do.

"Are you going to get us on the ground now?" She shouted back as we clutched at each other.

"I can't!" I informed her. "We're going too fast. If I don't set the exit of the portal correctly, we're just going to go splat even quicker. You're going to have to slow us down before---ack."

A sudden, sharp pain struck me between the ribs. It was sharp and precise as if something had pierced me. I looked down at my torso and it was one of her daggers within me. I saw Bennett below facing us as he fell. He had somehow stabilized his fall and accurately launched the dagger that Angel had used to penetrate him and gotten me with it. I don't think he had a way of stopping his descent, but this proved he wasn't out of the fight yet.

My grip on Angel loosened and my vision started to get blurry as my strength faded. We were starting to separate before Angel grabbed me by my coat and started infusing herself with aura. The sudden burning intensity of her heat jolted me back to alertness.

"Don't you dare think about dying!" She yelled from behind her mask. "You're the only way I'm getting to the ground safely."

"To think that you actually cared," I muttered to myself in pain, but I gave her a look of confirmation and yelled back. "Let's finish this!"

"Agreed!" With that she used her flames to rotate herself in midair and when I was at the apex of her throwing motion, she launched me down towards Bennett.

I sped through the air again and used a portal to get close enough to deliver a solid hook with my left before, spinning counterclockwise and using a portal that appeared at his left shoulder which I used to grab his trench coat, before delivering another fist to his face with a portal that had opened up by his right cheek.

With the gap presently between us, Bennett's strength advantage was completely neutralized as I continued my assault. The edge when it came to abilities, had also been inverted. Bennett may have had the ability to know when and where I was using my abilities, but since we were both plummeting in mid-air, there wasn't any way that he could react to my strikes in time, nor did he have the ability to brace himself from the blows. He was completely at my mercy.

I stopped my onslaught, long enough to see that we were starting to get close to civilization below, maybe a thousand or so feet above the nearest skyscraper. I needed to get back to Angel before we both turned to pancakes on the street or became impaled by an obtrusion below. I couldn't let my obsession with Bennett get the best of me again.

I managed to maneuver my way directly above him, safe from his reach. I had fought with Angelus in both of her personas before, but we had never truly fought together. Most of the time we arrived at separate intervals and then divided and conquered, but through that time I had developed a real bond with both of them, so I was trusting that she would understand what I had planned next.

I created a portal behind my back that was obscured from Bennett's vision. I struggled to maintain it as I was falling, but the power within me held it steady. Next, I felt the aura that I was looking for, my body tinged with an indigo blue light, the same color as my portals, different in nature from when I had first accessed the flames against Bennett. Instead of the burning sensation fueled with my own rage, I felt an indescribable lightness. A warm feeling that comforted me even in the face of death.

Bennett's expression twisted in confusion, perplexed by my sudden glowing. He crossed his arms in an x before him, his claymore still in his grasp, preparing for the perceived blow, but the thing is, my amplified aura wasn't meant as an attack.

It was a signal.

I think Angel understood what it was supposed to mean because I heard her act above me. I sensed a sudden rush of wind coming towards me from above, but I knew what she had done. The Southern Gent lowered his arms, peeking to see why I hadn't yet attacked him.

"Goodbye Bennett," I whispered silently to myself. That's when I opened a portal directly in front of me, between us, and a roar of black flames that Angel had unleashed came barreling out towards my lifelong foe, engulfing him below me.

The sudden power of the attack pressed him quicker to the city below, while also changing his trajectory. Bennett crashed against the side of a skyscraper, tumbled head over heels, but he had the wherewithal to use his claymore to slow his fall. Though it only happened to be a minor inconvenience to the laws of physics.

If Bennett had fallen from the top floor, his momentum would've been completely stopped and he could've pulled himself inside, but that was far from the case. Not only had he fallen from a private jet that had reached its maximum altitude, but my combined attack with Angel had made sure to push his speed past that of his normal terminal velocity. The powerful blade dug into the building, decelerating Bennett at such a rate that a man with much less size and experience would've had their neck snapped by the whiplash, but he tucked his thick neck in to avoid that. The problem was that he simply was going too fast to bring himself to a complete stop.

Finally, his blade hit a snag with so much force that he wasn't able to maintain his grip on the handle. When Bennett lost his grip on the weapon, he dropped into construction below, tearing through the wooden boards before being buried by debris from his crash.

I wanted to begin crying in relief when I saw his body land. After all these years, he finally knew how it felt. That was for the hero who had come before me, and all the innocents Bennett had killed along the way.

I didn't have time to celebrate though because if I didn't act, I would be next, along with Angel. I activated flying squirrel mode, spreading my arms and legs just enough to slow my descent and fell into a portal I created below me, which stopped my fall long enough that Angel crashed into me from above. We spun in mid-air for a bit after the sudden collision, with no control in our tumble.

Angel shot jets of flames to help slow our fall. I couldn't really tell how far away we were from the ground with the constant spinning, but I saw some bushes below and hoped that we had slowed down enough that I wouldn't kill us. I created an opening below us which deposited us into the bushes. We landed with a sudden thud into the shrubbery, with my dagger free side falling on top of Angel. Since I hadn't given myself nearly enough time to heal, my old injuries started to remind me why I was previously in a coma. I was seriously hurting, but that meant I was still alive.

Angel was still gushing flames when we dropped, so the bushes ended up igniting, but other than a few bumps and bruises, she was mostly unscathed. She batted the fire off her attire, which also made it through the fight other than a few scratches from our earlier encounters.

"Did we do it?" She asked as she knelt down to help me to my feet.

I held onto her elbow to help steady myself before looking around. Our perilous plunge had landed us in Centennial Park. From where we were, only a few people saw us, but attire in Peach City was all over the place these days. The Steampunk look we currently had going for us was almost as normal as a suit and tie, no doubt attributed to MyKey's rise. The park-goers simply gave us disapproving looks and continued on.

That's when the screaming began.

"Look. A plane!" A voice shrieked.

"It's coming right for us!" Another yelled.

"Run!" One more screeched.

Citizens not expecting that their Saturday stroll in the park would lead to a plane crashing towards them, started running in absolute terror. I know I told Marcus to look for a large strip of land, but I thought the word *empty* would be implied. The plane's descent was steady, and the landing gear had at least partially opened, so he could operate large vehicles not just propel them forward, but the way it was headed, the plane was definitely going to kill someone if nothing were done.

"Unfortunately, not yet," I remarked to Angel, answering her question. I began wading through the crowd to observe what I could do. If we stopped the plane suddenly, then the hostages on it would surely die, but if the wheels touched ground without crashing, we couldn't afford to let it run until it came to a complete stop. There were just too many citizens.

I winced as I got to a clear opening and reached for my side. The dagger from earlier was still buried between my ribs. I wanted to pull it out, but that might've made the bleeding worse. If only there was a way to cut it off without hurting myself further, I would've.

I paused for a second, staring at the wound. Optimism spread into my heart as an illuminated light bulb popped into my head. That was it.

I looked back over my shoulder to Angel. "Do you think you can make a few decorations to the plane for me?"

"What?" She cocked her head sideways. I don't know if it was because she was perplexed or perturbed by my peculiar question.

"I don't think the wings are working for me," I stroked my chin in a pensive manner as I looked towards the plane. "What do you think of it?"

The mask glanced at me and then towards the plane. She tilted her head up as if she understood my meaning and sent two slashes of her black aura to slice the wings off the sides of the plane. The wings fell into two portals that I created beside the plane and disappeared as I closed the openings behind them. I had an idea of where they had exited, but I couldn't be entirely sure.

The next part would determine if the city would view us as terrorists or not. Without its wings, the plane's speed of descent increased at a dangerous rate and there was no longer any way to control it mid-landing. I stepped in front of the statue of Pierre de Coubertin, which the plane was currently rushing to.

"Angel, do you think you and Emma can stop a plane?" I asked without turning around.

"I don't think we have a choice not to try at this point," she sprinted forward at full power before instantly transforming into Emma. I shielded my eyes as the sudden brightness of her light nearly blinded me.

In her inverted attire, Emma leapt up spreading her wings and went straight for the nose of the plane. White flames erupted from behind her as she pressed against the plane to stop its momentum. Though their flames don't always burn, with the extent at which they were currently using their ability, there was no telling if someone below would get injured from her projection of power. This is where I stepped in.

I created a portal behind Emma large enough to capture all of her flames, focusing on keeping it stable with one hand in front of me. With my other hand, I produced a portal directly above my head, which is where the aura shot out of. The flame shot up into the sky like a beacon, burning brighter than any Olympic torch had burned before it.

The plane was slowing down due to Emma's effort, but with her strength being significantly less than Angel's it wouldn't be enough to prevent a crash. I heard her yelling from the exertion of effort and the strain it was putting on her body, but her flames never decreased. I could feel liquid start to run down my eyes. I was bleeding tears again and my knees were starting to shake from the stress, but I refused to falter as long as Emma was still fighting.

The plane was nearly in my face now and I could feel the amplitude of her power as she continued pressing against it. I made my portal even larger, and Emma entered into it along with the nose of the plane. As she passed through, I closed the portal above me and created another one in the open field behind me where most of the crowd had cleared out of.

Instead of more white flames jetting out of this one, black flames raged about as Angel's feet began sliding out of that portal. She was pushing against the plane now and without having to worry about flying she had a steady base to gather her power and significantly stop the plane's momentum. When the last of the plane entered my portal, I closed it and used both hands to focus on maintaining the exit point. I was seeing everything through complete red now, but my will was unwavering.

Once all of the plane had departed the portal and was at a complete stop, that's when I collapsed onto my face and Angel dropped to a knee. I looked at the plane from my spot on the ground. I barely had enough energy to keep my head up to watch, but I had to make sure everyone was alright. After a few moments, the door to the private jet propped open and each of the hostages came strolling down the stairs, all except Marcus.

My breath caught in my throat.

I pushed against the ground to stand. My muscles screamed from the effort, but never underestimate the power of adrenaline. I slowly managed to get to my feet and stumbled towards the plane. I thought I was going in a straight line, but everything kept spinning as I wobbled over. I must've looked like one of the drunks that came stumbling out of the red-light district of the city at night. I finally got to the stairs, and it was more of me pulling myself up by the railings than walking up them. As I entered the main cabin, I fell to the ground.

Working my way back to my feet, I scanned the inside desperately. There were two visible feet laying on the floor of the cockpit. I leaned against the wall to stay on my own as I looked inside. It felt like my heart was repeatedly punching the inside of my chest as the apprehension made me hesitate before stepping inside. As I finally worked up the mental strength to look inside, I saw Marcus down on the ground.

"Marcus," I called out as I fell to my knees. I took my goggles and bandana off as I did. "Can you hear me kid? Please respond?"

I turned him over and held his limp body in my arms. Cradling his head as I spoke to him, "No, no. Don't do this to me kid. Come on. Wake up for me."

I put my ear to his chest and felt the faintest of movements. He was breathing very shallow breaths, barely audible. He must've exceeded his limit and fainted once the plane had landed. I began chuckling to myself as I sat there.

We won. For the first time since I had become the Peach City Phantom, I really felt that this was a true victory.

"You did good," Sammy stepped into the cockpit. He folded his arms and leaned against the door, looking at us on the floor.

I stopped my laughter long enough to give him my attention. I looked at Marcus's sleeping body, thought about Angel and Emma's combined efforts, then glanced back at my past self. "Yeah, we did. Didn't we?"

Sammy shot me a quick smirk before fading from the cockpit. I took the new communicator Toni had given me as a gift and placed it in my ear. "Toni? Toni, can you hear me?"

"I'm here," the familiar Italian voice of my patron responded back over the headset. He sounded bewildered, word must've started to spread already. "What is going on? My social media department is flooding my phone about destroyed buildings and planes crashing into Centennial Park."

"I wish I had a social media department," I replied jokingly as I sat there with the kid still resting in my arms. "After this, I'll probably need a P.R. department to clear this up?"

"Consider it done," he answered immediately. "Are you at Centennial Park?"

"Yeah, but not for long," I grunted. The pain was winning now and talking was becoming a struggle again. "Can you get here soon? There's four people that I would prefer you get to before the IPF?"

"I'm already about five minutes away. Like I said, flooding my phone. Don't worry about the IPF, my guys can get a situation under control pretty quickly," Toni said, assuaging my concerns.

"Thanks Toni," I leaned my head back on the side of the control panels and started to close my eyes.

"Anytime Devin. Get back to my place when you get the chance. I already called Susan and she's making preparations."

"Will do," I whispered back and took the communicator from my ear. I started to feel something shifting on my legs. Marcus was finally stirring.

"What happened?" He moaned.

"You did it kid," I congratulated him. "You can tell Tina you're a hero now."

He had a fit of coughing before smiling weakly. "Hero sounds nice."

I heard steps coming into the plane and I tensed up. We were both in a vulnerable state and if anybody wanted to start anymore trouble, there wasn't much that I could really do. The footsteps got closer, and Emma poked her head into the doorway, with mask in hand. She and Angel must've switched before she got onto the plane.

"Is everything okay?" Concern was in her voice before she looked at us. She nodded in relief at the sight before our eyes locked. We both smiled in victory before she gestured with her head for us to leave. "We should probably get out of here. Our fans await us."

I nodded and offered Marcus to her, so that I could stand up. She took him from my hands before giving him back to me. She placed her mask on and playfully put my bandana back over my mouth. She went to get my goggles and carefully placed them back over my eyes. Finally, Emma began wiping away at the blood from my cheek with her thumb. I started to pull away, annoyed that I was being treated like a little kid, but she held my face steady.

"Appearances are everything, my muse," she said chidingly, before finishing. She stepped back and smiled, satisfied with her work. "Now let's go."

We made our way down the stairs and were met by an ever growing gathering.

The crowds of people stopped and began murmuring about the sight they were faced with. It had been decades since the last costumed person with abilities had been officially confirmed. It wasn't just that superheroes were a dying breed, they had been hunted down to complete extinction. To be in public, was an affront to the Irregular Police Force, one that wouldn't be taken lightly either.

We were anomalies as far as the citizens were concerned and they weren't going to miss a chance to be a part of history. Phones, cameras within glasses, and other recording devices documented our presence.

"Obviously you're not one to revel in the glory, so do you want to get out of here?" Emma asked me from behind her mask.

I glanced down to Marcus and gently handed him to Emma. "No, not yet," I shook my head to her before taking my tonfas out. "Meet me at the Romanis or my place. There's still one more devil that I want to make sure returned to Hell."

I created a portal and stepped through, away from the crowd and noise. Where I exited was quieter despite the fallen debris that had resulted from the crash. Most people avoided it, heading towards the park to see the plane rescue or failed terrorist attempt, depending on how the story got spun, that had occurred.

I walked over calmly to the epicenter of the rubble. There was a horribly burnt hand sticking out from above the wooden planks. Still clutching my sides, I made my way over to the owner of the hand.

It was Bennett. He was somehow still alive, but just barely. The portal-flame combination attack had torched him along with his trench coat. His fingers twitched sporadically, indicating nerve damage had occurred. His eyes were dilated, looking up at something beyond me.

"C...Caro....Caroline," he sputtered as he struggled to speak. I saw his right hand reaching up for something and I followed the direction of his gaze to find his orange ascot. It had snagged onto one of the construction platforms. It fluttered in the wind as the breeze blew.

"Caroline," he repeated again. It must've been the name of the person that gave it to him and from what he told me that person was his sister.

I reached up slowly and took the ascot from where it was caught. His eyes tracked me as I did. I took it over to Bennett. Standing over him, I let the ascot fall to his chest. He clutched at it deliberately and squeezed.

"Thank you," he moaned before gesturing for me to come closer.

I cautiously viewed the surroundings. Ever since I knew him, he had always been steps ahead of me. I wasn't going to get caught in a last second 'I'm taking you with me' scheme.

"Relax," he coughed. Blood spurted out as he did. "My back is broken. Couldn't move if I wanted to."

I was still careful, but that put my paranoia at ease. I knelt beside him to listen.

"Hell of a fight. I wish we could do this again," he coughed again, blood started trickling out of his mouth. "Don't worry about others coming for Dr. Prince. You beat me fair and square. I didn't tell them who you really are, but the organization will send others for Peach City's Phantom. I did tell them your other secret though."

"Which one?" I demanded. My heart quickened at his confession. Did he tell them about those closest to me, how to neutralize my abilities, or any other fact that would put me at a disadvantage?

"Your mind," he tapped my head, lightly. "They're going to make you question your reality. I only hope you're ready for it."

My body went completely cold. A dead man has no reason to lie. If Bennett told the Underground that I suffered from schizophrenia or at least mentioned that I hallucinate, I was in a world of trouble. There were countless Irregulars or Enhanced that had the ability to mess with a person's psyche.

"Why are you telling me all of this?" I asked him curiously. We had been at odds for my entire life. He had no reason to confess any of this to me.

"Your purpose," he gave the ascot another tight squeeze before continuing. "It annoys me, but your resolve is special. It can even bring you back from the dead. Maybe you can put a stop to all of this. In a way that doesn't bring the memory of those you love to shame."

I felt a hint of regret in his voice. Bennett wasn't anything close to a good man, but maybe he had been once. I wasn't in a position to judge the totality of his moral currency. I mean, my body count was pretty high these days. After Dr. Green's death, I also understood the effect of having someone close to you taken too soon, and the effect it has on the limits you'd go to in order to avenge them. I'd never grow to like Bennett and I'd probably always hate him in my heart, but at least I got to see the humanity in him in the end.

"Is it time?" Bennett asked. He didn't clarify, but we both knew what he was talking about. I simply nodded at him grimly. "Well then, at least let me tell you one more thing."

"What is that?" I asked somberly.

"The name of your enemy. The organization loved how you called them the Underground, so they chose something in honor of that once I reported that I killed you."

My head snapped back in surprise. After all this time, I was finally going to be able to take the first step in pulling back the curtain on the group that had made the people of this city into their personal playthings. I leaned in closer as Bennett whispered the name quietly into my ear. When he was done, I gestured in confirmation and stood over him, withdrawing my bamboo tonfa with my left hand in the process.

He looked at me in what seemed to be gratitude or at least acceptance and nodded, never taking his eyes off of me.

"Farewell Hamilton," I raised my bamboo weapon and then brought it down on his head, ending a chapter in my life that had been open for far too long. I fell onto my behind after the final strike and began sobbing. It wasn't out of sadness or regret, they weren't even tears of joy. I was just done with it all and that was the only way I knew how to respond at the moment.

I must've stayed like that for a few minutes until I heard the sirens wailing close by. The initial sirens all understandably went to Centennial Park, but someone had finally taken notice that the side of a building had been slashed open and the construction destroyed.

I wiped away my tears and opened my last portal for the day. I collected my weapons and looked over my shoulder one final time at Bennett's body. I took a deep breath and turned back around. He was right, it was time to step away from the past and move forward. I strode through the portal and entered into the Romanis home.

When I entered, I saw Susan and Sofia conferring together. They turned in shock at my sudden appearance and started speaking in hurried tones as they came rushing towards me. I didn't hear any of it though because as soon as I had arrived and knew it was all over, I collapsed to the floor. Muffled noises approached me as my vision faded to black and I passed out, mission successful.

Epilogue

When I finally awoke, I got an earful from both Susan and Sofia about my recklessness and how I was supposed to be resting and not fighting. They took away all of my gear while I was unconscious and told me I was banned from going out again until I was completely healed. Toni tried to bargain on my behalf, but he was staunchly told to keep his mouth shut before he got in trouble too.

He respected their wishes and supported the temporary suspension of my nightly activities.

The one good thing though was that I got to see Tina and Marcus reunited. Emma had dropped him off at the doorsteps before leaving. She was still uncomfortable associating with a mob family, so she headed back to my apartment to wait for my return. Tina ran into Marcus's arms screaming. He tried to keep up the tough kid persona, but I could tell from the way he was shaking that he was crying underneath the dreadlocks that obscured his face as he held his sister.

With the two reunited after two days, I took them to Mr. Jenkins residence. He was surprised by the suddenness of their arrival. I knew from Tina, when she was staying at the Romanis, that the siblings didn't have parents since there was nowhere else she could go.

I explained the situation to Mr. Jenkins who was understandably grumpy at first, but when he looked at the two siblings holding hands at his doorsteps, I saw something in his eyes soften. He 'begrudgingly' took them in and treated them as if they were his own. We didn't need to have many more sessions after that, but he still visited or called me from time to time to update me on everything going on. He butted heads with Marcus every now and then, but they really bonded over the labor of the farm. Of course, he instantly fell in love with Tina and spoiled her. I was glad that they had found a way to become a family of their own.

Needless to say, the IPF wasn't particularly happy with the plane incident. The Peach City Phantom and Angelus had both been labeled as fugitives of the law. Even though we stopped a confirmed kidnapping, they claimed if we hadn't gotten involved then hundreds of lives would not have been put unnecessarily at risk. Angelus was branded as shoot-on-sight due to the incident in the processing facility, while at least I was wanted, brought in alive, but that was just so they could make a public example of me.

The city, on the other hand, was torn on how to view us. Due to the number of Irregulars he had managed to bring into the fold of the Romani mafia, Toni had the full support of the family and used those resources to effectively brand me not as a hero, but a vigilant protector of the city, someone that fills in where the IPF can't, or doesn't. The campaign was big enough to sway public opinion, but not mainstream enough to draw IPF ire.

MyKey was also making bigger waves in the underbelly of the city. After my show of respect in his domain, he had become more powerful and feared than ever. He made sure to capitalize on this, turning Angelus, his underground fight club's champion, and the Peach City Phantom into cult heroes.

Adkinson had been arrested and financially ruined. If there are two things that people don't want to be connected to, it's gotta be pedophiles and human traffickers. Since he was the only person left on the plane after Toni's men cleared the area, he went down for the entire affair and was connected with countless other kidnappings. Also for his troubles, Adkinson's former safe house suddenly had two new airplane wings as decorations.

There was never any mention of Bennett or his body from the authorities.

The city swept the other kidnappings under the rug by throwing the book at Chrome Dome. This way they were able to maintain their reputation which would've been harmed by the poor publicity from the 'rampant Peach City kidnappings'.

I was relieved in the days after the fight, but there was still one promise that I unfortunately had to keep. The day of Dr. Green's funeral had finally arrived. With me being out of commission for so long, it had been delayed, but with technology these days, they had maintained his body without it decaying further.

I sat front row at the ceremony. Emma sat to my right. She had never met Dr. Green, but she was there to support me. Sofia had an opportunity to sit at my left, but decided against it, choosing instead to sit beside Emma. It was a reflection of how our relationship had to be moving forward, close enough to support each other, but far enough not to hurt them. Nurse Gooding instead sat to my left and gently held my hand as the ceremony proceeded.

When it was my time to speak, I did my best not to tear up. I failed, but everything I said came from the heart, so I was fine with it. Just as Dr. Green had said, you need to be a stabilizing force for those that come to you, but you're not a robot. Never be afraid to show genuine emotion.

Finally, I stood before his grave by myself, looking down at the tombstone wishing that the second year had been pushed back by a few digits.

"I hope you're proud of me doc," I spoke to his grave, placing my hands in the pockets of my black dress coat. The coolness of the evening breeze had made it chilly, so I didn't intend to be too long, but I wanted one last moment alone with him.

"I think he would be proud of you," Sammy consoled me as he appeared by my side. "You grew into a man that most fathers would be proud to raise, and who most boys would love to grow into."

I gave a half-hearted grin to my younger self and faced the grave again. After a few moments of silence, I finally spoke again. Voicing a concern that had bothered me for the past few days. "How are the others doing?"

Sammy stood there silently, peering at the plot with me. He shrugged his shoulders defeatedly. "Barb is gone. I'm not sure where or why. Specky said you don't need us anymore," after a few seconds, "I tend to agree with him on that."

"So, you're all abandoning me too now?"

"Devin, we're a product of your condition," he informed me before kicking absentmindedly at the leaves beneath him. "There was a day that I thought you would celebrate this."

"So did I," I said soberly. "I'm going to miss you all."

"We're going to miss you too," he leaned into me and hugged my leg. I wrapped a loving arm around him in response. "But you have other people that can look out for you now. Goodbye, big me."

With that he faded from view and my mind. I wiped a tear when I heard footsteps approaching.

"You okay brother?" Emma asked when she arrived by my side.

"Yeah," I nodded. "Just saying goodbyes."

"Are you gonna be good?" She put a comforting hand on my elbow, looking at me with worry in her eyes.

I turned to face her, giving her a sly grin. "I will be."

"What happens next?" She looked at me expectantly.

I scratched at the back of my head and looked to the sky. "Well, when Susan and Sofia give me my toys back, we go after our enemy."

"We don't even know who they are yet?"

"Actually, we do," I corrected before gazing back at her. "The Third Rail."

She flinched at the name of the organization that had been responsible for all of the known kidnappings that occurred over the past year, including her own. "How'd you come by their name?"

"Call it a parting gift," I said soberly before turning back to my mentor's grave. "Speaking of which."

I took out the tea and chocolate bar that I had gotten for him before he passed away. I walked over to his tombstone and placed them down before it. "Rest easy, Mo."

As I turned back and continued walking towards Emma, I heard a voice, barely a whisper, from behind me. "Well done my boy," I paused to look back over my shoulder, but there was nothing there.

"Ready to go now? I'm kinda ready to celebrate," Emma was speaking of the private celebration at *Rifugio* that would celebrate the takedown of Bennett and the first real blow to our enemy.

Her question jolted me back to reality. My eyes darted behind me for a few more seconds before I turned back to her with a reassuring smile.

"Yeah, I can use a celebration right now. Just no reciting quotes when we arrive."

"Aww," she pouted as she turned to walk with me. "I thought you liked my quotes. It's kind of my bit."

"Alright," I conceded, "Just a few, but you might wear the audience out if you keep doing it constantly."

"When words are scarce, they are seldom spent in vain, my muse."

"Let's go, Em. We're gonna be late," I rolled my eyes and pressed forward.

Emma gently held my coat sleeve as we walked into the gentle autumn breeze. I didn't want to teleport or drive anywhere, but just enjoy the company of someone that had accepted me as family.

After all the pain and struggle I had suffered through all these years, I was finally taking the next step in life. I was moving past the trauma that had haunted me and now progressing towards something better. I didn't know what the future or The Third Rail had in store for me, Emma, Angel, and the rest of my allies, but I was going to put that on the backburner for now.

With all the death that I had finally worked through, I finally had some living to do.